THE DISINHERITED PRINCE
THE DISINHERITED PRINCE - BOOK ONE

THE DISINHERITED PRINCE

THE DISINHERITED PRINCE
BOOK ONE

GUY ANTIBES

CASIE PRESS

SALT LAKE CITY, UT

THE DISINHERITED PRINCE

Published by CasiePress LLC in Salt Lake City, UT, August, 2016.
www.casiepress.com

Cover & Book Design: Kenneth Cassell

ISBN-13: 978-1537211138
ISBN-10:   1537211137

AUTHOR'S NOTE

This is the first book in the Disinherited Prince series. The idea of the series came from a short story that I wrote some years ago. Although there are some references to events in this first book of the series to the short story, they won't take place any time soon. I'll leave it to the reader to discover just what that story was when it shows up as a book of its own in the course of the series.

Every series must have a beginning and for Book One of the Disinherited Prince series, I chose to keep the story and the action relatively compact, with the intent on showing how the main character of the book dealt with the dynamics in a turbulent four months of his life. I hope the concept is enjoyable and works for you.

I'd like to again thank Judy for her editing and Ken in the interior and exterior design of the book.

— Guy Antibes

Map of the Continent of Eastril

In the world of Phairoon

THE DISINHERITED PRINCE

Chapter One

~

THE OLD WARHORSE PLODDED ALONG THE FOREST FLOOR, its hooves making loud thuds as it plunged further through the thick trees. A man dressed in soiled but soft leather clothes guided the animal, with two boys, just reaching adolescence, clutching to him and each other. One of the boys shared the dark brown hair of the man, but the other boy, a bit younger and slighter, had light hair, nearly colorless.

A column of sunlight lit up a clearing, sending away the cool dankness of the forest. The man, skin brown and creased from a life spent outside, reined the huge horse to a stop.

"You two jump off. We have to be back at the castle tonight, or your father will have my head on a pike," the man said to Pol, the light-haired, younger boy. He slapped the older boy's leg. "Paki, you untie our things, and Poldon, you can find some firewood. I'll want a fire going in half a turn."

Pol looked up at the sun to determine the time. He stumbled on a fallen branch and picked it up, bringing it to the fire ring that had been used by many campers in King Colvin's forest. He and his friend had shortened his name to Pol. Prince Poldon came at the tail end of King Colvin's children, with a different mother and with a fragile constitution. Pakkingail was the son of Siggon Horstel, the King's gardener, an ex-soldier, and everyone had shortened Pakkingail's name to Paki.

Pol looked at Paki, who led the horse to a rock bench, which he climbed to untie their supplies. Pol and Paki had worn backpacks to carry their personal things. Paki looked over and grinned. It was a beautiful day in late spring, and both boys were anxious to get out and enjoy the weather.

Gathering dead branches at this time of year proved to be a quick and easy task. Before long, a fire was crackling.

Siggon looked long at Pol. "You're not overtired, Pol?" Poldon insisted on no honorifics when they were alone in the woods.

"I feel fine," Pol said. Not quite true, but the boy wasn't fatigued, just tired. At least he wasn't out of breath. Last year at this time he might have been. He had grown just a bit, and that seemed to have given him a little more strength and endurance. "I am hungry, though."

"We'll let this fire burn for a bit." Siggon examined the fire ring and tossed a few of the bigger pieces of wood on the fire. "Let's check around for evidence of game in the area."

Pol liked the fact that Paki's father would always turn a visit to his father's hunting preserve into a classroom for woodcraft. He knew that his two older brothers had never bothered to learn anything about survival. Pol knew he picked things up better and faster than his siblings, but that didn't gain him any respect, just more enmity.

"Something large recently came this way," Pol said as they walked in the forest.

"Why do you know that?" Siggon said, kneeling down at the sign that Pol had noticed.

"The leaves have been turned over, and the darker leaves are still damp."

Siggon nodded. "Is that right, Paki?" He looked at his son who had been whittling on a dry branch while they walked.

Paki scratched his head. "I think so." His face turned red with embarrassment, since it was obvious to Pol that he hadn't been paying attention. Paki used the pointed end of his work to disturb the leaf-covered ground. "If it was a smaller animal, there might not be any leaves turned over, certainly nothing as large as that."

"Good recovery, lad," Siggon smiled. Seemingly, Paki's antics never failed to amuse his father. "Can you find the direction that the animal went?"

Pol gave it a try, but Siggon showed them how to read the pattern. "Of course, if this was bare dirt, you wouldn't have as hard of a time, but you can't always rely on an easy way to track something, except for clumsy humans. They are always easier to track. You don't want a vicious animal circling back and attacking you."

The words struck a chord within Pol. Siggon looked at him and nodded. His statement held more meaning, and Pol knew it had to do with tracking non-clumsy humans, as he had immediately thought of them. Pol nodded his head once to Siggon to let him know that the message had been received. Pol had to be wary of the humans with whom he interacted. Paki was back to slicing the bark and nubs off of his stick.

Back at their day camp, the coals looked perfect, so Siggon removed a long, thin package from their bag. He unwrapped a damp cloth and waxed paper, revealing chunks of marinated meat speared on thin metal rods. "Our meat course," Siggon said. "We can start with some bread and cheese. One of my wife's helpers put together a savory spread." He laid out a small ceramic pot and a knife.

Pol sliced the bread, and Paki used the back of a spoon to smooth out the spread. Both of them laughed at each other as they took big bites of the bread.

"Do you want some?" Pol asked Siggon who shook his head.

"I'm not one for that kind of thing. You boys enjoy," Siggon said as he turned the meat.

It had begun to sizzle, and the sound and smell of the meat made Pol wolf down the bread. He didn't like the spread very much, anyway. He just watched the meat cook as the light breeze pushed the aroma of cooking meat his way.

Paki groaned and clutched his middle. In a moment, Pol's stomach began to churn.

"Something's spoiled!" Siggon said. "Quickly! Put your finger down your throats and throw it up."

Pol didn't want to vomit, but his stomach began to spasm, and he could feel his heart begin to beat in his ears. Paki had successfully brought the bread and spread up, and that made it easier for Pol to duplicate the action.

"Water, Paki," Siggon said. "You, too, Pol."

Both of them drank water and Siggon made them bring that up too. He eyed the pot of savory spread and wrapped it up in the damp cloth that once held the meat skewers. "Do you feel any better?"

Paki nodded, but still looked pale. Pol shook his head. "I've got a headache now." He lay down on the soft floor of the clearing and used his backpack as a pillow.

Siggon took a piece of meat off one of the skewers. "Mmmm. You two don't know what you are missing."

Pol rolled his eyes. "I don't want to taste it twice," he said, smiling weakly.

Kneeling at Pol's side, Siggon said, "Good lad. We'll let both of you rest up for a bit."

The young prince didn't like the look on Siggon's face, but he didn't like feeling so awful either.

Amonna Fairfield, youngest daughter of King Colvin, the monarch of North Salvan, stood still at the side of a door leading into her sister's rooms in the castle. She leaned towards the door to hear her sister, Honna, talking to her middle brother Grostin.

She heard Grostin laugh. "Serves the little twit right."

"Aren't you being a little harsh?" Honna said. Amonna didn't hear any compassion in her sister's voice.

"Pol needs all the harshness we can give him. I hope he dies," Grostin's voice chilled Amonna. Such a casual disregard for his half-brother. Why would Pol be dying? She still wanted to know.

"Poisoning is sometimes an inexact art," Honna said. "You want him to suffer, but not to die, right? That way he'll remember your act of kindness for years."

"Years!" Grostin barked out a single laugh. "Pol doesn't add to our family. He only detracts, doesn't he?"

There was a pause in the conversation, so Honna must have nodded or something.

"Well, you've certainly covered your tracks nicely using the kitchen assistant," Honna said.

Grostin chuckled. "Isn't it, though? Once I caught him with the ostler's wife, he was mine to command. I felt just like father, ordering my minion to put something less than nourishing in their food bag. I can picture them all writhing in pain in the forest…"

That was all that Amonna needed to hear. She quietly withdrew from the door and raced to Kelso Beastwell's office in the North Building, where he oversaw the King's Guards.

"What is all this fuss?" Kelso said, as Amonna ran into his office.

She felt her lungs were about to burst. She never remembered running so fast for so long. "Pol has been poisoned. He's with Siggon Horstel and his son in the King's Forest."

Kelso shot to his feet. "How did you find this out?"

Amonna kept her mouth shut, her eyes pleading with Kelso.

"Never mind. I'll send out men to find them. There is a clearing that they generally frequent. You will excuse me," he said, leaving Amonna, her chest heaving, leaning with both hands on the Chief Guard's desk.

Pol's eyes began to droop. He realized that all the poison in his system hadn't been purged. He looked up at Siggon's concerned face. "Am I going to die?" Pol said.

Siggon shook his head. "Not yet." He looked back at his son, eyes closed and looking pale. "I can't get both of you to the castle. I didn't bring the tools to make a travois, but we will have to make do."

Pol could see the war waging in Siggon's mind play out on his face. He struggled to raise his arm and touched Siggon. "Take Paki."

Siggon shook his head, but then he turned it towards the forest. "Riders!" He rose to his feet to greet the newcomers. Pol twisted his head to see five men dressed in the livery of the Castle Guard entering the clearing.

"I've got two sick boys," Siggon said.

"Poisoned, we hear. Why are you unaffected?" one of the men said.

"One of the cook's helpers offered a pot of savory spread. I don't like the stuff, but it's either that or the loaf of bread. I saved the pot, so we'll have the Court Magician take a look." Siggon wiped his brow. "I'm glad you're here. I hadn't yet figured out a way to get the boys out of the forest by myself. I'll take the prince if one of you will grab my son."

Once they were all mounted, they headed back to the castle. Pol sat in front of Siggon on the big warhorse. He looked ahead of him and realized that he couldn't focus properly. If he shut his eyes, his body hurt more. The forest opened up and the road straightened out.

Pol blinked in the direct sunlight, and that made his head pound in pain. He closed his eyes, but that only made things worse, so he returned to his squint. Even that seemed to take too much effort. The fact that the farmlands were mostly plowed, broke through the haze affecting Pol's mind. Gradually Borstall's outer edges passed Pol's view. He found that the range of his vision began to contract, since the pain in his head and in his body continued.

He felt as much as heard the clatter of hooves on the cobbled streets as they finally reached the castle. Arms pulled him off of Siggon's horse and the knowledge that he had made it home filled him with such relief that he lost consciousness.

The voice of Pol's father broke through. He lifted his eyes, seeing a blur in front of him. He blinked the vision clear and looked up into eyes of his father, the King of North Salvan. His father looked to the right, and Pol followed his eyes to find Malden Gastonia, the Court Magician, standing on the side of his bed.

"You really think it was poison?"

Malden lifted the savory spread pot. "That's what it is. This particular poison is rarely fatal, but with two young boys slathering huge amounts of it on their bread, they each ate a healthy dose. With Pol's constitution, I'm rather glad he pulled through. If Siggon hadn't made the boys puke most of it up, we might be burying one or both."

"He is out of danger, then, eh?" King Colvin nodded. "Good, then. I have things to do." He patted Pol's foot. "Glad to have you back, boy." The king turned and left the room.

Pol tried to sit up, but his efforts were futile. He'd often experienced severe weakness before, but somehow this was the worst he'd ever felt. "What day is it?"

"You ate your poison yesterday. It's just past midday, and you woke up to the one and only appearance of your father. Your mother spent the night, but you seemed to improve overnight, so I sent her to bed."

"But why are you here? You're not a healer," Pol said to the Court Magician. Pol knew the magician well enough to think of him as Malden, but he never had much to do with the man. All magicians seemed mysterious to him, since they were traffickers in secret knowledge and had special abilities.

"I don't usually interfere with the healers, but your mother asked, since she knows I have some talent using my power to help people. Siggon came last night to take Paki home. He can finish his recovery there."

"Who did this?"

"I know, but I won't tell you. Take care of yourself. I'm afraid this may be an escalation of your troubles here at the castle. This goes beyond a mere prank."

The 'prank' description told Pol all he needed to know. He stared at Malden. This was the first time the magician had ever admitted to knowing the chronic troubles Pol had with three of his four siblings. "Tell me."

Malden shook his head. "Let us say, you know the perpetrator, and there is nothing that can be done."

"Grostin or Landon, then. Landon would probably have sent assassins with arrows or swords, but Grostin…" Pol looked up at the magician. "You don't have to tell me."

Malden shrugged. That was good enough for a yes for Pol. He sat back and closed his eyes. Grostin, Landon, Honna. Any of the three would be capable of such a thing. He didn't think they would go so far, and that disappointed him. It seemed that they had finally decided to raise their antagonism to a higher level.

Pol felt isolated and alone, but not for the first time.

"How is your patient, Magician?" Amonna said, tiptoeing into the room. She saw Pol's face and smiled. It looked genuine to Pol. "Oh, you're awake. That's a good thing. I was very worried about you."

Malden sighed. "He could have died. Luckily, Siggon made the boys throw up their dinner. It saved Pol's life." The magician looked intently at Pol. "His physical condition could stand some improving, but we don't have an appropriate healer in Borstall."

"What's an appropriate healer?" Amonna asked. She flipped her long, dark hair back and pushed it behind her ears. Honna, her older sister, had already taken to wearing her hair up like the older women in court.

"There are a few good Healing monasteries that have combined magic with healing to achieve remarkable results." Malden patted Pol's arm, making Pol feel like some kind of pet. "You should spend some time in one, I think." Malden said.

Pol thought that Malden had more to add, but the magician looked at

Amonna as if there was more to be said, but not in her presence.

"Thank you for coming to visit," Pol said, changing the subject away from magical healing. "I heard you called on Kelso Beastwell to find us."

Pol noticed a faint smile on Malden's face. She must have found out that Grostin had done something. Pol still didn't think that Landon would do anything so sneaky.

"A rumor in the kitchen. I, uh, went there after dinner for a snack and overhead the cook's helper admit to a prank." She turned red while she said it.

Pol had long known that she did not lie well. "Grostin was behind it, wasn't he?"

Malden gave Pol a dirty look, while Amonna looked trapped.

"He was, wasn't he?"

"I can't say..." Amonna looked out the window and then turned around. "I can't say who did it. Can you, Malden?"

The magician shook his head. "No one told me Grostin had anything to do with it, as far as I know."

Pol looked at Malden. The magician's face was devoid of emotion, but that didn't fool him. Pol decided he'd have to give up and not say any more. Amonna was his only friend among the other siblings, and she had just proven that she couldn't be as open as she had been in the past, but she had come to visit. She didn't have to do that.

"No matter who did it, I'm glad you are here. I just woke up when Father visited. I do feel better. My whole body ached before I finally went under, riding on Siggon's horse through town."

"Poor dear," Amonna said. She moved to the bed and put her hand on Pol's forehead. "Still a little warm?" She looked over at Malden who nodded. "I suppose I'll leave you to your recuperation. You do know what that word means?"

Pol rolled his eyes. He suspected that he had a better vocabulary than any of his brothers and sisters. Mistress Farthia Wissingbel had said so, and he believed her more than he did Amonna at the moment. He watched her go. She turned and gave him a little wave before disappearing into the corridor of the infirmary.

Malden clicked his tongue. "That wasn't very nice of you, putting Princess Amonna on the spot like that. You may be right, but it is impolitic for you to say it to her." Malden smiled craftily. "You do know what impolitic means?"

Pol shook his head. "I learned the word last year. I learned a lot of words last year. I suppose I'm learning more than words this year."

"Indeed you are, young prince. Learn all you can about North Salvan and the Empire this year." Malden raised his hands when Pol made an ugly face. "I'd spend less time around your friend Paki and more time with Farthia Wissingbel. Just my opinion."

Pol pouted, just a bit, and said, "You can keep your opinions to yourself."

"I usually do," Malden said, smiling.

~ ~ ~

Chapter Two

~

"**M**OTHER," POL SAID, STANDING as Queen Molissa, his mother, walked into his rooms.

She waved her hand. "Sit down. I've come to see how you fare." His mother looked happy. Her face showed a sheen of sweat and was still a bit ruddy from being out in the sun. She must have just come back from delivering alms.

"You've been busy helping others. They need help more than I do," Pol said. He laid a book about the origin of the Baccusol Empire on the reading table. "I'd like to go with you again, but I'm not back to full strength yet."

He knew he still looked pale, and just getting ready for the day still tired him. He had thought his strength was on the mend before he took that poison, and now he felt more like he had when he was younger. He felt like an invalid again, and that had put him out of sorts until his mother's presence brightened up his day.

"You need to get out and play with Paki more. That boy helped put life into you."

Grostin's role in taking life out of him was left unsaid. "He did. Malden Gastoria said I shouldn't be playing with him, and that I should study."

Molissa leaned over to read the title of the book that Pol had been reading. "That will put you to sleep. It worked wonders to do the same to me when I was a young girl. Quite a bit has happened since that was written."

"I suspect there is much more to come," Pol said. "There always is, but the Empire is still here after all the centuries."

Molissa sighed. "I'm not sure that is a good thing, if you ask me." His mother had been politely requested to marry one of the kings or princes of the Imperial kingdoms shortly after her parents died in an epidemic in the country of Listya far to the west of North Salvan. She had chosen Prince Colvin, a recent widower with four small children. Pol never really knew how her mother felt about it.

Pol nodded.

"I'm worried for you and worried for us, I'm afraid," she continued. "I suspect the poisoner was paid by one of the siblings—"

"Grostin, I'd guess," Pol said.

"You are probably right, and that means there is nothing you can do." Molissa sighed. "There's nothing I can do. We only have limited power in this place."

"Do we have any power?" Pol asked.

She shook her head. "Not much. You are my heir and next in line for the Listyan throne, but that will never happen. Your father mentioned yesterday about appointing Landon as vassal-king of Listya, replacing the current regent, another one of your father's cronies. You and I represent a threat to Colvin's other children. Once Colvin gets a notion, he just lets it grow and grow. I think this is one of his grander ones."

"But what does Father think about their activities."

Molissa sighed again. "Boys will be boys. That's a clichéd saying, but I think he thinks their treatment of you is fair game. At some point, I worry about your safety in this castle if the King gets obsessed with putting Landon on my throne."

"I thought you and Father got along."

"That is the sad part. We really do. He's grown to care for me as I have for him. It's the children from his first marriage that work to drive us apart," Molissa said, fingering the hem of a sleeve. "I shouldn't be boring you with all this depressing talk. It will only serve to keep you from getting your strength back. Being strong is more than just physical strength. It's also the power to endure hardship." Molissa laughed. "That's coming from a Queen living in a castle. You should see how the common people live."

"I have," Pol said. He'd accompanied her mother in her alms-giving expeditions a few times.

She nodded her head. "Hardship is not just a lack of money. It can be a lack of many things. Respect, trust, love. You have to endure envy and jealousy on the part of people who would seek to put themselves above you."

"They are above me. We've talked about this before," Pol said. Her preaching sometimes got boring, and this was one of those times. It made Pol yawn.

"Oh, I've been taking you away from your rest." She got to her feet. "I'll be back. I'll instruct the cook to send your evening meal here."

"Will it be poisoned?"

Molissa laughed. "I assure you it won't be since I'll taste it first myself."

Later that evening, Pol heard a knock at his door. 'Dinner,' he said to himself. He rose to the door and opened it up.

"I heard you might be hungry," Paki said. He had dressed as a servant, rolling a wooden trolley into Pol's rooms.

"You'll need to watch me eat, so I don't get poisoned," Pol said, not able to suppress a grin.

"That didn't work so well the last time we ate together, did it?"

Pol shook his head. "My mother said she'd taste it first to make sure my dinner was digestible."

Paki laughed. "Only you would say digestible. Everyone else would say fine or something." He removed the cloth covering the trolley, revealing two plates. "One for you and one for me."

That was enough to get the boys eating. Pol wasn't very hungry, but he managed to keep up with his friend.

"So Prince Grostin did it?" Paki said. "That's what my dad thinks, but don't you tell anyone he guessed. His life wouldn't be worth a clod of dirt."

Pol nodded. "There's nothing we can do but be vigilant. Actually, there's nothing I can do. We will need to forget the incident. My father brushed it off. Amonna didn't admit it was Grostin, but I could tell. Landon would come at me with a bare sword, if he was brave enough."

"To fight a fourteen-year-old boy? He's six years older than you and is the size of a full-grown man."

"I know. He's more like the King, but Grostin… who knows who he is like. Malden Gastoria?"

Paki shook his head. "The Court Magician is a reasonable person and doesn't let his emotions take over, so my Dad says."

"Grostin isn't particularly emotional. He is cold and calculating. He scares me more than my other siblings." Pol stirred the remaining food on his plate.

"Yeah," Paki said. "Sneaky. The kind of person who wouldn't think twice about stabbing you in the back."

Pol looked up from his meal. "Or poisoning a treat."

Paki nodded. "So where do we go from here?"

"Malden wants me to stay away from you…not get distracted. Mother wants me to continue to play with you to lighten up my days. I'm sure we can find a middle ground, now that you're formally apprenticed to your father."

"Gardener Pakkingail. That's me." Paki made a face. "That wasn't my first choice."

"What was?"

Paki looked across the room without focusing. "I always wanted to be a scout. Much like what we were doing when we went out this week."

"You can still do that when you are older. Siggon is a great teacher, and he knows a lot about woodcraft."

After a snort, Paki looked intently at Pol. "You are the student. It's hard to be taught by my father. It's different when you are related."

Pol laughed. "I don't have to worry about that. My father doesn't want to teach me anything. He has others…" He thought of how bored he had become listening to the queen lecture him earlier in the day. "I know what you mean, now. It's hard to listen to my mother."

"Perhaps my father can find someone else to teach me, and he can do the testing. That will work."

"I don't know if anyone can replace my mother, but I'll talk to Mistress Farthia about it." Pol said. He couldn't successfully stifle a yawn, so he shooed Paki out of his room and went to bed early, exhausted from another day of recuperation.

In a few weeks, Pol had recovered most of his former strength. That put him in a positive mood. He walked the halls towards the family dining room that the children used for dinner. His parents generally had their evening meal with nobles, merchants, or important visitors.

He opened the door and found Amonna reading a book by the window. She didn't look very immersed in whatever she read, as she looked up and closed the volume.

"You are looking good, Pol. Now you need to get out of the castle and let the sun bathe your face."

Pol smiled. "I don't tan as well as you do," he said. That applied to the other siblings as well, with their darker coloring. "But I'm ready to resume my life."

"Life?" Grostin entered the dining room with Landon and Honna.

"What have you three been up to?" Amonna said, standing up. She went to the fireplace and pulled on the thick decorated rope five times, signifying how many were to eat. "I assume King Colvin and his wife will eat with notables?"

Landon smiled at his youngest sister. It turned into a grimace when his eyes landed on Pol. "Life. I see you retained yours," he sneered.

Pol resisted clutching his fists as anger filled him. "I am happy to say that I did."

He endured his evening meal with Amonna being the only sibling to directly address him. Their disdain of him seemed to have become even worse. Grostin's face looked as if he had a boil on his bottom. The thought made Pol smile, but he quickly suppressed it.

The others rose and sat in the easy chairs that were arranged in a window alcove.

"If you'll excuse me, I will return to my studies," Pol said. He bowed to Amonna, but the others didn't even recognize his presence.

As soon as Pol left the room, he made a face and tightened his fists and locked his arms straight as he stalked off towards his rooms. Pol vowed that he wouldn't return to the dining room unless invited by his mother or the king. He continued toward his rooms and ran into Malden Gastoria, sitting on a bench nearby.

"Ah, there you are. I thought we might have a chat while I checked on your progress. You look about normal, for you." He got up and followed Pol into his suite.

"I want to see your chest, so undress, my prince," Malden said.

Pol could hear mirth in Malden's voice. Pol wondered why the magician would be visiting him when he was feeling normal, but he carried out the request.

Malden felt the muscles in Pol's arms and worked his fingers. He put his ear to Pol's chest. "Oh. I should have listened to your heart long before now. Did you know you have a heart murmur?"

Pol furrowed his brow. "Don't all hearts murmur?"

"Yours sort of wheezes. A heart murmur is more of a wheeze, to me, anyway. It means your heart isn't pumping efficiently. It's probably why you haven't thrived in all these years." The easy smile had been dropped, and replaced with a look of concern. "No wonder you couldn't throw off the poison as easily as the disgustingly healthy Pakkingail Horstel. There's nothing that can be done here in Borstall. I had thought you had some other kind of malady." Malden looked drowned in his thoughts for a bit. "Your future may change for a bit. I don't think a heavy regimen of arms training is going to do you much good to build up your strength. You'll probably just get more and more fatigued."

Pol rolled his eyes. "I know all about fatigue."

"You do. Don't worry about restricting your activities, but I wouldn't run more than a few miles at a time." Malden tossed Pol's clothes at him. "You are good enough to do most things. I think you've recovered enough for now. If you have any noticeable changes, let me know."

"I am fourteen," Pol said. "I'm, hopefully, looking at a lot of change in the next few years."

Malden nodded. "Ah, yes. I didn't exactly mean puberty, but with your heart and your fatigue."

"I'll let you know at the soonest," Pol said.

"My Prince," Malden bowed with his hand over his heart.

That particular honorific had never meant much to Pol before, but with his new knowledge, it did now. He watched Malden leave his room, and then sat down and thought more about the encounter. Malden seemed genuinely interested in his well-being. He hadn't expected that of the magician.

Pol realized that he could learn to like Malden Gastoria. His father's magician didn't talk down to him, like other men in the castle. He seemed to act more like Siggon, an interested uncle. Pol didn't have any uncles, but he thought that Siggon acted like one. Malden might as well. It made Pol smile, and he ended the evening in a much better mood than when he had left the family dining room.

Pol had finally finished the history that his mother had said put her to sleep. He walked into the room that had once served as a nursery for the king's children. The toys were replaced by shelves of books. A slate board stood against a wall, and a large flat table served as a place to examine maps of the world, of the Baccusol Empire, and of North Salvan.

Farthia Wissingbel turned around after writing numbers on the slate board. "You're early."

"I am. Do you know much about anatomy?"

"I know a little bit about a lot of things, and anatomy is one of them," she said. She smiled at him. Pol put her down as another friend, although Farthia seemed more like an older sister than an aunt to him.

"Malden Gastoria thinks I have a heart murmur."

Farthia lifted up an eyebrow. "He does, does he? I suppose he would know. The man is a better healer than anyone else in North Salvan. If he told you that, why do you bring it up to me?"

Pol shrugged. "I want to know more about it. Do you have any books on such things?"

"I do, but there won't be much about a heart murmur. Anything that happens inside of you…well, we can't see inside of a human body, at least a live one. So no one can be sure what makes the heart murmur."

Farthia evidently didn't have the knowledge that Malden had, since he seemed to know from the sound of his heart that it wasn't working properly. "He said my heart isn't as efficient as it should be."

She nodded and went to the bookshelves and pulled out a book. "You don't have to read the whole thing, but there might be something about your condition in here."

"Why is such a book on our bookshelf?"

"I can't say. That book was in the crates that were put here when the nursery became a room of learning. It's not one of my personal texts."

Pol flipped through the pages and couldn't help but raise his eyebrows at some of the illustrations. Bodies weren't very nice underneath the skin. He looked at his hand and flexed his fingers, imagining muscles and tendons moving underneath. He had learned about those skinning rabbits with Siggon.

"So what are we talking about today?"

"Logistical problems. Your father requested that I spend a few weeks on the administrative aspects of rule." She looked at Pol. "Take a seat, and let's go over how you would figure out how to supply an army."

"Have you done that yourself?"

Farthia giggled. "I actually have. My father wanted to know if a certain someone was padding his purse and tasked me to make the calculations. It took a few times to scour the numbers and compare them to the actual figures before my father let the Emperor know about the culprit."

"Your father?"

"Oh, I never told you." She shrugged her shoulders. "My father works on special projects for the Emperor. He has his helpers. Before I came to teach you, I assisted him in his work. I learned as much doing that as my time spent as one of the few ladies enduring the abuse of being a female student at the University of Baccusol."

"I know what abuse is," Pol said.

"You do, don't you? I suppose my situation wasn't particularly life-threatening, but I did have my father available to help quell the anger from time to time. You don't have that luxury, even being the king's son."

"Not when my tormentors are my brothers and older sister."

Farthia pursed her lips and shook her head. "Let's get into our studies."

They spent a full morning on logistics. Once Pol figured out the basic point of what Farthia taught, calculating the needs of an army became less interesting. He endured it until lunch. He suggested that they eat in the classroom. Pol had no desire to go to the family dining room, and he wanted to know more about the political situation in the Empire. He never tired of hearing about the far-flung Baccusol Empire that covered the entire continent of Eastril except for the reclusive people in Shinkya. Since the Emperor ruled with a light hand, kingdoms and dukedoms did much on their own. They wrote their own laws, subject to the review by Imperial lawyers, but in Pol's eyes, every undefended entity was still treated as a vassal-state to Baccusol, the country from which the Emperor administered the affairs of the entire continent from the Imperial capital of Yastan.

"So what restrictions does the Emperor really make on the countries that make up the Empire?" Farthia said, expecting a quick answer by tapping her fingernail on her wooden surface of her desk.

"He restricts all countries to a maximum armed force of two thousand men. Countries can fight each other, but the loss of men and material is minimized. The law of the Empire, the Codex, is contained on one hundred pages. The country heads administer all other laws. The Empire has been in place for seven hundred years, even though specific country boundaries have changed somewhat since the founding of the Empire."

"You do know your politics, Pol," Farthia said. "That could have come right out a textbook. What is the implication of your father's alliance with Listya?"

Pol put his hand to his chin. He'd seen Malden Gastoria do such a thing, and he wondered if the gesture helped one think. "It is marginally legal. Father can have a vassal-king or duke that rules under the laws of North Salvan. I think it might be against the Codex since the countries aren't physically adjacent." Pol was unsure of that, but it seemed right to him.

"Right, again," Farthia said with a lowered voice. "I suggest that you don't openly take that point of view, however."

Pol nodded. "My father does not take dissent lightly."

"Especially when he wants to put your older brother on the Listyan throne. He has been more vocal in his desire to do so, and I think that will eventually lead to more pressure put on you."

Hence, Pol thought, the cause of anger and resentment. Pol might represent a possible threat to Landon, if the Emperor decided that King Colvin had overreached. After his mother, he was first in line, not Landon. But that didn't mean anything to his father or any of his siblings, with the possible exception of Amonna.

"I think I have been given a message about that, already," Pol said.

Farthia looked confused, and then she understood. "Oh. You have indeed. Vigilance. Always vigilance. Even in the Emperor's city, one must stay on one's toes. My own father knows that all too well."

"What is next?"

"A treatise on the religions of the world." She pulled a thick book from one of the shelves and put it on the map table. "I'll be traveling to Yastan and will be gone for a month or two. I want you to read this book while I'm gone. Malden Gastoria has agreed to take my place, and he will be teaching you other subjects, and working on your mathematics and writing skills. I leave tonight."

Pol pursed his lips. He liked his tutor and would miss her, especially if the actions of his siblings were to get worse.

"What's interesting in here?" Pol said as he hefted the book. It was so dense that he wouldn't bring it back to his rooms, since the book was much too heavy for a fourteen-year-old boy, healthy or not.

"Get to know what others believe. There's even a religion on the continent of Volia that claims its god is sleeping in their cathedral. Just read it. I don't think you'll find it quite as dry as one of your history books, but it may be close. Promise you'll read it while I'm gone?"

"I'm sure parts of it will be interesting," Pol said to be polite. He knew he wouldn't be able to generate the enthusiasm that his tutor did about their studies.

"You are dismissed," she said.

Pol gave Farthia the customary bow and left.

On his way back to his rooms, Pol's thoughts turned to what Malden Gastoria might teach him. He had to admit that the man intimidated him. However, he'd rather be intimidated by the magician, if he continued to be friendly, than assaulted by his brothers and sister. Any time that he could justify away from them was time well spent.

He laid down to rest in his room. Fatigue had caught up with him, as it did from time to time. He rang for his dinner, and when the servant came, Pol said he wanted to study, so the servant followed him as he made his way back to the classroom.

The servant lit the lamps and set the meal on Mistress Farthia's desk, while Pol dragged the heavy book on religion to the large table and began to read. The sooner he started reading, the sooner he could complete Farthia's task. He examined the table of contents and decided to start with the chapter on the sleeping god that Farthia had mentioned.

Pol pulled out a piece of paper and wrote down the chapter's number. If he skipped around, he might as well record what chapters he had read. He soon found out that whoever wrote the book had no intention of making the descriptions of the religion entertaining.

The sleeping god, called Demeron, really existed in a crystal dome, if this book was to be believed. The crystal was opaque except for a small oval that revealed part of the face, and that face was purportedly not quite human. The sleeping chamber itself was a wonder, built out of strange metal with designs that looked like writing that no one knew. The whole thing sounded like a prank to Pol, so he was a bit disappointed when he read the description.

The religion itself wasn't too far off some sects in Baccusol, the book pointed out. There were priests who preached the waking of the sleeping god that would usher in a new level of life. In the few temples and churches that Farthia had taken him to, priests or clerics of one kind or another preached a coming of their god that would change the world. Pol found that he wasn't very interested in religion, but he felt he had to learn how others lived when the opportunity presented itself.

Farthia admitted that with all the gods worshipped, none had actually changed society. There were plenty of miracles sprinkled around, but magicians could create a miracle with powers that mimicked what a god might do. He wondered what miracles Malden Gastoria had performed. Did he perform a miracle in bringing Pol back to life from the poisoning?

Pol finished making notes of the sleeping god sect and pulled out a map the world of Phairoon and located the city of Fassia in the upper part of the Volian continent.

One chapter down and forty-seven more to go. How could there be so many religions? Pol yawned and rose to look out the window. The room looked down on the central part of Borstall, revealing a number of spires and domes of the eleven religions practiced openly in his city. They were pretty, but Pol didn't feel a desire to belong to any of them.

~ ~ ~

Chapter Three

~

A FTER A RESTLESS NIGHT FILLED WITH GODS AND PRIESTS chasing him, Pol awoke and decided he needed some exercise, so he went to the family dining room early for breakfast. He breathed a sigh of relief that his siblings hadn't shown up yet, so his plan of going early had paid off.

He finished his breakfast just as Landon entered with his older sister Honna. Pol endured sneers from both of them, and neither spoke to him, even though he had wished them a good morning. He exited the dining room, wishing that he had finished sooner, but it felt good to walk the castle's corridors after scurrying about for the past weeks.

Pol looked down at the courtyard from a tall window and saw Farthia just getting into a carriage. Malden Gastoria helped her in and closed the door. They had a few final words, and as the carriage left, Malden waved with a slight smile on his face. He turned around to re-enter the castle, and looked up to spy Pol standing in the window. Malden gave another little wave to him, before moving out of sight.

Honna walked up beside Pol. "Making nice with Malden, the mad magician?"

Pol narrowed his eyes. "Malden's not mad. Different, but not mad."

"Twit," Honna said, turning her face into her characteristic sneer and pushed Pol backwards.

He fell over something and landed on his shoulders, and his head slammed into the stone floor. He noticed Landon's face leering before the pain in his head made him pass out.

"Not again," Pol said as he came to. Back in the infirmary, he looked up at Malden. "How long was I out this time?"

Malden frowned. "An hour? I suppose they pulled this prank while you were at the window looking at Farthia leave."

Pol nodded, but that made his head ache. "This time it was a prank," Pol said. "They've used that trick enough times in my life. I thought both of them had outgrown something like that."

"When you get older, pushing someone backwards gets more dangerous. Your lack of strength didn't help you avoid hitting your head."

"I know. I tried to get to my breakfast early, but not early enough."

Malden took Pol's pulse. He closed his eyes and whispered something. The magician's eyes opened, but were unfocused. "I'll be eating my meals with you, for now. Perhaps breakfast in your chambers and dinner in mine, unless King Colvin eats with his family."

"They will hate me even more if I do that."

Malden shook his head. "Do you really think they will change their minds? I don't."

The magician's frank opinion shocked Pol. "You should be defending them. Saying their anger will eventually go away. That's what most people say. They will outgrow the pranks," Pol said.

"Oh, I'll concede that their anger may end some day in the distant future, but they will never like you. Prince Poldon Fairfield is an unwelcome threat to them, especially Landon, since he has his heart set on ruling Listya."

Pol felt deflated. In a fair world, he would be the one in line to sit on the Listyan throne, but what was fair or honest in the world around him? He shook his head and made it ache.

"Spend today in bed. I'll send along Paki to cheer you up." Malden stood up and left Pol alone in the same room he had used to recover from the poisoning.

Amonna poked her head in the door an hour or so later. "Are you feeling any better?"

"I felt just fine this morning before breakfast," Pol said. He rubbed his forehead and the pain didn't seem as bad. "My headache has improved, if that's what you mean."

She smiled. "It was. I'm sorry about Honna's prank."

"Honna and Landon," Pol said, correcting her. "I'm sure they aren't sorry."

Amonna just nodded. She gave him a weak smile. "Get better. Perhaps we can spend an afternoon in the classroom reading."

"I'd like that," Pol said. At least she acted friendly. He didn't expect her to actually take any time out with him. Amonna wasn't filled with anger, but there were always a lot of 'perhaps' in their conversations that never came to pass.

She patted his hand and said goodbye, leaving Pol alone in the room again. He looked out the window and let a healer check on his heartbeat and pulse. The healer didn't say a word and left him alone.

Pol began to get restless when Kelso Beastwell walked in. He was a tall, broad man who had served faithfully as his father's Captain of the Guard. His father commissioned Kelso to train his brothers in the use of arms. All of the older siblings attended some kind of weapons classes, especially Landon and Grostin. The two sisters had learned basic defenses using whatever was at hand and knew how to carry and use small knives, at least Amonna had told him that. Pol had no reason to doubt her word.

"It's about time you commenced your training. The king told me to let you grow up a bit, but from what I heard today, it's time for you to get started. You need to learn to defend yourself."

"I'm not interested in fighting my brothers," Pol said. "They would only hit me harder."

"Not so," Kelso said.

Pol thought, what did he know? Kelso had never been poisoned or the object of such hate. Pol found himself too tired to fight back. Thoughts of doing so only made his head hurt worse.

"I don't want to learn. Perhaps if you can teach me some exercises that I can do in my rooms…" Pol offered an alternative, and that would be all Kelso would get out of him.

Kelso had the look that told Pol that he had succeeded in avoiding any physical activity. It looked like he had won, this time.

"It is my wish, Prince, that you improve and return to your studies. If you change your mind, I'm sure we can teach you something to improve your chances to survive in this life." He gave Pol a short bow and left him alone with his thoughts.

Malden Gastoria thought his siblings wouldn't get any worse. Pol knew otherwise. He could see all kinds of nastier tricks they could play on him. It seemed that their actions took a turn for the worse, and Pol would have to find a way to make them hate him less. He could make that his goal. He nodded to himself, but he wracked his brain for some kind of solution to his dilemma.

Maybe avoiding his siblings was the wrong approach. Perhaps his defensiveness made things worse. He snapped his fingers and thought he had found the answer. He would make more of an effort to be a friend to them all.

Tomorrow he would show up for breakfast at their normal time and extend a hand of friendship. Pol wasn't so naive as to think that he could let his guard down, but he would do what he could to show them that their intimidation efforts wouldn't make him angry with them.

Breakfast couldn't come too soon for Pol. He had to wait, pacing the floor of his sitting room, waiting for the right time to bound into the dining room. Rain began to patter against the windows as the sky turned darker and darker.

The time had come, so he walked quickly to the dining room, only to find his mother and father as sole occupants. Where were his siblings?

"I am sorry to intrude," Pol said. Bowing his head to the King and Queen of North Salvan.

"You're not intruding, my dear," his mother said. "The other children poked their heads in the door and quickly left, just like you. Have a seat and tell us how you feel after yesterday's accident."

Accident? Pol thought that it was more like assault. "How did you find out?"

"Malden, as usual," the King said. "Although I don't think he termed it an accident." He looked at his wife.

Pol restrained a smile. So Malden had supported him while he described the incident. Good for the magician.

She waved off her husband's stare. "We need to all get along," she said, uncomfortably.

Their comments confused him. He thought his father would defend his children, and now his mother was…or was she? Perhaps she had come to the same conclusion that he had. He couldn't help but nod his head while he looked over at the buffet table. "I'll get something," he said, hoping to change the subject and get out of their line of sight. Pol knew he didn't hide his feelings very well. He sighed at the thought, because none of his siblings could either.

"We haven't really had the chance to chat, just the three of us," King Colvin said. He looked at his wife. "It might be a good idea to get something out in the open."

Pol quickly began to eat. He didn't want to be in the position of having to say anything about Landon's claim to the Listyan throne, but if his father was obsessing on Listya, Pol would certainly be made uncomfortable. The King's mind could be transparent sometimes.

"I intend on placing Landon on your throne, Molissa."

Even though she knew it was inevitable, his mother turned red. "I know you will do what is best for my country."

"Our country," his father corrected. "It remains my country, not Landon's. He will serve as a vassal-king to me."

For how long? Pol thought. Listya was across the continent, and that would probably be far enough away from North Salvan for Landon to do whatever he wanted.

His mother cleared her throat. "How will Hazett III accept the concept of a king having a vassal-king? It's never been attempted during the Empire before. Dukes were the highest ranking vassals to kings, and there are none in the Empire that I know of now."

The king waved his fork around. "Details. Details that I have taken care of. The petition is already on its way to Yastan."

So that was one reason his tutor had left so abruptly. The petition had to be on the carriage with Farthia Wissingbel. So his teacher traveled all the way to the Imperial Capital as his father's messenger? If she didn't know Emperor Hazett III, her father certainly would. Did she know what his father had included in the petition? She might. That didn't mean she supported it, since he felt that she didn't like Landon all that much.

"What about Pol?" his mother said.

Pol nearly winced at her question. He didn't want the King's focus on him, and he couldn't help but squirm in his chair. He quickly put another morsel in his mouth to keep from saying anything.

"Pol? What about him? He is weak. Smarter than my other children, but weak, and who knows how long his health will hold up dealing with the stresses of ruling a kingdom?" The King spoke of him as if he wasn't seated at the same table. What kind of a compliment did he just hear? Smarter than the others, but not up to the stress. His father might just be right. This conversation was already wearing him out.

"It's all right, Mother. I never have thought about ruling your country. All I'm really interested in right now is learning as much as I can about the world, and Mistress Wissingbel is teaching me to be a scholar, not a king." Pol knew that wasn't entirely true, but the fib would serve the purpose of hopefully avoiding his father's attention. The last thing Pol wanted his father to do was join his siblings in disliking him.

"See, Molly?"

His mother shook her head at the King. "I told you not to use that nickname in front of the children."

"I don't see what's wrong," the King shrugged. "Very well."

"If you want me to sign something to keep me from taking the Listyan throne, I'll consider it, Father. If it will stop the 'accidents,' I may be willing," Pol said.

His mother shot him a warning glare.

"In the future, when I'm closer to a proper age, of course." Pol put his head down and took another bite, rather proud of himself for coming up with the offer. He didn't worry about his health lasting in the near term; at least as long as Malden was around, but his siblings might not wait for his health to fail; in fact, it appears that they had already stopped waiting.

"Of course," his father said, with an eye firmly on his wife. "Something to think about." He straightened his tunic and stood. "I'm done, and I think we've talked enough. Are you finished, my queen?"

"I'm not quite done. You go on ahead, if you wish, Husband."

The King nodded to the both of them and left.

His mother took a drink of watered wine from a goblet and put it down on the table a bit more forcefully than called for, and that made Pol jump. He'd never seen such anger on her face, and it also showed how tightly her hands were fisted.

"To mention that to you! I'm sorry, Poldon. I must apologize for the

King."

Pol put his hand up. "No apology necessary, Mother. I'm serious about a letter of abdicating my right to the Listyan throne. It may be the only way I can survive for the next few years."

His mother looked shocked, and then after a long moment, tears formed in her eyes. "Oh, my dear one. You are wiser than your years."

"The King did say I was smarter."

She narrowed her eyes, but Pol could see the playfulness in her face. "Smarter than your siblings doesn't mean you are smart, just relatively so."

Pol nodded.

"I wouldn't be surprised if the King is looking in the Imperial Codex and in the law books of North Salvan for the rules on abdication. It is horrible what Colvin's three oldest children have done to you. Their meanness only gets worse."

"It might have stopped forever in the forest if Siggon hadn't—" Pol said.

"I know what Siggon did. You don't have to describe it at breakfast," she said.

Pol wondered about Mistress Farthia's journey. "Did my teacher leave for Yastan just to deliver Father's petition?"

"Let's say he took an easy opportunity to make sure his petition got into the right hands." His mother looked worried. "I had always thought you would take my own father's place..." She looked out the window and then back to Pol. "But your health needs to improve. I can wait."

Pol smiled to comfort his mother. "Maybe I'll take my father's place here in Borstall." Pol knew his siblings wouldn't permit something so bold, and they definitely wouldn't wait.

His mother looked a bit shocked at Pol's comment. She smoothed her face and lifted her chin to look more like a queen and less like a mother. "Over the dead bodies of your brothers and sisters, and that even includes your friend, Amonna, my dear. There is nothing more to say, for now." His mother and he were in precise agreement on that.

~~~

Chapter Four

~

THE CONVERSATION WITH HIS PARENTS hadn't quite gone the way he had expected. He thought his father would demean him, and his mother would step up to defend Pol's right to the Listyan throne. Instead, the King unexpectedly threw him a compliment, and his mother chided him for naiveté.

He shook his head while he headed towards the classroom and passed a window looking out at the Royal Gardens. His mind needed some kind of distraction, so Pol decided to stroll in the gardens. Perhaps the change in scenery would help him to process the disturbing breakfast.

No one disrupted his stroll down to the ground level of the castle and out the door leading to the gardens. He walked, taking in Siggon's handiwork. The colors seemed to ring like bells in his mind, a visual music that Pol hadn't quite realized before. He sat on a bench under a small tree and looked about at the pathway and the vibrant borders.

Someone pushed hard in the back, enough to spill him onto the gravel path. He heard laughing and wondered which of his brothers had played with him this time. He hadn't even had an opportunity to prepare his mind to act calm and friendly.

"Only you, My Prince?" Paki said, grinning, as he leaned against the tree and swept the cloth hat from his head in a bow. "I hope you're not hurt." A look of concern replaced his grin.

Pol got to his feet, brushing the gravel from his knees and hands.

"Nothing permanent." He tried to say it as seriously as he could, showing him the abrasions on his palms.

Paki winced and bowed his head. "I'm sorry."

After giving his friend a mock glare, Pol broke into a smile. "Don't be. I would have expected much worse from…"

Paki raised a hand to keep Pol from continuing. "I know," Paki's gaze went up to the castle. He turned back to Pol and put his foot on the bench, facing Pol. "What brings you to my domain?"

"Your father's. You still don't strike me as the gardener type."

Paki frowned, but then brightened. "To tell you the truth, neither does my Dad. I'm his apprentice until further notice, though. He's teaching me how to be a scout, but a scout who knows all the plants in the forest. I'll get to know what can be used for healing and which herbs for cooking," Paki got closer to Pol and looked around, "and what can be used for poisons." He jerked his head. "I'll not be letting someone get to me again."

"I'd like to get in on that instruction," Pol said, "but I'm afraid my father won't allow it."

Paki puffed out his chest. "Did you ask him?"

Pol laughed. "Why would I do that?"

"You won't know if he doesn't allow it if you haven't made the effort to ask."

Pol wondered about that. He made the effort to ask his mother about taking the Borstall throne, but perhaps that question was impertinent. "Knowledge is power."

"What?" Paki said. "Where did that come from?"

"Something that I learned from Mistress Farthia. I guess I've been learning more statesmanship than I thought. Your learning woodcraft along with your gardening gives you more knowledge. Maybe no one would give you a chance to be a scout if you didn't have that knowledge. It's the same thing ruling a country, supposedly, but you really don't get the chance if you're not born the right way."

Pack sat down next to him. "Born the right way? You're a prince by birth. Doesn't that count for anything?"

"Not to my siblings. They have the birthright, but I'm afraid all I have is the knowledge."

"Then why don't you make use of your knowledge?"

Pol considered the question in his own mind. What knowledge did he have that would make him valuable to anyone? His father said he was smart, but then he dismissed Pol in the next sentence as too weak. Maybe knowledge wasn't the source of all power.

Suddenly he knew he'd have to seek out Kelso Beastwell. He needed the kind of knowledge that he could use in his own defense, and Kelso could teach him how to use weapons and build up his strength. He might not get strong, but his father had all but told him that he was useless in his present state. Malden Gastoria told him that he wouldn't get a lot stronger, but one didn't necessarily need strength. If Amonna and Honna could get some training in, so could Pol.

"You're thinking again," Paki said as he gently shook Pol's shoulder.

"Keep shaking. I think you've dislodged an important thought. Why don't you give me a more detailed tour of the garden? It sure is colorful."

Pol spent the next few hours roaming around the garden until Siggon called Paki away. He sat down on another bench and was trying to fix in his mind what he had just discovered when Malden Gastoria walked up to him.

"Lunch in my rooms, Prince Poldon," Malden said. "I came out when I overheard that you were noticed wandering the gardens by certain people." He flashed his eyes towards the castle.

The magician's rooms were on the other side of the castle from the Royal Family's quarters. The walk wore Pol out a bit, but he made it without a single wheeze. It seemed that he had nearly recovered from his poisoning.

"Come in," Malden said. "You haven't been here before, have you?"

Pol shook his head.

"No revived corpses or boiling blood here, I'm afraid. We will be talking about magic, however. In fact, I'd like to test you to see what kind of potential you have."

"Me? I'm no magician."

Malden squinted his eyes and took Pol's hand. His eyes went unfocused for a moment, and then he looked at Pol. "You can be, you know. It takes a certain mind, and I'm sure you have that kind of mind. Your siblings don't, except for Grostin, perhaps, and I'd never teach him anything."

"Refuse to teach a prince?" Pol said.

"I'd leave your father's service first. That is between you and me, right?"

Malden said it so calmly, but Pol's heart began to race at the implications in the magician's words.

"You don't trust him? His mind is too devious?"

Malden nodded. "Let's leave it at that." He took a portfolio from his bookshelf. His books were haphazardly arranged. Mistress Wissingbel's bookshelves in the classroom were a model of orderliness. He untied the two strings that held a number of thick pages."

"I want you to examine this board intently. Tell me what you see." Malden pulled what he called a board from the portfolio.

Someone had painstakingly painted lots of different colored dots on a black background. Pol couldn't see the point of the exercise, and he let Malden know it.

"Patience. Keep looking. There is a pattern in there, and I want you to tell me what it is."

Pol put the board on his lap. He leaned over and squinted his eyes and looked quickly from one side to the other to see if he could pick up something, but the dots still looked like dots.

"You have to let your eyes take over. Don't try too hard, or you will fail."

"Fail?" Pol said. "I either pass or fail this test?"

Malden nodded. "I'll give you a few more moments." He stepped to a rope pull and jerked it three times, twice. "I have called for lunch. They always give me more than enough for two, so we'll get enough to eat. I'm afraid I may not eat quite as fancily-made food as you do."

"It's all right," Pol said, waving his hand, still concentrating on the board. He rubbed his eyes and kept them closed. Relax, he told himself. He opened his eyes and something materialized. It was a shape… an animal?

"I saw something! Am I doing magic?"

Malden shook his head. "No. This is all preliminary to your testing. Keep looking until you can see the shape as long as you look at it. A momentary flash is insufficient." He picked up a book on a side table and began to read.

Pol closed his eyes again and relaxed, just as he had the first time. He took a deep breath and slowly opened his eyes. He cried out in frustration, but then let his eyes relax without closing them and all of a sudden the shape of a horse appeared in front of him.

"It's a horse! I can see it. Not very well drawn, though."

Malden lifted his eyes from the book and nodded his head. "Take the next one and tell me what that is. It's the same technique. It is very hard to create an image with the dots, so give the illustrator some latitude, that's a good prince." He went back to reading as Pol pulled the next board from the portfolio.

It took him half the time to figure out the image, and then he flew through the others once he had the technique down.

"Good. You passed the first qualifier. If you can't detect the pattern, then your mind just won't be able to handle the magic technique. Rest for a bit until our lunch is delivered." Malden pointed to a couch on the other side of the room.

Malden had to wake him when lunch finally arrived. Pol rubbed his eyes.

"Headache?" Malden said while he directed the servant to put their meal on his small dining table.

Pol shook his head. "No, just rubbing my eyes from sleeping." His comment brought on a yawn. He joined Malden at the table. "This isn't quite the same as I get," Pol said, "but I'm hungry enough that it doesn't matter. I didn't eat very much at breakfast."

"You ate with your mother and father? Is that a common occurrence?"

Pol took a bite of bread that he had just buttered. It wasn't quite as fresh as what he usually ate. "The first time in the history of the world."

"Can you share any of it?"

Pol munched on his bread while he thought it out. The king hadn't said anything that Malden couldn't figure out by observing the family.

"I don't think it will hurt," Pol said. "He sent Mistress Farthia to Yastan with a petition to allow him to install Landon as a vassal-king under Father."

"King to king. I knew he didn't want to reduce Listya to a dukedom. Your father has a chance of getting his way. Does it make you feel disappointed?"

"I shouldn't be. Father said that I'm smarter than my brothers and sisters, but I'm so weak that I couldn't survive ruling for very long."

Malden nodded. "I can see his point, but I disagree with him. By the time you're twenty, you will be capable of ruling better than any of your siblings—"

"If I last that long," Pol said interrupting the magician.

"That's right, if you last that long. What do you intend to do about that?"

"I thought that if I was nice all the time around my siblings, I mean aggressively nice, that they might just ignore me."

Malden prodded and pulled a tiny bone out of his fish. "That won't work."

"I wanted to try, but then I ran into Paki."

The magician narrowed his eyes. "He's not a good influence."

"I disagree. He told me that I should ask more questions and be more prepared."

Malden raised his eyebrows. "He did?"

Pol nodded. "I told him knowledge is power, but then I realized that knowledge alone isn't power. You need to mix it with other things to make it powerful. A scholar may know everything about the world, but that just makes him a scholar. Paki is learning how to be a scout while he apprentices with his father. Siggon is continuing to teach him the things that he was just starting to teach the both of us."

"Where is the knowledge?" Malden asked.

Pol furrowed his brow. "What do you mean?"

"I agree with you that knowledge is power, and that it isn't everything. I'd like you to explain Pakkingail's relationship with what you just postulated."

"Oh. He wants to be a scout. Scouts need to know a lot of things, but Paki will know about plants that grow in the wild and plants that are cultivated. He'll know which ones can be used for healing, health, and…and for killing. Just knowing what the plants are isn't enough, so his father will teach him how to use them."

"Go on," Malden said.

"So it isn't about just knowing something, but you need to know when and how to use that knowledge. Isn't that right?"

"It is. Wisdom is where you know when to use that knowledge and how much to apply it. The process is both simple and complex. Simple, because knowledge can often be easily obtained. It is complex because there are many factors known and unknown that create an uncertain environment for applying the tools to deliver the results derived from knowledge."

Pol blinked a few times. He asked for Malden to repeat what he just said.

"So it is like an arithmetic problem except the numbers aren't all known. Missing pieces to a pattern. Wisdom is making the right guesses with the information at hand?"

"Patterns." Malden smiled. It made Pol uncomfortable. The entire conversation had unnerved him. "I am going to give you some knowledge. Magic is made by finding patterns and then tweaking them, like this." He reached forward and put two of his knuckles on either side of Pol's nose and twisted.

"Hey!"

"That is tweaking, except you do it in your mind."

Pol remembered the times when Malden's eyes lost their focus. "Like when you heal? Did you tweak my pattern when you did that?"

"I knew you would get the essence of magic quickly, helped unexpectedly by your friend Pakkingail."

A few things made sense all of a sudden in Pol's mind. "So you have to nearly go into a trance to detect the patterns. How do you go about 'tweaking' the pattern?"

"That is the hard part. Visualization is absolutely necessary, but manipulating the pattern takes a lot of practice. There are those who attend monasteries and never learn how, even if they can pick up the patterns in the boards with ease."

"I can do that now."

"A preliminary step only. I think we can set aside the magic lessons for now. It could be dangerous for you to learn much in the way of magic all at once, and you've gotten a tiny taste. Finish your lunch, and we can start on the list that Farthia gave me."

Pol shook his head. "Mistress Wissingbel gave me a large book on religion to read. I thought my lessons consisted of reading that."

"We won't be talking about religion. Studying that book is something you are to do on your own. You need to continue to learn sums, political and military history, and some geography, maps, and what the various dukedoms and kingdoms in the Baccusol Empire contribute that is unique... or not unique, as the case may be."

After clutching the dinner knife in his hand, he remembered that he wanted to talk to Kelso Beastwell about self-defense. "If I can't use magic to defend me against my siblings, I wanted to ask the Captain of the Guard to teach me defense and help me exercise to get stronger."

"Are you finished with your lunch? I'll ring for a servant to clean up."

He rose and pulled on the rope. "I think you need more tools to defend your knowledge, so I will go with you to Kelso. We can do that now, since there is no reason to put off teaching you some basic things."

The servant soon came, permitting Malden to lock up his rooms. They walked through the castle corridors. Pol looked back at Grostin, who pointedly ignored his brother when they passed him.

"You can call me Malden, by the way," the magician said.

Pol had always thought of the magician as Malden Gastoria. "If I can do that, then you can call me Pol."

The magician nodded and turned his head towards where Grostin had headed. "Has he ever acknowledged you?" Malden said.

"Yes. I'd at least get a sneer or some snide comment, but not in the last few months."

Malden nodded and put his hands behind his back as they continued down to Kelso's office close to the practice yards. "Ever since King Colvin probably began thinking about giving Listya to Landon?"

"I suppose so."

The magician raised his index finger. "That's a pattern, Pol. Look for patterns of behavior everywhere you can. Sometimes you will notice a change in a pattern, and when you do, there is a technique for backtracking and finding the original pattern. Grostin used to show his meanness. That is a pattern. Now he ignores you, and the pattern has changed, and something caused Grostin to change that pattern. I want you to look for things like that, large or small. Consider it as preparation for learning about magic. Although I am loathe to admit, pattern observation is generally more useful to a magician serving a monarch than any magic he is called upon to perform."

"Oh. Observation gives you knowledge and putting it in a pattern is the tool to make sense of it. That is where the power comes in?"

"Close enough," Malden said. "Even if you never pick up magic, recognizing patterns can serve to help you all of your life."

"As long as I use that information wisely?" Pol said.

"You really were listening. Very good!" Malden clapped Pol on his shoulders. That made Pol feel like he had been appreciated for his ideas.

They talked about patterns a bit more until they found Kelso examining weapons in the armory.

Kelso looked up from a table filled with swords. He put the one he held into a barrel next to the table, point down.

"Sorting the good from the bad?"

The Captain of the Guard nodded. "Sorting out the blades that are only good for practice," he said. "What brings you two into the armory?"

Malden patted Pol on the shoulder. "The prince has something to talk about with you. It is time for me to go." The magician looked at Pol. "Tomorrow at dawn, my rooms." He turned and walked out.

Pol watched Kelso's eyes following Malden out the door. "I've reconsidered your offer. Can you teach me to defend myself?"

"May I ask what has caused this change of heart, Prince Poldon?"

Was this a change in Pol's own patterns? He quickly concluded that he should change what he normally did in order to survive. "I thought I could change my behavior and that would make my siblings like me more."

Kelso snorted. "Not bloody likely. The stakes are too high to let a bit of a smile and a courtesy mollify the competition for your father's throne. You've made the right choice, but we can't just deal with defense. You will have to learn offensive tactics as part of your defense. It's a vital element in changing control in a fight. If you can't wrest control from your opponent, you are bound to be defeated."

That fit into what Malden had said about magic. Tweaking the pattern. Pol thought if you could make a pattern unstable with an unexpected offense, then the control could change. He smiled at the concept, and that still served to let Kelso know that he agreed.

"I don't know how I can go on an offensive if I am so... so—"

"Small? Weak? I didn't say attack with all your might. You couldn't really do that against Landon, right?"

Pol had to admit that was exactly what he feared. In a sword fight, Landon would certainly prevail no matter what defense Pol put up, or so he thought. "Right."

"First of all, like I tried to tell you in the infirmary, you need to build up some strength. It's not only getting stronger, but gaining confidence in your physical actions. Let's talk while I get these sorted out."

Pol looked around the table. "One barrel for good swords, another for practice, but what is this third barrel?"

"Scrap. Swords with loose hilts, bent blades or edges that won't take sharpening are scrapped and made into new weapons. A good soldier always avoids using a defective blade, since it can put him in unexpected peril at the wrong time."

Pol nodded. Kelso talked about swords and what criteria he used to sort them. After a while, Pol began to help him classify the blades. He'd return tomorrow afternoon for the beginning of physical training.

With a free evening, Pol ate in his rooms, and then headed back to the classroom to continue reading the text on religions. After three chapters, Pol had read enough. He looked at his notes and searched for patterns between one religion and the next.

He had read only four chapters, and already he could see similarities. After recording his observations, he searched the bookshelves for any books on magic, but couldn't find any. That couldn't help but be an intentional omission by Mistress Farthia and something to discuss with Malden tomorrow.

~ ~ ~

Chapter Five

~

THE COURT MAGICIAN KNOCKED ON POL'S DOOR. "I have received permission from your father to eat breakfast with you in the family dining room."

Pol opened the door, rubbing sleep from his eyes. "I'm not quite ready, come in. I won't take long." He let Malden in and showed him to a seat in his sitting room while he went back into his bedroom for a quick face wash, and to run a brush through his straw-like hair.

"This is a pattern change," Pol said when he entered his sitting room.

Malden stood looking out the window and turned. "It is. Glad you noticed. I thought you'd rather like the food you're used to. My morning meals are simpler, as you know. The King agreed. I'd like to see how your siblings interact with you when you have an ally in the room, at least I'd like to think I'm an ally."

"More of a bodyguard?"

The magician shrugged. "Perhaps something like that, too. It is a change in a pattern. One that we initiate, remember that."

"It didn't work out too well the last time I tried."

"That doesn't mean you can't learn from every tweak. Even for a magician, you try to learn from every experience, both the good ones, but especially the bad experiences." Malden walked to the door. "Ready?"

Pol narrowed his eyes. "Why shouldn't I be?"

"There is always a risk of something unexpected happening when you initiate a change. We will talk about it after."

Amonna arrived at the dining room and slipped through the door just as they arrived.

"Allow me," Malden said, opening the door for Pol.

When Pol stepped through his brothers and youngest sister turned to look. Malden bowed to each of them.

Landon sneered. "Not brave enough to show up on your own?"

Pol ignored him and showed Malden to the buffet table. He was relieved that a buffet had been set up this morning. Not having to order relieved Pol of an awkward period of waiting for their food to arrive.

"What are you doing here?" Grostin said, looking at Malden and ignoring Pol.

"My Prince," Malden said, nodding his head towards Grostin, and then at Landon, " Your father suggested that Pol, rather than eating in my rooms at the start of each day, enjoy his food more taking his breakfast here, as befitting his rank."

Landon snorted. "Rank?" He held his nose. "Yes, I do believe Pol is rank."

"I stink less than you do," Pol said, losing a bit of control.

Pol's oldest brother lifted his chin. "You won't say that when I'm the King of Listya."

"I'll be able to smell you all the way from Borstall, then," Pol said, "and I'll still be able to say it."

"Juvenile talk," Grostin said.

"Ah, you have been listening? And will you join your brother in Listya? I'll bet you'll do really well as his Royal Poisoner," Pol said.

Malden gripped Pol's arm.

Pol growled. "If you don't mind, I'd rather enjoy my food than the disgusting repartee."

Grostin frowned. "What is repartee?" He looked down at his plate and at Landon, who shrugged.

"Talk, banter," Pol said dismissively.

"Don't look down at me," Grostin said to Pol, and then he glared at Malden. "Use regular words in the presence of your betters, magician."

Malden blinked his eyes and moved his head back in surprise. "I will, My Prince."

Grostin grunted and looked down at his plate.

"How are you feeling these days?" Amonna said, looking at Pol.

At least one of the three acted civilly to him. "I am gaining a bit of strength every day."

"And knowledge," Malden said, looking carefully at Pol's brothers. "Since Mistress Wissingbel has journeyed to Yastan, I have taken Pol under my wing, so he can continue to learn in her absence."

"What do you know?" Landon said with a sneer in his voice.

Malden's eyes lost focus and Pol wondered what kind of magic he'd perform.

Landon stood up, knocking the chair backwards. "What the…" He looked down at his plate.

Pol could see it float an inch or two above the table.

"I will lower your plate," Malden said, and the plate dropped. A few particles of Landon's breakfast flew off. The magician blinked slowly and turned his gaze to Landon. "I know how to do that, do you?"

"I—" Landon sputtered as he picked up the chair.

"You don't?" Malden said. "Just as Prince Grostin doesn't know as many words as Prince Pol does, you don't know the slightest bit of magic. In magical abilities doesn't that make me your better?" Malden shook his head. "No, it doesn't, does it?" Pol could tell that was Malden's way of defusing his demonstration. The magician continued, "We'll quickly eat our breakfasts and leave you alone." Malden winked at Amonna, who looked rather amused. She chanced a glance at her oldest brother and wiped the smile off her face.

The rest of breakfast proceeded in silence. Pol knew enough had been said and done already, and he wondered what kind of reprisal he could expect.

Once they had finished, Pol and Malden made their way across the castle to the magician's chambers.

"You shouldn't lose your temper," Malden said. "It puts you at an instant disadvantage. If their temper matches yours, you will be caught in a fight that you can't win. If they remain calm, you look smaller and more vulnerable in their eyes, and they'll know you'll be easier to prod into rash behavior."

"But they make me so mad."

"They angered me as well, but what did I do?"

Pol considered the magic episode. "You showed them your power."

"But why?"

"To teach them?"

Malden smiled. "Teach them what?"

"That you have talents that they will never attain."

"Good. I also distracted them from your own anger, didn't I?" Malden said.

"You made it look like I know more than they do."

Malden smiled again, looking ahead as they walked. "Don't you?"

"Father says I do."

"Don't tell them that. You'll only get them riled up. You must interact with them carefully. Even I overdid it with my interaction with Prince Landon." Malden smiled. "At least we gave them something additional to think about today."

Pol didn't share Malden's confidence, but then the magician never did lack in that area from Pol's perspective.

Two weeks later, Pol sat with Kelso in the squad room of the Palace Guard. With Malden close most of the time, the siblings had generally ignored him. Pol followed Kelso's training and exercise regimen every day and did even more practice up in his rooms in the evenings. He wondered what would happen when Mistress Wissingbel returned and he lost his bodyguard.

"You have the exercises down, Prince, but not the intensity. In order to get strength, you need to challenge your body. Your flexibility would have improved, if you weren't so young. People your age are quite flexible anyway. You need to exert yourself. I know it's not in your nature, but trying isn't enough. Muscles are paid for with sweat."

Pol sat down after demonstrating the moves that he had learned. "I don't like the exercising," Pol said.

Kelso put his hand to his bearded chin. "Then we need to give you some goals. Would that work better?"

"Like keeping score?"

Kelso nodded. He pulled out a sheet of paper and dipped a pen in an inkwell. "First of all, we are going to use weights. We will increase your repetitions, but go down to lighter weights and then increase them again once you've gotten comfortable at that level. The idea is to work you hard enough to where you are uncomfortable. Once we know what you can do, then we will chart out a plan. The goal is to get some improvement in your strength from today. In the meantime, we will talk about two elements for those who lack strength. It may not seem noble to you, but you can certainly master how to move with stealth."

"Like a hunter?"

Kelso broke into a grin. "Exactly. You learned some of that with Siggon, right?"

"I did."

"Then you'll spend more time with him. That way Pakkingail and you can figure out your own games. Siggon knows more than how to move quietly in a forest from his scouting experience. You'll be doing some training on the castle grounds, but at night. Can you handle a little less sleep?"

Pol nodded.

"Good. I'll let Malden know what the new plan is."

Why did Kelso have to get Malden's permission? Had the king directed Malden to be his bodyguard? He had only been joking in the dining room with his siblings, but it looked like he might have spoken the truth, after all. It didn't matter, not really. A pattern change. Pol knew that the less predictable he could be, the more power he could acquire at the expense of his siblings.

Paki stood looking towards the gardens in the dark. Pol had moved faster than he had, using a different route, and now faced Paki's back. Pol grabbed hold of the bar of chalk in his pocket, walked up to his friend in the darkness, and struck a line down Paki's back.

"What?" Paki turned, his face filled with shock. "How did you?" He put his hands on his hips. "Magic? You've been spending too much time with Malden Gastoria."

Pol laughed. He had used everything he had learned before his poisoning along with new walking techniques that Siggon had taught him. Kelso had reviewed the plans of the castle, allowing Pol to take short cuts. The short cuts were the real disruption in the pattern that Paki saw, and Pol had the confidence that he could succeed.

"I've spent time with Kelso. I learned about the benefit of shortcuts."

Paki clapped Pol on the shoulders. His friend had grown noticeably taller in the last month. "You'll have to share your knowledge. It will help me stay one foot in front of my father," Paki said.

Pol felt wonderful. His planning and hard work had paid off. Kelso had him running as much as he was able, but even if he lasted a bit longer, Pol tired quickly and just couldn't gain the stamina that he wanted. Still, he had slipped through the castle grounds more quickly than Paki, who was in much better shape.

Later in his bedroom, Pol fell onto his bed. Sleep came quickly, crowding out the vision of his victory.

He rose early the next morning and decided he would track Grostin before breakfast. He put on dark clothes to match the clouds that had rolled in that night and stationed himself just around the corner from Grostin's chambers.

His brother surprised Pol and walked out much earlier than expected. He looked around the corridor before heading just past Pol in the opposite direction from the dining room. Pol hugged the wall as Grostin walked past.

He slithered along the wall and padded his way to the next intersection, and then ducked behind the edge of a tapestry. Grostin didn't look back while Pol followed him.

His brother stopped and looked around before he turned into the servants' quarters. Why would he be heading that way? Pol had no idea, and he couldn't place Grostin's actions into any kind of pattern that he knew.

Pol let just a slice of his head appear in the next corridor, just quickly enough to see Grostin knock on a door. A young servant girl grinned at Grostin and pulled him into her room.

What did that mean? Pol turned to go back to his rooms. He had just about made it past when someone hit him square in the back. Pol lost his breath.

"No bodyguard this morning?" Landon said.

Pol fought for breath. He leaned over, hands to knees, fighting for air, when Landon kicked him in his rear, sending Pol sprawling out on the stone floor. His brother stepped on his back and stalked off towards the dining room.

He finally caught his breath and felt for bruises. He'd be sitting tenderly for a while, and perhaps Paki could tell him the condition of his back. So much for stealth, he thought.

Pol shuffled to his rooms. His back and rump ached. He pulled the rope for breakfast. He'd eat in his rooms this morning. If Malden showed up, Pol could easily share his food, since his new injuries had taken away much of his appetite.

Kelso and Malden both shook their heads when Pol told him about his victory and his defeat.

"Why would Grostin be sneaking into the servants' quarters, anyway?" Pol said.

Both men broke out in laughter. "You're a bit young, but Grostin obviously was having a dalliance."

"Dalliance?" Pol furrowed his brow until he understood. "Oh. He would be kissing the servant?"

"Perhaps more," Kelso said.

Pol blushed. "That's not proper."

"No, but I'll bet Landon was about to do the same, or perhaps he was returning from such an encounter when he caught you."

It embarrassed Pol to agree. "Stealth must include ingress and egress."

"Good word choices," Malden said.

Kelso rubbed Pol's hair. "You can't let up until you are sure you are safe. Vigilance throughout the entire mission. Paki wouldn't know that since when you marked him, the game was over. You didn't play a harmless game this morning."

"And I lost."

Kelso nodded. "You did. Learn from it, Prince Poldon. Be lucky you escaped with a few bruises to your body and your pride. It could always be much worse."

A guard intruded on their conference. "Mistress Wissingbel has returned."

Malden looked at Kelso. "She would have just barely made it to Yastan before she turned around and came back. I'll be leaving you both," the magician said, as he walked out of the room.

Kelso dismissed the guard. "You rest up for a couple of days, but continue your exercises."

~ ~ ~

Chapter Six

~

A SERVANT SUMMONED POL FROM HIS ROOMS just after he had finished his lunch. Malden had excused himself from his duties for the afternoon, and Pol still hurt from his bruises. Mistress Wissingbel waited for him in the classroom.

"You came back early," Pol said as he entered the room.

"No sense staying in Yastan when my father and the Emperor have launched a Processional."

Pol tried to remember what a Processional was. The Emperor's tour. He would pick five or six kingdoms and visit them, nearly unannounced. "Where is he going?"

"Waring, a corner of East Huffnya, Tarida, North Salvan, Finster, and then he'll finish up going through Boxall on his way back."

"Did you deliver the petition?" Pol said.

"You know about that? I did, thirty miles north of Baccusol, catching up with my father who accompanies Hazett Pastelle."

Pol knew that was the real name of Hazett III, Emperor of Baccusol. "Can you tell me anything?"

Farthia looked into Pol's eyes. "He might approve the petition if Landon marries. The Emperor is a great believer that a headstrong youth is softened by a serious relationship with a woman." She made a face. "In some things, I think Hazett is a naive romantic. Just because he loves his wife and children, he thinks that every marriage is a success."

"That's not true, is it?"

She shook her head. "For many it works, but there are plenty of headstrong young men who take up mistresses if their wives don't please them. That isn't applicable to all men, and I know women who have a similar point of view."

Pol thought of Grostin's dalliance and blushed. "I understand."

Farthia looked at Pol sideways. "I'm not sure that you do." She gave him a sly smile.

If Landon became the King of Listya, Pol would be disappointed, but not terribly so, since he never had thought he'd be ruling anything but his own life. "When will the Emperor arrive in Borstall?"

"Three or four weeks. He had already started when I caught up to him. Now your father has to find a suitable mate for your elder brother before the Emperor shows up. That will make granting the petition a bit more certain."

"But there hasn't been a vassal-king under a king before."

Farthia looked sympathetically into Pol's eyes. "There is always a first time, my dear Prince. I think it will only help your situation, but I could be wrong. Now, tell me all that has happened while I've been gone."

Pol took the rest of the afternoon and told Farthia everything that had happened, from the prank that had led to a concussion to Landon's attack the day before. He finished by going over his sessions with Malden.

"My, you've made tremendous progress. Maybe I should have stayed away," she said.

"I'm glad you are back," Pol said. Although he had grown to know Malden Gastoria better, Pol preferred learning regular subjects from Mistress Farthia. "I'm still learning, but I don't feel as lost as I did just before you left."

"As I said, progress. Now what do you want to learn before the Emperor arrives?"

Pol thought for a bit. "Protocol? How do I act around an Emperor? As a prince, I can just act, especially since I am the youngest, but I don't want to embarrass Mother and Father in front of the ruler of the continent."

"What about the book on religion? These are your notes?" Farthia walked over to the map table that held the book and Pol's papers.

"I went through about fifteen religions. There are a lot more, but many of them are similar. The god worshipped may be different, but the organization of the religion and the various priesthoods are similar."

Farthia skimmed the papers. "I see you jumped ahead to the Church of the Sleeping God."

"You mentioned it. If you take out the fact that their god is in their central cathedral in Fassia, the organization is similar to others."

"So what does that tell you about religion?"

Pol laughed. "You're sounding like Malden Gastoria."

She pursed her lips, but Pol could tell she could have just as easily laughed at him. "Questions?"

"Not just questions, but piercing questions. Hard questions that force me to think about the answers."

Farthia nodded. "Get used to it. If you ever end up in a monastery, as Malden and I think you will, all of the questions will be like that."

"How can you be certain I'll be in a monastery?"

"That or Baccusol University, but I don't think you would flourish at the university. As a prince, you'd get too many privileges. No, a monastery is where you need to go."

Pol shook his head. "Don't I get any say in what I will do or where I will study?"

"You might. But the truth of the situation is that your siblings look at you as a threat. Look at what's happened since I have been gone. Do you call that a healthy situation?"

"Father said I was smarter..."

"More reason for them to fear you, Poldon."

Those were words Pol didn't want to hear. All of the progress that he thought he had made and effort he had gone through to exercise and learn stealth seemed like a waste.

"So what do I do now?"

"Your fate won't be decided until after the Emperor's visit. Malden thinks you are ready to learn more about magic."

That took the sting out of the current circumstances. "I get to go beyond discerning patterns?"

Farthia shrugged. "I'm no magician and that's why I don't have any books on magic."

Pol flushed.

Farthia broke into a wide smile and put fists in her hips. "You looked, didn't you?" She twisted her head and glanced at the shelves holding all the books in the classroom.

"How can I learn magic if I don't have any books?"

"You'll read the appropriate books after you've been assessed. Malden has what you need, and it's time that you meet with him. He should be in his rooms by now."

"Where has he been?"

"Conferring with King Colvin. He is a member of the King's Council, after all. Go now."

Pol left Farthia looking more closely at his notes on religion as he closed the door.

When Pol knocked, Malden yelled at him to come in. He sat at his table looking through a few open books.

"I don't know why King Colvin seems to think I'm competent at scheduling events for the Emperor's visit." Malden shook his head. "What do you think we should do?"

Pol shrugged. "When I read about historical events, such things are recorded. A tournament of some kind is held in conjunction with a festival to make the people happy. It gets everyone excited, even if they have no real connection to the Emperor. I would think a state dinner would be nice, and if the weather is appropriate, perhaps an Imperial hunt in Father's hunting preserve."

"Well, I guess that takes care of the outline." Malden bowed his head over a large paper and scribbled what Pol had told him. "I've been worrying about that for the last hour, and you just spout a good program off the top of your head."

Pol laughed, although it seemed more like a giggle, and that embarrassed him. "Actually I got that from the last novel that I read. *The Red Knight's Curse* or something like that. Mistress Farthia would know exactly where the novel is."

Malden laughed and jotted that down, too.

"Well, let me get to the point. I think you need to learn some magic, enough to help you with stealth. Landon sneaked up behind you, and I know a technique that will let you sense the presence of someone near."

Pol's eyebrows went up. "Real magic? I thought you said I would have to wait years."

"Maybe you'll only have to wait a few days, since I think you are talented enough." He pulled out one of his dotted boards. "Tell me what this is."

Pol thought back to how he had successfully read the other boards. He shut his eyes and let them relax. He opened his eyes and saw the word 'Magic' spelled by the dots "Magic. It says magic."

Malden grinned and rubbed his hands together. "Great. That didn't take you any time. Have you given any more thought about detecting patterns?"

Pol knew that Malden was aware of his activities. "Of course. I look for patterns all the time now."

The magician nodded. "So there are patterns that you need to identify around you. This is an easy visualization. Picture the dots on this board in your mind and think of people as colored dots moving around you."

"Is that it?"

Malden shook his head. "It is much, much harder than seeing 'Magic' on the board. Close your eyes and picture a pattern."

"Does it have to be dots?"

Malden paused. "No. If you know the plan of this room, then you can picture the walls and where the furniture is placed. The layout becomes the pattern. Don't try hard, just let the visualization come. Take your time, just let the image appear."

Pol leaned back and shut his eyes. He thought of the layout of the room and concentrated on relaxing. His mind thought of the room as black. Furniture and walls were a shade of lighter gray. He noticed that there were two large dots.

"I see two dots in the room. One is red and the other is a pale yellow or a yellowish gray." He furrowed his brow and shook his head. "I can't tell the difference in the color."

"Keep your eyes closed." Malden stayed silent. "Now, where is the red dot?"

"By the door," Pol said, pointing towards the door.

"Open your eyes." Pol blinked his eyes open to see that Malden stood by the door.

"That makes me the pale yellow."

Malden nodded enthusiastically. "I'm absolutely amazed you succeeded on your first try."

"Does that make me a magician?"

"Is a baby who holds a rattle a warrior?"

"No."

Malden folded his arms. "That's your answer. But you definitely have potential. So we know you can detect people in a room with your eyes closed. The theory goes that your location's physical layout is like a painting, and that becomes the pattern. People moving about are aberrations to that pattern."

"But how would I tweak that pattern?" Pol said, using the term that Malden introduced to him.

"No tweaking. That can be dangerous. If you tried to move me, I might feel the urge to move or I might be thrown across the room. The results are very unpredictable to the unpracticed. You will need to train to know how far you can go and what you are capable of. For now, we will work on identifying the dots. You will have to be able to do it with your eyes open."

"Then Landon can't sneak up on me any more?"

Malden shook his head. "Landon may approach you again, but it won't be a secret. You'll sense him coming if you are consciously aware of your location."

Pol folded his arms. "That will do me a lot of good when he starts kicking me and Grostin joins him."

Malden shook his finger at Pol. "Don't forget Honna."

Pol raised his arms with mock exasperation. "How can I forget her? She'll join in using her pointed shoes."

"But you'll know they were coming," Malden said, smiling.

Life might become more complicated using the location spell. Pol could always turn and run away. Now he had another good reason to know how to defend himself. "I think I need more lessons from Kelso Beastwell."

Malden nodded and sat down at his books again. "Never said you didn't. But know this, Prince Poldon, you have been tested and have passed."

"That was the test?"

Malden tapped his finger on the table. "A test. There isn't a specific one. You have to manifest the ability to set up a pattern in your mind and interpret it."

Pol was unconvinced. It seemed too easy for him, but at least his actions met with Malden's approval. "Will I get more lessons?"

"Hopefully, we can carve out some time. I know Mistress Wissingbel wants to cram protocols into your head, so you don't make a fool of yourself when Hazett III comes. That is, unless all the behavior that you need to learn was in that red knight novel." Malden smiled and clapped Pol on the shoulder.

"But what about my siblings learning the proper behavior?"

Farthia doesn't care about them." Malden smiled. "She only cares about you." The magician colored. "Well maybe some other people, but of all of King Colvin's children, you are her favorite."

~ ~ ~

Chapter Seven

~

POL STOOD ON THE DIRT OF THE INDOOR PRACTICE HALL of the armory. He looked around at the empty space. He liked the smell of the aromatic wood they had used to build it. Pol used his toe to draw a cross in the hard-packed dirt and assumed the pose that Kelso showed him. He ground his teeth at the thought of going through all of this training for a single morning of playing for the Emperor.

"Why do I have to participate in the tournament?" Pol said. "I'm only fourteen."

Kelso eyed Pol with an impatient look. "You'll celebrate your fifteenth birthday in the fall, My Prince, so you will be competing with other boys thirteen and fourteen." He shook his head. "King Colvin set the age categories to show off his three sons in the different classifications."

Pol didn't care about being shown off like some prize horse, especially since physically he was no prize. He didn't expect that he would have a chance to do anything other than embarrass his father and mother in front of the Emperor of Baccusol.

Pol knew he had to give his full attention to Kelso and his training in order to give him any chance at all not to look totally clumsy out in the field with boys of similar age.

~

Pol had improved in the last two weeks of intensive training, but unless he put his opponent away quickly, he discovered that he couldn't last more than a few minutes before fatigue began to hit, and then he would be fighting for breath, and he could feel his heart labor.

"I don't want to be made a laughingstock." Pol stopped practicing basic forms, which were now second nature, and stood straight up. "I can't understand why you are forcing this on me. Can't there be a tracking event where I can sneak around?"

That made the older man laugh. "Just your style, along with your brother Grostin."

Pol could feel his face heat with anger. "Don't compare me to my brother." He crouched down and let his eyes lose a little focus, so he could pick out the patterns that he could detect from Kelso. Malden had shown him how to use a touch of anticipation magic to discover the next move an opponent would make. Malden called it a 'sip' of magic, and it took Pol ten days to get the hang of it. Pol needed to create every bit of advantage that he could.

"That's more like it. Just do that for a few minutes and then a good touch," Kelso said. "It looks like you've got to get a bit angry to get going." Kelso sighed. "How can you do that on the tourney field?"

"Pretend that my opponent is Grostin or Landon?" Pol said.

Kelso cocked his head. "If that works, use it."

Pol wasn't so sure, but he knew that the magical technique would help him survive in the tourney, if practiced along with the pattern recognition technique. He just didn't have enough time to learn all the moves and counter-moves that an opponent might throw at him.

Kelso's compliment made him smile and gave him some motivation. He had never expected to develop any skill in using a sword, but with the magic helping him anticipate his opponent's moves, Pol found he had sufficient confidence not to dread disappointing his father in front of the Emperor. He finished with Kelso and washed up before heading up to the classroom.

Luckily, his siblings had duties to perform preparing for Hazett III's visit that kept them away from Pol, so he could walk the castle corridors without too much worry. He took the opportunity every time to practice the location magic that Malden had taught him.

Pol had improved on that technique. With practice, he didn't need to create a picture of the surrounding castle plan before the dots appeared in his mind. His new senses detected the layout as he walked. Pol only needed to close his eyes to get the image started, and then it seemed to stick in his consciousness while he moved throughout the castle. Malden continued to test his mastery, and Pol had failed to recognize the magician's familiar red presence only once.

"You must have just returned from the practice yard," Farthia said. "Your hair is still wet from washing up."

Pol grinned. "You are too smart, Mistress Wissingbel."

She returned his grin with a smile. "Of course. I am a graduate of the University of Baccusol, and you haven't graduated from anything."

"You speak the truth. What will we be learning today?"

She turned around and waved her hand at the bookcases. "Something you won't learn in any of these books. We are going to discuss emotional control."

"I've been lectured about controlling myself since I was a baby," Pol said.

"Not behavioral control, but hiding your emotions. This is an area where all your siblings are adept when they choose, and you, being the baby of the family, are unschooled. I have left that aspect out of your training since you've had your relationship issues to deal with."

"Can I be taught such a thing?"

Farthia nodded. "You can, but it requires a great deal of patience along with some practice."

"My time to learn is just about gone. The Emperor will arrive in a week or two," Pol said.

"I don't intend that you become an expert. In the kind of control I'm talking about, you have to develop a sense of the situation in conjunction with learning to suppress your feelings. Malden says you are beginning to learn to split your mind, something magicians can do quite easily."

Pol was uncomfortable with Malden sharing his magical progress with his tutor, but what could he do? He pressed his lips tightly together. "I have begun to learn a few things."

"You can build on developing an awareness of the emotions being displayed, so you can recognize when someone is trying to manipulate yours. Then you use that information to control your emotions. Learning to be an expert takes a lot of practice, but I suspect you do more of that than you think."

"Perhaps you can tell me how?" Pol said.

"I know you're an introspective boy. You often think things through before you respond to my questions. Do the same thing before you say something that will anger your siblings. You can use that technique before you let your emotions get the better of you."

"Before I lose my temper?"

Farthia shrugged. "For lack of another suitable example, yes. You should instantly recognize situations where something is better left unsaid. Then you suppress your emotions. As Malden might say, it's a matter of detecting a pattern and not letting others use the pattern to get a response from you. Let me try to put it another way. Think of the emotional framework in the social situation you find yourself in, and then in this situation, avoid breaking the pattern, so that you don't react negatively and make an emotionally-charged situation worse."

"Not tweaking then," Pol said. "Magician Malden talks about tweaking patterns if you are a magician."

She waved her hand, and then nodded. "Whatever works. In this case your goal is to make other's unable to tweak your own emotional pattern." Farthia put a finger to her lips. "I think that's how Malden would explain it." She gave her head a little shake. "We will go through various scenarios. Playacting, if you will, to practice."

Pol thought such an exercise would be boring, but as Farthia explained situations and began to badger Pol, he realized that he could turn suppressing his emotions into a game. If he could keep from making an outburst, then he won. The key was recognizing such situations, but Pol quickly found out that any social situation could be made into a game.

Farthia suggested a test the next morning.

Amonna had just sat down at the table in the family dining room. A servant walked in to take her breakfast order, and Pol decided to have much the same thing. He hadn't seen Amonna since the announcement.

"How are you this morning? Are the preparations close to finishing?" Pol said.

Amonna rolled her eyes. "You don't know how much work all of this is. I had to be measured for eight dresses. Eight! The Emperor will only be here for three or four days."

Pol smiled. "I've never been measured for a dress before, so I can only imagine."

That made Amonna giggle. He had missed talking to his only friendly sibling. Since the other three had stepped up their campaign against him, he rarely saw her.

"What are you laughing about?" Grostin said as he opened the door and stepped in. "Do we have to order today? I don't have much time."

Pol didn't like Grostin's attitude or his whining, but he set his deeper emotions aside and attempted to suppress those emotions.

"Pol told me a joke. More of a funny comment, really. It made me laugh," Amonna said.

Grostin grimaced and pulled the cord. He posed in a ridiculous way, tapping his toes impatiently, waiting for a servant to appear. It looked ridiculous to Pol, and he just about laughed. But he only laughed deep inside and kept his expression as calm as he could.

The door opened and Honna stepped in. She made a face when she saw Pol sitting at the table. "Why are you here? I thought you had taken to always eating with Malden Gastonia, your nursemaid."

Pol struggled to give his sister a bland smile. "Why are we all here? For breakfast, of course."

Amonna giggled again, and received glares from Grostin and Honna for her trouble.

The game seemed to be working.

"Where is Landon?" He would be the true test, Pol thought.

"Practicing on the field, where else?" Honna said. She put her hand to her mouth. Pol knew that his oldest sister had slipped up and answered Pol in a normal fashion.

"Oh," Pol said. "All I've trained for is swordplay for the fourteen-year-olds. I imagine he will be competing in multiple events."

"All the events," Amonna said. "Grostin is only doing swords like you."

"Unlike Pol," Grostin said. "I will win."

Pol would normally have taken issue with the comment and said something he would later regret. He stayed silent as he thought his emotions through and decided to say nothing.

Grostin and Honna quickly ate and left Amonna and Pol finishing their breakfast.

"That wasn't so bad, was it?" she said.

"So bad?"

"You were actually civil this morning. Usually you get all red in the face and stomp off."

"I do?" Pol said.

Amonna bobbed her head up and down.

"Hmmm." He struggled to maintain his outward state and not let the anger he felt get the better of him. "It's time for class. I hope to see you later."

"Oh, King Astor of South Salvan arrives at the castle today. Father sent a bird to him the day after Mistress Wissingbel returned with her news. He is bringing his daughter Bythia to meet the Emperor Hazett. I think Father hopes that Landon will be taken by her. She's only a little older than Grostin and just at a marriageable age."

Pol felt his breath taken away. The reality of Landon's elevation to king made Pol's stomach turn, but he continued with the game. "I look forward to meeting her." Pol forced a smile when he rose and bowed to Amonna. As he walked out of the room, he hoped his face hadn't turned as red as it felt at the moment.

He reflected on his actions in the breakfast room. Pol knew he had done well, but he detested how he had to grovel, for it seemed like that when he controlled his emotions. It made him feel like he was lying, but he hadn't uttered a single falsehood.

Pol had made sure to choose his words carefully and not react. It startled him when Amonna had actually noticed. He had never realized that he had been so emotional, but as he thought back to his reactions in past confrontations with his siblings, he had always fallen victim to his siblings' tweaking of his pattern, making Pol get upset and flee from the room.

They had all probably gotten a big laugh out of teasing him and making him mad in the past. He hoped he could make that stop. He now looked at the concept of controlling his reactions as a defensive tool in dealing with his siblings, and that thought made the deception palatable.

He walked into the classroom to see Malden and Farthia Wissingbel in an embrace, which they quickly broke.

"Excuse me," Pol said, feeling that he had intruded on something he shouldn't have, and that made him breathe faster. "I am here to report back from breakfast." He kept his eyes averted from the pair, still standing together, and sat down. "Would you both be interested in learning how I succeeded in keeping my emotions hidden?"

Pol looked out the window. He reminded himself that the game was still on. He had never, ever considered the relationship between Mistress Farthia and Magician Malden to be a romantic one. He concentrated on his breathing, and once it was under control, he blinked slowly and turned to face the pair of them as they sat down on the other side of the map table.

"I told you he learns quickly," Malden said. The magician tried to suppress a smile, but Pol could tell he was amused by Pol's embarrassment.

"You are telling me something I didn't know? But this is impressive." Farthia moved her eyes from Malden to Pol. "Proceed."

The story didn't take too long, and Pol didn't leave anything out, talking about what he felt and how he reacted. "I continued to practice the game when I walked into the room."

Farthia blushed. "And you won, Pol. You really won. How do you feel about it?" That sounded more like a question Malden might ask.

"It's not that I'm lying, but it is some kind of deception, isn't it?" Pol said.

Malden nodded his head. "I'm glad you are that perceptive. It is closer to restraint than deception, but look how you survived in the breakfast room. Could you have controlled the situation if you had lost your temper? There were certainly opportunities to do that."

Pol knew he had just demonstrated what Malden had told him before about controlling the pattern without using magic. "I maintained the pattern rather than disrupt it, didn't I?"

"If you want, think of it as a weapon of survival. Your siblings know it well enough, but not at the conscious level that you do now. There is a proper time to tweak the pattern, non-magically, but it must be done with the consequences firmly in your mind beforehand. They perceive it as teasing or something worse, goading you to a precipitous action that makes you look small in their eyes."

"Pre-meditated, but I accept the fact that I'm smaller than all of them."

Farthia's face brightened up. "Premeditated, good word! Malden is right. Continue to practice until it becomes less of an effort. You might not like to hide your emotions, but the consequences of a lack of control outweighs the pain, and you have already had to feel more than enough of that pain."

"Oh. So my siblings aren't perfect at this kind of thing?"

Malden looked at Farthia and nodded to Pol. "In a social setting they are when they want to be, but they can be provoked to break out of control. You've done that before when you've argued with them, and they lost their tempers."

Pol thought on the magician's words. "So if I had learned this a few years ago, none of this would have happened?"

Malden moved his head from side to side as he weighed Pol's conclusion. "Perhaps not so intensely, but with the throne of Listya suddenly at stake, your very existence is viewed as an impediment to them. Your behavior will not change that."

Pol wasn't very pleased with Malden's reply. "I'll have to think on that."

"Now," Farthia stood. "It's time for Malden to leave and see to Hazett's visit while we go over sums."

~ ~ ~

Chapter Eight

~

POL JOINED HIS MOTHER AS SHE WALKED with two ladies-in-waiting. He had an afternoon free, since his father had called Mistress Farthia and Malden to provide him with additional counsel prior to the Emperor's visit.

"Are you distributing alms?" Pol said.

His mother nodded her head. "I do it once a week, and you know I've done it for years. Why?"

"Can I go along? It has been a long time since I went with you."

The grin on his mother's face gave him the answer. They walked to together to the kitchens.

"Siggon's wife prepares the baskets," Molissa said. "My ladies-in-waiting choose the recipients, so it won't take too long."

Pol took his mother's hand. "This is something that you don't need to do."

Molissa smiled, a bit too condescendingly in Pol's estimation. "I feel more like a human if I do something like this. I know it's just a gesture, but I'd rather make the gesture than cloister myself in the castle. Your father gets out to inspect the city and the kingdom, and I don't want to just do needlepoint all day long."

Pol followed her to the kitchens. Eight guards were grouped around a table filled with baskets. Each guard picked one up as the queen approached them.

"Who has the list?"

One of the guards spoke up. "I do, Your Majesty. We'll be going to Bangate South. It is the roughest area in Borstall."

Pol's mother nodded. "It's not as if it's the first time I've set foot among the lowest of my people. My son will be joining us," she announced proudly to all in the kitchen

The guard bowed. "As you wish, Queen Molissa."

"I'll catch up to you," Pol said. He ran to the armory and strapped on one of the sharpened practice swords and slipped a knife in his boot. He caught up with the small procession before they left the castle grounds. Pol slid up to walk beside his mother.

"You added some paraphernalia," she said, looking down at the sword swinging at Pol's side.

"Just a few weapons. I've trained on the sword. I'm not particularly good, but I'll feel better escorting you with something to defend your honor."

"What about us, My Prince?" one of the ladies-in-waiting said.

"I will do my best to protect all three of you." Pol couldn't help but grin.

The women giggled, which surprised Pol. He didn't know how to take the laughter. Did they discount his ability to defend? Pol had to admit that the guards would do any fighting if they chanced upon a street brawl, but since Pol was capable, carrying a weapon made him feel more useful.

"It would be better to stay out of our way, Prince Poldon," the lead guard said, "but stay close to the ladies, just the same."

'Just the same' meant that he could be a line of last defense. The women began to talk amongst themselves, and Pol turned into a hanger-on for the long walk to the southwestern edge of the city close to Bangate, the southwestern exit.

As they walked through Borstall, people bowed and praised the queen. Pol guessed they had seen her pass by plenty of times, but Pol had never been to this part of Borstall before, other than to proceed directly out Bangate towards the Royal Hunting Preserve. At least he had an inkling of how common people lived by accompanying his mother.

They moved from the merchant section, closer to the castle, and soon passed tenements. People began to crowd the streets. Families scurried across Bangate Road, and the condition of the buildings began to get worse. The party turned down a lane, and soon the city began to reek with the unpleasant aroma that Pol had associated with the poorer sections of Borstall.

The ladies began to pick their way more slowly along the streets, as waste of all kinds were littered about. A sluice ran down the center of the lane towards drains that were embedded in the pavement every so often. The smell became oppressive to Pol. Even on still days, when some of the city smells invaded the castle, they had never been this bad.

His mother kept the scarf around her neck in place, while the other two ladies pulled theirs over their mouths and noses. The buildings became more dilapidated. Some of the woodwork was bare and showing signs of rot, where others had many layers of paint peeling off.

"Here is the first address," the lead guard said. He held his basket out to the queen.

"Come with me, Pol," she said, holding out her hand to stop her ladies-in-waiting. "My son will accompany me this time."

Molissa knocked on the door, and a toothless woman answered. Pol thought the woman was old, but then as he looked closer at her face, the lack of teeth turned the woman into a crone. She wasn't even close to his mother's age.

"Come in, My Queen." The woman mumbled. "I am so graced by thy presence." She used formal language, which surprised Pol, and then shuffled back into the tiny multi-story house.

"May I see your baby?"

Baby? Pol thought. This woman is young enough to have recently given birth? His musing was immediately halted when he stepped inside. The smell of human waste mixed with vomit and other smells made Pol rock backwards. How could a person live in such a state? He didn't put his hand to his mouth, although he felt like gagging. Pol thought of his recent lessons of maintaining the pattern. This time he wanted to maintain the pattern of a polite visitor, regardless of the smell.

Pol had volunteered to come, and he told himself that he would learn from this experience. He followed the two women through a front room filled with broken furniture and refuse. They climbed up the narrow, creaky stairway to a tiny room in the front of the house. The baby seemed lethargic in the crib. His mother lifted the baby up and looked into the child's eyes.

"She needs to go to a healer. There are coins in the bottom of the basket. Don't show them to your husband until you've had your daughter looked at," Molissa said. "What about your other children?"

The woman's eyes shot down to the floor. "They are out, My Queen."

Begging or thieving, Pol thought. How many men would take alms offered by the Queen of North Salvan and use them to drink? But then he looked around at the filthy walls and thought if he lived in this condition when he was older, he might take up drinking.

"I will, My Queen. As soon as you leave."

Molissa pushed the baby girl into Pol's arms. "Take her downstairs. We will escort you to the healers right now."

The woman just about fainted and put her dirty hand to her forehead. "My Queen. I am undeserving."

"Why?" his mother said with a gentle smile. "All lives are valuable in my eyes. Let's give your daughter a chance in life, shall we?"

The woman nodded, speechless at the attention from her country's queen.

Pol carefully preceded the women down to the ground floor and out into the narrow lane. He would never have thought the air in the lane would be appreciated, but compared to the closeness of the stench in the room, he did.

"We will be heading to the local healers. You walk with us," Queen Molissa said.

Pol held the baby while they walked ten minutes to a local healer's office. The queen took the infant and its mother followed them inside. Pol regretted that he felt relief leaving the house and paced outside taking deep breaths.

The lead guard walked up to him. "It's always something." He gave Pol a sympathetic smile. "It looks like you've held up well. First time?"

Pol shook his head. "I've escorted my mother a few times before, but not in an area like this." He looked around at the people. Pol tried to find a pattern in South Bangate. The people walked passed them with shifting eyes and frightened looks on their faces as they eyed the guards.

What kinds of lives did these people live? How did they perceive his father, the King, when he lived so well, and they lived so poorly? He continued to observe the passing throngs until his mother touched his shoulder. "Thank you for your help," she said. "I know it wasn't easy for you."

"Just the smell," Pol said.

His mother scrunched up her nose and smiled. "It was awful, wasn't it?"

His mother had never shown her reaction to the awful house in front of the woman. If she had, the woman might have instantly gone on the defensive, even with the Queen of North Salvan in her house. Pol thought of how well his mother controlled her emotions. With his mother it was more than emotion, it was deportment, as Mistress Farthia would describe it.

His determination to maintain an even emotional state had nearly succumbed to the city stench. His mother hadn't spent much time educating him while he grew up, but she had just taught Pol an unexpectedly valuable lesson.

The next seven baskets were given to astonished and grateful citizens. None lived in such dire circumstances as the first woman. They headed back towards the castle, which had just come into sight. Pol looked up at the towers and considered wandering into the kitchens to get some food.

Shouting in the street interrupted his thoughts. Two carts were piled up in front of them cutting off their path. Pol looked behind them and saw a number of shabby men drawing swords. He instinctively pushed the women together and herded them into an alcove between buildings.

He glanced at the lead guard who nodded his approval to him. The guards took positions around the women, drawing their swords. Another four or five men approached them from the carts.

Pol became anxious and fought for his breath. He began to sweat, so he wiped his hands as he moved his sword from one hand to the other. He drew in slow, heavy breaths and tried to be as calm as he could. He looked at the men approaching and frantically thought about perceiving a pattern, anything to help save his mother's life. He pulled the knife from his boot and now held weapons in both his hands.

The men attacked. Pol flinched at the first clash as the guards began fighting. The guards held the advantage in Pol's eyes since the attackers were poorly equipped. He remembered Kelso telling him that any weapon was dangerous. A dull sword could still break bones, and a hard thrust with one could still kill a man.

He gripped and re-gripped his weapons and tried to ignore the screams of the women. He looked back at his mother, surprised that she observed the confrontation with a calm, but concerned face. One of the men evaded a guard and attacked Pol, who had stepped away from the women, so they wouldn't be exposed to an errant strike. He worried more about his own slashes inadvertently hitting his mother, than he feared the attackers.

The man stopped to grin at Pol. "You are going to die today, little prince," the man said. He thrust his sword, but Pol used a sip of magic to predict the man's movements and slid aside to poke the man's arm with his knife. Kelso had taught him to use the knife for offense and the sword for defense just last week, but Pol had no idea he would be putting his lessons into practice in a real situation.

The man began to quickly wear on Pol's defense and showed frustration on his face. Pol's breathing had begun to increase, and he knew he had to stop the fight or the thug would wear him out. Pol recognized what the man would do on his next stroke, and in desperation, Pol slid his sword against the man's edge all the way to the hilt on the next thrust. He followed his parry to plunge his knife into the taller man's chest.

The man fell back, jerking the handle of the knife out of Pol's grasp as Pol quickly fell back to guard the women. He realized that he had just killed a man, but Pol quickly erased all thought from his mind to identify the next threat, even though he could hardly take a breath.

"Here," his mother said. Pol quickly turned his head as his mother offered him another knife hilt-first. Her assistance seemed to pump a little energy into Pol, and his breathing eased just a bit.

Pol nodded his head to his mother as a guard tripped on the body of the fallen thug that Pol had killed. One of the attackers rushed to the guard and looked at Pol for a moment before he raised his sword to strike the tripped man. Pol didn't wait for the man to strike, but threw his mother's knife into the man's stomach. He watched as the attacker fell over on the guard's back. The guard threw him off and finished him off with his own sword. He gave a little salute to Pol and re-entered the fray.

The overmatched ruffians began to back up while a squad of more guards pulled the carts aside and joined the fight. The new arrivals chased the remaining attackers who fled back into the town. Pol sat on the ground taking huge breaths. He could hear his heart beating in his ears and felt light-headed. The street began to tilt as dizziness overcame him. Pol dropped his sword. He noticed his mother picking it up and laying it close to him.

"Stay here. I'm checking on our guards," she said. She looked at the lead guard, who held his bleeding forearm. "Don't let them get away. The King will want to question the attackers."

Pol looked up at his mother. He had never noticed how strong of a person she really was. "Are you all right, Mother?"

"I am fine. You just rest. You did as well as any today," she said, surveying the carnage in the street. She left him to help the injured men, urging the ladies-in-waiting to follow. None of the guards was killed, but all of them seemed to be clutching wounds, except for the guard who Pol had saved.

Leaning against a wall helped clear Pol's head. He still breathed heavily, but the dizziness had stopped.

"Thank you, My Prince." A guard bowed deeply to Pol. "It is the first time my life has been saved by a fourteen-year-old prince. I am your man forever." The guard bowed his head again. "If you ever need anything, you seek out Darrol Netherfield. That's my name."

"Saving you helped me save my mother. You don't owe me anything."

"Forgive me for differing, My Prince. The debt is mine, no matter what you may think."

"Netherfield, over here," the lead guard said. "I need you to help me figure out what happened."

The guard bowed again. "I am called to consult with my leader," he said apologetically and left Pol sitting alone on the ground.

~

"Our hero," Malden and Kelso said together.

Pol had accompanied the guards to return the sword that he had borrowed from the armory. "It wasn't much."

Kelso shook his head. "Fourteen-year-old princes generally do not kill two of the enemy in a skirmish, and yet you managed brilliantly. Tell me all about it."

"Yes," Malden said. "No magic?"

Pol shrugged and gave a detailed blow-by-blow account.

"It looks like a knife is your friend," Kelso said. "All of your practice with two blades made the difference."

"Even picking up some throwing skills," Malden added. "Good for you."

Pol wasn't particularly proud of his deeds, but he had saved at least five lives, including his own, by taking an active defense.

"One thing though, the first attacker knew who I was, and I got the impression that he was out to kill me, not Mother."

Malden looked at Kelso and nodded. He turned back to Pol. "You don't tell anyone this, but I think you were the target of a hastily-arranged assassination attempt."

"Grostin wouldn't do such a thing," Pol said looking at both men. "Would he?"

"We interrogated a few of them that we caught," Kelso said. "They all claimed that the King of South Salvan hired them to kill the both of you. They had South Salvan coins on them."

Pol squinted his eyes. "That doesn't mean King Astor hired the men. Anyone could pay the thugs in South Salvan money and make it look like King Astor ordered them to kill."

"You could be right. All the more reason not to say anything. Stay within the castle grounds until the Emperor arrives, and if you leave, I'll have a squad of guards out to accompany you. Your mother shouldn't be out delivering alms until after all this is over," Malden said. "I'll let King Colvin know of my opinion when I report to him on the incident."

Once Pol would have thought his mother would do anything her husband asked of her, but after seeing her so calm in the midst of the melee, he wondered if that were the case.

Malden grabbed Pol on the shoulder. "Your mother said you nearly collapsed in the street."

Pol nodded. "After the fight, I could hardly breathe, and my heart began to pound. I was dizzy, but I sat down and recovered."

"The extra effort saved a guard's life and likely your own." Malden put his hand to his chin. "When did you decide to go with your mother?"

"I didn't have anything this afternoon, since Mistress Farthia and you were meeting with Father. I chanced to encounter my mother on her way out to give alms, and I decided on the spur of the moment to join her."

"Who knew you accompanied them?" Kelso asked.

Pol thought. "Any number of people. I went to the kitchen with Mother and her two ladies and ran to the armory for the sword. I honestly can't remember saying anything to anyone. She did announce to the kitchen staff that I'd be going with them."

"That's an assassination attempt organized on the fly," Kelso said. "Couldn't be King Astor, since he isn't here yet, plus I don't see why he would see you as a threat to his country." He looked at Pol. "It still might be your brothers' work."

Pol could understand pranks and tricks, but assassination involved the intent to kill. "I'd rather that not be the case," he said, trying to mask the feelings of fear and anger fighting within him. His stomach began to churn, and he could feel his heart pump again, making Pol feel a bit nauseous. "I don't feel well."

Malden grabbed a bench and pulled it behind Pol. "Sit for a bit." The magician looked at Kelso. "I've got to get back to King Colvin. Let Pol rest up for a bit and let him choose a new knife." He nodded to Kelso and hurried out the door.

"You rest up for a bit," Kelso said. "I'm going to find the best knife I've got here."

~ ~ ~

Chapter Nine

⁓

POL HUFFED AND PUFFED AFTER A PARTICULARLY HARD SESSION at the training yard. He could still tell he had a long way to go to fight as well as the instructors that Kelso had assigned to tutor him. It only showed that the men who had attacked his mother were inexperienced and raw in their sword skills.

He felt drained of energy and sat down for a moment.

"Tired?" Paki said, coming from nowhere to sit next to Pol on the bench. "The rest of the thirteen-fourteen group of fighters in the tourney are crying foul now that you have real life experience, and they don't."

Pol shook his head. "As if I care. I could just as easily have died in the street. If I hadn't been training for this stinking tournament, I would be."

The group of boys for the next higher age classification took the training ground. Pol looked on with weary eyes. "My stamina is still the same. One match and I'll be done for the day."

Paki shrugged. "Then win your one match. No one expected much of you before you had to ruin one of your advantages."

"Advantage?"

"Your poor health. It's still well-known you can only go so far, so go so far. You don't have much more to prove."

Pol barked out a short laugh. "You think the tournament is my only focus? I'm training so when better assassins come for me, I might, just might, have a chance to survive. Whoever tried to kill my mother and me will try again."

Paki grinned. "Then find out who it is and kill them first!"

A trainer called to Paki. "Get out on the field now, or we'll kick you out of this practice. Move it!"

Paki had ended up in the next oldest group from Pol in the tournament. If his friend wanted to be a scout, that meant he had to stand out in the tourney.

"I'll talk to you later," Paki said, jumping up and running to his instructor.

Pol got up and returned his sword inside the armory. He noticed that no one currently used the straw-filled dummies at the time, so he grabbed a few throwing knives and began to practice tossing knives into them, trying to figure out the pattern of the throw.

"You are getting better," Kelso said from behind.

The Captain of the Guards surprised Pol, and his throw clattered against the wooden backdrop.

"It's something I can improve. I avoided getting killed only because those who attacked my mother weren't very skilled with a sword," Pol said. "My only real success was through using knives."

Kelso looked at Pol intently. "Not so. You were only able to get close to one of the assailants because you learned enough to parry off his attacks. Don't underestimate the use of a sword. Knives have notoriously short reaches unless thrown, and that's why swords were invented."

Pol considered Kelso's words. His implications made him a bit upset that Kelso didn't understand Pol's point the same way that Pol did. The sword did put off the attacker, though. He gave a little bow to Kelso as the man went outside, and then walked over to retrieve the knives.

He didn't care what Kelso said. He would become an expert with knives, if only to be able to defend himself without running out of breath so quickly.

Pol threw a last brace of knives, hitting the target close to where he wanted to with each blade, until he had to leave for a hastily-arranged class with Mistress Farthia. His father had taken up a lot of her time, but perhaps the king had learned all he needed from her.

He hurried to his rooms, washed his face and changed his clothes, ending up just behind Farthia as she entered the classroom.

"Excellent timing, Pol," she said, turning around and adjusting her hair.

"Sit. We have quite a bit to discuss."

Pol gave her a little bow and sat at the small table in the room.

"As you know, King Astor comes to Borstall tomorrow, one week before the Emperor is due to arrive. I thought that I'd give you some advanced warning. Both kings seek an alliance in marriage. Your father is so wrapped up in Landon's elevation that he has invited them for their visit."

Pol thought for a minute. "Bythia Hairo and Landon? That is so Emperor Hazett will approve Landon's elevation to vassal-king while he's here in Borstall?"

"Why did I ever pull you from your practice?" she said in mock dismay.

"Because I want to know what is expected of me when the Emperor stays in Borstall," Pol said.

"That is right. We've never discussed how to behave during this stop on the Emperor's Processional. Since I have been back, I've been doing just that for King Colvin and his court."

"I know that King Astor is a rival. North Salvan and South Salvan have had different ways of thinking about a lot of things," Pol said. "Father is far fairer in treating his people than King Astor is. I don't think Father should trust him."

"Malden has tried to point that out to your father, but it appears he isn't listening to any counsel that will put off Landon being made King of Listya."

"It's a mistake that even a fourteen-year-old can see," Pol said.

Despite thinking that Mistress Farthia would want to talk more about King Astor's visit, she had Pol learn more than he ever wanted to about the different degrees of genuflection that were proper to use in front of Baccusol's Emperor.

Malden put his head in the door. "Are you finished with him, Farthia? I'd like to talk to Pol, if you don't mind."

"He's all yours," she said.

Pol eagerly arose and escaped from the classroom. He didn't think he'd have any use for such detailed protocol, but he remembered everything that Farthia had taught him. Pol refused to give anything to his siblings that could be used to criticize him.

"It seems that your father has wrung all he's going to out of Farthia and me. I thought you might want another session on magic. We've managed to pretty thoroughly neglect your studies since she returned from Yastan."

Pol wasn't so sure he wanted to continue magic studies, since it only distracted him from learning more about how to defend himself from assassins, but he did want to tell Malden about his progress in recognizing patterns.

Malden ushered him into his chambers. "Since you are so gifted, I think we need to accelerate your magic studies. If you had known how to defend yourself, you might have not put yourself into such peril."

Pol didn't appreciate all of the attention that developed from the alms-giving incident. It seemed that every conversation that he had recently devolved into a discussion of that afternoon.

"I'm tired," Pol said.

"Of what?" Malden said. He narrowed his eyes. "You don't look particularly tired to me."

Pol looked at Malden for a moment and tried to come up with something to put off the lesson. "I've done a lot of sword work lately, and I've improved my knife skills."

Malden didn't look like Pol's excuses swayed him. "I don't care about that. I don't suppose you've practiced locating people?"

Pol actually had kept that up, but he hadn't told anyone. "A little. I've been trying to see patterns as much as I can. I think I've made progress doing that."

"What about controlling your emotions?"

Pol sighed. He felt put upon. "That, too. It's so much to do. If I practiced everything at once, I'd still be in my rooms figuring out what to wear."

Malden nodded. "I see your point. Today you will learn how to push a coin across a table."

"What use is that?" Pol asked. He felt a bit irritable but decided that he had already gone too far in acting surly.

"It is a first step in letting magic interact with the physical world. Locating people affects no one and the predictive magic that I taught you doesn't change what your opponent will do, but pushing a coin is an actual manifestation of power. Do you understand?"

Pol did. "Okay. I don't know how you would find a pattern surrounding a coin sitting on the table. What is a pattern if it doesn't move?"

Malden smiled. "Good question. The answer is that the coin represents a pattern of inactivity, but it takes up time and space. It sits in front of you, and you can see it and touch it. The tweak is to move it from an idle state to a moving state, along a grid, from square to square, if you will."

Pol thought he had the gist of what Malden said. "Like the game of Kings and Castles?"

"That's an apt comparison. Watch." Malden's eyes lost focus and the coin moved from one end of the table to another. Pol looked at Malden's eyes, and it seemed like they guided the coin.

"I've seen that kind of thing before, even from you," Pol said. Malden had performed tricks at state dinners before. Pol didn't think that the magician liked doing that.

Malden waved the comment away. "The point is to have you do it. This is the most basic physical magic that an acolyte learns in a monastery. Remember how you look at people's color? This time I want you to imagine a grid of squares on the table, like the Kings and Castles board." He pulled out a paper and used a charcoal to draw vertical and horizontal lines. "Like this. The coin is here, you want to tweak the pattern so the coin goes there." Malden pointed to a blank square. "I want you to locate the coin with your eyes closed.

Pol shrugged his shoulders and was able to get into the same trance he used to find people. He saw Malden's dot, but then he sensed the table and pictured the grid lying over it and growled with frustration.

"I can't see the coin,"

"Try until you do. The coin is part of the pattern."

Pol tried five or six more times until he sensed the presence of the coin in the grid that Malden had talked about, and then as he concentrated, Pol suddenly felt that the coin was part of the pattern. He visualized it moving one grid over and then another, and another. He left the trance and realized that he had moved the coin.

"You didn't move it, did you?"

Malden shook his head, grinning. "Very good. Knowing how to do that would get you admitted into any monastery that taught magic."

Not that it would do him any good, but Pol smiled with the praise. "Can I try it again?"

The pair of them worked another hour on moving the coin. Pol finally was able to fully visualize the coin moving from square to square on the pattern in his head. He looked at the carpet in front of the door and pictured a long part of the grid to the carpet and moved the coin over the table and onto the floor in the precise place that Pol desired it to be.

"How is that?"

"Very good. I had hoped to get you to successfully nudge the coin, but you surprised me, as usual. Shall I order dinner to celebrate?"

After sword training the next day, Paki pulled Pol aside. "My Dad would like to talk to you."

Paki stood to the side of the door to the armory, while Pol took off a padded jerkin and put away his sword.

"This way," Paki said.

Pol followed after him and soon realized he was headed for the Royal Gardens. They entered the garden, and Siggon rose from planting some flowers.

"Kelso said you might want some resume training in botany and other things."

Pol figured that 'other things' meant woodcraft and stealth. He nodded his head. "I think I do."

"Good. Figure out a time when you can be with Paki and me for an hour or two every day. You need to learn a lot. Come see me tomorrow. Wear something suitable for spending a night in the forest."

"I will," Pol said. He looked forward to learning from Siggon again. He expected that his training would be at a different level than the casual instruction before his poisoning. "I have an appointment with someone else right now, if you will excuse me."

Pol hustled inside the castle and changed his clothes and ran to Malden's chambers. He was thoroughly out of breath when he knocked on the magician's door.

"I'll be right there, Pol."

Malden knew who stood at his door, so Pol looked out at the pattern, as he called it and saw three people in Malden's rooms. He knew Malden's color, but he had no idea who the others were.

"You have guests?" Pol said, as Malden opened the door.

The magician's eyes widened a bit at Pol's question and then broke into a grin. He looked over his shoulder. "I do indeed. Come in, and I'll introduce you."

Pol walked in.

"Prince Poldon, this is Valiso Gasibli." Malden pointed to a short, dark, curly-haired man. He had a thin mustache and a patch of beard underneath his lower lip. "And this is Namion Threshell. Both of them come to Borstall from Volia and are passing through on the way to the Deftnis Monastery."

Namion looked much younger than Valiso, perhaps Landon's age. They both had a certain posture, tight like the drawn string of a bow. Valiso, especially, looked dangerous.

"They carry messages for me."

Pol didn't ask why since it wasn't his business. "I thought we were going to spend some time tonight." Pol looked at Malden, somewhat embarrassed for barging in.

"I am sorry we will have to postpone our session until tomorrow. I hope you don't mind."

Pol chewed his lip for a moment. No one said a thing in the awkward silence until Pol said something. "I'm to train with Siggon for a bit, but I wanted a time to give him. If we might work in the afternoons after sword practice?"

Malden looked at the other two. "Early in the morning would be best to work in the gardens. See if Mistress Farthia will allow you a late start, then you can spend some time with Siggon right after an early breakfast."

Pol hadn't expected Malden to solve his timing issue, but he appreciated Malden's suggestion. "I will. Excuse me for barging in." Pol bowed slightly to the two men, who bowed deeply to Pol. "Tomorrow, then?"

Malden nodded while Pol didn't waste any time escaping from Malden's rooms. He couldn't help but wonder what business those two men had with the magician. He would try to work up the courage to ask Malden about them the next time they met.

He strolled back to the kitchen and decided to eat an early dinner and then read more in the religion text in the classroom. Later, when his eyes began to droop reading about a sect in southern Volia that worshipped a crocodile god and practiced child sacrifice, he jerked his head up.

Pol didn't want nightmares about little boys being killed and eaten by priests, so he closed the book and put his pen and paper on the proper shelf. He rubbed his eyes and looked at the book on the table.

Patterns, he thought. He sat down and put his two palms on the table and pictured a grid, including the book. If he could move a coin, he could move a book.

The grid solidified in his mind, so Pol tried to move the book up a few inches from the table's surface. He focused on the book and it did, indeed, float above the table surface, but after a moment it drifted down again all on its own. Pol looked over at Mistress Farthia's desk.

He imagined a larger grid that included the desk and moved the book from the map table to the other surface. Pol noticed that as he moved the book, that he became winded. He wiped his forehead and unexpectedly found that it was sweaty. So there was a limit to his talent. He stood up to bring the book back to the map table and felt a bit dizzy.

He sat back down for a minute or two. Would Malden be mad at him? Pol didn't know. He finally stood up and carried the massive tome back to the map table. Pol sought out his bed and slept that night, wondering what he had just learned in the classroom.

~ ~ ~

Chapter Ten

~

W HY DID THE EMPEROR HAVE TO COME? Pol thought as he plucked weeds and removed dead flowers from the garden. If King Astor had stayed in South Salvan, then the constant threat of injury or death that Pol felt might be significantly less if what the thugs had said were true. Pol just wanted to live without any stress. He wanted to ride out into his father's hunting preserve and hunt with Paki and learn stealth from Siggon without having to worry about arrows or poison. Such a vision of happiness didn't seem to be a near-term possibility.

Siggon called both boys into the little wood and lectured them about being aware of where one's body was and how to conceal it. Pol found the instructions enlightening. He thought of the trees and bushes being the pattern and his movements as a disruption that needed to be minimized in order not to be noticed.

They practiced moving among the trees. Pol did much better than Paki.

"How did you do better than me?" Paki said.

Pol looked at Siggon and then at his friend. "I tried to become as close to the woods. My thoughts were to be as close to the trees as possible."

"I've never told you that," Siggon said, "but that is the key to moving through any territory or within any building without being seen."

Paki groaned. "How can anybody do that?"

His friend obviously didn't get it, but Pol did. He looked at Siggon who just nodded.

"I have to go to the armory," Pol said. With only a few days left to train, Mistress Farthia had given Pol the day off from study in order to get some individual training from Kelso Beastwell.

Pol entered the armory and found Kelso talking to Valiso Gasibli.

"Prince Poldon, I'd like you to meet—"

"We've met before in Magician Malden's chambers." Pol bowed to the man. His eyes hadn't warmed at all since he met him the first time.

"You'll be training with Valiso Gasibli as soon as he returns from Deftnis."

"Training?"

"Val, I've known him for awhile, has a certain expertise in knives and other things that Malden and I think would be useful for you to pick up."

"What other things?" Pol said.

Valiso smiled, but coldly. "Wars are not just fought on battlefields. I am an expert on the silent side of wars."

"Poisons? Assassinations?"

"That may be part of it, but the silent side doesn't dwell on death and destruction as much as learning things that your opponent doesn't want you to know."

"You are a spy?"

Valiso bowed to Pol. "That might be a better description of my talents than assassin."

"Stealth?" Pol said to Kelso.

The Captain of the Guard nodded. "Siggon and I can only teach you so much."

Pol looked at Valiso and nodded his head. "I will call you Val and you can call me Pol."

"I suppose that means you will work with him?" Kelso said.

"I will. Does that mean I won't be spending time with Siggon?" Pol actually meant to say with Paki, but that might seem too selfish.

"What you are doing with him is fine for now. Siggon was the best scout in his prime. He knows tricks that I'm sure Val doesn't."

The spy nodded his head. "I will leave you now to take my companion to the monastery in Deftnis. I will return, and then we will spend the time you currently use training with a sword for other pursuits."

A change in tutors surprised Pol, but if he could learn to get comfortable around the man with the cold eyes and the cold smile, he might learn something useful that wouldn't rob him of breath and make his heart pound in his head every session.

Pol watched Valiso walk out of the armory and turned to Kelso. "Do you trust him?"

"As much as I trust any man. He's not a mercenary, although he occasionally sends the shivers down my spine. The Emperor uses him, and he's coming to tutor you as a favor to Malden Gastonia. We worked together seven years ago in our war with Tarida to the north. That's the war where your grandfather died. Hazett lent him to King Colvin for a season. He saved a lot of lives on both sides, he did."

Pol wondered how a spy could save lives.

"You doubt me?" Kelso laughed. "Let me say that we knew what the Taridans were going to do as quickly as they did, and the war lasted just a few days after the unfortunate death that brought your father to the throne. Without the information that Val extracted, the war could have gone on for months."

Pol could extrapolate what that would mean, not only for the armies, but for the civilians caught up in the war's path.

Two mornings later, Pol worked alongside Paki, weeding patches in the Royal Gardens. Pol looked for patterns among the flowers, and to his surprise he found more than he thought he would. Not only were flowers more similar than they were different, but the number of sets of leaves was always the same. He had thought flowers grew totally at random, but as he pulled the weeds and deadheaded the flowers, he could perceive patterns, not necessarily order, but patterns.

After half an hour of doing that, Siggon pulled the boys aside and took them to a grove of trees that stood in its own enclosure at the end of the gardens.

"We will do additional work in here now that you two have warmed up by doing some constructive work," Siggon said. "So, let's review what I've taught you in the past. It's been weeks since the poisoning."

Pol had to admit that this session bored him, but he learned nothing new, and Siggon made them practice walking without disturbing the ground for most of the time.

Eventually, Siggon dismissed Pol. The morning's program didn't involve much physical exertion, so Pol washed his hands and changed his clothes before he made his appearance in front of Mistress Farthia.

"I see you have been working outside," she said from her desk, looking up after placing her finger on the passage that she had just read in the new-looking book in front of her.

"I have. How did you know?"

"Flushed face." She looked back down and placed a bookmark in the book and closed it. "Now what should we do today?"

"No religion, please." Pol said, bringing a smile to Farthia's face.

"That's fine. The Emperor's arrival has been delayed, so he will arrive in another week or so. King Astor has come, as you know. I found that you weren't included in the dinner for Bythia, Landon's soon-to-be intended."

Pol stood, trying not to betray any emotion. "I know, Malden told me not to expect to interact with my family until the Emperor arrives."

Farthia frowned. "I think you should. Not to intimidate, but you must assert your position, as lowly as you might think it to be. There is a dinner tomorrow night. My assignment for you is to attend. I talked to your mother, the Queen, and she has agreed to set a place for you. It will be in the family dining room."

"My brothers and sister are likely to put up objections."

Mistress Farthia shook her head. "Not this time. They can't demand your place be removed in front of your mother or a visiting royal family."

Pol wanted to make a face, but Farthia gave him a stern look. "You must go. Consider it a test for the Emperor's visit, and no one really cares if you attend any more events until then."

"Even my mother?"

Farthia took a breath and looked away from Pol. "She knows how tortured you are when attacked by your siblings. Queen Molissa has seen them interact with you enough. Now let's go over trade routes between Borstall and the Volian Ports..."

Kelso rubbed his hands together. "We will work on patterns today."

"Magic?"

The man laughed and shook his head. "No, not magic, but tendencies of your opponent to repeat strokes and combinations."

Track thought back to his only real sword fight. "I already know what you are talking about." He recounted his fight with the attacker on the street and pointed out the patterns that he saw then.

"I remember you mentioned something about that, but I didn't know you actually saw it as a pattern."

Pol considered his next words. "Malden has been teaching me about magic, so I had patterns on my mind."

Kelso nodded as if he knew, and that was fine with Pol. He had never told anyone about his magic lessons, not even Paki.

"Good. I wondered if I had waited too long to tell you. You've done well enough for a fourteen-year-old, but I still doubt you have the stamina to last an entire tournament unless you put your opponents away as quickly as possible."

Pol had wondered about that as well. "So my strategy is to fight until I see a pattern to exploit and then win as soon as I can?"

Kelso put his hand on Pol's thin shoulder. "That's the size of it, My Prince, but the matches will end more quickly if you already know your opponent's patterns of fighting. Think of the tourney as five or six sparring sessions. How do you feel after each one?"

"You know how tired I get."

"And no knives are allowed, no shields either. I know the other boys in your classification will be waiting for you to get fatigued enough so that you won't last. I know you've improved your physical condition and your sword work matches up with the boys Grostin's age, but there is only so much you can do."

They worked all morning long until after time for lunch. Pol finally developed a scheme for taking care of his opponents quickly, under Kelso's expert tutelage. Kelso gave Pol a wooden sword to practice with imaginary opponents in his rooms until the day of the tournament.

Pol dragged himself up to Malden's chambers after he had washed and changed.

"More tired than usual?" the magician said.

Pol could only nod as he dropped to the couch. "I learned fighting patterns and how to exploit them. Kelso gave me some hope, since I didn't really feel I could last through all those matches."

Malden chuckled. "That's quite a change, My Prince. I've never seen you express hope in anything before."

"What?" Pol furrowed his brow. He didn't know what the magician was getting at.

"You expect to win all of your matches, don't you?"

Pol squinted his eyes at Malden. "Of course. I have Father's reputation to uphold, and finally I have a chance to do something useful with this scrawny body of mine." He pulled on his tunic. "I've got to get better so I can learn from your friend."

"Friend?"

"Val."

The magician's eyebrows shot up. "Val? You know him that well?"

"He will be another tutor when he returns from the West. We met in the armory the morning after you introduced us. He scares me, but we decided to call each other by nicknames. He is Val and I—"

"You are Pol?"

The young prince nodded. "I am. He is going to teach me how to spy."

"I don't know if he'll teach you all about that. But I arranged for him to augment your weapons training. I think you need some additional perspective, and learning a bit about Val's trade will give you an edge, no matter what happens in the future."

"Unless I am killed."

"Death has a habit of stopping a person's endeavors, doesn't it?" Malden said drily.

Pol gulped, but continued on. "Now what do we have to do?"

"Nothing. I want you to rest up for the next few days. It looks like Emperor Hazett's arrival has been put off a bit more. The tournament will start the day after he arrives. Tonight you will be attending the family dinner with the Hairos?"

"Farthia told me that I am required to attend."

Malden nodded. "I have an assignment for you, as well. Sniff out patterns. Listen to what Landon and Bythia have to say, and if you can, pick up patterns to understand what the adults talk about."

"I am a spy?"

"Not at all," Malden said. "It is an exercise in quick pattern recognition. You might find that there are bits and pieces of the conversation that won't make as much sense as you hear it, but you will once you reflect on what was said and the pattern becomes clear."

"So I'm making information out of nothing?"

Malden nodded. "Not nothing, but out of little bits here and little bits there. That's what an astute spy does. A good spy like Val can connect the words up in a flash."

"But what does this have to do with magic?"

After shrugging, Malden smiled. "I told you most of what I do doesn't involve magic at all. This is a lesson on that aspect of what a good magician does."

After closing his eyes and attempting to pick up patterns in the room with his eyes closed, Pol walked around his sitting room, nervous about the dinner. His mother had sent him a note that explicitly commanded that he come to dinner and that he was not permitted to back out.

He walked along the corridor to the family dining room. He nearly turned around and fled back to his room. Pol had successfully avoided all his family since Mistress Farthia had returned with news of the Emperor's visit, and now that day was nearly upon them.

Four guards stood at the door, two in the livery of North Salvan and two in South Salvan's colors. He took a few deep breaths and walked through, struggling to meet the eyes of his siblings as they swivel towards him. A girl a bit older than Amonna turned her head along with the others. None of those eyes gave him an encouraging look, even his youngest sister's.

"What are you doing here?" Landon said. "Shouldn't you be out grubbing in the dirt?" Pol had expected such a greeting from his oldest brother.

Pol lifted his chin and tried to smooth out his face. Landon's anger hadn't pierced his newly formed reserve. Another time, weeks ago, it might have, but not now, so he just ignored the comment. Pol noticed they all stood holding drinks, so Pol walked to the buffet, now arrayed with a few snacks and various carafes of wine and other spirits.

He looked at the servant manning the buffet. "Any fruit juice?"

The servant looked a bit embarrassed. "I was told to remove it." The man gave a quick glance at Grostin.

"Watered wine?" Pol said.

A look of relief made the servant smile. "Yes, of course. This is a sweet wine that should work well."

Pol nodded and took a sip. The drink was still too strong for him, but a few more sips were all he would chance anyway.

A man in South Salvan colors slipped into the room. "King Aston and Queen Isa."

All of them turned to the door. Farthia had prepared him for this. He bowed, but not deeply. Pol noticed that Landon bowed deeply and Grostin barely at all. The girls had long since mastered a royal curtsey.

The announcer stepped to the wall, when Malden, of all people, entered the room. "King Colvin and Queen Molissa." He gave Pol a wink and left the room, urging the South Salvan man to leave with him, just after his father and mother entered.

Pol gave his father a bow and his mother a separate bow. Again he had done it properly, as far as he could tell.

"Sit, sit," His father said. "We actually have place cards on the table."

Pol hadn't noticed and walked around looking for his place. He sat between Amonna, who sat on his mother's left, and Honna. Queen Isa sat on his mother's right. Bythia sat next to her mother with Landon next to her. Pol nearly smiled at the thought that he formally had a place at this dinner, just as Farthia had predicted.

No one talked to him. Amonna and Bythia seemed to have hit it off since she had arrived at the castle. Pol sat across from Queen Isa, but he had nothing to say to a grown woman. He looked down the table and could only grab snatches of his father's conversation with King Aston.

"Pol?"

His mother had broken Pol's concentration. "Mother. I'm sorry. I was listening to another conversation."

"Queen Isa wanted to know what went through your mind when we were attacked in the city."

Pol looked at the queen. He really hadn't noticed the woman's poor complexion compared to his mother's. He took a sip of the wine, his second, and described his feelings without getting too graphic. Farthia had drilled him about how to treat that subject if the Emperor should ask, so he was prepared.

"I assure you I wouldn't have done anything so bold," Queen Isa said. Was it an act of boldness to give alms to the poor or an act of kindness? Pol didn't get the impression that Queen Isa was very kind. He would remember that comment as part of a possible pattern.

He listened to his mother talk and draw information out of the queen. His mother skillfully kept the conversation going and Pol listened for patterns in his mother's questions and in Isa's answers. He suddenly found a thread and continued to listen as the pattern established itself in his mind.

The South Salvans wouldn't be so overt, but he got the impression they wouldn't bat an eye at something subtle. Pol listened for a signal of intent, but couldn't find one. Bythia changed the subject when she asked her mother about clothing styles. Pol wouldn't find anything of interest in that.

Servants arrived with dinner, and Pol pretended to concentrate on his food while the others picked at their meals. Landon drew Bythia into a conversation with Honna and Grostin about the upcoming tournament.

Pol discovered that his three oldest siblings had the impression that the common folk were going to let them prevail in the tournament. While he understood what Landon claimed, he realized that they were boasting without true confidence, and Pol decided to detect the patterns in that line of their conversation. Pol knew that the boys he practiced with every day had no intention of going easy with him. Paki didn't express any reluctance about mixing it up with Grostin, so Pol knew Landon's talk was all bluster.

"Will you be participating?" Bythia asked Pol.

Pol could feel a blush creep up from his neck, but he bit the inside of his lip to calm down. "I will be. Swords for thirteen and fourteen-year-olds. Grostin will be in the next higher classification and that is swords-only, as well."

She giggled. "Wouldn't it be interesting to see the both of you in a match. Perhaps the Emperor will let you fight."

Where did that comment come from? Pol looked at Grostin, sitting next to Landon. He looked a bit too smug. Unlike Landon's boast just earlier, Pol saw the confidence exude from Grostin. His brother had something up his sleeve, and whatever it was, it would not benefit Pol.

"Grostin is much better than I will ever be."

"What does that matter? A friendly match among brothers?" Grostin said, puffing up his chest. Who was he trying to impress? Bythia?

Pol turned to look at his mother, whose eyebrows were slightly raised. He recognized, for the first time, that her expression was part of her pattern of being subtle when she was unpleasantly surprised. He wondered if his training had given him that insight.

"Wouldn't it be fun?" Amonna said.

Pol sighed a tiny bit, a very controlled sigh. His sister was in on it, whatever 'it' was.

Landon returned to his boasting. His oldest brother was the least subtle and seemed to resent not being the center of attention.

"What events are you in?" Pol asked.

He pierced through Landon's studied disregard because it gave his oldest brother a chance at more boasting.

"Lance, sword, and melee," Landon said.

"Not melee." King Colvin had interrupted his conversation with King Astor, wagging his finger as a sign to prohibit Landon. "It's too dangerous for a man in your position."

Landon assumed a smug grin. His gaze went to everyone at the table and lingered, so it seemed on Pol. "And what position is that?"

King Colvin colored and glared at Landon. "My oldest son and heir."

Landon looked a little crestfallen. Did he want his father to proclaim him rightful king to the Listyan throne during the dinner?

Pol had seen enough and had no desire to stay, but Mistress Farthia was quite adamant about his enduring through dessert. He continued to look for patterns, since everyone began to ignore him again. He didn't feel like initiating any conversation or participating on subjects that were ostensibly above him.

Pol did have opinions when they talked politics, but his brothers' comments were simplistic. He had no desire to demonstrate a superior grasp of geography and the interactions of the various kingdoms, so he restrained himself from correcting them as he had in the past, much to their ire.

Pol did listen when his father brought up that the Taridans were arming again and that he'd bring that up with the Emperor since Hazett's Procession had just come from that country. Their northern border with Tarida had always been a subject of skirmishes, and under the loose rules of the Empire, the exact border was defined by whoever could defend it.

North Salvan and South Salvan generally clashed about trade routes between the countries on the west side of Volian continent and Eastril, the continent that held the Baccusol Empire. Borstall traditionally took the lion's share of shipments and transported them to the rest of Eastril. Pol didn't think a royal marriage and the installation of Landon far to the west in Listya would solve that rivalry. He mentally shrugged. Landon would better serve his country by marrying an eligible high-ranking Taridan than Bythia. However, Pol knew his father was getting increasingly anxious to get the Emperor to approve of Landon's elevation, and that meant a wedding as quickly as possible.

Dessert rolled around, and Pol quickly devoured his serving, allowing him to make his excuses to his mother and father and to the King and Queen of South Salvan. With relief, he headed for his rooms while the other siblings had after-dinner drinks with their parents.

Pol sat at his desk and began to jot down the patterns that he had noticed. He tried to separate his true feelings and hoped that he did a good enough job for his observations to look objective. His breath caught as he again reviewed Grostin's statement. His brother would assault him, and Pol had to be prepared for that.

~ ~ ~

Chapter Eleven

~

KELSO HANDED A WOODEN SWORD TO POL. Previously he had sparred with blunted metal weapons that would be used by the two youngest age groups in the tourney.

"I have been instructed by the king to assess your abilities in a sparring match with your brother Grostin," Kelso said. "Out in the yard."

So his humiliation would be very public. Pol didn't know about the wisdom of that, but from the expression on Kelso's face, it looked like he hadn't been given a choice.

"Same rules as in the tournament," Kelso said, and then reviewed the rules. Thirty or forty spectators watched. Pol's eyes looked on Amonna, Bythia, and Landon. Paki gave him a nod, but Siggon didn't look very pleased.

Kelso took Pol aside. "Make this as short as possible. If Grostin prolongs the match, he'll have you as soon as you lose your strength."

Pol already knew that but nodded anyway.

Both brothers stood facing each other wearing padded jerkins and wooden swords. Pol noticed that Grostin's sword was brand new and had sharper edges than Pol's. He grimaced. His brother really would enjoy hurting him. Pol didn't feel the same, but he was determined to make a good showing, even though Grostin was more than a head taller.

Pol tried to improve his spirits by reminding himself that he had fought a life or death battle before and had prevailed. Grostin certainly hadn't. At least he'd get Grostin's threat over sooner than he had expected, and he would just have to accept the public humiliation.

The circle of spectators grew, and now both kings were in attendance. Grostin would revel in Pol's disgrace. But then what kind of disgrace was there for a sixteen-year-old boy, already growing into a man, against a boy who hadn't yet begun?

After gritting his teeth, Pol walked into the center of the ring. Grostin spoke in whispers to Landon and the two girls, and they all laughed. Pol's heart sank when Amonna joined in without hesitation. He truly felt alone.

Grostin strutted to Pol. "Ready to be hurt? I mean hurt, really bad?" Pol didn't appreciate his brother's taunting.

He looked at the way Grostin waved his sword. It was much heavier than it should be. Someone had converted his practice weapon into a real one.

Kelso also looked at Grostin's weapon and cringed. He put his mouth close to Pol's ear. "I'll call the fight the minute you hit the ground. Beware of that weapon."

"Why don't you make him change it?" Pol said.

Kelso looked pointedly at Landon and frowned. "I'm sorry." He backed away.

Pol observed Grostin's warm-up and could see clumsiness in his swings. How could Pol put that to use? Perhaps Grostin wouldn't be able to swing accurately, so he could push Grostin's blade away with parries. Thrusts might be more problematic.

"Fight!" Kelso said.

The spectators had grown to more than Pol could count. He had to ignore the onlookers and maintain his concentration on Grostin.

His brother ran at him, sword raised high. He swung down, but Pol found he had a speed advantage if he used a sip of his magic to predict the timing of the blow and stepped away from the strike. It left Grostin open, so he poked Grostin in the side. A point could have been called, but Kelso remained silent. Perhaps his tap was too light.

Grostin stood upright and swung his blade wildly. Pol could tell that it weighed more than a regular sword because Grostin had trouble stopping his swing. Pol poked his brother on his upper arm again. Still no point was called.

He took a chance and looked at Kelso, who stood still, looking away from Pol. He would get no help from Kelso. Had everyone betrayed him?

Grostin thrust again, but this time Pol jumped back and parried with his wooden sword. It was like hitting the side of the castle's stone wall, but he managed to make Grostin miss; however, his brother stepped closer and threw a punch at Pol, which knocked him to the ground. Even the crowd groaned. That would have disqualified Grostin from a tourney match. Pol glanced at his father who now frowned.

He had to roll over to miss a downward slash that ended up sending up a plume of dirt. Pol backed up. His brother was so wild with his swings that he couldn't find a pattern. Grostin began to put the sword over his head and began to pound down like chopping wood. That drove Pol back and back again. He stumbled on the wooden walkway in front of the armory and rolled over just as Grostin drove the sword into the planks.

Pol heard a plank break. He looked at Grostin's sword and half of the blade had broken off, revealing a flattened iron rod. He backed up, but no one moved to stop his brother who advanced on him. Pol could see murder in Grostin's eyes as he scrambled into the armory, in hopes to find a metal blade. Grostin ran at him, and as his brother swung, Pol parried with his blade, but it broke in two from the ferocity of the swing.

Scrambling backwards he slammed into the wall. Grostin advanced. Pol bit his lip. He refused to die, so he looked for the pattern in the room and found Grostin's advance as part of it. He tweaked the pattern like he had done with the big religion book, and, in his panic, threw Grostin across the room. His brother slammed into the wall. His head jerked back and his eyes rolled up.

All of Pol's energy departed, and he could only lie there, looking at Grostin's comatose body.

Kelso ran in and picked up Grostin's sword. He looked at Pol and nodded grimly. No one had seen Pol use magic, so for all anyone knew, they had fought, and Pol had managed to overcome his brother.

Guards kept the crowd from entering the empty armory. His father pushed the onlookers aside and looked at Pol and then at Grostin.

"How did you?"

"I shoved him against the wall and he hit his head. It was that or let him kill me. He wasn't going to stop, Father."

King Colvin didn't look happy at all. He hoped his father directed his anger at the lack of honor that Grostin showed rather than at him. Malden talked his way through the guards and quickly looked at Pol and then attended Grostin, who began to stir, but then he went limp again.

A healer arrived and directed two guards to carry Grostin to the infirmary.

"He is concussed as far as I can tell," Malden said. "Prince Poldon is weak from the fight. I'll help him to his rooms.

Pol lifted up his broken sword. "According to tourney rules?" He waved the sword at Kelso, who looked away. "Who told you to take a blind eye?"

His father took up Pol's cause. "Yes. I'm interested. Who threatened you to allow Grostin to use that travesty of a sword? Landon?"

Kelso looked up at the rafters of the armory and nodded his head. He looked King Colvin in the eye and took a deep breath. "I'll be leaving North Salvan when either of your two oldest sons become king, sire."

"Not until then," Pol's father said and put his hand on Kelso's shoulder. "Don't succumb to their requests again. That is a royal order. If you want me to put it in writing, I will."

"I would appreciate that, Your Majesty."

Pol wondered what dire threat Landon had made. His oldest brother stood at the door, his face red with anger.

"You cheated, you little slug." Landon said. "Grostin—"

Pol's father raised his hand. "Grostin lost at two touches. I saw them both. Kelso should have stopped the match then. A blind man could see he swung a weighted sword." He looked at Kelso, who looked thoroughly chastened. "Bring it to me."

The weapon was an iron bar, flattened and slipped into a hardwood shell. "Who made this, Landon?"

"Uh," Landon stuttered, but didn't give his father the name.

"Who!"

Landon gave him the name of a blacksmith in town. Banson Hisswood, the King's Landsman and principal advisor, stood at the door looking on.

"Banson, arrest the man. Right now I can't trust the Captain of the Guard." King Colvin looked evenly at Kelso. "I will interrogate him myself."

Banson bowed his head and quickly left.

King Colvin looked down at Pol, who finally felt a bit of energy returning. "I should have stopped this when I heard about it, but I wanted to see how you performed." He leaned over and helped Pol stand. "You have shown your father and your king what honor is."

"I'll take him to his rooms, My King," Malden said.

"You already said you would, so do so. I have King Astor to see to. If you will excuse me."

By the time they stood in front of Pol's rooms, Pol felt much better. "I'm a bit hungry."

Malden looked in both directions as he led Pol into his rooms and closed the door. "I'm always hungry when I've overdone a spell." The magician grinned, and that relieved some of the anxiety that Pol felt.

Pol was afraid. He'd been caught out and he had no idea what the consequences were. "Magic?" He tried to look Malden in the eyes, but failed.

"How do you think you are at one side of the armory, helpless, and Grostin has obviously been thrown across the room so hard you knocked him out? That is one impressive feat for a fourteen-year-old. I've never taught you how to do that."

Pol nodded as he shuffled to the rope and rang it twice, which meant he wanted food served. "Yes, you did. I used the same technique to move Grostin that I used to move the coin to the rug in your rooms. I just put more effort into it, since I really, really wanted to survive."

"So now Grostin knows," Malden said.

"Will he ever admit it? I'm not so sure. He might not even remember that part."

Malden shrugged. "Who knows, but you will need to be prepared for your talent to be revealed at some point, as raw as it is. You've certainly impressed me. What magic did you use when you saved your mother?"

Pol shook his head. "I used the anticipation technique. It helps defend, but not attack. I had the benefit of a knife in my other hand. Kelso taught me how to use it."

The magician shook his head. "Kelso. Landon even admitted intimidating him. I don't know how your father can permit him to run a kingdom. I would strip him of his ability to inherit. Grostin, too."

"That won't happen," Pol said. "By the time the Emperor arrives, today will only be a memory. I've seen such things happen before. Time softens the embarrassment of my siblings' misbehavior."

"Spoken like a wise man. You're too cynical for a young prince."

"I've been the focus of too much anger." Pol wished he didn't have to think so poorly of his brothers and, he had to admit, of his father. The King would forget soon enough, especially if it meant putting Landon in complete control of the Listyan throne.

Malden snorted. "You certainly have. I do have some news that will help you out, though. The Emperor's Procession is an excuse for Hazett III to test the men of his empire for magic. Farthia only found out this morning from a message her father sent. He is accompanying the Emperor, you know."

Pol did know. "So no matter what Grostin reveals, everyone will know soon enough, anyway."

"They might. I said you'll need to be prepared to have everyone know, but I will see what I can do to keep you from being tested. Your life might be more complicated if all know you are a budding magician."

Pol looked out the window from his seat on the couch. "I can't see being treated any worse." His mind went back to the murderous words of Grostin. He still didn't understand why his brothers hated him so.

Continuing to practice for the tourney didn't appeal to Pol the next day. He dreaded talking to Kelso again, so he skipped his practice to spend more time with Siggon and Paki.

"We saw your match with your brother," Siggon said. "Kelso is a spineless twit. I thought he were a better man."

As much as Kelso disappointed Pol, he didn't want the man disparaged. "Who knows how he was threatened. His life? The lives of his family? Imprisonment when Landon inherits? Would you stand up to Landon, Father's heir?"

Siggon's gaze turned to the ground as he thought for a bit. "Maybe not. Your father defended Kelso well enough. I heard every word he said." Siggon spit on the ground. "Your brother did something very dishonorable. He'll find it a hard time to gather men to battle if he continues to soil his reputation."

"It wasn't nice," Pol said. "And he didn't win in the end."

Paki ruffled Pol's hair. He probably thought he could since he was quickly getting taller than Pol. "How did you do it? I could see your strength leaving you."

"It's a secret, for now, but I'll let you know sometime in the future," Pol said.

Paki frowned, obviously disappointed not to know, and shook his head. "I saw those touches. You beat him fair and square."

"I might not have been able to get those in if he had a blunted metal sword. Whoever built Grostin's wooden sword made it much too heavy for Grostin to wield."

Siggon put a foot-long metal bar into Pol's hand. "But he didn't. You won up front, so remember that. No matter what happened in that armory, you beat Prince Grostin fair and square. We are through weeding for now. I want you to go into the little woods and hide this. When you return, Paki and I will try to find it."

"That isn't stealth."

"No, but sometimes you need to hide something valuable and don't have much time. Use your imagination."

But not magic, Pol told himself. He took the bar, which was about half an inch thick, and hefted it in his hand. Siggon knew the little wood intimately, so Pol had no idea where he should put it.

He slipped into the woods after closing the gate and looked around. The first thing he would have to do is use stealth to hide it, so he wouldn't be creating a trail for Siggon to follow. His first inclination prompted him to put the bar as far away from the entrance as he could, but then he thought about patterns and decided that might be where most people would hide it.

He continued to walk around the entrance and closed his eyes. If he used magic principles, he would be tweaking the pattern. He could do that without magic if he could perceive a pattern that most people would use. Most people would bury it, Pol thought. So he wouldn't do that. He looked up at the leaves and thought he could hide it overhead, but Pol didn't have the strength to climb a tree this morning, still feeling the aftereffects of his duel the previous day.

Pol turned around and looked at the thick hedge. He would slip the bar directly into the hedge at Siggon's eye-level. That way if he looked straight on, he'd see the end of the bar. The leaves were thick enough to hide the bar anyway. So he carefully walked to the hedge and placed it deep in the branches. Pol made sure he could find it, so he placed a rock directly underneath where he placed the rod. He decided to create some diversions, so he quickly ran far into the little wood and picked up a few sticks about the same size as the iron rod and buried one in the leaves. He did the same thing two more times at random places and carefully walked back to the gate and opened it.

"You took your time," Paki said.

"Do you want to find it, Paki?"

His friend grinned. "Of course I do. Follow me.

Siggon smiled at Pol and followed his son along with Pol, strolling with his hands clasped behind his back.

Paki looked like a bloodhound, keeping his head down and kicking over the leaves. He reached one of Pol's diversions. "Here it is."

Pol had made the diversion look like he had tried to cover up a bit of digging. It worked for Paki, who leaned over laughing and pulled out a stick.

"What's this?" His smile turned into a confused expression.

"A stick," Siggon said, patting his son on the back. "My turn."

Paki's father roamed around a bit and found the diversion at the far end of the woods. "This must be it," he said. "This is more skillfully hidden, Paki." He reached down and grunted when he pulled up another stick. Siggon looked around. "I'm not up to rooting around the entire woods, so where is the rod?"

"I won?" Pol grinned and looked at Paki.

"You won." Siggon looked up at the trees, and then peered at Pol's clothes. "I know you didn't climb any trees and it's not on your body."

Pol led them to the hedge and stood close by. "Can you find it now?"

Siggon looked around and spied the rock. "Here." He bent over and peered through the hedge. "Are you playing with us?"

Pol couldn't contain his joy. "Look straight ahead."

Paki pushed his way past his father and looked into the hedge. He came away frowning.

"Straight ahead."

Siggon chuckled as he looked down at the little rock and looked straight ahead at his eye level. He rooted around for a bit and then laughed, pulling out the rod.

"Are you sure you're only fourteen?"

"Fifteen in the fall," Pol said, trying to contain the giddiness that he felt from winning.

"Okay, Paki. What did you just learn?"

Paki furrowed his brow and put his forefinger on his chin. "That Pol can hide the rod really well?"

Pol knew what Siggon was getting at, even though Paki didn't.

"What does a person normally do when they want to hide something in the woods?"

"Bury it."

"Right, but Pol didn't do that. In fact, he set up false trails to mislead us. Those false trails kept us focused on the object being buried, right?"

Paki nodded. Pol just kept smiling.

"When someone struggles to climb a tree, the bark generally leaves marks on your clothes, so Pol didn't do that. If he were a little stronger, maybe, but not this morning. So I gave up because I couldn't get the burying out of my head. I was as stuck on burying as you were, son."

Paki's eyebrows shot up. "So he did the unexpected?"

"And did it well. He went close to the gate where you immediately ran deep into the forest, and hid the rod so I couldn't find it by casually looking in the hedge."

"Eye-level and straight ahead so you could only see the end?" Paki said.

Siggon grabbed Paki by the neck and rubbed his knuckles on Paki's scalp. "Finally, he gets it."

"Did I pass?"

"I think he should," Paki said.

Pol looked up at Siggon. "Like a scout or a spy?"

Siggon grinned. "Right, like Prince Poldon, and that's even better."

~ ~ ~

Chapter Twelve

~

"YOU LOOK PROUD OF YOURSELF," Malden said, opening the door.

Pol nodded. "I hid something, and Siggon couldn't find it."

"That doesn't sound like much of an accomplishment."

Malden's dismissal of Pol's accomplishment punctured Pol's mood.

"I mean, tell me the whole story," Malden said. The magician must have seen the disappointment on Pol's face.

Pol told him, and Malden brightened. "So you used the pattern concept to hide the rod?"

Pol nodded. "Call it a non-magical tweak?"

"It is. I think you've gone far with that concept. I know I told you we wouldn't be meeting together again, but I wanted to talk to you about your future. I talked to your father and to Farthia about you. We are concerned that Grostin or Landon will be successful if they keep trying to remove you."

"You mean they will kill me if the pattern stays the way it is."

Malden walked to the window and looked out. "I'm afraid so. There's not much your father can do about that. He's already told them to stop, but..." Malden shrugged and turned around. Pol knew that his father wouldn't really punish his sons. He might be angry with them, but they would be around for a long time, and Pol wouldn't. "I'd still like to send you to a monastery and sooner than later."

"Leave Borstall?" Pol said. "I won't leave my mother alone to fend on her own against my brothers and sisters."

Malden looked at Pol and put his hands on his shoulders. "You put her in peril while you are here as well."

"What does Father say to that?"

"He doesn't believe me. Even after Grostin's deception, King Colvin still defends his two older boys."

The thought saddened Pol, but there wasn't anything he could do other than be there to protect his mother. She had already been attacked once. If Pol left, his mother would be exposed to three vindictive stepchildren.

"Leaving for a monastery always is an alternative, right?" Pol said. "I'd rather not think about it right now, but things may change. I'll think about it then."

Malden nodded. "Don't wait to make up your mind until it's too late. That's all I wanted to say. I think Mistress Farthia is waiting for you in the classroom."

Pol expected his tutor to also press him about going to a monastery, but Pol would give the same answer that he had given Malden.

"Come in," Farthia said. "I heard you had an awful experience yesterday."

"You weren't there?"

Farthia shook her head. "It's not something a lady would attend unless she is very young or very reckless."

What did that make his sisters? He didn't really care about Bythia. If she married Landon, she was a lost soul along with his brother. Pol frowned. "It wasn't pleasant."

Farthia leaned back in her chair. "Pleasant! He might have killed you, so I heard."

"That was the look in his eye." Pol had said enough about his duel. "What are we going to do today?"

Farthia straightened out the front of her dress. "Monasteries. You are going to learn about monasteries."

"I just came from Magician Malden's chambers, so I expected that you would try to talk me into leaving."

His tutor looked a little abashed, and then she pursed her lips. "It's still a place where you should go for awhile. I'd hate to see you permanently damaged by your brothers."

"And sisters," Pol said.

She nodded. "Let's not talk about them. What do you know about a monastery?"

"It is a place of learning and developing certain skills. The teachers are called monks, and the students are called acolytes. Few acolytes become monks, so people come and go. It is more concentrated learning than in a university, and you live in the monastery."

"Right, a place of total dedication for a time. Monasteries are safe havens. They are like churches in many countries."

Pol had read about that enough in the last weeks. "Sanctuary."

"There are few incidents of non-sanctioned violence inside a monastery's walls, if you will. Do you know what I mean?"

"If someone does violence in a monastery, they won't leave the grounds without severe punishment and might be subject to death."

"You've been doing some reading on your own?"

Pol stood up and walked to the bookcase. He pulled out a book. "Here. This is all about monasteries."

"Why are you letting me teach you about them, if you know what a monastery is?"

"Because I want you to understand that I'm not going to one as long as my mother is exposed to danger in the castle."

Farthia's mouth made an 'O'. "That is why you look so sad?"

"It is," Pol said. "I know it would be a good place for me to learn without feeling I'm liable to be attacked at any moment, but I can't leave Borstall."

"I understand, and monasteries don't typically admit women. They go to nunneries that do much the same thing, at least in most countries of the Baccusol Empire."

Pol knew that in some countries, especially outside of the Empire, nunneries were more likely to be a religious order than an educational one.

"Let's keep the option open. Monasteries accept men of any age, although generally not as young as you."

"But since I'm a prince…"

"Since you are King Colvin's son, allowances can be made. If you were exceptionally gifted, you might as well."

"Magician Malden said the Tesna…" Pol stopped. He didn't know if Farthia knew about his magical ability.

Farthia gave him a sideways glance. It looked like she knew, but she let the comment go. She took a deep breath. "For now, bury yourself in the religion text. I think there won't be time for anything once the Emperor arrives."

"So, it is definitely tomorrow?"

She shook her head and waved a small parchment letter at him. "My father sent me this along with a few other messages from the Emperor early this morning. His arrival has just been put off for another week. I think we are done, for now."

Pol rose and bowed to his tutor before he left.

He paced back and forth in his sitting room and wondered what he should do. The religion text had lost all appeal, and Pol needed a diversion of some sort from thinking about the tourney. After his match with Grostin yesterday, he didn't know if he should return to the armory, so he found the wooden sword that Kelso had lent weeks ago and cleared out a practice area in his sitting room.

Pol stood in the middle of the room, trying to make sense of the last day while he proceeded through the patterns that Kelso had taught him. He laid his sword down and sat on the couch. He questioned why he needed to participate in the tourney anyway. What benefit did he get from doing so? He really didn't care how his father perceived him, since King Colvin was anxious to steal away the throne that rightfully belonged to Pol. Not that Pol wanted to rule, but Landon would be a disaster ruling wherever he went. His non-participation wouldn't matter to his mother. Pol knew that. So why did he need to compete?

He rolled around various reasons and only came up with one good one. It was his duty as a prince. Pol didn't care about what his siblings thought. He didn't care about what King Astor of South Salvan thought, and he didn't even care what Emperor Hazett thought. He would participate because he was a Prince of North Salvan, and the people would want him to win.

Would Grostin or Landon do something to stop him in the next week, now, before the tourney started? Pol thought it likely since Grostin probably chose the timing of the duel to push him out of the tourney, but he now had another week to come up with something, and that made Pol restless.

So how would Pol do it? He picked up his sword and closed his eyes, imagining an opponent. Grostin would do. He smiled and began to play out a fight with his brother. Pol remembered the wild swings, and then he found what he sought, a pattern in Grostin's moves that he hadn't noticed while fighting before. His memory had served him well. He dredged up about all of Grostin's moves, except this time, Pol fought with a strong blade.

He imagined the weight of the heavy blows, but none so heavy as what he actually deflected in his match. He saw opportunities, like his weak touches, but this time, in the tourney, his touches couldn't be so weak. Two solid touches would win a match judged fairly.

So how could he win quickly? He had thought about that dilemma before, but he realized that he could scout the competition and find their pattern. If he already knew their tendencies, then he could use his magic to anticipate their next move even better. Pol hadn't intended to return to the practice field, but he put his sword away and walked to the armory.

There were plenty of his possible competitors still practicing. Pol decided not to put on a padded jerkin and mix it up with anyone, but kept behind the railing and observed patterns. All ages were practicing, but most of the boys in his classification were at the far end of the field.

Pol passed Kelso on the way. "Hello, Kelso," Pol said. He felt uneasy around the man because of his actions the previous day.

"Prince Poldon. How are you feeling?"

Pol could see genuine concern in Kelso's eyes, but he didn't feel he could forgive him quite yet. He looked across the field. "I'm still a bit tired, but I'll be fit enough by the time my part of the tourney starts."

"You aren't going to practice?"

Pol shook his head. "I'm here to observe my competitor's styles." He was careful not to use the term patterns.

Kelso looked at Pol with shrewd eyes. "You are quite a fellow, if you forgive me for saying so, My Prince."

"I'm just another fourteen-year-old," Pol said.

"No, you aren't. I should know since I have talked to all your competitors. They would say they are picking up styles, but that's something their fathers would tell them to say. I know you really can, and that will give you a competitive edge."

Pol returned Kelso's gaze. "I need every edge I can find, so I need to observe my opponents more. You know I'll run out of energy at some point."

"Yet you can find a way. You did with Grostin. I have my suspicions of how you defeated your brother. Your victory made my complicity in the match the lowest point of my life. I hope you can find it within yourself to forgive me."

"I wasn't angry with you because I know your arm was twisted." Pol knew he said words of placation, but it felt right to do so. He still felt hurt that Kelso had betrayed him.

Kelso nodded. "When Val returns, know that no one has the strength to twist his."

"Thank you for your admission and for telling me about Val. Now I've got to observe my competitors before they leave the field."

"Of course," Kelso said.

Pol could feel the man's eyes on him as he strolled to the far end of the field and took up a position looking at his competition. Pol turned his concentration to those practicing. He picked out the boys that had practiced at the same time he had and focused on memorizing their faces and their patterns.

Since he had been practicing with these same competitors, Pol didn't take too much time to identify how he could score quickly on most of them. A few were as wild as Grostin, and they just took a little longer. Wild swings, although unpredictable for deciphering a pattern, made for obvious openings.

Kelso walked up behind Pol. "Are you finding the information that you need?"

"I am. Are there any participants who haven't been practicing here?"

Kelso nodded. "There are undoubtedly some. Maybe not so much for the younger boys, but the competition is open to anyone at the highest level, and there will be those who come to make a name for themselves."

"Does Landon have a chance at winning?"

Kelso pursed his lips. "Probably not, but you never know. The melee event requires a bit of luck to rise to the top, if your father relents and lets him participate. Grostin, if he recovers from getting his bell rung by a certain someone, has a better chance, but I think you have the best. The other two haven't really applied themselves like you have."

"But I have to," Pol said. "It will be difficult as it is with my condition."

"You've learned that there is more to a match than utilizing sheer strength."

Pol didn't care to respond. "I think I've seen enough, for now. With

Emperor Hazett's arrival delayed a week, I'll have more time to practice and observe."

"Do that. The good fighters competing will be doing the same in their classifications."

Pol nodded to Kelso, who bowed back, and sought out the Royal Gardens and Paki. He needed a diversion.

He entered the gardens and heard giggles. If a visitor entered the garden, Siggon and Paki generally found something else to do, so Pol wouldn't find his friend here.

Now that he had come this far, his route into the castle was closest through the gardens. Normally, Pol would find that a pleasant experience, but he spied Amonna and Bythia talking and giggling on the path he wanted to take.

"Pol, come here," Amonna said catching Pol's eye before he could find a way around them. The request had the ring of a command to it.

He looked at the two girls and did not see a friend. It didn't seem that they were mad at him, but he could see a look of mockery in Amonna's eyes that he hadn't noticed before.

He gave them both a little bow and just stood for whatever kind of question they would torment him with.

"Have you been to Listya?" Bythia said. She narrowed her eyes a bit, for what reason Pol was unable to fathom.

"Once, about four years ago. I was only eight. My mother and King Colvin wanted to check on how the king's regent ruled. I remembered the country as hot and muggy. The countryside was lusher than North Salvan. Perhaps South Salvan is hotter than here."

Bythia giggled. "It is. Were there bugs?"

"As large as my hand," Pol said. He teased of course, but this wasn't a formal inquisition. "The buildings all had moss or mold growing on them. As I think back, the people looked a little green as well. I think my mother has spent enough time in North Salvan for it to wear off. Of course, I was born here, so I am greenless."

"You're joking!" Amonna said, laughing.

Pol narrowed his eyes like his sister did moments before. "Am I?" He turned and walked away, wondering what to make of the girls and wondering what they made of his performance.

He sighed once he entered the castle. Where had Amonna gone? His one-time confidante seemed to have transformed into Bythia's best friend. Pol knew that Amonna had already ceased to support him, but now that he had sure knowledge of that, he felt more alone than he ever had.

~ ~ ~

Chapter Thirteen

~

POL SHOWED UP FOR GARDENING, since the Emperor had put off his visit. Siggon taught Pol and Paki snare-making for the morning's instruction. Since he had been taught this before, Pol made short work of making one from the bundle of materials that Siggon threw at the two boys' feet. Paki took a bit longer.

Pol's friend spit on the ground. "I hate doing that." Paki shivered with distaste.

"Your life might depend on finding food in the woods," Siggon said. He rose and walked off into the garden.

Paki snorted and pointed at Pol. "You'll always have a servant close by to find stuff."

"I haven't lived my life yet, so I can't agree," Pol said.

"You know the booths for the Emperor's festival are open. Let's go sneak to the grounds and find something good to eat. Anything is better than a gamey old rabbit."

Pol hadn't done anything fun for so long that he eagerly agreed.

"I'll need different clothes. I don't want to be recognized."

Paki nodded. "I already thought of that. I brought some of my old clothes and one of Dad's hats with me." He grinned and beckoned Pol to follow him behind a garden shed hidden by greenery.

Pol changed and both boys left by a secret door at the back of the woods, and sauntered to the large field just outside of Borstall's walls where the festival and tourney had been set up. Flags flew above the tourney field, which had already been plowed, dragged and raked for the competition. The festival booths were to one side of the tourney grounds.

The boys walked along the rows of booths. During the tourney, Pol could picture the place crowded with people, but he was surprised at the numbers that had evaded work to walk between the booths with the tourney a week away.

They stopped at a puppeteers' booth and stood behind much younger children. Pol vaguely recognized the setting. The puppeteer talked about the god Demeron and how he slept, alive, yet not alive, under a crystal dome in the city of Fassin. Priests were plotting to kill the god and make off with the golden statues that adorned the inside of the god's temple. The story had a hero that saved the priest's beautiful daughter at the last minute and saved the day.

Pol rather enjoyed the show, but on a different level than the children who cried, laughed, and clapped together with Paki as the events in the story unfolded.

"I know the real story," Pol said.

"Real? That wasn't real," Paki said. "I enjoyed it too much for it to be real."

"There is a real sleeping god, but he sleeps under a crystal dome in a cathedral, not a temple, in the city of Fassin in the northern part of Volia."

"You're kidding!" Paki said, guffawing in a most unsophisticated way. That was part of Paki's charm.

"No. Maybe I'll go there someday." Pol smiled, since he likely wouldn't last long enough to chance a trip to the Volian continent.

"On your Processional, after you've expanded the Baccusol Empire?"

Pol hit Paki in the shoulder. "I'm not delusional."

"Yes, you are!" Paki's eyes lit up as they passed a vendor selling candied apples on a stick. "I want one of those."

After not finding any money in the pockets Paki had given him to wear, Pol shook his head. "No money. Do you have any?"

"Why do we need money?" Paki stood close to the vendor's booth and when the man looked in the other direction, he stole two apples and thrust one into Pol's hands. "Here, now we run!"

"I can't run," Pol said, but he followed Paki as best as he could down the lane between the booths amidst calls for guards.

Paki turned a corner and four guards stood to block their way. Paki reversed course and took off. Pol knew the men would catch him once he tired, so he just stood, looking stupid, he thought, still clutching a candied apple. Two of the guards took off after Paki. Pol just gave up the booty to one of the guards.

It wasn't long before Paki returned between the two guards, with his hands tied.

"Stealing from a vendor is a misdemeanor, you know. It's a good thing the Emperor isn't here, or we'd have to cut off your hands."

Pol knew bluster when he heard it. "What happens next?" he said. His adventurous spirit had left him.

"We have a detention shack on the grounds. You can cool off there and reflect on your evil deeds while we scare up a magistrate. Perhaps the king will come and adjudicate; then you'll be in real trouble."

Pol had no doubt about that. He followed the guards without making the same kind of fuss that Paki did. Once inside, guards locked the door, and the two boys sat alone in the dark roughly-made jail.

"I'm sorry, Pol. I was caught up in the moment."

"And now we are caught up by the guards," Pol said. "I don't know what my father will do."

"Laugh it off? That's what Dad does when I have my little run-ins."

Pol's eyebrows shot up. "You've done this before?"

Paki nodded and grinned. "I generally get away with it, but my luck isn't always alive when I try."

"Did you stop to think about me? This is an embarrassment to my father. The people will laugh at him for having such a stupid son that would steal treats at the festival."

Paki shrugged his shoulders. "Give them a different name. Say Malden is your father or Kelso Beastwell."

"Malden's not married, and don't you think the guards would know Kelso?" Pol put his head in his hands and shook it. How could he get talked into this, but Paki had gotten him into trouble. Pol tried to feel guilty, but all he had done was catch the candied apple and run from the vendor.

Should he have given the apple back to the vendor after Paki took off? Pol didn't know, and the situation had confused him at a time when he dreaded being confused about anything. He had to find a way out of this prison and get back into his regular clothes and into the castle. He looked at the solid lock on the door. "Maybe there is another way."

He stood up and looked closely at the lock. After concentrating and not coming up with any inspiration, he shut his eyes and tried to probe in the lock for a pattern. He had to succeed, he just had to. He shut his eyes again and concentrated. Suddenly, like the time he pushed Grostin, Pol felt something click inside of him, and he could perceive the works of the lock. It was a stationary pattern that he could tweak a bit here and a bit there. He did so and opened his eyes.

Pol took a deep breath and pushed the door. It opened! This time he couldn't feel any loss of strength, but after the run and the shock of being arrested, Pol might not be a good judge of his physical condition.

"What have you done?" Paki said.

Pol looked back at him. "I opened the lock."

"How did you do that?"

"Magic," Pol reluctantly admitted. "Malden has taught me a few tricks."

Paki's eyes grew a bit, and then his practical nature took over. "Then let's get out of here."

If Pol wanted to punish Paki for his misdeed, he would have left him alone, but he untied Paki's hands, and they sneaked out of the detention shack. No one was around, so they both took off for the castle.

Pol ran out of breath halfway to the city, but they found no evidence of a pursuit. The guards had probably enjoyed the candied apples, anyway. They slowed to a walk.

As they got closer to the castle, Pol gave Siggon's hat to Paki. "Now I want to be recognized, so we can get back in if the door we used is locked."

To their delight, the door was still open, so they slid inside and locked it. Pol quickly changed his clothes. They turned a corner and found Siggon tossing pruned branches into a cart.

"Where have you gotten off to? I've been looking for you all morning. I was about ready to comb the drinking establishments and the jails." Siggon laughed and commanded Paki to help him with the branches. Pol just waved and hurried into the castle.

Once he reached the sanctuary of his rooms, he sighed and lay down on the couch. No sooner had he closed his eyes, than Kelso knocked on his door.

"Grostin has asked your father for a rematch, and he has agreed with conditions, My Prince."

"Conditions?"

"Wooden swords are the same for each, and the match ends at two touches."

Pol gnashed his teeth. "Is there no way out of this?"

"Your father, the King…"

The walk down to the training grounds took forever. Pol wasn't mentally or physically prepared for another match. The 'trick' that he had performed in the detention shack had taken more out of him than he had realized.

He hadn't seen Grostin since his previous match. Pol wouldn't prevail this time, but he had no reason to. He didn't feel guilty for what he had done to Grostin. The end of that match was a matter of life or death, of that Pol was certain. He wouldn't let his brother win too easily, either. If Pol could get a touch, he felt he would retain his honor, at least to himself.

There seemed to be as many people in attendance as the last match. Grostin had already donned a quilted jerkin and evidently wanted to show off in front of the crowds warming up. Pol paused and watched him perform. Someone had taught him a few new moves. He had been coached, but that might mean Pol could pick up his patterns more easily.

He found a jerkin his size and soon practiced with a real sword, so the wooden sword wouldn't seem so heavy. Pol limited his warm-up so he could preserve what little reserves of strength he had.

Kelso called both of them together. Pol looked over the audience and saw the two kings conferring while he continued to survey those who would watch his defeat. The Captain of the Guard stepped into the center of the field.

"This is a princely rematch of the two younger brothers of our King Colvin. This time, the king has graciously offered to judge the match."

Pol heard the buzz from the crowd intensify. At least Grostin wouldn't be threatening the judge this time. He watched his father have a few good-natured last words with King Astor. It appeared they had become fast friends in the short period of time the South Salvans had been at Borstall. Pol knew it wasn't always so, and he wondered why.

His father raised his hands to silence the crowd. "I want to make sure that this match is conducted to match the rules of the tourney." He raised two fingers. "Two touches and the match is over. I will personally provide swords to each of my sons."

Kelso delivered the two new wooden swords.

"You get to choose, Poldon. That is my rule." King Colvin looked at Grostin who looked disappointed.

Pol took each and swung them. The balance of one of the swords seemed to suit him better than the other, but they were much the same.

"When I drop my arm, the match begins." The king took a few steps back from the boys and raised his arm. In a moment the match was on.

Grostin sneered, but that didn't matter to Pol. The sneer was an intimidation tactic, and it didn't work on Pol. If Grostin was truly overcome with hate, the wild swinging would appear again. His brother looked over his shoulder towards a man Pol didn't recognize. The man pushed down with his arms, which Pol took to mean calm down, so the man was Grostin's coach.

His brother took a deep breath and resumed his guard. Of course he couldn't resist attacking first. Pol concentrated on looking at Grostin's footwork. That hadn't improved, but as Grostin slashed and Pol parried, clearly his brother had a more compact, controlled swing.

The pattern was even more evident, but Grostin just overpowered Pol and eventually after a flurry of thrusts and swipes, Grostin pushed the tip of his sword into the padded jerkin and Pol couldn't help but gasp at the sharp pain. His rib felt like it had a hole in it, but Pol let Grostin gloat while he quickly slapped Grostin on his rear end with the edge of his blade. That part was not padded and Grostin winced before he turned and glared at Pol.

Pol expected the rush from Grostin in much the same fashion as his earlier flurry, but this time Pol used his knowledge of his brother's pattern and the little sips of magic that gave him the information to anticipate Grostin's moves, which meant he used much less energy to deflect his bother's onslaught.

For a moment Pol thought he had a chance, but then something from the crowd hit him in the neck and distracted him enough for Grostin to score the winning point, a vicious slash against his arm. Pol went down.

Grostin raised his sword for another blow. "Do that, and you'll be spending the night in my dungeons, Prince," King Colvin said.

Grostin made an unpleasant face and withdrew, but not before Pol saw his brother nod to his coach in the crowd and lift up the corner of his mouth in a sly smile, but Grostin walked tenderly out of the training grounds.

Pol's father and Kelso helped him up. "Your brother didn't pull the blow like an hon—"

"That's enough, Kelso," the King said. "Take Prince Poldon to the healers. I would guess he has a broken rib and maybe a broken arm."

"My arm is bruised, but my rib really hurts," Pol said. He thought he could tell the difference and his arm only hurt where Grostin had hit it. He thought that the pain of a broken bone would go up and down his arm and inhibit his movements.

"Still, you see a healer. I'll send Malden down to check you."

"I'm right here, My King," Malden said. "You can walk, Prince?"

Pol nodded, but he had barely enough strength to take off his jerkin.

"Sit for awhile," Malden said. "I can look at you here as well as in the infirmary."

Kelso and Malden helped Pol to the large table in the armory. Someone had rolled up his jerkin and put it under Pol's head.

Malden started with the arm and concurred that it was only bruised. He prodded the red mark below Pol's heart and when he touched the welt on his skin, Pol couldn't help but wince.

"You're lucky. I think it is only cracked, or there is a deep bruise. You'll still be able to participate in the tourney," Malden said. "Two days in your rooms doing nothing more taxing than reading Mistress Farthia's religion text should do the trick."

Pol smiled through the pain and nodded.

"No need to walk all the way to the infirmary. I'll help you to your rooms," Malden said.

King Colvin came into Pol's view from the table. "What is this smudge of blood on your neck?"

Pol instinctively put his hand up to his neck and looked at the speck of blood on his hand. "Someone used a pea shooter on me, but that was no pea, and they were very accurate."

"Prince Grostin found a way to cheat yet again, eh?" Kelso said.

Pol remained silent.

"You had him figured out until that…whatever it was hit your neck," King Colvin said.

"I'd like to think so, Father, but…" Pol managed a shrug.

"You did well again, Poldon," his father said, patting Pol's forearm. "It's too bad."

"What?" Pol said.

The king shook his head. "Never mind. I must attend to King Astor." He looked at Malden. "Take good care of my boy."

'My boy.' Pol took that as a high compliment from his father, who rarely interacted with him. His most intimate moments with his father always resulted from Pol being ill or injured. Life was so unfair.

"Let me look at your neck," Malden said after Pol collapsed on his couch.

Pol winced as the act made his rib injury hurt.

Malden looked closely and grunted. "That was a metal pea. It looks to me that it had a rough texture on one side that brought out the blood. Your brother is rather creative."

"Or whoever is helping him."

Malden chuckled. "So you think he has help?"

"I do. I can't see Grostin hiring the thugs or making that illegal practice sword by himself. How did Grostin get an idea for the peashooter and then find an expert? I saw a man who was coaching him from within the crowd. I'll bet he was the one."

"Grostin would deny all of what you said."

Pol ground his teeth. "Except for the sword."

Malden pulled up Pol's tunic to look at his chest again. "Right. Now I'm going to use a bit of magic on you, but it's a secret between you and me."

"We already have secrets. One more won't matter."

Malden laid his hand on the wound and closed his eyes.

"It helps to close your eyes if you are trying to do something beneath the surface, doesn't it?" Pol said.

"Quiet." Malden continued until Pol could feel the pain in his rib start to burn.

"What are you doing?"

"Fusing bone. It's an easy enough technique. The pain will be gone in a few days instead of a few weeks."

Pol had never heard of bone fusing before. "That doesn't seem like a tweak to me."

Malden nodded his head. "Quite the opposite, really. I re-established the pattern of your bone, and as I apply magical power to do that, the cracked bone fuses again. Consider it accelerated healing." Malden helped him pull down his tunic. "How did you know about looking past the surface?"

"Another secret, but it's mine. Promise you won't tell my father."

That got a smile out of the magician. "I won't."

"Paki and I were arrested yesterday at the festival fair."

"I know you were."

"How did you find out?"

Malden thought a bit. "I get reports from the guard. Not Kelso's group, but from the city guard. I read a report about two boys who were able to somehow escape from the detention shack. You were late for our session yesterday, so it must have been your friend and you."

Pol shook his head. So much for the secret escape. "We got out because I tried a bit of magic on the lock. Nothing worked at first. I couldn't access the pattern of the lock until I closed my eyes. Like when I did when I first learned to notice people around me."

"Good, so far."

Pol felt a bit frustrated with Malden's nonchalance. "Suddenly a picture of the workings of the lock popped into my head, and then it was only a matter of tweaking the pattern. The tweaking involved moving the pieces to get the lock to open."

"I am impressed, as always. That is something you would learn in your second or third year at the Tesnian monastery. How did you feel afterword?"

"I didn't think it affected me, but later on, I could feel less energy."

"Make sure you get plenty to eat. You need it to continue to heal your rib and to build up some energy for the upcoming tournament. King Colvin has decided that the two youngest categories, the one that you and Prince Grostin are in, will fight with wooden practice swords. Not swinging a steel sword about will help you get through the day a bit better."

That put a smile on Pol's face. "I worried about Paki fighting Grostin in that age category. My brother might take out his anger on my friend."

"Always a possibility." Malden turned towards knocking on Pol's door. "I'll get it."

Mistress Farthia walked into the room following a gesture from the magician.

"I am bringing a formal invitation to the both of you. It seems there will be a small state dinner tonight honoring King Astor and his wife. Close advisors are invited, and I guess they considered me a close advisor of our invalid here," Farthia said.

"I will still be hurting," Pol said. He glanced at Malden and was rewarded with a conspiratorial wink.

Farthia shook her head. "No excuses, except you can use your injury to retire from the dinner a bit sooner than the others."

Malden brightened up. "Oh, and I'll probably be needed to attend to the prince."

She gave the magician a scolding look and thrust two sealed parchments into his hand and left.

"Formal invitations. This is a state dinner. Good practice for you, Prince Poldon."

Pol scowled. "Grostin will be there lording it up."

"I didn't heal your neck, My Prince. Just flash it to him and your father if the conversation gets unbearable. King Colvin knows about the cheating, remember?"

"I do. I hope he doesn't forget."

Malden pursed his lips. "Not an irrational hope, but you won't be able to count on that."

~~~

Chapter Fourteen

~

POL MANAGED TO TALK MALDEN INTO ARRIVING AT THE DINNER at the same time. A small state dinner meant there might be fifty or more attending. Pol wondered where he'd be expected sit. When the both of them were announced, a servant led Malden to a table next to Mistress Farthia. Pol wished he could sit with them, but that would never happen.

Pol was led to the end of the royal table stretching across a temporary dais. Amonna had already arrived and luckily separated Grostin from him. There wouldn't be room for him when Emperor Hazett and his retinue arrived, if his presence was requested. Pol still felt that he was too young for state events. All of the adults in the room intimidated him, although he didn't feel the same in regards to his siblings.

Landon sat on the other side of table with Bythia, who sat next to her mother.

"Aren't you too damaged to attend?" Grostin said.

Pol leaned back and saw the pillow that Grostin sat on. "I should say the same to you. Does your bottom still hurt?"

Grostin ground his teeth and turned to say something to Honna, who sat next to his mother. Pol sat down.

Amonna leaned over. "That wasn't very nice, Pol."

"Tell my broken rib that and my bruised arm." His arm went up to the wound on his neck. The bruise had faded a bit since the match.

"You were injured?" Amonna looked a bit confused. She turned to

Grostin. "You said you didn't do any damage when you won."

Grostin made a disagreeable face. "No lasting damage." He chuckled and turned back to Honna, who leaned over and gave Pol an angry look.

"Can you at least give me a smile?" Pol said to Amonna.

"Like this?" She grinned at her brother.

Her smile made Pol laugh. At least she hadn't absorbed the talent for scowling that her other siblings had. "Just like that."

"What's on your neck?" she asked, touching the scabbed spot.

"It's a bite from an angry insect," Pol said, loud enough for others to hear.

His mother turned his way and gave him a nod and a smile that looked more like a grimace. He hadn't talked to her since the match, and he wondered if his father had told her anything.

"Are you all right, dear?" his mother said. "I heard you were hurt."

"I still am, but I seem to be recovering just fine. Maybe a little faster than my opponent."

Grostin glared at him for a moment and then turned back to Honna. Pol hoped his brother would get a stiff neck from looking at his oldest sister all night.

His father rose from his seat. The babble immediately stopped. "I wanted us to get together and enjoy each other's company in a more relaxed gathering before His Excellency Emperor Hazett III arrives in Borstall. He is obviously behind schedule, so we haven't been told how long he will stay. The tourney will begin the day after he arrives. The Emperor might not attend all the events then, as he might be recovering from travel.

"I have received word this afternoon, that he intends to test for magic potential while he is here. Some of you already know and have sent out riders to inform those outside of Borstall. We haven't had a magician of note from North Salvan in a decade, so who knows who might show the potential that our Emperor seeks?

"Magician Malden will work with the Emperor's magicians administering the testing. That is all the business for this evening. Enjoy your dinner and spend some time and some coin supporting the festival fair since they had to set up their booths somewhat early."

The king raised his hands and the audience applauded.

"There!" Pol's father said to King Astor, loud enough for Pol to hear.

"I'm hungry enough. Let's get dinner served." King Colvin snapped his fingers and signaled for dinner to commence.

"How are you getting on with Princess Bythia, Princess Amonna?" Pol said.

"She is like a best friend."

"Like? She isn't your newest best friend?"

Amonna looked across the table at Bythia and Landon. "She won't be here for long, but at least I can keep company with her."

Pol followed her eyes. The pair seemed to be getting along just fine. Although Pol couldn't hear what was said, it appeared that Landon did all the talking, and from his gestures, it looked like mostly boasting.

"You've been keeping busy," Amonna said. "I've hardly seen you these past few weeks."

Pol hadn't changed his habits as much as his sister had. "I spend my early mornings in the gardens training with Siggon and Paki. Then it's the rest of the morning in the classroom. In the afternoons, I train for the tourney, followed by a session with Malden, if he is available."

"What is Malden teaching you, magic?"

"About magic, I guess, and he has a lot of practical experience with politics."

Amonna's eyes narrowed a bit. "I thought you weren't training to rule."

Pol shrugged. "I'm not." He lied. Malden and Mistress Farthia taught him subjects that weren't as directly related to rule as his brothers might have learned, but Pol knew how to connect the subjects to their practical application. "But I have to learn more than geography, religion, numbers, and history." He shrugged again.

"I'm glad I'm past all that."

She should be if she was to be married off to another royal family, thought Pol. Amonna had a more pleasant personality than a thorough intellect. Did he have a thorough intellect? Pol had to admit that he thought he did. He pressed his lips together and didn't say anything while dinner was served.

Grostin looked over and began to engage Amonna in conversation, to the exclusion of Pol. Honna joined in, and as quickly as that, Pol ate by himself. His mother caught his eye and gave him a sympathetic smile.

Pol ate more than he normally did because of Malden's suggestion. He looked over at Malden and Mistress Farthia engaged in a lively conversation, and Pol realized that they were a pair, more suited to each other than Landon and Bythia. He could see that they liked each other, and although Pol had caught them in an embrace in the classroom, their intimate behavior at the dinner made him feel more isolated.

He mused that when he sat in the classroom reading the religion text or just puttering around in his rooms all by himself, he didn't feel as lonely as he did surrounded by people. He looked down at his cleared plate and rose from his chair. He walked over to his mother and father.

"I'm still hurting from my injuries. May I be excused?"

"Certainly," his father said. "How is your neck?"

Pol's hand went up to his wound. "Healing like the rest of my body."

His father glanced at Grostin and grunted. Pol looked at his brother, but Grostin hadn't noticed the king's glance.

Pol bowed to King Astor, who turned to them. "Quite a match today. I thought you had figured your brother out and might have gotten that last touch," Astor said. "But your brother is older and taller. The match always goes to the bigger man."

Pol knew that wasn't the case, and King Astor's comment bothered Pol. He looked over at Landon, who turned his eyes away to Bythia. Landon had been listening, so his brother would feel good about the comment.

"Your Majesties," Pol said, and then bowed before leaving the room.

Pol stewed about King Astor's comments when he reached his rooms. Kelso had specifically told him that size wasn't the principal factor, although it wasn't to be dismissed. Technique and strategy could prevail, especially in tourney sword fighting.

He wondered if King Astor had been subtler than he gave him credit for. Was he referring to the suitability to rule Listya? Pol thought that he just might.

He collapsed on the couch and felt a twinge of pain in his ribs, and then he rubbed his bruised arm. A twinge was better than the agony he had undergone earlier when Grostin first jammed his sword into him. Bigger and stronger? Pol wished he were seventeen, but would he still be undersized at that age? If so, a twenty-year-old Grostin would still be much bigger than a seventeen-year-old Pol.

The thought frustrated him. He would think about it more tomorrow.

Pol decided to adhere to the schedule that he had provided Amonna at dinner. Siggon still toiled in the gardens with Paki and the other gardeners. Today's lesson would be making fire without a tinderbox. Pol could see the advantage of that, even without being a scout. Siggon tossed branches and a few logs down on the ground underneath a tree in the little wood.

"This won't take too long, if you can get the hang of it," Siggon said. He pulled a cord out of his pocket. "If you can use a shoe lace or some other kind of cloth strip, it makes the process easier. You will need a knife to cut wood and file off some shavings. "We'll do it all together."

Pol enjoyed learning from Siggon. Paki wasn't as serious as Pol, and that made their learning more fun. Siggon had them trim a stick and split a larger branch. Soon they had their strings wrapped around a central stick, with a rounded end on the top and a sharper end on the bottom.

Pol began to move the bow back and forth as fast as he could, rubbing the stick on the split branch below, but Paki's strength put Pol's efforts to shame when the other boy had the sharp end smoking before Pol. Eventually they both generated enough heat to make the tiny coals that they transferred to the shaved kindling and the fires were started.

"Can you remember how to do that?"

Paki turned up a side of his mouth and confidently nodded. "It's easy."

Pol had to agree. "If the forest is wet, isn't this much harder?"

Siggon nodded. "That's no different from using a tinderbox. If you can't get dry shavings, you won't have a fire."

After Pol untied the cord around his bow, he gave it back to Siggon. "And if I don't have a cord?"

Paki's father looked at his son. "Do you know?"

A frown appeared in Paki's face.

"Twisted bark?" Pol said.

"That's the idea. That will work. Braided stalks can work if they aren't too dry. You can rip the cloth from your shirt and twist that as well."

"I've got the concept, so the real limitation is dry tinder," Pol said.

"Indeed it is." Siggon got up and fetched a bucket of water to douse the small fires.

Pol gave a nod of his head to Siggon and said, "Now I get to be tested on religion."

He jumped up and headed for the classroom.

As usual, Mistress Farthia had arrived before him and had her nose buried in a sheaf of papers.

"What are you reading?"

Farthia smiled at Pol, but she looked distracted. "Reports on the Emperor's Procession. My father sent these along, so King Colvin might know what to expect."

"Why are you reading them, then?" Pol said.

She narrowed her eyes. "Are you accusing me of something?"

"Only of reading the reports. What do they say? Any secrets?"

That made his tutor laugh. "Most of it is about the magician testing."

Pol didn't like the testing coming to North Salvan. "What happens to those poor souls who are identified with magical talent?"

"Most are sent to monasteries unless they are closer to the imperial capital."

"Does Emperor Hazett own the magicians?"

Farthia laughed. "Are you afraid of becoming a slave?"

"Me?"

"You. I imagine you haven't changed your mind about protecting your mother in the past few days?"

Pol knew the answer to that. "No."

"Then you can refuse."

"I can just like that?"

Farthia nodded. "A prince has a certain amount of privilege. If you are in line to a kingdom or a dukedom, you can certainly refuse." She shrugged. "Actually, anyone can refuse, but why would they turn down a chance to learn a very useful and lucrative trade? Most people in the world don't live like magicians do."

"I know that," Pol said.

"You do, don't you?" Farthia squinted her eyes a bit and smiled, making her eyes crinkle.

Pol asked one more question. "Will I have to be tested at all?"

Farthia nodded. "It's best to do it. Landon and Grostin certainly will since they weren't old enough when magicians came through Borstall a decade or so ago. You are not quite old enough, but most twelve-year-olds are included in the testing, anyway"

"I gathered that from Malden."

"And you will be identified."

The thought frightened Pol. He worried about having a talent that Landon and Grostin did not. His siblings were angry with him enough for just being a bit smarter than they were. "Maybe I'll be sick."

"No you won't. Be brave, like I know you can be. It's not the end of your life."

Pol looked at the books and the map table, anything but in Mistress Farthia's eyes. "It could be."

Malden repeated Farthia's words nearly verbatim as they discussed the testing.

"I know you are worried about your mother and yourself, but if that is the case, perhaps King Colvin will let your mother travel with you to the monastery."

"To stay?"

The magician shook his head. "No, but while on the trip, things might settle down in Borstall somewhat. If you are gone, no one will be thinking of you."

"Grostin will," Pol said. "I'm a threat no matter where I am." He leaned over and buried his head in his arms.

"Are you serious about that, My Prince?"

Pol jerked his head up and down. "I am."

"You could always abdicate your line to the throne."

"Give up my right to rule Listya and North Salvan?"

Malden paused for a minute. "If you aren't a threat to the succession, then why would they want to attack you?"

"I'd no longer be a prince."

"You would be, but you'd never rise above prince. You'd still live in the castle, but you wouldn't be in line, that's all. There have been others, although they generally got disinherited due to poor behavior or poor health. Disinherited is more serious than abdication," Malden said.

"That's me. Poor health."

Malden shook his head. "I'm talking more about mental health."

"I'm not crazy, am I?"

"Some might think you would be if you gave up succession rights," Malden said.

"Can I think about it?"

"I'm not seriously suggesting that you do that. Your entire life would change."

Pol nodded. "That's what I'm trying to do...change my life, so I can save it."

~ ~ ~

Chapter Fifteen

~

POL SUCCESSFULLY STAYED OUT OF EVERYONE'S WAY while
he continued his restricted activities. Paki asked him to sneak into the
fair again, but Pol had learned his lesson and scolded Paki that he should
have, too.

The Emperor was due the next afternoon when Pol walked into his
classroom. Mistress Farthia had a pen in her hand, dipping it in an inkwell.

"What are you doing?"

"Copying down the events planned for the Emperor's visit. I just got
this, and my father would like his own copy. The king's scriveners are making
a more formal copy for Hazett III. I've noticed something a bit odd. Come
look over my shoulder."

Pol examined the documents while Farthia turned the pages over.

"It's as if I don't exist," Pol said. "My siblings are included in official
events, but not me. Is it because of my age?"

Farthia snorted. "Hardly. I wonder who put this together. This is a
deliberate affront."

Malden walked into the room with a sheaf of rolled up papers. "Did
you see this, Farthia?"

"I just did. Pol has just been expunged from the family."

"I'll bet it's one of your siblings, My Prince. I'll find out who." Malden
left the room.

"No matter what, we are your supporters, Malden and I."

Pol didn't know what to say. His emotions roiled inside of him. He felt anger, isolation, but most of all he just hurt. Would he ever feel a moment's peace in his life? Pol never saw himself as a threat to anybody, but this relentless ill will had just about made him give it all up.

"I don't know what to do."

"Fight it. Your siblings have no right to treat you this way, and quite frankly, I think your father has been much too lenient about their relentless campaign against you," Farthia said. "I am not a subject of King Colvin. I am an Imperial Citizen, so I can say these things and feel this way."

"But that doesn't help me."

Farthia put her arms around Pol and hugged him. He didn't know how to react to such intimate contact and felt foolish standing there letting a fully-grown woman embrace him like that. Even Amonna never clutched at him, and he couldn't remember his mother being so, so close. He could feel his cheeks redden.

She let him go and stood apart with her hands on his shoulders. "I'm sorry, Pol, but I understand how you feel."

How could she? But then he really didn't know her past at all.

"I'll just stay in my rooms. I think I might prefer that, anyway. I'm only fourteen."

"But you are still your father's son and a Prince of North Salvan. It is proper protocol that you attend a certain number of events. Do you want to know which ones?"

Pol nodded. He clutched his fists as anger replaced his shock. "Maybe if I show up for a few."

They spent the next hour going over the events. Farthia explained each one in detail and who should attend. Together they decided that Pol should go to three or four of the events, including the first night's dinner with the Emperor.

"I don't care if you're not on the list. No one can deny your participation, except for King Colvin.

"But what if he is the one who struck my name?"

Farthia gave Pol a look of reproof. "Does this seem like something your father would do?"

Pol had to shake his head.

"Let's go through the list one more time," Farthia said, when Malden poked his head through he doorway.

"Honna. The Queen put the list together, and Honna offered to make a few rough copies and distribute them."

Farthia looked at the list. "This isn't her handwriting."

"She probably just crossed out Pol's name and gave it to a lower level scrivener. They wouldn't question a princess, would they?"

Farthia stood up and walked to the window. "This castle has become a snake pit," she said. She turned to Pol. "One day, perhaps in idle conversation, your oldest sister and brothers got together and realized that you had made it through your illnesses and represented a true threat to their inheritance." She shook her head in disgust. "I just can't... no, I can believe it. I saw the same petty squabbles when I grew up in Yastan. It is a disease that too many nobles catch when they feel threatened."

Pol sought out his mother, with Farthia's initial copy in hand. He found her in the Royal Gardens sitting with the Queen of South Salvan.

He bowed as politely as he could. "I need to speak with you, Mother." He dragged a foot through the gravel. "Alone, if we can." He bowed quickly to Bythia's mother.

The woman laughed. "I have other things I can do. I will talk to you later, Molissa." She didn't look offended, and that made Pol sigh with relief.

"What is so important?"

"Look at this." He gave his mother the list of events.

"Oh," she said after she looked at the first page, and her face turned red as she continued to turn the pages faster and faster. "That girl!"

"Honna?"

Her mother nodded her head. "She asked me so nicely to copy the events for the scriveners. Her behavior encouraged me to believe that perhaps once Landon left, we could get closer, but she acted a part, didn't she?"

"To my disadvantage."

The queen snorted. "To put it mildly, as you always do, Poldon. This list came from Mistress Farthia or Magician Malden?"

"Mistress Farthia. She noticed the lack of my presence as she made a personal copy for her father."

"What am I ever going to do?" His mother put her hand to the side of her face. She was emotionally upset and generally that would make Pol try to make her feel better, but in this instance, he let her feelings go without any consolation, since he must have felt much the same way.

"See this little dash next to the first night's state dinner. We decided that I would intrude on three or four events that we both decided were appropriate for me to attend."

His mother went through the list and nodded her head. "You don't mind losing the visibility?"

"When have I ever been interested in that?"

"I want you to meet the Emperor."

Pol agreed with his mother. "I will and, I'll be tested for magic."

"The Emperor doesn't do that himself, you know."

"But I'll pass the test. Malden thinks I'll rate high in potential."

The queen looked shocked. "You? How did this happen?"

Pol shrugged. "Malden had a feeling that I might. He tested me a few times, and I passed. You know when I defeated Grostin the first time? I had to use magic to keep him from killing me."

"Kill?"

Pol nodded. "I'm pretty sure he poisoned me in the hunting preserve. That's when all this started, and I think Grostin had someone hire the thugs that attacked us. He had to have had help in making that fake practice sword."

The queen waved her hand. "Spare me the details. I told your father I didn't want to know, and I don't." She took Pol's face in her hands. "If you have magic and are an heir to the throne, Emperor Hazett will be thrilled."

That wasn't what Pol wanted to hear. "And that means we are both in even more danger if that happens."

The Queen paused for a moment, still holding onto Pol's face. "I know, but I want what is best for you, my only child. Can you keep your magic a secret?"

Pol could feel fear begin to grip him tighter than his mother gripped his cheeks. "Malden doesn't think so because Landon and Grostin will be tested as well. He knows they don't have a bit of talent."

She took her hands away from his face and held them together in her lap. "We will survive whatever happens, together. I promise I won't tell Colvin. I'm not sure how he will react. He thinks you are too frail to rule or do much of anything, although I think that attitude has been softened by the pluck that you demonstrated when you fended off Grostin's attacks." She looked at the sundial on the castle wall. "It is time for me to leave you. I will tell Colvin about the slights, so feel comfortable about showing up for the events marked in your program."

Pol felt much relieved as he bowed and watched the Queen walk out of the garden. He wished that his life had been different, but he wouldn't trade the queen for anyone else as a mother.

He walked back to his classroom. Farthia had gone, so he read more in the religious text. He had gone through about half of the big book. He had read about rulers being advised by the clergy, and sometimes that helped and sometimes it didn't. Then an idea came to Pol about advisors.

Malden walked in. "Farthia isn't here?"

Pol shook his head. "Can we talk for a bit?"

After shutting the door, Malden took a chair across from Pol at the big map table.

"First of all, Farthia and I decided that I should attend some of the events. I talked to my mother and she agrees, since she originally came up with a program that actually included me."

"She or one of her ladies-in-waiting."

That didn't matter to Pol. "When I gave her the papers, she became angry at Honna and agreed that I should attend a few of the events."

"Is this what you wanted to say?" Malden said.

"Only part. I told Mother that I would pass the magician's test."

Malden pursed his lips. "I would hope that the king discusses handing Listya over to Landon before the Emperor finds out."

"Mother agreed to keep it a secret."

"It won't be a secret for long, anyway. The Emperor's reaction will be less predictable, but at your age, I think his enthusiasm will be muted a bit."

Pol bit his lip and hesitated to say what he had been thinking. "What if the Emperor knows ahead of time and agrees not to say much about it?"

"And how…" Malden's face broke out into a smile. "Ranno, of course."

"Who, or what is Ranno?"

"Farthia's father. He has a unique relationship with the Emperor," Malden said. "I'll find Farthia and have her send a message to him. If she can't find anyone, I'll ride out and intercept the Emperor's train myself." He ran out of the classroom, leaving Pol stunned by the turn of events.

Pol stood with his family in front of the castle steps. The Emperor was a few minutes away. His retinue had already stopped close to the tourney grounds to set up a camp for the many officials and servants who supported the Emperor during his Procession. Hazett III would stay in the castle with some of his staff.

Amonna smiled at Pol, but her smile didn't go very deep. Was she in on his being snubbed? He looked over at the royal family of South Salvan standing on the other side of the steps. Bythia looked at Landon and then at Amonna. Her eyes never drifted towards Pol. Her ignoring him was too obvious for him.

Honna had done a good job of setting everyone against him. His father didn't seem affected, but King Astor seemed less friendly than before. Pol wondered if that was his imagination. He didn't know. The entire welcoming business made him nervous. Farthia had said her father got her message about him, but they hadn't heard if the Emperor agreed to minimize the attention to his talent.

Pol's hands were damp with sweat. He looked down through the gate. Crowds lined the street, and a set of banners had just turned the corner far away. The last vestiges of the setting sun put a golden hue on the scene. He could hear the buzz of the crowd turn into cheering. The Emperor had arrived in Borstall.

The banners seemed to barely move closer to the castle. Pol wiped his hand on the back of his legs. His stomach began to flip as he could now see the Emperor waving to the crowds. He looked down the line at his father and mother. They held hands, and that always surprised Pol.

Pol blinked. His nerves now made him breathe more heavily, and he could hear his heartbeat, as he usually did when he was fatigued or very nervous. Pol knew he feared meeting the Emperor. He had to stay strong for just a few more minutes. He looked at the gate again, and Emperor Hazett III entered the courtyard where Pol had played since he could walk. The man rode a gigantic white horse, decorated with golden hoofs. The white leather saddle was chased with gold and silver.

Emperor Hazett was a youngish man, perhaps a decade younger than his father. His short dark hair held not a speck of gray, and his face was clean-shaven. He didn't wear armor, although Pol noticed he sat rather stiffly, indicating that he might wear a boiled leather cuirass under his flowing tunic.

The man's eyes were sharp as a hawk to match the thin prominent nose. He wouldn't call Hazett III handsome, but he did have presence.

An older man dressed in light armor rode just behind on a smaller horse, but then all horses would be smaller compared to the massive beast the Emperor rode. The man jumped off of his horse and grabbed the reins of the Emperor's horse as he dismounted.

Hazett stood as the two kings approached him. Each lowered their gaze and bowed to one knee.

"King Colvin, how nice of you to host part of my Procession, and King Astor, it is good to see you again. Introduce me to your families."

And Honna had written him out of this entrance? Pol pressed his lips together in anger, his fists held tightly to his side. The nerves had disappeared.

King Astor beckoned his family towards the Emperor. He introduced his wife and Bythia to the Emperor. He chatted briefly with them, and then dismissed them to their places.

"King Colvin."

Pol's father had his family line up in front of the ruler of the Baccusol Empire.

"My wife Molissa."

"It is nice to see you again, Queen Molissa. Does Colvin's regent manage Listya properly?"

His mother nodded. "He does, Your Excellency."

"This must be Landon." Hazett clapped Landon on the shoulders. His brother flinched at the gesture. "You can be braver than that, my boy. Stand tall, proud, and do honorable things."

Hazett looked at the Queen with his eyebrows up.

The queen curtseyed. "Honna, Your Excellency."

"Of course. You probably have broken many hearts, and there will be many more to come."

Pol noticed the gleam in the Emperor's eye and realized that his seemingly innocuous comments came with barbs. He pursed his lips to refrain from smiling as he remembered what Hazett said to Landon. The Emperor had a sense of humor. How would he treat him?

"Grostin, right?"

His middle brother affected a languid gaze that looked a bit ridiculous on him. "I am, Your Excellency."

"I am sure your mind spins and whirls with ideas…to help your father, the king, of course."

Grostin looked flustered. "It does, Your Excellency."

"Amonna. I hope you don't break as many hearts as your sister. You are quite pretty, though don't do anything to spoil it."

That comment was not barbed, but Pol could see the meaning behind the banter. The Emperor had been well briefed on his family. Now Hazett III's gaze turned to Pol.

"Prince Poldon. I am thrilled to meet you. I have heard admirable things through Ranno, your tutor's father. I understand you and your brother crossed practice swords in rather exciting ways. I trust we will see more of you before I leave."

Pol noticed the added inflection on the word 'practice'. It seemed the Emperor had even been told about their sparring matches before he arrived in Borstall. Every introduction meant something. Did Mistress Farthia tell her father everything, or did the Emperor always find information to make the introductions more memorable?

The Emperor dismissed the family and turned around. While they stood at the steps, there were more ceremonies concerning the Procession. Torches were lit as the sky darkened with the evening.

Pol realized that the Emperor had only addressed Pol by his title among his siblings. He hoped his brothers and sisters didn't notice. How would he tell? They gave him the same dirty looks they always had, with the exception of Amonna, who just looked confused.

Mistress Farthia talked to the older man who still held the reins of the Emperor's horse. That must be her father, Ranno Wissingbel. Pol saw an intelligent man from his perspective. Perhaps he would get a chance to meet his tutor's father. He looked like he might have interesting stories to tell, like Kelso did.

Pol tried to pay more attention to the ceremony. He might never see another Processional for decades, when he would be much older, if he lived that long. The thought of dying early made him sigh.

The ceremony lasted much too long for Pol, but finally it came to an end. The two kings stood on either side of the Emperor as he ascended the steps into the castle proper. The queens followed and then the children. Pol brought up the rear.

"Prince Poldon, right?"

Pol looked into the man's eyes. "Ranno Wissingbel, am I correct?"

Ranno's eyes crinkled into well-worn creases around his eyes. "You are. I suppose you've been taking good care of my Far these past few years."

Pol blinked. Far? Then it dawned on him. "Yes, uh, Far. I usually call her Mistress Farthia."

"You would, and that's the right way. I noticed you listened intently to My Emperor's comments. Did you enjoy them?"

Pol could feel his face blush. "I did, mostly. I'm afraid mine will be noted by my siblings."

Ranno nodded knowingly. Mistress Farthia had told him everything. "Don't you worry about that."

"I always worry about that, Sir Ranno."

"Just Ranno will do, if I can call you Pol. That's what your friend Paki calls you, right?"

Pol stopped on the top step as the others disappeared into the castle. "How did you know that?"

The older man just chuckled. "It's my business to know the important things."

"My nickname is hardly important," Pol said.

"I'm sure it isn't to some," Ranno smiled. "You've got to hurry along. I'll just walk with my daughter and her best friend."

Pol looked behind him to see Malden and Farthia, 'Far', just walking up the steps. He hurried inside. Up ahead, the Emperor chatted with the two kings as the families dispersed, probably to get ready for the state dinner to be held in an hour.

~~~

Chapter Sixteen

~

POL STOOD AT THE DOOR while his father's chamberlain announced his arrival at the Emperor's Reception. This was to be a state dinner, but Hazett III turned it into a reception that allowed a hasty expansion of the attendee list.

Only a few courtiers bothered to look his way as others filed in to be announced behind him. He headed for Ranno, Malden, and Mistress Farthia, standing by a drinks table. Before he reached it, someone bumped Pol's shoulder.

"Don't you think we didn't notice," Honna said. Pol thought he could see venom dripping from her mouth. "You are a non-person, always have been and always will be until something untoward happens." Her threat was quietly given, but he could see that his two friends and Ranno had noticed the nasty expression on his sister's face.

"Am I another heart to be broken?" Pol said with little emotion, rather proud of his comeback.

She reddened and stalked off.

"She doesn't like you, lad," Ranno said. He certainly didn't care about honorifics.

"Never has," Pol said. "Lately, that is all she talks to me about, how much she doesn't like me."

The crowd hushed. King Astor and his wife were announced, followed by Pol's parents. "Emperor Hazett III," the chamberlain said, and then rolled off a number of additional honorifics that Pol had never heard before.

"How long do I have to stay?" Pol asked Mistress Farthia.

"A bit longer. You can't leave until the Emperor recognizes your presence," she said.

Pol had expected a reception line and wanted to line up closer to the front, but the Emperor walked through the crowds, kings in tow, meeting and greeting the attendees. Pol noticed that he tended to avoid the better-dressed nobles and made a point of speaking to the less-impressive attendees.

"Does he always do that?" Pol said to Ranno.

"What?"

"Speak with the more common people."

Ranno nodded and smiled. "Good that you noticed. His Processions are for him to get in touch with his subjects. The nobles can come to Yastan, to see him if they have to, but the merchants and others…" He shook his head. "You really are a smart lad."

"Observant," Pol said.

"Smart and observant," Malden said. "He is a boy with hidden talents."

Pol could see Ranno accept Malden's words, and that worried him. The Emperor had already made Pol seem a bit more special, and Honna certainly noticed it.

The Emperor made his way to the four of them.

"Ranno, I see you haven't wasted any time in locating the fair Farthia." The Emperor seemed to be a natural at this kind of banter. "Malden," the Emperor said and gave the magician a sharp little bow of the head. Malden returned it with a deep bow.

"I am honored that you would remember my name."

"Posh," Hazett waved away Malden's comment. "You do the Empire a service working for King Colvin."

"Indeed, My Emperor," Pol's father said from behind.

Pol just stood there, hoping the Emperor would just acknowledge his presence and move on.

"Farthia." He nodded to his tutor as he hoped he would to him.

The Emperor's eyes swiveled and fell upon his. Pol looked down at the floor.

"Up," Hazett said and lifted Pol's chin. "Look me in the eye, Prince Poldon. Do you like it here in Borstall?"

"I have lived here all my life, Your Excellency."

"Indeed, but do you like it here?"

Pol became flustered. He hadn't expected any kind of an interchange at the reception.

"I am among friends," he waved his arm towards Malden and Farthia, "and my mother and father treat me well."

Pol began to get hot, and his face turned red.

"We will talk again, perhaps after the tourney." The Emperor turned away and began to circulate through the crowd again.

After seeing that his siblings were safely out of hearing distance, Pol sighed. Hazett had called him Prince Poldon again. It disturbed him like nothing else. What must his father think?

"My, you've come up in the world, My Prince," Malden said, smirking.

Farthia tapped the magician playfully on the shoulder. "Don't embarrass my student."

"Your student? He is our student. I'm going to ride his coattails all the way to the Baccusol throne."

"You'll be gray when that happens," Farthia said.

"So will you." Malden made a face at her.

"Are you two finished?" Ranno said. "I'll have to have another word with Hazett. The man has much too playful a personality than what is good for him."

"Is he a good leader?" Pol asked.

"Better than his father, young man, and his father was very good. Holding onto an empire is a tricky thing, much more difficult than setting one up. Hazett keeps himself visible and gives plenty of rope to his vassals, not that he isn't adept at knowing when to jerk them back from doing something too stupid."

Farthia put her arm through her father's and grinned at Pol. "See? You get a wonderful lesson in politics, even here."

She looked happier than he had ever seen her. Perhaps she didn't have to feel so proper when joined by Malden and her father. Mistress Farthia had never mentioned a mother.

That reminded Pol he should visit his mother somewhere in the crowded hall before he left. He bowed to the three and went off to find Queen Molissa. He spotted her standing next to Bythia's mother. Pol looked around for Bythia but couldn't see her. That was a relief, he thought.

"I made it," Pol said, smiling.

"Why on earth wouldn't you?" the South Salvan queen said.

"My youngest son was left off the event list. Luckily, I noticed the oversight, and I'm glad I did." Queen Molissa turned to Pol. "We both noticed that the Emperor sought you out to say hello."

If they noticed, then his siblings would know, and that didn't bode well for Pol. Well, Malden and Farthia said he needed to be here, so here he was.

"What did the Emperor have to say?" Bythia's mother said.

"He asked me if I liked it in Borstall."

The woman put her hand to her mouth. "What did you say?" She looked a little shocked.

"I said I'm happy to be here when I'm among friends. He had already acknowledged Mistress Farthia and Magician Malden, knowing each by name."

"And you, too, My Prince," Queen Molissa said.

"He did call me Prince Poldon again. I thought that a bit odd."

Both queens looked at each other. "He did?"

Pol nodded. "He even remembered my name. I think he has a talent for that. Ranno said he has a playful personality."

"Ranno?" Bythia's mother said.

"Ranno Wissingbel, one of his advisors. He is Mistress Farthia's father, and she's my tutor," Pol said.

"That man is the Emperor's Instrument. I would watch out for him. He helps keep the Empire in line," the South Salvan queen said. "And you called him Ranno?"

"He asked me to, and he asked if he could call me Pol. I said he could."

"Pol?" She looked at Molissa.

"That is Poldon's nickname."

Pol heard the Emperor's voice coming his way. "If you will excuse me," He bobbed his head at the two ladies and escaped before having to talk to Hazett again.

He wandered around. Not being as tall as the rest of the people at the reception became tiring for Pol. He found Malden standing by himself.

"Where is your lady friend?" Pol said.

Malden barked a laugh. "She left the reception with her father. They had some catching up to do since she never had a proper amount of time with him earlier this summer. Why?"

"The Emperor keeps calling me Prince Poldon. Is there any significance to that?"

"Twice, you say?" Malden looked a little surprised. "Did he call either of your other brothers 'Prince'?"

Pol shook his head.

"This is not good. To do that indicates that he recognizes you as Colvin's heir." Malden looked down at his wine cup as he swirled the red liquid. "Ranno said Hazett was playful, but this is too much. I'll have a talk with Ranno. He may have unwittingly put you into even more danger. This is exactly what we didn't want happening."

Pol became alarmed. "What should I do?"

"You look tired. I would go back to your rooms and retire for the evening. Make sure you lock your door. You need to rest up, for tomorrow the tourney starts with fourteen-year-olds trying to beat up on each other."

That suited Pol just fine. He bowed to Malden and left without making eye contact with another soul.

~ ~ ~

Chapter Seventeen

⁓

POL WISHED HE COULD HAVE SLEPT THROUGH THE TOURNEY, but at sunrise he heard a knock on his door. He had to get up to unlock it.

"Siggon!"

"I'll be your squire for the tourney, Pol. Get washed up. I've got a basket of breakfast that you can eat after you are trussed up in your jerkin and your colors. You need to win quickly, so I can get back to my garden. With all the trespassers in the castle, I'll be working through the night to put things back in order.

"Colors?"

"Everyone gets a tabard in the tourney. Yours will be scarlet and silver, your father's colors. Hurry."

They walked down to the training ground where Pol picked out a good wooden sword and Siggon helped him secure his jerkin and arrange the tabard, so it wouldn't be in the way when he fought.

Both of them picked food out of the breakfast basket. "Don't eat too much, lad. You need your energy, but you'll not be wanting stomach cramps interfering with your sword work."

"Are you going to help Paki, too?"

Siggon nodded. "A whole morning watching little boys play with sticks." He ruffled Pol's hair. "The matches will be fought at once in the tourney field. Each round will get smaller and smaller, so preserve what precious energy you have. The Emperor will arrive for the final matches of the three age classifications. They will also take place at once. If you make it all the way to the final match, you will have the most time to recover. Make the most of it."

"I know. It's part of my strategy."

It seemed that the festival grounds and the tourney field blossomed with flags and pennants overnight. Pol could feel the excitement from all the people. By the time they reached the tourney field, most of the thirteen to fourteen-year-olds were lining up to draw lots for partners.

Siggon patted Pol on the back and walked to the edge of the field and sat on one of the benches. It looked like being a squire involved making sure your charge got to the field on time.

While he waited in line, Pol stepped aside a bit and began to warm up. Soon the other boys were doing the same. Pol stood at the table.

"Poldon Fairfield."

The man at the table looked through the list. "No Poldon Fairfield here."

"Prince Poldon?"

The man looked up, shot to his feet, and bowed. "My Prince, I am sorry." He sat back down and checked the name of Prince Poldon. Pol would have rather entered as any other boy, but he nodded and graciously, in his mind, took the number the man gave him. Another man pinned the cloth badge on his tabard.

He looked around and began to watch the unfamiliar participants warm up. There were two that looked competitive, so he played at stretching as he watched them. He could easily detect their patterns. It seemed that the better boys had developed more definitive patterns, and that only made it simpler to come up with a match strategy, and that would also make it easier to use his magic to anticipate their moves.

A trumpet sounded, and the participants crowded around the table. The two men who signed them in put a pot on the table and began to draw out cards with names on them and hung them on a board. Pol looked for his number, and it finally came, number seven. He would fight a boy that he recognized as a decent competitor, but he didn't think he would have any trouble with him.

His partner found him.

"I get to fight a prince, eh?" the boy said.

"Just think of me as Pol Fairfield. No prince, just a competitor. We've sparred before."

"We have?"

Pol nodded. "You just didn't notice since I haven't wanted to draw attention to myself. Just give it your best, and I'll do the same."

The boy smiled. "Right." He gripped his sword and walked out onto the tourney field as the competitors found spaces for their match.

Men walked onto the field and would act as referees for the first matches. They looked like off-duty guards.

"Are you a soldier?" Pol asked the man assigned to them.

"I was and will be a miller until I'm called up again, My Prince."

"Don't give me any advantages. I want to fight fairly."

"You want a fair field?" the ex-soldier laughed.

Pol just smiled at the pun on his last name. "I do."

After a bit of warming up, Pol watched his opponent get loose, and that reminded Pol of the boy's patterns.

"Start after two short bursts on the horn. Two good touches win the match. I won't be counting a light tap." He looked at Pol and the other boy until they both nodded their understanding.

The horn blasted, and Pol jumped back just as he intended to do each and every match. His opponent liked to attack, so Pol let him push him back. Practicing on a full field for weeks gave Pol a second sense where the other matches were. Perhaps it was his magic location visualization at work, but he had other things to concentrate on.

He began to go on the offensive. His opponent kept his sword high, so Pol moved past his opponent and sneaked out a tap on the other boy's thigh.

"Not hard enough," the referee said.

Pol grit his teeth and barely dodged a blow on his back when he hesitated, expecting a touch called. The match had gone on long enough, so Pol concentrated on the boy's patterns and scored a touch on the inside of the boy's forearm as he cocked his arm for a strike.

"Touch," the referee said.

His opponent took a moment to rub his forearm.

"Begin."

Pol reached out again when the boy cocked his arm and slapped his sword on the boy's wrist hard enough to disarm him.

"Match. Seven won. The winner to the north side of the field. The loser can watch from the south or exit the field."

Pol watched his former opponent sit on a bench next to a man who wrapped his arm around him, probably his father. Pol threaded his way through the other matches and found only one other boy waiting for the next round.

Each match played out in much the same way. Pol made sure he varied his style and touches, since the squires were giving advice to their charges. Siggon had gone off for some reason. He studied each match as well as he could, reinforcing the patterns that he had memorized for each boy.

Pol made it to the last two pairs. If he won this he would be in the final match along with the winners of the eighteen year and sixteen year classifications.

His opponent was one of the new boys. This one was a head taller than Pol. He had watched him in a close match the previous round and thought he knew the boy's pattern, but his new opponent was as good as Pol thought he was. Pol was worried about his stamina, though. He could rest after this match, if he could get through it.

Pol looked at the way the boy stood, and his magic revealed that he would run towards Pol. His squire must have told him about Pol's backing up, so Pol would jump to his right, the boy's left, and quickly touch him in the side.

The horn blasted two times, and Pol shifted to his right as his opponent ran past him. The boy turned, but not before Pol hit him in the side. His opponent clearly favored his left side, but the referee didn't call a touch. Pol couldn't lose his concentration as he fought on and on. He had touched his opponent four times before his opponent barely tapped his elbow after a clinch and a push off.

Pol realized then that the match was rigged. His father and the Emperor hadn't arrived yet, so Landon or Grostin had had words with this man. Pol had to do something dramatic, or his strength would give out. His opponent had figured the judge would let the match go on, so he began to fight more recklessly. Pol couldn't rely on patterns alone, but he detected a lunge. The boy lost his footing, and Pol slapped him soundly on the back of his head with the flat of the blade.

His opponent fell headlong into the dirt of the tourney field and slowly rose to his feet.

"Touch?" Pol said to the judge.

The man refused to meet Pol's eyes and stayed silent.

"What is your name?" Pol said.

The judge ran off the field. His opponent could barely focus his eyes as Pol helped him to the south side of the field and into the arms of his squire.

"You beat Dirron fair and square a number of times in your match," he said.

"I'm sorry."

"No offense, My Prince," Dirron said blinking the daze from his eyes. "You were the offended one."

Pol watched as the two of them left the tourney grounds. That made sure Pol had won.

He had made it into the finals, but his victory had lost its savor as he dragged his way to the north side, approaching his opponent in the finals. Pol didn't know if he could recover well enough for the final match, but he had to make a good showing to show respect for his father.

The Chief Judge declared both boys as opponents in the finals to be held just before midday and excused them.

Paki caught Pol just as he left the field. "Have you seen my father?"

Pol shook his head. "He left before my first match. You need to get ready!"

His friend looked worried. "We were to meet after your last match."

Could his brothers have waylaid Siggon to disadvantage Pol? He couldn't think of another explanation.

"Let's go look for him. You don't have much time. The sixteen-year class has been called to line up. I'll take the festival grounds and meet you at the armory."

Pol and Paki split up. Pol looked around the fair grounds and ran all the way to the castle. He just reached the armory when Paki returned.

"He's not in the gardens or the woods."

"Let's look in the stables."

The boys ran around the armory and began to search the stables. Horses whinnied as they slid past them in their stalls to rummage around in the straw.

Pol heard a moaning above him. "Up!"

Paki garbbed a ladder and scampered up to the loft. "Dad's hurt pretty bad."

Pol just couldn't get up the ladder as quickly and felt his heart beating in his chest. He had used up most of his energy running around looking for Siggon. Pol didn't care and found the old stable master walking into the stable.

"Siggon has been beaten, please get him to the infirmary."

"You'll have to help me, since all the boys are at the tourney grounds." The man looked more angry than concerned and reluctantly helped Pol and Paki.

Pol did as much as he could, getting Siggon down from the loft.

"You go on, Paki. I'll get him help. You'll be late for your match."

Paki nodded and left once they got Siggon down from the loft.

"Do you have a wheelbarrow?" Pol said. "I can't lift him that far."

The stable master put his hands on his hips and looked at Pol. "You don't look so good yourself, My Prince," he said.

"We've got to get help for Siggon." Pol sat on the ground, beginning to wheeze when the man returned with a wheelbarrow. Then both of them struggled to get Siggon in the barrow.

"I've got a bum leg," the man said. "You'll have to manage mostly on your own."

Pol narrowed his eyes in anger, but Siggon's pitiful moan stopped that emotion. He needed to get Siggon to the infirmary, and if he had to do it himself, he would. It took him longer than he wanted with the minimal help the stable master offered, but eventually he made it.

Only one healer was on duty. The rest were set up to assist the injured at the tourney, so it was another effort to get Siggon on a bed.

"One of you will have to help. I can't do this all on my own," the healer said.

The stable master shook his head. "I have horses to mind. I've been gone too long already." He left the infirmary and walked away, rolling the empty wheelbarrow.

Pol took a deep breath. "I will stay if you give me some water and a moment to recover."

The healer began to take Siggon's clothes off, but struggled. Pol had little left in him, but he assisted the healer in disrobing the royal gardener and sat down as the healer examined Siggon.

Pol was astonished at the amount of bruises on Siggon's body. This was a brutal attack. The healer had him wipe down Siggon's face and while he did, Siggon grabbed hold of this wrist.

"You must return to the field. You won, didn't you?" Siggon said. Each word seemed to be filled with pain.

"I'll stay with you. There are only the two of us here to take care of you."

"Leave me." Siggon winced and his hand dropped.

"He is concussed," the healer said. "I could see his eyes were unfocused. Continue to clean him up. The worse injuries seem to be a few broken ribs and his head. I couldn't find any other broken bones other than his left index finger. I'll wrap that up."

Just then a man and a woman walked in. The woman's hand was covered with blood.

"Kitchen accident," the man said. "What's wrong with Siggon?"

"He was beaten," Pol said. It was because of Pol, but the boy couldn't say it.

"You watch him, and I have to attend to the woman," the healer said from across the room.

Pol continued to wash Siggon, and then Paki's dad woke up again.

"Keep him awake. Don't let him go to sleep."

More patients came and went. No one else could talk to Siggon, so Pol continued to talk to his friend's father. He might miss his match, but that wasn't important. Pol had a responsibility to see Siggon well again.

Siggon again told him to go, but Pol encouraged Siggon to talk about his war stories when he scouted for King Colvin and for Pol's grandfather, King Jaben. The storytelling brought a smile to Siggon's face as the memories flowed. The minutes turned to hours until another healer walked in.

"There you are, My Prince. The match was called for your opponent because you failed to show."

"I had one of your patients to care for, didn't I?" Pol looked at Siggon, who had closed his eyes. "Siggon." Pol nudged him. "He was awake just before you walked in."

The healer's eyes grew wide and he ran to the bed. He pounded on Siggon's chest as the man's face began to turn pale. "He just passed."

"No! We were having a conversation."

"Must have bled out in his brain," the healer said. "I'm sorry. Doesn't he have a son?"

Paki ran into the room. "How is my Dad?" he said. "Prince Grostin beat me." Paki had a deep bruise along his chin. "A bee stung me and Grostin took advantage of it."

"Siggon didn't make it," Pol said. "I'm sorry."

Paki pushed past Pol. "He can't be dead!" He broke into uncharacteristic tears and broke down over his father's body. Pol noticed the little circle of blood on his forehead. Grostin's peashooter had struck again. He suspected that both of his brothers were behind Siggon's death, but Pol had no evidence to prove otherwise. He clenched his fists and pounded them on his leg in frustration.

However, Pol knew he couldn't have prevailed against his opponent. Not after the entire effort of finding Siggon and taking him to the infirmary. At least Siggon seemed to enjoy his last minutes recounting old times.

Paki sat up and gave Pol an angry look. "You caused his death. If he hadn't asked to help you today, he'd be alive. You can leave. Go!"

Pol hadn't expected Paki to turn on him, but he was in so much shock and hurt from Siggon's death that he shuffled out of the infirmary, head down, barely noticing the ground pass beneath him.

~~~

Chapter Eighteen

~

WHILE POL WAS TRYING TO TAKE HIS MIND OFF THE HORRIBLE MORNING by reading the religion textbook, Ranno walked into the classroom with his daughter.

"Prince Poldon, I'd like you to describe this morning's events. My father senses a conspiracy," Farthia said.

Pol closed the book. He wasn't getting much of what his eyes saw. "Three events. First, someone bribed the judge for my last match to ignore my touches. I was getting fatigued and had to hurt my opponent to end the match. If I had to fight much longer, I wouldn't have had any energy for the last match. Second," Pol found his eyes watering. He took a deep breath to collect himself and wiped the wetness out of his eyes, "Siggon was beaten senseless. He had left the field before my first match ended. Paki and I found him in the castle stable loft. We struggled to get him to the infirmary. With only one healer and Paki's match about to start, I sat with him and talked with him until..." Pol felt a shudder go through is body. "...Until he died from head injuries, I guess."

"I had one of my healers look at the body. He also had internal bleeding that didn't stop. He wouldn't have survived the beating even if Malden attended him."

"That doesn't help cushion the loss. He died because he wanted to help me. Grostin—"

"Prince Grostin?"

Pol nodded. "I'm certain he's behind it all. If anything underhanded or sneaky happens, Grostin is likely to be behind it. Paki hates me now. My best friend hates me, and for good reason since his father died because of me." Pol buried his face in his hands.

Ranno put his hand on Pol's shoulder. "I'm sorry, lad, but this is what happens in noble families."

"It isn't very noble, is it?"

"No. You said there were three events?"

Pol clutched his hands and tried to smooth out the jumble in his mind. "Paki had a mark on the side of his forehead like I had on my neck."

Pol showed Ranno the nearly healed mark on his neck. "A man, who is expert at using a pea shooter, shot me when I fought Grostin. It cost me the match. The same thing happened to Paki. My friend called it a bee sting, but I know what it was."

"Will Paki let me see it?"

"Just don't tell him that I sent him. He's probably home with his mother. She's a cook in the kitchens. He's really mad at me."

"I know how that works," Ranno said. "We'll investigate. Will you help me?"

"You have the Emperor to attend to, don't you?"

Ranno shook his head. "Not while we are camped. The beatings seem more like something your older brother would arrange, and the pea shooter and the judge are more Prince Grostin's style." Ranno looked at Farthia, who nodded back.

"I don't think Landon is smart enough to arrange anything," Pol said. He shouldn't have said that, but he felt so badly, he knew he had lost control over his emotions.

Farthia dragged a chair next to Pol and put her arm around him. "You think you know who did it, but my father is an expert at investigation. Let him help prove what happened."

"No one will care," Pol said. "If you find my brothers are the culprits, my father will just say 'boys will be boys' and leave it at that. There have been other incidents, as well as their constant sneers and nasty comments." Pol looked down at his hands. They felt dirty after what happened. "I'm sorry. I'm really upset, and I can't think properly."

"Do you have anything to attend today?"

Pol shook his head. "Dinner tomorrow night after the tourney."

"I suggest you stay in your rooms," Ranno said. "I'll be by a few times because I know you can help me."

"I don't know how."

Ranno squeezed Pol's shoulder. "Let me worry about that."

Pol relaxed on the couch and closed his eyes. He rang for food and a servant knocked on the door.

"Come in," Pol said.

Paki brought a tray of food.

"What are you doing here? I thought you hated me along with my siblings."

After putting the tray on the table in the room, Paki sat down and put his feet on the low table in front of the couch. "I suppose I can relax in here."

"Whatever you want," Pol said. "I feel badly about Siggon. I really do. You know that."

"I do. I threw you out of the infirmary because I was hurt. I still hurt, but not as much. My mother ordered me to deliver the food." He jerked his thumb towards the table behind him. "Mistress Farthia's father helped explain things. What were Dad's last minutes like?"

Pol felt much better with Paki willing to talk to him. "He didn't expect to die, so there weren't any last words to you or your mother. The healer told me to keep him awake with the head injury, so we talked about old times, and then I got him telling me old war stories. He had lots of experiences. He was in some pain, but he kept talking and seemed to think just fine until he stopped talking. I was distracted with another healer with a patient coming in, and then he just slipped away. Ranno, the Emperor's advisor, said that he died from bleeding inside his body, as well as bleeding inside his head."

Paki looked at his feet on the table. His eyes were moist. "At least he didn't die alone," he said and sighed. "I didn't want to lose my father."

"And I didn't want to lose my friend. He volunteered to help me, and then he intended to help you."

"Can I take back what I said?"

Pol nodded. "We're still friends and I'll let you know what Ranno comes up with."

"You missed the final match because of my father. Competing in front of the Emperor. That would have been a high honor," Paki said.

"I couldn't desert Siggon. In the end, I know I made the right decision."

Paki nodded. "Let's have something to eat. Suddenly, I'm hungry."

The two of them avoided any serious talk for most of the meal that they shared.

"So what are you going to do?" Pol said.

"I'm still a gardener's apprentice."

"I'll talk to Father and see if we can't get you into the scouts a bit early."

Paki brightened. "You think he'd do that?"

"I can ask." Pol managed a smile. "It's the least I can do." Pol looked at his spoon. "No, it's not. Siggon died in my service. I'll ask for a pension for your mother as well."

Paki left, and at least Pol had one problem less to worry him. He drifted off on the couch.

A hand shook him awake. Pol looked up into Malden's eyes.

"Keep your door locked."

"I didn't feel like it," Pol said. "Did you hear about Siggon?"

The magician nodded his head. "Ranno is hot on the trail. Unfortunately, I don't think anything will come of it. Even if Prince Grostin is responsible, which he probably is, your father will only slap his hand."

"That's what I told Ranno. Will the Emperor help?"

Malden pressed his lips together. That meant no.

"Hazett is known for not meddling in the internal affairs of a country unless it impacts the Empire. If King Colvin lets Grostin go free, then he goes free. At least as long as he stays in North Salvan. As for you, stay in your rooms. I'd like to keep you company, but I'm running around helping to get the magician testing going outside of Borstall. The testing starts the day after tomorrow."

"I can't expect anything else." Pol didn't feel like going out anyway. "I'll be at the dinner tomorrow night. Until then I think I'll rest. I ran out of energy today."

"I'm sure you did."

Pol didn't do much the next day. He wandered down to the kitchens for breakfast and found Paki's mother hard at work.

"I am sorry for your loss," Pol said.

"We all are. It's a horrible thing what someone did to my man. Paki's not my only little one. I have others to keep me company and help around the house," she said. Pol could see a pattern of pain and justification. "I knows you were with him in the end and I appreciate he didn't die alone." She gave Pol a hug, which surprised Pol, but he stood there and took it. If his being by her side gave Siggon's widow comfort, Pol would endure the embarrassment.

"I can't say I'm glad, but I wouldn't have it another way. I would have felt worse, having him die up in the loft."

She sniffed and waved Pol away. She turned and cried away from his sight.

Pol grabbed some food and took it up to his rooms. He locked the door and looked out the window. In the far distance, he could make out flags fluttering over the tourney and the festival fairgrounds. Others wouldn't feel Siggon's loss, but Pol did. He didn't want to walk around all that activity, thinking of how Siggon had died.

After lunch Ranno showed up. "We found the pea shooter, but he won't talk. That man is very shrewd, and is, as it turns out, from South Salvan. I'm not about to employ any aggressive questioning techniques in your father's kingdom, but here is what hit you." He put out his hand. The little ball of metal had rough edges. "Bound to hurt."

"It did," Pol said. "What will you do with him?"

"I took him to Kelso Beastwell and Banson Hisswood. Showed them the shooter and his tiny weapons, which they confiscated along with the blowpipe we found on him. There was only one witness and not enough proof to do anything other than hold him in a cell overnight. That shooter is a dangerous man. He knows how to keep his mouth shut and refuse to talk."

"That means one of my siblings must have hired him."

Ranno nodded. "I think Grostin is the most likely since he benefitted. I was glad to learn that his opponent schooled your brother rather well in his championship match. If his opponent got 'stung', it didn't work. Landon fared much the same. He hasn't made it into the finals in any event. He talked his father into letting him fight in the melee, and if he does win, that will mean, in my opinion of fighters, that he paid off all his opponents. I've notified Hazett of that possibility. He will know if that happens and will mention any cheating to King Colvin."

Pol sat down and offered Ranno to do the same, but he remained standing. "No progress on Siggon's attackers?"

"There weren't any witnesses in the stable, if that's what you meant. I talked to the stable master, and he claims he was asleep when Siggon must have been beaten. Paki and you must have woken him up when you tore the place apart trying to find him. I'm sorry."

"It's frustrating that they got away with a murder."

"A lot of murders and assaults occur where the perpetrators are not caught. It's a matter of finding the evidence. I'm sorry, lad."

Pol didn't expect Ranno to find any evidence, and he was very impressed that Ranno found the peashooter. If Ranno acted as the Emperor's Instrument and took the time to help a fourteen-year-old prince, Pol couldn't be more appreciative. "Thank you."

"There is a big dinner tonight. Are you going?"

Pol nodded.

"Sit with us. We will protect you."

"Us?"

"Malden, Far, and me. Hazett knows that's what we will do."

Pol considered. "If it's acceptable to the Emperor."

"It is."

Pol saw Ranno out and sent a servant with a request for an audience with his father. He received a note to talk to him right after the dinner.

Pol looked out at the sea of people in the great hall. He spotted Malden, who stood with Ranno, and made his way through all of the long tables.

"How are you?" Mistress Farthia said.

"I'm better in every way, but that doesn't mean I'm good." Pol said. "I still feel bad about Siggon."

"You will for a long time," Malden said. "He was a good man."

Pol couldn't say anything else. He looked around the room and found that they were seated higher than most in the room. Ranno sat closest to the dais table, and he sat Pol down next to him. Malden sat at his right.

"Are you seated here because of me?"

She nodded. "Father should be up there." Mistress Farthia pointed to the dais table with her chin. "He outranks everyone here but the two kings and Hazett."

That surprised Pol. He knew Ranno was an advisor, but he didn't think that he was a noble. Pol looked up at the dais. None of his siblings had been seated at that table. That might have upset Landon, at least.

His siblings were on the other side of the room, still close to the dais table. That was just as well. He looked closer, and both Grostin and Landon had bruise marks on their faces. Landon had been mauled during the melee. Pol smiled. Served them right.

King Colvin introduced the Emperor. Hazett announced the winners of the various events, who met with polite applause. Pol wondered if his father was disappointed at the results.

"I would like to point out that the fourteen-year-old event yesterday was marred by tragedy. A squire, Siggon Hostel, was viciously attacked and later died from his injuries. Prince Poldon withdrew from the finals to be by his side at your castle infirmary when Hostel expired. I think that act of grace deserves some applause. Stand, Prince."

Pol turned red and stood with the help of Ranno and waved to the diners. Luckily, the applause didn't last very long. Pol looked over at Grostin, who looked angry. Let him look angry, Pol thought. His brother was responsible for Siggon's death.

The Emperor thanked King Colvin and the citizens of Borstall for their hospitality, and then he announced the magician testing. Some of the crowd didn't know about it, so the noise level in the room increased for a moment until the Emperor raised his hand.

"We have already started testing in the surrounding towns and villages and will continue tomorrow. All those who were not tested when the last evaluations were conducted over a decade ago are commanded to attend. That means everyone, including castle staff and the nobles here. It is one of the few duties to the Empire that I take to my states. I am sure you will all comply. Now, let us eat!" He raised his hands, signaling the commencement of the meal.

Servants filed through the hall. The dais table was served first, and then the sound level increased once their food had been served.

"I can't get out of the testing, can I?" Pol asked Malden.

"Would you defy your Emperor?" Ranno said. "Malden will be conducting the testing for those residing in the castle. That will include your friend Paki."

"And Grostin, Landon, Amonna, and Honna?"

"It will," Malden said. "I've already determined your siblings have no talent, but that will be formalized tomorrow."

"What if I don't show up?" Pol said.

"You've already been tested by me, so I'll merely write in the results."

Pol put his fork on the plate and sat back. "I'm doomed."

"You have been for quite some time," Ranno said. "I say make the best of it."

That was easy for Farthia's father to say. After considering Ranno's words, Pol wondered what that might be. He couldn't see any worthwhile path.

The dinner was a tasteless affair. Pol merely went through the motions of eating. He felt incapable of enjoying the food that he put in his mouth. He felt bad for his past and bad for his future. Magic wouldn't be an escape for him. It only meant higher expectations, not from his father, but from Emperor Hazett III. The notion that the Emperor might want Pol as his creature scared Pol nearly as much as his siblings.

The Emperor yawned. It looked affected to Pol, and then Hazett rose. "We begin in the morning. I must be on my way in two days." He raised his hands and all dutifully clapped.

"I will see you tomorrow," Ranno said, who got to his feet and followed the Emperor out.

The night wasn't particularly late, but his father left soon after. He walked past Pol.

"See me in my study as soon as you can. I have other meetings tonight," the King said rather brusquely.

~~~

Chapter Nineteen

~

POL NODDED AND EXITED THE DINNER within moments. He made his way to his father's study. Two guards flanked the doors when Pol knocked.

"Come in, Poldon."

He walked in. Pol didn't get many chances to meet with his father in this room. His last visit took place months ago, and even then he was with his mother. Pol bowed.

King Colvin waved his bow off and pointed to a chair. "Sit and tell me what you want. I assume this isn't just a visit."

Pol shook his head, suddenly afraid. He looked around the room to memorize it. His skill in detecting patterns had grown in the past weeks, and with it came the ability to remember much of what he observed.

"Out with it. Stop ogling."

Pol cleared his throat. He had to petition his father for a pension for Siggon's family. He looked out the window and then down at the rug until he heard his father tapping his finger on the desk. "I, uh, feel responsible for Siggon Horstel's death. I came to ask a boon. Could you provide his family with a decent pension? Siggon died helping me, and if he hadn't been my squire yesterday morning, he would be alive today."

"You want nothing? I thought you wanted some recognition for yourself."

Pol shook his head. "Nothing for me. I have everything I need." Except peace and quiet, he thought. Pol wished he could tell the king to tell his siblings to stop their evil deeds, but he knew he wouldn't be able to muster the courage. His father wouldn't lift a finger to stop them, anyway.

"Who do you think did it? I have talked to Ranno Wissingbel. He thinks it was Grostin," his father said. From the tone in his voice, he didn't believe what Ranno told him.

"Ranno doesn't have any proof other than the fact that there really was a pea shooter that distracted me in my match with Grostin, and the same person shot at Paki, uh, Pakkingail Horstel."

King Colvin nodded. "A similar mark was on the boy who thoroughly defeated Grostin in the championship match for his age group, but there were no witnesses, so my hands are tied. Ranno couldn't find any evidence at the stable, either."

Pol doubted if they were really tied, but Pol couldn't change the past, only the future. "I don't ask for myself."

King Colvin nodded. "I know. Your heart is in the right place, and in this case, I think your head is as well. I will provide a pension to Siggon's widow. Siggon's current pay for as long as she lives in North Salvan. Will that be acceptable?"

"Fully acceptable, Father. I will leave now."

"Not so fast, Poldon. Ranno told me something else. He says that you will pass the magician test tomorrow. Is that correct?"

Pol wanted so much to lie to his father, but he couldn't. He knew he blushed, and his father would know he'd been caught out.

"I will, Father. Malden found out that I had talent not long after my poisoning. He has taught me a few things, so I know I will pass."

"But you are only fourteen. Magical ability doesn't usually manifest itself for two or three more years."

"The test will reveal magical talent at my age."

His father made a face. "I know that, but you can actually do magic? Show me."

Pol looked at his father's neat desk. A thin volume, perhaps a diary sat on his left. He concentrated focusing on the little book and moved it from one side of the desk to the other. His father moved his chair back and looked at the book in its new location.

"I didn't really believe one of my children would have talent." Pol's father looked intently at Pol. "You look a little pale. Does magic sap you of your strength?"

Pol nodded. "I haven't practiced very much with the tourney coming up. I had to save my strength for my matches."

His father looked at him as if he had seen Pol for the first time. "I still want you showing up for the testing. Don't be alarmed if I show surprise. Your having magic only complicates your life, you know."

"I understand, Father."

The king nodded. "I think you really do. Rest up for tomorrow."

Pol rose from his seat. He was surprised that his little trick didn't take more out of him. Perhaps his full stomach helped.

"One more thing. My petition about Landon taking the throne of Listya was not granted. Our Emperor wants to think more on it. Make of that what you will."

So that was why his father was in such a foul mood. At least he granted Pol's wish. He left his father's study more confused and more afraid than when he had walked in. At least Paki and his family wouldn't suffer financially from the loss of Siggon, but his father now knew he could perform magic. He didn't know how that would make a difference in the long term, since he would be found out tomorrow when tested publicly.

The rejection of the petition really worried Pol. If the Emperor delayed making a decision because of Pol, that would put him in greater jeopardy. His mind roiled on his walk back to his rooms. When he opened the door, the room was dark.

The servants should have arrived to start a small fire and light the lamps. Pol stood in the doorway and located two bodies in his room. He had no weapon available to him, so he was about to turn and call for the guards, when someone pushed him into the room from behind. Pol hadn't even tried to sense the corridor.

He stumbled into the darkness and tried to roll underneath the couch, but a hand caught his foot. Pol struggled, but his assailants seemed to be full grown men. He yelled for help, but as soon as the first sound came out of his mouth someone wrapped a gag around his face.

Pol felt the punches and the kicks. Something hit his upper arm, and he heard, as well as felt, it crack.

"That should be enough to keep him out of testing," a voice said. Pol didn't recognize it, but he would remember it if he heard the voice again.

"Time to go," another voice said. That was Landon. Pol was sure of it. He hurt so badly that he couldn't summon any magical force. Shortly after he was pushed into his rooms, Pol lay in a great deal of pain, likely bleeding on the carpet.

After a few moments of agony, Pol began to scream for help. He saw a few embers showing in the fireplace. That was enough to let Pol know where he was in the sitting room. He couldn't get up from where he lay, but he struggled to inch his way forward. He didn't know how many bruises shouted at him with pain, but he eventually slid up the wall, and with his good hand, he pulled the rope as many times as he could before collapsing to the floor.

Pol had no idea how long he hurt, but eventually a few servants and guards opened the door. They lit lamps and from the looks on their faces, Pol must have been a mess. He thought of Siggon and the man's internal injuries that bled inside until he died. He didn't feel so bad inside, but his arm was a source of excruciating pain.

When they moved him, the pain in his arm overcame everything else.

Pol had seen the ceiling twice before, but he could barely open his eyes. He woke up in the infirmary, and Malden sat at his side. Pol tried to talk, but he could only mumble.

"Don't try to talk. Your face is swollen. Your own mother didn't recognize you."

"Time?" Pol managed to say.

"Oh, it's early in the morning. I hope you don't mind me using magic on your arm. It will continue to hurt for a week or so. Your arm was broken in two places, full breaks, not cracked like your ribs. The rest of your injuries are bruises and contusions, especially on your face. The healers had to stitch along the side of your forehead. You'll likely have a dashing scar to wow the ladies."

That was the last thing that interested Pol.

"Landon."

Malden put his finger to his lips. "Don't tell anyone who your assailants were. Ranno is collecting evidence, and there was some in your room. You'll put yourself at even more risk if you point out anyone who was there."

"Petition denied." Pol struggled to relay his father's message.

"I know." Malden put his hand on Pol's forehead. The stitches stung when the magician touched them. "That probably was cause for the attack. Landon probably wanted to punish someone, and with the Emperor calling you 'Prince Poldon', you were the best target."

"No test," Pol said slowly. "King knows."

"Ranno doesn't know if your father told Landon. It doesn't matter at this point, but staying silent is your best path, after all."

Pol thought about it through his dazed mind. Ranno had talked about what was best. Pol tried to assemble a pattern where that kind of behavior would fit. He did and recognized it as a defensive one. Malden had other duties, and his father hadn't even suggested a bodyguard. Perhaps it was time to ask for one.

"I'm going to give you something to make you sleep," Malden said. He lifted Pol's head and poured some foul tasting liquid down Pol's throat.

The magician didn't say a word, but Pol began to drift.

~

Pol woke in the sunlight. He squinted as he looked at the bright light. His puffy eyes must have gone down since his early morning talk with Malden. He also felt a bit better. Malden might have done more work on his injuries before he left.

A healer poked her head in the room. "You are awake?"

"I feel enough pain to know I'm awake," Pol said. His words didn't come out as mumbles. He touched his upper arm and felt a couple of lumps underneath the skin. They throbbed to this touch, but Pol remembered how badly his arm hurt the previous night.

"I'll fetch your mother."

Queen Molissa rushed into the room, brushing her fingers through her disheveled hair. She sat on the bed and adjusted her dress. "The healers let me spend the night. You have Malden to thank again. I observed him working on you."

"I'm fortunate," Pol said. He wished Malden had been around when Siggon had been found. Perhaps he could have saved his life, even though Ranno had said Siggon's injuries were too great for the magician to heal.

"You are. We are all amazed that you were able to get to the servant's bell. You left a trail of blood across the room."

"I didn't want to end up like Siggon Horstel. I still feel responsible for his death, but Father agreed to a generous pension for his family."

"He told me when he stopped by early this morning. He is attending to the Emperor who had demanded that he join him observing the castle testing."

"I told him that I can perform magic and gave him a demonstration. I'd be caught out today, anyway."

"No, you won't," his mother said.

"Malden said he would have to declare me tested. I didn't have a choice. That's why I gave Father a demonstration, so he would know ahead of time."

His mother looked worried. "We will need to talk as soon as Emperor Hazett leaves. I have something important to tell you. I wanted to put it off for years, but I can't any longer, not after this."

"Whatever you want," Pol said. "I think we both need bodyguards."

"Your father asked if I wanted one this morning."

"Say yes," Pol grabbed at his mother's arm with his good hand.

She took his hand and kissed it. "I will if you will."

"I decided when I woke up for a few minutes this morning that a bodyguard would have helped. The castle is presently a dangerous place."

"I know, Poldon. Once this business with Landon is over, perhaps life will settle down."

Pol nodded, but he didn't think that would happen. He seldom yearned to be fully grown, but he did this morning. His body protested every time he turned or changed position in his bed. If he was bigger and stronger, he might not have suffered so many injuries, but then his heart sank as he remembered how Siggon fared against his attackers. As he thought of losing his friend, Pol shook his head.

"Are you in pain, dear?" his mother asked.

"My head, my body, and my heart," Pol said, and truly meant it. He closed his eyes, and when he opened them again, his mother gently shook him awake.

"Emperor Hazett is here," she said.

Pol looked up to see Ranno and the Emperor standing at the foot of his bed. He tried to get up, but his mother pushed him back down.

"No need, Prince Poldon," Hazett said. "I see you went to extreme lengths to avoid testing today." The Emperor chuckled while his mother gave Pol an indulgent smile and patted his healing arm.

"Malden—," Pol said.

Hazett raised his hand. "I was told of your potential before I even arrived. There is no need to test, but I would like a demonstration. I heard from King Colvin that you were able to move things."

Pol nodded slightly. "I can. I'm not up to much, but I'll try." Pol struggled to sit up, and Ranno rushed to help.

"Take it easy, boy."

"Here," the Emperor pulled a small knife from his pocket and laid it on the foot of the bed. "Can you put this in my hand?"

"I can when I'm in better shape." Pol concentrated and found the pattern in the room that he needed. He tweaked the position of the knife from the bed to above the Emperor's outstretched hand and let it drop. He could feel his energy level lower. "It made me a bit tired, but I did it."

"See, Ranno?" Hazett said. "That is at least a Third level spell, not only horizontal, but vertical." The Emperor grinned at Pol. "It is too bad you are so frail, but don't give up hope! You can get stronger."

Frail. Pol kept his mouth shut. He had nearly prevailed in the swordsman competition for his age group, but the first words out of the Emperor's mouth after seeing him do something good was a description of his physical state.

"He just performed while severely injured," Ranno said.

Hazett nodded and looked at the small knife in his hand. "There is that." He looked back to Pol. "We will speak again before I leave tomorrow, if you are up to it."

Pol blinked. "You don't have to, My Emperor."

"I want to, Prince Poldon." Hazett nodded to his mother and left without Ranno.

Farthia's father looked back at the doorway. "He likes you, Pol."

"That only makes things more dangerous for my son," Molissa said.

"I know. He needs a bodyguard and the best one I know he's already met."

"I have?"

Ranno nodded. "I've contacted Valiso Gasibli. He had already intended to come back to Borstall to train you. With your friend Siggon's death, you will need to continue training in stealth and other things. Val has worked for me in the past and can serve as your bodyguard and, as your tutor, and he already knows Malden Gastoria and Kelso Beastwell."

At this point, Pol didn't know if he could still trust Kelso, but at least Val came highly recommended from two people that he currently trusted.

"I accept," Pol said. "Have you found any more evidence of my attackers?"

Ranno sighed. "Enough. I've talked to Banson Hisswood about the men who did it, except for one, and he will keep an eye on them. Their sort can't keep still."

Pol knew who the one was, Landon, and he figured his brother to be untouchable.

"I've got to get back to His Excellency." Ranno made the title sound like a joke. "Valiso should arrive in Borstall in a few days. We caught him on the road, and my men sent a bird back to say he is hurrying to get back to Borstall." Ranno bowed to his mother and pinched Pol's toes as he left.

"Farthia certainly has a colorful father," Molissa said. "He works for Hazett, but he insists on doing so in his own way. He must be very good to avoid reprimand from the Emperor for his antics."

"I think he is," Pol said. "I'm sure he does more than accompany Hazett III," Pol said. "Kelso introduced me to Valiso Gasibli. Val is a dangerous man, I'm sure of it. If he worked for Ranno, I guess that Ranno is some kind of spy master."

His mother giggled. "Spy master. That sounds so sinister. That would be only one of his duties as the Emperor's Instrument."

"Look at me, mother. I hurt and would hurt a lot less if Magician Malden hadn't helped treat me. I need a sinister person to look after me, and help me look after you."

Pol had just finished some honeyed gruel for his midday meal, when the Emperor walked into his rooms. He entered by himself and closed the door behind him.

"My Emperor," Pol said scrambling to sit up.

The Emperor put his hand on Pol's shoulder. "Relax. You still have some healing to do. I must say you look better today. It's a wonder what a day can do to one's constitution. I've taken care of a few things for you, but I will be leaving soon, and I wanted one last chat with you. Just you and me, Prince Poldon."

Pol recognized the Emperor's style of banter and tried to keep from smiling.

"I want you to stay alive, Prince Poldon." Hazett waggled a finger at Pol. "That's not an easy command to fulfill, is it?"

Pol shook his head. He knew the Emperor had to know everything about his family, and that made Pol feel disgraced.

"It doesn't look like you will ever rule North Salvan, or even Listya where you have the right to rule, after your mother, of course. Don't lose hope, though, Prince Poldon. I look after exceptional people, and you, my boy, are an exceptional person." The Emperor waved away his comment. "Of course, this is between you and me, only. If you ever need my help, in any way, seek Ranno or me. I can always use someone with your honor and sensitivity."

"I'm only a boy, My Emperor," Pol said.

"And I am only a man, really no different than any you might pass on a Borstall street."

Pol knew the Emperor didn't really mean that, but he understood his point.

"Endure and follow the counsel of Malden Gastoria and Valiso Gasibli. They are both good men, although Valiso has a certain sinister style, I admit."

The Emperor rose and patted Pol on his leg. "Get well, and come see me when you are older. I can always find something for you to do." He smiled enigmatically to Pol. "Keep our talk a secret, even from our friends?"

Pol nodded, so astonished that he couldn't speak.

The Emperor gave him a tiny wave and quietly left his room.

~ ~ ~

Chapter Twenty

~

"SO FATHER AND THE EMPEROR DECIDED TO KEEP MY RESULTS A SECRET, after all?"

Malden nodded to Pol, who had just been moved to his rooms. "Since you weren't tested, there is no reason to think otherwise."

"The Emperor said he'd take care of things when we talked in the infirmary just before he left. I didn't believe him. I guess I should have," Pol said, amazed that his magic hadn't been revealed after all. "Still, a lot of people know I can do magic."

"Those that do, know how to keep quiet. Farthia, your mother, and I have no reason to blurt it out to anyone. Your father won't, for obvious reasons."

"Paki knows." Pol said. "I'd like to talk to him about it, but—"

"Don't say anything. Paki might not be the most reliable confidant. Not at this point, anyway," Malden said. "Interestingly enough, Paki showed some talent in the test. Not enough to get the Emperor excited, but just enough to justify sending him to a monastery with you for further training, but not enough where he could attain an exalted level, like you." Malden grinned.

Pol snorted. How could he live long enough to be exalted at anything? "Paki's good at doing simple non-magical things. He wants to be a scout like his father."

"Why don't you let him train with you and Valiso? The man's not a woodsman, but much of what he has to teach a scout could be put to good use. Paki gives you an extra bodyguard, although he's still a bit small."

"Bigger than me," Pol said. "But then isn't everybody?"

"Give it all some time. That's one thing you have, time. I'd still give a monastery some thought. With Paki's talent, he could justify going along with you."

If Paki could go with Pol, then a monastery wouldn't be so bad. Perhaps Val could protect his mother, the Queen. With Pol out of the way, there might be less pressure on his siblings. Why did there have to be pressure at all?

"Even with evidence that Landon beat me up, Father still refuses to act? Doesn't he love my mother?"

Malden toyed with a penknife. "Colvin is not a perfect man."

"That's not an answer." Pol instantly regretted the sharpness of his words, but Malden didn't seem put out.

The magician sighed. "He loved his first wife more than he does your mother. His four children are all that he has left of her, so he is reticent to do anything that will damage her memory. That is what I think, anyway. When confronted with Grostin hiring the peashooter, Colvin brushed it off as a foible of Grostin's youth. He did reprimand him. Of course, you wouldn't know it."

Pol understood that. Grostin was hard as rock.

"Landon was a different story. Listya is where Colvin thinks Landon should be. If he hadn't submitted the petition to the Emperor, your father might have acted differently, but in this case, he told Ranno that it was his prerogative to ignore Landon's involvement. I'm sorry, My Prince."

Pol had always thought that his father loved his siblings more than him. He knew that his mother loved the king and that the king loved her, but he couldn't really comprehend a man loving more than one woman. Pol had never thought such things through, but Malden made sense, even though it was hard for him to accept.

"He will still let Mother have a bodyguard?"

"She arrives in a few days. Her bodyguard is a female scout from the forces stationed on the border with Tarida. She comes highly recommended by Kelso and a number of officers. That guard, paid directly by Ranno, will be your mother's shadow when she is out and about."

"Ranno?"

"Another gift from Hazett. The Emperor's advisor also pays Valiso. That will reduce the possibility of your brothers bribing them to look the other way. Your father agreed to it all. I don't know how he could refuse Hazett, since the Emperor holds the granting of the petition over Colvin's head."

"Since you know everything, and I know nothing, has my schedule been changed?"

"Instead of instruction from Siggon early every morning, you will get your instruction from Valiso then and again in the late afternoon. Farthia from mid-morning until noon, and then after lunch for another hour. Mid-afternoon, you and I will delve into other things, shall we say?"

"There is enough to teach me all that time?"

"You know less than you think you do, My Prince. There is even more to learn at a monastery."

Pol groaned. It all sounded so boring and tedious.

Valiso didn't arrive for three more days. Paki had agreed to train with Pol, and they both showed up in the morning to meet with Pol's new bodyguard.

"You're going to be awful sick of me, Pol." Val said. He turned his eyes at Paki. "You'll not be quite as sick since you won't have me sticking on you like a leech."

That made Paki laugh. "It's Pol who needs it."

Val glared at Paki, and that was enough to make Paki shrink at that look.

"We will learn a bit each day." He ticked off the list on his fingers. "Fighting with knives, throwing knives—"

"Kelso taught me how to do that," Pol said.

Val turned up his lip. "Not like what you'll learn from me. Let's see… poisons, potions, observation, deduction, sword fighting." Val looked at Pol. "Not like Kelso taught, and the defensive and offensive art of using magic. Malden might join us when we get to that."

Paki's jaw dropped. "Are you a magician, too?"

Val's eyes glazed and a bright ball of flame appeared between the three of them.

Paki's eyes grew. "I can learn that?"

"Maybe not a ball that big, but Malden says you should at least produce something to see by. You'll get a few sessions on basic magic from him in the afternoons after you have done your gardening job."

Pol's friend frowned. "I still have to do that?"

Val nodded. "It gives your family a bit more coin to work with. Are you against helping your mother and your siblings?"

Paki shook his head.

Pol now had a sense of what Malden had told him a few days ago about having enough to learn.

"We will start with knives." Val took them to a cloth-covered table. Pol could see lumps underneath, and then Val removed the cloth to reveal at least twenty kinds of knives. "Let's talk about what these are and what they are good for."

"I don't know why you have to bring him into the family dining room," Grostin said. "He looks like a criminal."

Pol sat down to eat while Val sat on a chair against the wall, munching on a plate of food he had served himself.

"Valiso is not a criminal. He has worked for Emperor Hazett III. He is both a tutor and a bodyguard."

"You need a bodyguard?" Honna said, quickly putting food in her mouth so she could leave.

"I guess you haven't noticed what's been going on around here. I've been beaten up in my own rooms and had to fight my way out of an attack in the city." Pol didn't mention the peashooter or Siggon's death. "Father suggested it."

Grostin snorted. "I heard Hazett, our Emperor, forced him to agree to bodyguards."

"How often have you been beaten up, Grostin? When were you ever attacked?" Pol said.

Pol's brother jumped to his feet. "Are you accusing me of something?" Grostin had balled his fists.

"I've accused you of nothing. You have received no injuries of any kind, so you don't need a bodyguard. What about you, Honna?" Pol looked her in the eyes as calmly as he could. He refused to lose his temper or make a direct accusation.

She shook her head and left the room, glaring at Grostin. Pol felt that was a good sign.

Bythia and Amonna walked into the room together, with linked arms.

"Who is this? Your bodyguard, Pol?" his younger sister asked.

"Valiso Gasibli. He will be teaching me different methods to defend myself, since I can't fight for long with a sword, and he will also look out for my princely person."

Amonna giggled. "Princely person, eh? He looks dangerous."

"He is. That's the point," Pol said.

Bythia stared at Val and then grabbed Amonna. "I'm not hungry right now."

Amonna glanced at Val and nodded her head. "We'll be back after you've finished."

Val moved his plate to the table. "Now that we are alone, we'll eat together." Val snorted. "I can see why you feel threatened. Have they always been this way?"

Pol nodded. "Worse since father petitioned Hazett to make my oldest brother vassal-king."

"That's what Ranno told me. Hurry up and finish your breakfast, so we don't let Paki get himself hurt playing with knives in our classroom."

Pol smiled at the thought of their private room at the armory called a classroom, but Val was right. Perhaps for a while, they would grab breakfast in the kitchens. However, they had not seen Landon. Pol wanted Val to get a good look at Landon and have his brother get a feel for how dangerous Val looked.

~

"Now that we have gone over these knives, I want to show you a special collection," Val said. He uncovered a set of knives that he had arranged before they had arrived.

"Pol, why do you learn the patterns of other swordsmen?"

"So I can anticipate their moves. It makes it easier to defend."

Paki looked down at the knives. "Those are really lethal, but aren't they all smallish?"

"You are looking at assassin blades. All of these are easily concealed and have specific purposes. A good assassin might carry four of more of these on his or her person."

"Are you training us to be assassins?" Paki said.

Pol shook his head. He was excited to experience a new kind of training. "If we know how assassins will use these blades, we have a chance to counter their attacks."

Val grimaced and rubbed Pol's hair. "Bright boy. You will learn how to use these along with the other knives we have talked about in the last ten days. I want you both to be proficient enough to be able to pick out your favorites. Every fighter uses the knives they are most comfortable with, and that is different for every person."

Kelso put his head into the room. "Pol, King Astor and his party are leaving Borstall. Your presence is requested in the front courtyard."

"I'll be back," Pol said.

Val began to gather the knives. "No need. We can end here. But I warn the both of you, our training will be getting more intense from here on."

Pol ran out the door and straightened his clothes. He didn't care to run up to his rooms and change just to say goodbye to King Astor, Bythia, and her mother. With Bythia gone, perhaps he could get some time with Amonna and find some way to repair their relationship. Pol didn't think Bythia was a very good influence on his younger sister.

King Astor stood talking with Pol's father when he walked into the courtyard. Mounted men in King Astor's colors sat atop impatient mounts. Pol stood next to his mother. He looked around for Amonna, but she hadn't arrived yet. Landon, Honna, and Grostin, looking as disagreeable as always, stood off to the other side of his father.

Pol heard Amonna laugh, and the two girls hurried down the steps. Both were dressed in traveling clothes. Pol had a sinking feeling.

"Will you miss me?" Amonna said to Pol. "I'll be spending my time until the wedding in South Salvan. It's warmer during the winter there, anyway," she said. She put her face close to Pol. "Bythia might have stayed here, but she is scared out of her wits when your bodyguard is near. Not me, but..." she shrugged and ran over to Bythia who was saying farewell to the others.

Pol wondered if Bythia was disappointed their trip hadn't ended with a formal betrothal. He didn't care. The girl never treated him as a human, anyway. He suspected she and Landon would do just fine as husband and wife when the Emperor got around to approving his father's petition.

"You are losing your only ally," Val said, as he slipped just behind Pol.

Bythia looked at Pol, and then her face froze when she noticed Val, who gave her a little bow and a wave. "She is skittish around me, and that's how I like it," Val said.

Pol could see that. He looked around and noticed his mother's ladies-in-waiting standing back by the steps. A new woman looked very fit and somewhat tanned for a noblewoman, but her eyes looked everywhere, constantly moving from place to place.

Malden and Mistress Farthia stood on the other side of the siblings and bowed as King Astor and the queen had a few words. Astor just looked over at Pol and nodded his head. The act didn't seem unfriendly, but then what did Pol expect since he hadn't really interacted with the King of South Salvan? The queen just ignored him, although she plainly liked the rest of his siblings as she bantered with them for a bit before being helped into the carriage by the King who got in on his own.

Pol stepped forward to assist his sister. "I'll miss you," he said to Amonna, as she was about to step inside.

She paused and pecked him on the cheek. "Take care of yourself."

Pol nodded as she disappeared inside. Bythia gave him her hand, but she said nothing.

In a moment, Pol stood watching the coach depart. He would miss his sister, but the sister he really knew had been absent from the castle since Bythia had arrived.

Val stepped up to Pol's side and pointed to one of Astor's troops, just leaving the grounds.

"There's your pea-shooter," Val said. "Ranno didn't want you to know that he was part of King Astor's men until after they had left. I guess they are as good as gone."

"So that means that King Astor was in on Siggon's death?"

Val shook his head. "No way of knowing. The thugs that did him in were probably local boys."

"So anyone could've hired them, including the pea shooter?"

"Could and did. Astor didn't know Siggon, but any one of those three could as well as King Astor himself." Val pointed with his chin at his siblings just turning to walk back into the castle.,

"Does my father know who the pea-shooter works for?"

Val shook his head. "I can't say for sure, but knowing Ranno, no. He tries to protect the Emperor and the Empire and that means knowing when to say something and when not to. I'm sure he has his eye on Astor though. Think of it, a united North and South Salvan along with Listya? That could be the birth of a challenger to the might of Baccusol."

Pol turned back to King Astor's entourage, fading into the hubbub of the avenue leading away from the castle gates. He hoped Amonna would fare well in South Salvan, but he had his doubts. Why didn't his father worry about these things? Pol shook his head and walked slowly with Val towards the castle.

~ ~ ~

Chapter Twenty-One

~

CASTLE LIFE RETURNED TO SOME NORMALCY. Pol felt the absence of Amonna, and oddly, the anticipation of the Emperor's visit had brought interest to his life. That life had changed, however. Paki was closer to him than ever before, but Val's constant presence reminded Pol that he still lived amidst constant danger.

"It is a letdown," Mistress Farthia said as they began their instruction in the classroom. "I miss my father, even now. I think he liked you, even more than Hazett did."

Pol didn't know how to respond and just nodded. He had told no one about his secret encounter with the Emperor of Baccusol. Now that Hazett's visit was over, Pol could believe that his meeting had been a delusion, but he really knew otherwise.

Farthia pushed Pol's shoulder. "Tell me, you were surprised and pleased by the Emperor's attention."

"If he had never come, Siggon would still be alive. I wouldn't have lost a friend, and Paki's father would still be alive. I wouldn't have a scar on my face, and my arm wouldn't be hurting." He hoped that would cover up the clandestine discussion with Hazett.

"Malden said that would take a while to heal."

"What? Siggon's death? That will never heal."

"No, young prince, your arm. We all grieve along with you. As for your lament, I seem to recall that your siblings' tricks were getting more and more vicious before I left for Yastan."

Pol thought a bit. "You're right, but everything got worse."

"That's because your father pressed the petition on the Emperor and stirred up your two older brothers. If you want a cause for all the trouble, I'm afraid your father is more to blame. His obsession with putting Landon on the throne of Listya has gotten so bad that he refuses to punish his children for attacking you."

Farthia brought up a reason that Pol didn't want to face. His father could have stopped the attacks and the pranks and the disparagement that his siblings had constantly rained on him at any time. When everything got worse, King Colvin didn't aggressively seek the attackers who went after Pol and his mother in the city streets. The peashooter was only pursued when Ranno took over the investigation.

"My father isn't behind the attacks," Pol said.

"I never said he was, but he enables the behavior. Landon and Grostin can do what they please, knowing King Colvin will do nothing. Look how he allowed Grostin to cheat in the tourney."

"Landon didn't get any special help in his contests."

"Your oldest brother is lazy and coddled. Do your really think anyone would have believed it if he had won anything? The biggest evidence of that was when Ranno confronted your father in Hazett's presence, identifying Landon as one of your assailants."

"Ranno said he was going to keep it a secret."

"That meant my father didn't shout it out for all to hear. Hazett was not happy that King Colvin only scolded his son for assaulting you in your own rooms, but although the Emperor felt free to complain, that was all he did. You weren't meant to survive, that's what my father thinks," Farthia said.

Pol refused to think his own father could be so callous, but the proof seemed to be right in front of him. He thought for a moment and realized that his father's actions only fit the pattern that Mistress Farthia had described. It erased the feeling of relative complacency that he had felt earlier after King Astor had left.

"I don't want to talk about it anymore."

Farthia squinted and pressed her lips together before saying, "As long as you don't let your guard down, you can think what you like."

Pol lifted his chin. "I will. Valiso Gasibli is always by my side, reminding me that someone could attack me at any time."

That got a nod from Mistress Farthia. "Today we will learn how to count up receipts and introduce you to the purpose of specific taxes."

"That's for rulers," Pol said, suddenly feeling irritable.

"No, that's for merchants and innkeepers and successful farmers and blacksmiths. Rulers need to count as well, but much of what you'll be learning for the next while applies to rulers and to the ruled."

Pol slumped back and folded his arms. Why did she have to be so reasonable? He sighed and sat straight up in his chair. He knew when he needed to pay attention.

Val's classroom instruction came to a stop, once the knives were all identified and thoroughly discussed.

"Now you have to learn how to use these, and to properly use any knife, you need to be physically fit." He eyed Pol. "As fit as possible."

They started each day with calisthenics and a run. Paki had to run much farther than Pol, but Paki told Pol he didn't mind. Anything was better than gardening.

"I will demonstrate the technique," Val said, facing a clothed straw dummy. "You will learn the same moves. Don't vary them until you can perform exactly as I teach you."

"But we're not training to be assassins, are we?" Paki said.

Val looked a bit put out by Paki's comment. "Like I said. You need to learn the moves in order to counter them." He assumed an attack pose.

"Or recognize certain cuts on a dead person," Pol said.

Val stood up and gave Pol the grimace that served as a smile for his tutor. "You hit the target. You need to learn both. There are more chances that you will see the work of an assassin than you will have to defend against one."

Pol hadn't yet seen proof of that, since he had always been the one attacked.

After showing them how to stand, Val taught them the basics of using a short, curved blade. The slash resulted in a cut throat. Pol shivered at the thought of being killed that way.

"Now both of you."

Pol sighed and did exactly as Val had taught. Paki took a couple of tries, but he got the hang of the move.

"Now how would you defend against that?"

"Wear a gorget," Paki said.

"Those are quite uncomfortable to sleep with, so most targets would take them off."

"Distance," Pol said. "Do something to keep the attacker away. That would work for most knives unless they are thrown."

Val moved his head from side to side. "That works for awhile, if you are strong and aware and have something to keep the assassin at bay. Simple wooden chairs work well, and swords work better. But I will teach you moves that you can try."

The rest of the session was spent with wooden rods about the same length of the knife. Val drilled them in attacking and defending.

"This works if you are awake and aware," Val said. "Unfortunately, if you are neither, your life will bleed out onto the floor."

Every session turned into a variation of that until all of the assassin knives were tried out on dummies, and the boys worked with Val on one-to-one defensive measures.

As the sessions wore on, Pol created a notebook on what he had learned and went over the techniques for a while after dinner, practicing with various items in his rooms.

Malden's classes sapped him of even more strength. He started every session moving something from one place to another. But as he practiced more, his abilities grew.

When Pol first used magic to move the big religion text from the map table to the desk, he could feel his energy drain. Now he moved chairs and tables with relative ease. He could still feel his energy decline, but not like before. He had doubted Malden's claim that practice made a magician stronger, but Pol had proven himself wrong. He felt uncomfortable with the fact that he could be wrong, but he was.

Most of Malden's sessions consisted of recognizing patterns. Sometimes they strolled through the Royal Gardens or in the armory or the stables. Malden pointed out something, and Pol had to discern a pattern and how it might be tweaked.

Rarely did Malden show Pol how to do anything. King Colvin didn't often use Malden as a magician, but often called him away from their lessons to act in the role of a counselor since the magician's advice must have been generally sound, Pol thought.

"Why doesn't Father use your magical ability?" Pol said when they walked through the closest marketplace to the castle. Pol looked around and saw Val following a few paces behind.

Malden smiled and looked off towards the castle looming over the rooftops. "King Colvin has a basic distrust of magic. Before I came, the border with Tarida came under attack, as it does from time to time. The old Court Magician at the time claimed he could shield your grandfather from an oncoming hail of arrows. The magician didn't realize that there was a flight coming in from the enemy that had sneaked along his flank and didn't account for that in the shield that he made. That's how Colvin vaulted from Prince to the King of North Salvan."

"Would you make a better shield?"

Malden barked out a laugh. "I wouldn't want to make a magical shield in the first place. A battlefield is a poor place for magic. Patterns shift and change and do unexpected things. If you are injured, you lose your ability to tweak. There's a limitation on what you can do, and that limitation ebbs and flows during the course of a battle. You need a quick mind to survive, and even the fastest thought might not be enough in a war."

"But I learned patterns for sword fighting and how to find people trailing me."

"Can you do both at once?" Malden said.

"No."

"Neither can I. I suppose if you could split your mind into a million pieces you might find an advantage in a battle. I haven't heard of anything like that. No, it's better to learn how to do magic on a small scale. You'll live longer."

"Healing isn't small scale, but it must take a long time to learn."

Malden nodded. "Simple things are simple, and most magicians can heal something they see. I spent a few years learning how the human body functions, so I can find more patterns to tweak or un-tweak, as the case may be."

Would Pol ever get the chance to take years to learn healing? Not while his mother was still in danger, and with his father excusing his children's behavior, Pol didn't know when that would be. Sometimes he really felt he should spend time in a monastery learning magic.

He clutched his hands into fists from the frustration that he felt. Pol felt bound by circumstances and powerless to make any kind of choice affecting his truncated future.

Val shook Pol from a deep, dreamless slumber. Pol sat up and blinked his eyes, looking at the darkness of an early morning.

"What time is it?"

"Half past the fourth hour. Paki was ambushed. A woman found him crumpled up in an alley. He's been taken to the infirmary where Malden is looking after him. He will survive."

"Let's see how he is," Pol said getting out court clothes.

"No. Wear practice clothes. We're not going to see Paki yet."

Pol didn't understand. "Why not?"

"Scene of the crime. We are going to find out who did this, so we have to inspect the place where he was beaten up."

"Like me and like Siggon?"

Val nodded. "I'm sure they are connected, but with King Colvin's reticence, we will do our own investigation. I can't see who it would be other than your brothers. They probably want to continue punishing you through him."

"Life was too quiet," Pol said, feeling disheartened by the dishonor of the assault on his best and possibly, only friend.

Val led him out of the castle and onto the streets after gathering knives and a sword to distribute on Pol's body. Val had clearly come to his rooms fully armed, along with a long thin rod that he twirled in his fingers. Val spoke to the guards for a few minutes as Pol rubbed a bit more sleep from his eyes.

"What is the rod for?" Pol asked.

"I'll demonstrate in due time."

The point on the end of the three-foot rod didn't look very sharp, so Pol didn't think Val would use it as a weapon, but then what did Pol know?

They passed an alley, but a woman stepped out. "Sir Gasibli? I was told to wait for you here. I'm glad you've finally come. A thing like this doesn't make a lady feel very safe out on the streets of Borstall."

The woman looked overdressed beneath the black knit shawl she had wrapped around herself. Val spelled a ball of flame about the size of his fist.

The light splashed on the woman's face revealing more face paint than Pol had ever seen on a lady of the court. This woman must work in an unsavory line of work, Pol thought. He hesitated to even think the word for her profession.

"Over here," she said.

Val moved the flame in jerks as he tweaked the pattern towards the entrance to the alleyway.

"I take this little lane on my way home from work. Generally all I have to do is watch out for garbage, but tonight I tripped over the boy in the dark.

"Stop," Val said. He knelt down and looked at the ground. "What kind of pattern do you see?"

Pol stood over the light, which Val had made brighter. "Those two lines. They dragged Paki in here?"

Val nodded. "That means he was out before they brought him here." He glanced at the woman and pulled out his purse and laid an Imperial gold eagle on her palm. "For your trouble. You should be getting home."

She gave a remarkably lithe curtsey to Val and scurried down the passageway.

"Note her shoe prints. They will be over the ones we're looking for."

Pol hadn't thought of that.

"We'll head back into the street and see where Paki's scuff marks start. Keep to the side of the alley."

Val kept the light jerking ahead. Pol thought he could do that, but he kept his thoughts to himself. He concentrated on finding clues. Pol walked on one side of the alley and Val on the other. Their own shoe prints had covered some of the others, but through it all, the long line of Paki's shoe heels kept going all the way out the alley.

"They end here," Pol said.

"Tell me more."

Pol got down on his haunches and looked at what the prints might say. "They backed a vehicle into the alley and lifted Paki. These are deeper right close to the wheel marks, right?"

Val used the rod to verify what Pol pointed out. "More," Val said.

"These carriage marks, no they are thick, so it's probably a cart with thicker wheels. The men got out and removed Paki."

"What do you notice about the cart?"

Pol didn't know what Val was getting at and shook his head. "I don't know much about carts, other than they aren't made as nicely as carriages."

"See this one wheel mark. Is it straight?"

"No, it wavers. What does that mean?" Pol asked.

"A wobble. Find enough variations from a normal pattern, and you discover what personality the cart has."

Pol furrowed his brow. This was so new to him. "Personality?"

"What makes it different. If it is different enough, you might be able to tell it apart from others. Think of it as a variation of a pattern. You're a budding magician. I think you know what I mean. Look here."

Pol followed the rod to a section the wobbling wheel. "The iron rim is held by nails? Is that different?"

"It is. Usually the rim is made of a piece and slipped over the wheel while hot. Heat makes the iron rim bigger. When it cools, it fits the wooden wheel tightly. This is a somewhat common repair of the broken rim of a wheel. They just slice a break and nail the ends of the rim to the wood." Val pulled out a piece of paper and a charcoal stick. "Draw the pattern of the nails. It's certain to be unique."

Pol had no idea what unique was, but he did as Val asked. "This is different?"

"Five nails on one side and four on the other. One of the nail heads has cracked off, see?"

Pol looked down as Val shifted the light closer. "Oh, the middle one."

Val nodded. "Let's go back to where the woman found Paki. Keep looking at the footprints. When you find something unique, point it out to me."

"Variations on any kind of pattern?"

Val grunted his assent, and had Pol measure footprints and some of the boot heels. Pol found it easier to draw the ones going back out of the alley. He ignored the shoe prints of the woman, Val, and his own.

"Isn't there an easier way of doing this?"

Val nodded. "They do it differently in Yastan, but then they have more resources. They would make plaster casts of the prints, but once day comes, everything here might be obliterated with more foot traffic."

"Oh. The evidence will be gone."

The man grunted again. Pol thought that rude, but he had to admire Val for his detection ability.

"Where did you learn to do this?"

Val smiled as if recalling a pleasant memory. "Working for Ranno."

"But you stopped?"

The smile faded. "Personal reasons. Too personal to be telling a young lad like you."

Pol knew when to change the subject. "Isn't that blood?"

"It is," Val said. "No blood until now, so they beat Paki while he was unconscious. Your friend didn't even know they were going at it, most likely."

Pol examined the ground. "Maybe four of them?" He looked at the footprints on the collection of papers he now held.

Val nodded. He poked his rod around a bit and closed his eyes."

"Are you performing magic?"

Pol's bodyguard nodded again. "Picking up patterns." His eyes popped open. "No sharp instruments, just blunt weapons, but they can draw blood easily enough. There's nothing more to see in the dark. Let's check in on Paki before tucking you in for what's left of the night," Val said.

"Can Malden do your kind of magic?"

Val snorted. "I hardly can do anything compared to him. He is one of the best."

"Then why is he in Borstall?"

Val shook his head. "You'll have to ask him."

~~~

Chapter Twenty-Two

~

PAKI DIDN'T LOOK LIKE HE WAS GOING TO DIE. Pol had already seen that happen and didn't care to lose Siggon's son. Malden had already left by the time they entered the castle's infirmary. The lone healer on duty showed them to Paki's bed. He didn't merit a private room like Pol did.

His friend didn't move. The injuries had swollen his face, so Pol barely recognized him. So that was what Pol had looked like when Landon and his thugs beat him nearly senseless.

"Do you know how to heal?" Pol whispered to Val.

His bodyguard shook his head. "I can close wounds and join a blood vessel that I can see, but that's about it. Not trained for that, but you pick up things, you know."

Pol didn't know, but he nodded anyway.

The healer drifted to their side.

"How badly was he?"

"Bad. Malden performed another one of his miracles. I wish he'd spend more time with us. He complains about a loss of energy." The woman shook her head. Pol didn't know if it was out of disgust or dismay. "The poor boy had both of his legs broken. His chest was nearly caved in. You can see how they treated his face. There is more you can't see. Malden will be back before noon. He says he did enough to get Master Horstel through the night and the magician said he needed rest."

"He won't wake up?"

The healer shook her head. "That won't happen. Magician Malden put him to sleep."

"Time to go," Val said.

They walked back to Pol's rooms in silence until Val spoke up, "Tomorrow, instead of knife practice, we will go look at carts. I guess that a castle cart was used since the guards had no record of Paki leaving."

"They have records?"

"Especially of boys who get into trouble."

"Me?"

Val nodded. "You and Paki are probably right at the top. The other boys are servants or the children of high-level courtiers that have apartments on the grounds."

Pol didn't know of any who had young children, but Pol didn't know as much about the castle as he might have, since it had never interested him. Val had only been at the castle for a short time, yet Val already had figured out the list and that there were other boys. Pol felt pretty useless, but then Val thought he needed to learn, and that's why they walked the empty streets of Borstall before the sun rose.

"Up!" Val said, pulling on one of Pol's feet. The sun streamed into his bedroom, but Pol could barely pry his eyes open. "We have work to do."

Pol struggled to sit and rubbed his face. "What work?"

"Carts. We need to look at lots and lots of carts."

Pol threw on his court clothes. "Will these be acceptable?"

"Today, they will be."

Pol staggered into the sitting room. Val had littered the floor with the sketches they had made earlier that morning. "Do you want me to make sense of this?" Pol asked.

"Think of it as a pattern to solve," Val said. "Did you know the very best Seekers are magicians?"

"What is a Seeker? I haven't heard of them."

"That's what we call ourselves, Seekers. We make sense of things by seeking a pattern."

"Investigators? Like what guards do?"

"More or less, but on a higher level."

So you're a Seeker, not an assassin?"

Val smiled, barely. "I am many things, and a Seeker is one of them. I am teaching you what I know."

Pol noticed that Val didn't say he wasn't an assassin. The man remained irritably opaque. Pol smiled at his mental turn of the phrase. "You want me to be a Seeker?"

The man shook his head. "I am not interested in whatever you become, but I want you to learn what Seekers do. You are a prince. Princes aren't seekers."

Pol didn't know how to respond. His mind was still muddled from lack of sleep. "So we will Seek this morning?"

Val pointed to the papers. "Remember these, especially the pattern of the nails in the cart. Our mission this morning is to find it."

"But I want to see Paki," Pol said.

"You will. He'll still be in the infirmary when we return. You may rely on that. Poor boy."

"Why is he poor?"

Val responded with a smirk. "Because he isn't going to learn as much as you will this morning."

Pol needed some food, so they ate in the kitchens before setting out. Paki's mother stopped by.

"You haven't seen Paki, have you?" she said.

Pol blinked in alarm. "No one told you?"

She gave Pol a blank stare. "No, My Prince."

"He's in the infirmary. Someone attacked him last night, but Malden has been treating him.

Her eyes grew. "Magician Malden is caring for Paki?" She tore off her apron and told the others that she would be gone for awhile. She put her hand on Pol's arm. "Thank you, thank you for letting me know, My Prince."

Pol watched her run out of the kitchen. "No one told her," Pol said.

"Not very kind, do you think?"

"No." Pol felt really bad that he had to be the one to tell Paki's mother; however, her eyes brightened when she found out Malden had seen to her boy. That made Pol less guilty about Paki's attack. It was certainly the result of his being Pol's friend. He had to set that aside for a bit, since Val and he had a job to do, a task that probably no one else cared about, but Pol did.

They ate well and left for the gardens.

"We look at the most obvious places first. The simplest explanation is usually the best."

Pol thought criminals would be more devious. "Why?"

"When we think too much about what the criminal would do, we overlay our own motivations, our own tastes and values. Criminals generally don't think the way we do, so what do you think happens?"

"We head in the wrong direction, a direction of our own making?" Pol knew that had to be the correct answer. Mistress Farthia had taught him something similar when they talked about good and bad rulers.

"Good. I won't have to teach you that. Most criminals don't think any more deeply than others. People will think of the simplest solution first, so we look for an easy answer, and it's more often right than wrong."

Pol kicked at a pebble on the gravel walkway in the garden. "I learned that concept from someone else."

Val nodded. "Learn to pull in all your knowledge to apply to a problem. It will help you detect a pattern."

"As long as we don't use our own bias?"

"Generally that's correct, but if we are stumped, sometimes we have to introduce our own bias to shift our perception of the pattern and once we do, we have a chance of finding the right one."

Pol shook his head to get his confusion out. "I thought you said we go for the simple, first."

Val patted Pol on the head. "Everything is a bit more complex than you might think. Simplest first, and then you can complicate things."

Val continued to confuse Pol until they walked into the garden storage yard. Three carts stood, unhitched, in a row. Pol looked at the tracks that led to the carts, but they were backed into place and what the horse hooves didn't obliterate, the last of the two wheel tracks did.

"Inspect, while I ask a few questions," Val said, as he gave Pol his iron rod. It was heavier than Pol expected.

Pol took the measurements and compared them to the notes he remembered on the paper. They were all the proper width. He looked all over each one, but couldn't see the tracks on the underside of the wheels where they touched the ground.

He tried to push the carts forward, but couldn't summon the strength.

"Just a moment," Val called to him while the bodyguard talked to one of the gardeners. Pol nodded to the man, who he knew when he worked with Paki for a bit before the Emperor came.

Val and the gardener, Jed, moved each wagon just a bit. None had any nails.

"Not these," Pol said, somewhat disappointed.

"Jed's pretty sure the fourth and missing wagon had a nailed wheel," Val said.

Pol put his hands on his hips. "Then why did you have me check the wheels?"

Val put his arm around Pol's shoulder as they left the yard. "The gardeners like you, but you are still a fourteen-year-old and their prince. Words don't come quite so easily to a member of the royal family."

Pol didn't quite know how to take that comment, but he just swallowed hard and let Val tell him what the gardener said.

"Paki spent a little extra time late last night cleaning the tools and oiling them. He was probably taken an hour or two after sundown, after he finished most of his work. There were a few pieces left undone, which meant he was abducted towards the end of his task."

"How can you tell that?"

"Simple. If a boy is supposed to finish a task that he usually completes, but doesn't, what happens to the pattern?"

"It is disrupted," Pol said.

"The kidnappers tweaked a natural pattern. So we aren't looking for Paki to have left in the middle of the night, are we?"

"No," Pol said. "Any time after eight hours after noon?"

Val nodded. "You do catch on, eventually. We'll need to talk to the guards again. They only looked at the late-night logbooks."

The guard at the gate sent them to Kelso Beastwell's office. The Captain of the Guard hadn't arrived yet, but the clerk pulled out the logbook

Val put it on Kelso's conference table and pulled up a chair for Pol to sit right next to him. He opened the log up and flipped the pages until they reached a few pages from the end.

"Look at the entries. There is a time, a description, and those who enter and leave."

"I've never been stopped."

Val gave Pol a disgusted look. "The guards won't stop nobles if they know who they are. I'm sure they miss some people, but they wouldn't miss a garden cart. You'll be on the logbook for the early morning guard shift."

Pol didn't question Val, but they ran down the entries together. Only two carts were recorded, and none of the entries declared the cart to be from the gardeners.

"That doesn't mean anything. How is a guard going to distinguish what part of the castle the cart came from?"

Pol looked at the time. "When did the gardeners last see Paki?"

Val smiled. "That's more like what I want to hear. What would be the pattern?"

"Smuggle Paki out of the castle after dark, but not so late that their departure would be particularly noticed." Pol looked at the two entries. "The later one. That must be it. We write down the names of those who left with a cart, and then we can get closer to what happened, right?"

That got an approving nod from Val. "So, do you know these two men?"

Pol looked at the names and frowned. "No. I have no idea who they are."

"Who might?"

"Who might what?" Kelso said as he walked into the room. "What are you doing here looking through one of my logbooks? They are sacred to me." Kelso put his hand over his heart.

"Sure they are," Val said, lifting a corner of his mouth in a wry smile and shaking his head. "Sit down and give us a hand, will you?"

Kelso followed Val's suggestion and took a chair opposite Pol and Val. Pol didn't trust Kelso, but he seemed intent enough as Val brought the Captain of the Guard up to date.

"And Paki?"

"Malden took care of him, so he will recover," Pol said.

"I am glad to hear it. I would feel most awful about the boy. How can I help?"

"If you could talk to your guards about these two entries. We are pretty sure that the later one had an unconscious Paki riding along."

"Why wouldn't they just dump him in the hayloft, like his father?"

"Would you link the two beatings?" Val said.

Kelso shook his head. "You know I wouldn't and you wouldn't either, unless you were sending some kind of message."

"But they could have just put a knife into him," Pol said. "They didn't have to beat him up while he was unconscious."

"That's the message," Val said. He looked at Pol. "They probably thought they beat Paki, but not enough to kill him."

"They only succeeded not killing him because of the lady that found him."

"A lady of the night?" Kelso said with a twinkle in his eye.

His comment embarrassed Pol, but he had another idea. "There is a pattern. Siggon wasn't killed either."

"Not immediately," Kelso said.

"Then that is the link, beaten within an inch of their lives. Not killed. To kill would have indicated an assassination, and whoever hired the attackers, told them not to kill. The attackers, both times, might have been a bit over-zealous. That's what happened to Pol, as well, and Prince Landon was in on that," Val said.

"I suggest you share your theory with Malden. He's more acquainted with the mental aspect of this kind of thing," Kelso said.

"He's helped you in the past?" Val said.

Kelso nodded. "But the magician is in a ticklish position here because one of the siblings probably ordered it. The castle is unsettled about the King's pre-occupation with Listya. It shows in his actions more than King Colvin thinks it does." Kelso looked at Pol. "You know this, don't you?" he said a bit uncertainly.

"I know he's in a ticklish position," Pol said, confirming Kelso's statement.

"Then let's keep him out of the ticklish position, at least for now. Our goal is to find the thugs first." Val glanced at Pol, and then again at Kelso.

"Do you know the men who took both carts out of the castle?"

Kelso looked down at the log. "I wouldn't, but we can talk to the guards. I don't mind interrupting their sleep. Let's go." He grabbed the logbook and exited his office, leaving Pol and Val looking at him.

Pol and Val caught up to Kelso as he began walking up the stairs to a dormitory. Ten beds were lined up on each side of the barracks. Half of them were occupied. Kelso went to each man and uncovered their faces, and then covered them again. Midway through he found one of the guards and pushed him onto the floor. He did the same with the slumbering guard just one before the last bed in the row.

"Up, you two," Kelso said.

The men blinked and rubbed their eyes. They rose a bit unsteadily and stood next to two unoccupied beds. One kind of stood at attention, and the other just sat on his bed, struggling to keep from falling asleep.

"The Horstel boy was kidnapped last night, hidden in one of the garden carts. Neither of you realized that the cart belonged to the gardeners. Here are your entries. Do you personally know the men who accompanied the carts?"

Both of the men shuffled over to Kelso and looked down at the entries.

"Tilbon Carter and Ferad Placer. I know them. They picked up their cart from the kitchen. They came in with a load of hardwood and the cooks sent them away before unloading, not wanting a disruption to their cookery and were told to come back after it later. Right?" The one guard looked at the other, who nodded.

"You'll probably see an entry before midday noting them coming in the gate. Tilbon's about seventy and Ferad is his son-in-law, thin as a rail," the other guard said.

"That was the earlier entry. What about the other?"

Both guards shook their heads. "Their cart was a manure cart. Every so often the stable master has too much manure for the gardens and has it removed. It typically leaves the castle later in the day, just before all of the horses are stabled. I never saw the men before except for one. There were four of them. I know I've seen the man who talked to us before."

Val nodded. "Did this man take out manure that last time?"

The guard shrugged. "It wasn't recently."

"And you didn't check the cart?"

"For manure?" The first guard shook his head and made a face. "No."

Pol thought of a question. "Did they bring the cart into the castle?"

Both of the guards looked at each other and shrugged their shoulders.

"So if this cart didn't come into the castle with the identified man's name, then those are our culprits. We can go arrest at least one of them."

Kelso put his hand on Pol's shoulder. "Not so fast, My Prince. That is probably a false name."

"Oh," Pol said. "I didn't think of that."

"Anyone who would abduct Paki from the castle won't care about lying about his name, will he?" Val said.

Pol could feel his face turn red from embarrassment. "No."

"But your point about checking if the cart came in will just about prove it's the garden cart. The manure was probably thrown over something covering Paki. I don't know a guard who would be bold enough to dig very deeply into the load."

That was enough for Kelso. "You may be called to identify any of the four men, so get thinking about what they looked like. Don't make up any stories, though."

"Yes sir," the guards straightened up for attention.

"Back to sleep. That's an order."

"Yes, Captain." The two of them saluted and quickly returned to their beds.

~ ~ ~

Chapter Twenty-Three

~

AFTER TALKING TO THE STABLE MASTER, who claimed he had never ordered a cart in the first place, Val asked Kelso to get written descriptions of the manure carters when the two guards woke up.

"One more stop before we go out into the city and look at the scene in the daylight," Val said. "Let's see Paki."

They stepped into the infirmary and found that Paki hadn't regained consciousness, but Malden had kept the boy under on purpose.

"Where are the boy's clothes?" Val asked the healer. The one that attended to Paki at first had gone home, since her shift had ended.

"In a bag. It will have a tag on it," the healer said.

Pol and Val followed the healer to a closet. Inside were shelves with burlap bags. Val began looking at the tags. "Here it is," he said.

Pol untied the string while Val knelt down on a knee and put his face into the opening.

"Blood, sweat, and manure," he said.

"So now we know what happened. There was a pattern to the robbery, but how will we find the attackers?" Pol said.

"Back to the alley," Val said. "We might find something in the daylight that we missed last night. My magic fire is a poor replacement for the sun, you know."

Pol went back to where Paki recovered and stood looking down at him. "We are trying to find the criminals, Paki. I don't know if we'll be successful, but we are making the attempt. I'll tell you all about it when you wake up."

On their way out, Pol passed Paki's mother going into the infirmary.

"How is my boy?" the cook said, worrying her hands. "I can never stay with him for more than a few minutes."

"Better, but still not awake. Malden wants him to stay asleep for a bit."

She nodded grimly and walked inside, leaving them standing in front of the infirmary.

The alley looked much the same to Pol, except he could see that there were new footprints all over the place.

"How can we find anything since the dirt has been walked on?"

Val frowned. "We won't find anything at all if we don't look, My Prince."

"Oh," Pol said, considering his bodyguard's words. "We still might find something?"

After a shrug, Val knelt down by bloodstains on the wall where Paki had been found and poked around with the same metal rod he had used the previous night. "This is the place. Can you see a pattern? Remember part of reconstructing an event consists of seeing the structure of the actions. That structure is the pattern. They brought Paki here, of all places. Why? What made them think of using manure to hide Paki in the cart? We just keep asking more stupid questions until we find something odd or out of place."

"Does this happen every time?"

Val shook his head. "There are enough times when there aren't sufficient clues to lead to something else, and then you can't go any further."

"So someone gets away with whatever happened, even if it's a death or something nearly as bad?" Pol asked.

"It's a sad fact," Val said.

Sad for whom? Pol thought. If every criminal knew they would certainly get caught there would be a lot less crime or rebellious acts or whatever one wanted to call what happened here. He tried to imagine what happened during Paki's abduction. "Maybe they chose this place at random, or they wanted to dump Paki in an area away from where they lived. The manure in the cart might mean that the attackers knew how the stable master operated his stable."

"Those questions are a start," Val said, still looking at the streaks of blood. "Some tracks remain, but still no signs of a struggle. That's what we saw last night, and it is confirmed in daylight. It looks like they just propped Paki next to the wall and beat on him. No handprints on the wall or smears from Paki's clothing. See where no one has walked right by the walls?"

"Who would beat an unconscious person and not kill them?" Pol said.

"I think the pattern that we built holds up, even today. The beating must be a statement."

"But they could just do the same to me."

Val lifted the side of his mouth in something resembling a smile. "Not with me around, they wouldn't. That is the difference."

That made Pol feel even worse about being responsible for Paki's current condition. Pol moved over to the wall and forced himself to look at Paki's blood. He stepped on a rock, or was it?" He furrowed his brow and bent down to find the object.

"What are you looking for?"

"I stepped on something. Right there." Pol pointed to the spot. "It's probably a pebble."

"Pebble in this alley?" Val took his rod and began to stir in the dirt. A corner of yellow metal poked out of the thick dust. "What's this?" He picked up a tiny, nearly-square block of gold. "You know what this is, Pol?"

Pol shook his head. The object was about as big as the tip of his little finger.

"This is a South Salvan Lion. It's a cube-shaped coin that is only traded in South Salvan. A hired thug would never leave one of these to throw us off, but that also says that the attackers were locals. South Salvans carry these around in special leather pouches where these are stacked one on top of another in a purse with leather tubes. It's too easy for these to work their way through a pocket, if they are new as this one is. A Borstall local might just put one of these in his pocket, not knowing that it is a coin that can quickly rub a hole in a pocket."

"A break in the pattern?"

Val held the Lion in his palm and moved it with his finger. "This one is new, so someone brought these unspent into North Salvan."

"King Astor?"

"It could even be our pea-shooter. A smart man wouldn't pay the thugs off until after the job had been done, but that obviously wasn't the case. They didn't trust the payor, so they demanded payment up front. We can make a guess that the entire crew was made up of local men. It doesn't help us find them, but it's a possible piece of the puzzle." Val got to his feet and gave the Lion to Pol. "Do you have a leather purse or pocket?"

Pol nodded and put the Lion in his purse. "Are we finished here?"

Val looked at the bloody wall one more time. "I think we are. Let's see if Kelso has come up with anything."

"Could we see how Paki is doing?" Pol desperately wanted Paki to wake up and would have preferred to spend the day by his friend's side, but he had to admit that finding those responsible for the beating took priority.

"That's on our way," Val said.

Pol knew that the infirmary and the headquarters of the Guard were not in the same direction, but he appreciated Val's comment. To Pol, it made Val more of a person on his team rather than a hired bodyguard or just a tutor in odd military techniques.

They walked in silence, but Pol could only think of the South Salvan Lion in his pocket. What if King Astor had funded Grostin's efforts? He still thought that Landon would have joined in on an abduction. That was the pattern he saw if his eldest brother had participated. Grostin wouldn't care to dirty his hands with such a mundane task.

Pol wanted to talk about the situation with Val some more, but as they approached the infirmary, Val seemed to be lost in his own thoughts.

Val lifted his head up into the sky and smiled. "What would you do if you lost a valuable coin?"

Pol shrugged, but then thought of the possible patterns of behavior a person might go through. "Look for it?"

Val nodded. "You go see to your friend, and I'll get Kelso to put some guards in various places to see if a stranger goes looking around at the ground for something." Val quickly walked off in the direction of the armory, so Pol would have to wait to talk to Val for a while.

Pol stepped inside the infirmary and ran into Malden. "How is Paki?"

The magician grinned. "You can ask him yourself. He's awake and out of danger. I'll talk to Valiso and you later, but I'm already late for a meeting with King Colvin." Malden clapped Pol on the shoulders and rushed out of the infirmary.

After opening the door to the ward, Pol heard his name. Paki had been moved to a different bed. He sat up, still wrapped up in places like a corpse.

"How are you?" Pol said. He couldn't keep from smiling.

"I'm sore all over. Malden said his work speeds healing, but it's not without pain."

Pol rolled his eyes. "I know that well enough."

Both boys laughed. "If I sit up or move my head quickly, I still get a bit dizzy, but that's getting better by the minute. If it wasn't for Malden…"

Pol didn't finish Paki's sentence. "We've been out trying to find who did it."

"Any luck?"

"We've assembled more information than I would have thought possible. Pol pulled out the Lion and showed it to Paki.

"My Dad had one of these. He said it was worth a few months' wages, but he said he would keep it until the need came. It didn't look like that. The corners were worn down. That looks new. What does this have to do with me?"

"One of your abductors had this. This coin is so new that the edges probably cut a hole in his pocket, and it fell out while he beat you. You can add this to your collection once we are done with looking into your kidnapping." Pol then told Paki what they had found and how they had made their discoveries.

"I wish I could have gone with you."

"So do I," Pol said. "But then we wouldn't have needed to go anywhere if you weren't injured."

Paki laughed. "That's what I would prefer, not to have to look for anyone, but you've learned a lot?"

Pol nodded. "I didn't know that looking around for criminals required a process. It's like learning a complicated new game. There are rules and practices to follow. We're not done yet, but it looks like you aren't in the kind of shape to join us."

"Another week in here and a week at home before I can go back to gardening."

"So another week, and then you can join us. This is mostly 'think' work."

Paki looked sideways at Pol. "I'm not good at thinking. You know that."

Pol nodded. "I'd like you to learn as much as you can. It seems that even dumb questions are encouraged."

Paki brightened. "That I can do."

It felt good to laugh with his friend again, thought Pol.

Buoyed by Paki's recovery, Pol felt relieved and looked forward to meeting with Val and Kelso. He found both of them in Kelso's office examining a large, well-worn map of Borstall laid out on Kelso's table.

Kelso looked up at Pol. "The cart was abandoned behind a blacksmith's shop hidden amidst a number of broken carts in line for repair."

"The blacksmith didn't know of it?"

"No. He's well enough known to the guard who found it," Kelso said, looking back down at the map. "They found it here." He pointed to a spot on the map. "The alley where Paki was beaten is here."

"So since the blacksmith's shop is so close, does that mean this is more evidence of a local band?" he said.

"Why?" Val asked. Pol thought back to Mistress Farthia's classroom. This was no different.

"Someone not familiar with the city would have a hard time finding the blacksmith's. I'm not sure I could," Pol said.

"A decent assumption, and it fits into the pattern that the group were made up of local thugs," Val said.

Pol looked down at the map and wondered what else might fit the pattern that had emerged. "At least one local person who isn't a noble. They knew about the manure carts, they found an alley, although they could have just chanced on one that wasn't all that far from the blacksmith's shop," he said.

Val gave the ghost of a smile to Kelso. "He has a good mind, don't you think?"

Pol blinked at the compliment coming out of Val's mouth. He thought the man despised him.

"Smartest of King Colvin's bunch, but not the most conniving." Kelso looked nervously at Pol. "I'll leave it at that."

"I'm glad you didn't just assume all the men were locals. There are many alternatives that fit into an investigative pattern, and if one can't think flexibly, you'll miss where the actual pattern diverges from the one in your mind."

Pol couldn't help but smile that he had caught onto something important while working on the investigation. At least, he knew that some of what Malden had taught him worked with what Val was teaching. Common sense made up a lot of it, but common sense in a structure…the patterns.

"Is anything else new?" Pol said.

"The names given at the gate were all false, but one of the guards thought he remembered the face of one of them on a previous arrest when he worked the city patrols," Kelso said. "I have him combing though the city logs."

"So we wait?" Pol asked Val.

"No. That coin is too valuable to leave behind. I want to spend a little time across the lane from the alley, seeing if anyone will show up. A guard has been dispatched to stand at the alleyway, so the attacker won't go close until we have gotten into position."

They hurried back to the alley. Val nodded at the uniformed guard, who took one more look at the alley and then left. A cobbler's shop stood across the street from the alley. Val took Pol inside.

"Keep your eye on the alleyway," Val said. "I'll let the store owner know what we are doing."

Pol looked back and saw some coins changing hands. It appeared that one paid for permission to look out from the window. Pol had never been in a shoe shop before and inhaled the strong aroma of leather, glue, and shoe dye. He actually liked the smells and listened to the sounds of the cobbler working behind the counter.

He never had spent much time among the people of Borstall except within the confines of the castle and when Paki and he roamed the streets, but Pol had never actually gone into shops. The closest he had come to buying anything was at street vendors and market stalls. If Paki hadn't been so seriously injured, Pol would be quite excited about following Val around and getting exposed to other people's lives as well as learning to investigate.

They stood looking out at the alley for the rest of the morning. Pol quickly got bored and wondered what he could do while waiting. Val paid the cobbler to buy some food for them and for the cobbler as well. Pol took over looking while Val went to relieve himself in the back of the shop, and Val did the same for Pol.

Pol walked to the extension of the shop that ran beside a miserable little garden before backing up against an alley that paralleled the street. After he had used the outside convenience, he peeked through the gate, and then he poked his head, looking up and down the alley. Pol noticed three dodgy-looking men walking his way.

"Hey, you!" one of them cried out, pointing to Pol.

The prince ducked back into the gate and ran into the shop. He had lost his breath. This was not the time to begin to wheeze, so Pol took a deep breath. "Attackers coming from the back yard!" He sat down, trying to calm his heart.

The cobbler scrambled into a nearby closet to hide while Val pulled his sword. "Get ready to use one of your knives."

Pol hadn't brought any weapons with them. "I don't have any," he said, nearly wailing.

"Go to the cobbler's bench. He uses sharp things. Quickly!"

After frantically sorting through the cobbler's tools, he found a wickedly curved short knife, with the sharp surface inside the curve. Pol also picked up a long awl.

Someone shook the door, and then it flew open. Two men entered.

"There were three!" Pol said.

"Defend my back, but if there is a lot of fighting, just get out of the way," Val said.

One of the men sneered at Val. "We want the prince. We've already taken care of his little friend." The thug looked at Pol. "Saw you gazing out the front window, all moon-faced."

"Who hired you?" Pol asked. If he were to die, he'd like to know who ordered it.

"And wouldn't you like to know," the thug said, looking at Pol, but he lunged at Val. The man groaned as Val dispatched the man with incredible speed.

The other man pushed his dying colleague into Val, who tumbled to the floor, and went after Pol, who got down on one knee and dropped the awl. He used his left hand to keep the attacker at bay, and his right hand gripped the curved knife behind his back. The man leaned over and Pol jumped at the man's feet and took the curved knife and sliced the tendon behind the man's foot. He sliced the way Val had just taught him a week ago, and felt the blade go all the way through the man's stocking and into the tendon.

The attacker fell over. Pol fought for his breath. He could hear the swishing sounds of his heart in his ears. He took another deep breath, and picking up the awl, he plunged it into the man's chest. He felt it slide against something hard, (maybe a rib, he thought?) and then it went in all the way.

His strength escaped, and he fell to the floor. Pol looked on as Val got up and extricated his sword before two more men entered the shop, waving the naked blades of their own poorly-made swords. It was back to two to one, but Pol had lost his ability to help his bodyguard.

Val flailed as he backed up, seeking more room to maneuver. He took a slash to his sword arm, but one of the men had surprising talent and gave Val a fight. The other man passed by his fellow thug and tried to slip to the side of Val.

Just as Pol yelled out a warning to Val, the closet door opened and the cobbler hit the sneaking man soundly on the head with a large wooden mallet. That distracted the other attacker enough to give Val the opening he needed, and soon three out of four were messing up the floor of the cobbler's shop.

Pol struggled to sit up and leaned against the wall just beneath the multi-paned shop window. His heart still thrummed in his chest, but his strength began to return. He gazed at another man he had killed, and then looked up at the cobbler standing over the bodies.

"Thank you," Val said, holding his arm.

"I have something to bind that with," the cobbler said. The man eyed Pol. "You are the youngest prince aren't you? I saw you at the tourney."

"I am" Pol said, still sitting beneath the window. "You helped us out."

The cobbler nodded his head to Pol and gave him a half-smile. "I thought I was a coward, but I couldn't just stand in the closet and not help."

"I'll see you get a reward," Val said.

"A cleanup crew and removal of the bodies will suffice." The cobbler pulled his tools from the man Pol had killed. He smiled grimly again. "I always keep my tools sharp," he said to Pol. "You should too."

Pol nodded and found enough energy to stand.

"I'm sorry, lad," Val said. "Bodyguards can make mistakes, and I just committed a big one. I let you get too close to the window. People can see in as well as seeing out. I forgot that for a moment. You shouldn't."

That got another nod from Pol. "I guess we both learned something, then." Val's admission surprised Pol. He would have never guessed that Val would make a mistake.

Val rewarded Pol's comment with a long stare. "I learned a few things, My Prince. Let's get back to the castle as soon as we tie up the man who still lives." He gave the cobbler a curt bow. "I'll make sure to send some men over shortly."

~~~

Chapter Twenty-Four

~

"THEY WERE THE ONES AS FAR AS I CAN RECALL," the guard on duty the night of Paki's abduction said. "The one that's tied up in the cell, he's the criminal I remembered." The guard shook his head. "I don't know how you found them." He talked to Kelso, who sat behind his desk. Pol and Val stood behind the Captain of the Guard.

"It's a secret," Val said, winking at Pol. Both Val and Pol had agreed to leave out the fact that Pol had killed one of them.

Kelso looked up at the guard. "That's what I wanted to know. You are dismissed." The guard left the room to continue his slumber in the dormitory.

"Time to talk to your prisoner?" Kelso said, standing up from behind his desk. He rummaged around and pulled a ring of large keys from a drawer in his desk. He led them through a door behind his desk into a corridor Pol had never noticed before, and they followed Kelso to another door that took them to the cells.

A man leaned over the prisoner with the door to the cell wide open. Val loosened the sword in his scabbard. The man turned at the sound.

"Malden!" Pol said.

The magician turned and stood up. "I wanted to make sure your prisoner felt up to an interrogation. I'd like to stay if it is permissible."

"Certainly," Kelso said, asserting his authority in the jail. "Is he ready to talk?"

Malden nodded. "I put him to sleep, but will awaken him after you've told me what you know." He looked at Val.

The bodyguard told Malden everything, including Pol's role in fighting off the thugs.

"You have recovered?" the magician asked.

"I have. Before my tourney training, I couldn't have moved fast enough to avoid getting killed, but I only lasted for the one man. I lost my energy soon after that."

Malden checked on the prisoner and then turned around again. "The mighty Valiso Gasibli makes a mistake, eh?" The magician smiled, but amiably.

"I've made plenty of mistakes, but I rarely have witnesses," Val said. He glanced at Pol.

Pol shrunk back a bit. "I generally make mistakes," he said. His bodyguard's comment sent a chill down Pol's spine. He knew how ruthless Val could be when training Paki and him, so it would be no surprise to know how he would act in secret.

"Not this time," Malden said. "You don't have to be here when this man is questioned."

"Yes, I do," Pol said. "I'm still in training, aren't I?" He looked at Val, who nodded.

"Very well." Malden checked the prisoner's bond, and his eyes lost a bit of focus. All attention was on the prisoner as the man began to stir.

"Let me go!" the thug said as he began to struggle in his bonds.

Val drew his sword and put it to the man's throat. "The rest of your little band are dead, all three. Why did you attack us?"

The criminal glared at Pol. "You won't get me to say anything." The man turned his head towards the wall.

Val looked at Malden and nodded. The magician looked at the prisoner as his eyes lost a little focus again. Pol tried to imagine what kind of pattern Malden had tweaked, but he couldn't. Val obviously knew.

"Turn around and look at us," Malden said.

The prisoner obeyed.

Pol could see that the prisoner's anger had lost its edge. Did Malden cast a truth spell or something on the thug?

"Tell what happened this morning. Why were you walking down the street in front of the cobbler's shop?"

"Mo had dropped something in the alley. We had to wait until the guard left the entrance."

"A South Salvan Lion? Newly minted?" Val asked.

The prisoner nodded. "We were in the alley on the other side of the street and then cut over when Solly saw him." The man pointed his chin at Pol. "We all got mad and split up to take care of the prince."

"Who hired you to beat up Paki?"

"Mo worked for a week or two in the gardens a long time ago. He also did a few odd jobs for the stable master." He looked from Malden to Val. "He's the one who paid Mo the Lion to take care of Siggon's whelp."

Malden looked back at Pol. "Paki."

"I understood," Pol said.

"Did you beat up Siggon, too? Did the stable master help?"

"Yeah, we took care of Siggon. He just looked on."

"Were you supposed to kill them?" Pol said.

The prisoner managed an angry look at the prince. "No, but..." He shrugged his shoulders even though bound.

"That's enough," Kelso said. The Captain of the Guard sighed and held the door open for the others. Once they were back in the passage to Kelso's office, he sighed. "Too bad we can't use that in front of the magistrate."

"What?" Pol said.

Malden put his hand on Pol's shoulder. "Magically-enhanced interrogation is not permitted as evidence."

Pol didn't understand. "Why not?"

"Think about it, My Prince," Val said.

The command silenced Pol as he began to ponder what just happened. "People don't trust magicians?"

"That's part of it," Kelso said. "Some magicians can also plant responses."

Malden patted Pol on the head. "Those can only come out when you use magic to question."

"Oh. I didn't know that."

"You do now," Val said. "However, we don't need a magistrate to charge our friend in the cell with attacking a member of the royal family, do we?"

"No. I'm a witness, you're a witness and the cobbler is too."

"Right," Val said. "Who will we talk to next?"

Pol smiled because he knew the answer. "The stable master."

"Good boy."

The stable master hadn't been very cooperative when Paki and Pol found Siggon beaten and dumped in the hayloft. He tried to remember the entire episode and related it to Kelso and Val as they walked back to Kelso's office. The Captain had to fill out a form for the prisoner, so Val and Pol left him to it.

"The stable master sent the stable boys off to view the tourney," Pol said to Val. "He helped me, but I felt that he grudgingly gave me help. Paki had to go off to his match."

"Can you piece that into a bigger pattern?"

"Perhaps the stable master and Siggon weren't the best of friends? That might have made it easier for him to order the attack on Paki," Pol said. "That would fit into one pattern possibility."

Val nodded. "Let's talk to one of the gardeners next. You know them a bit, don't you?"

"I do," Pol said. "Bibby was a good friend of Siggon."

They walked through the stable yard, with Pol leading them to the gardening storage area.

Pol found Bibby weeding with his back to them in a flowerbed. Pol nudged him with his foot so that the young man fell forward onto his face.

"Paki?" Bibby said. "Can't be him since he's in the infirmary. He turned around and quickly scrambled to his feet. "My Prince!" He bowed low. Pol caught the sly smile on Bibby's face.

"You can cut out the bowing and scraping. It's just my bodyguard and me. We've a few questions to ask."

"How is Paki?"

Pol grinned. "He'll survive. He would have kicked you harder than I would."

Bibby just nodded in agreement.

"We have a few questions to ask you—"

The gardener put up both of his hands in protest. "I had nothing to do with the missing garden cart. You know that."

Pol looked at Val, who gave Pol a blank look. It appeared that the prince would be questioning Bibby on his own.

"I really wanted to talk to you about Siggon."

"We still really miss him. He worked harder than any two of us and still had time to work with you and his son."

"I miss him, too," Pol said, realizing again that he really did. He found himself sighing with regret, but turned it into taking a few deep breaths. "Did he have any problems with the stable master?"

Bibby whistled. "Did he! The stable master always thought that Siggon was after his job. You know that couldn't be further from the truth. Siggon loved the garden, and especially the little wood where you three trained all the time. The stable master is an old fart—a stinky, smelly fart!"

"Thank you," Pol said.

Pol told him what injuries Paki suffered and that Siggon's son wouldn't be back to the gardens for a while. Val signaled to Pol that it was time to go.

They walked back to the stable, and found the stable master yelling at three of the boys about not properly mucking out the stalls.

"Get on with you!" the stable master said to the boys. When he noticed Pol and Val walking towards him, he smiled. Pol recognized the smile on the stable master's face. His teachers had long ago told him to disregard a smile that didn't extend to the eyes.

"Can I have a minute of your time?" Pol asked.

"Of course, My Prince. Shall we go outside where the smell of the horses isn't so strong?"

Even Pol could notice that the boys hadn't been diligent in replacing the hay. They walked towards the tack room.

"In here?" the stable master said.

Pol didn't smile at the man's discomfort. The stable master's behavior told Pol all he needed to know about the man's involvement, but Pol wanted to know who had funded the thugs that the stable master hired.

Val went first to check out the tack room for safety's sake. He soon returned and motioned Pol and the stable master into the room and stood by the closed door.

"So, how can I help you, My Prince? Need to arrange for horses for yourself and your bodyguard?" He eyed Val and Pol could see a faint shudder in the man's shoulders.

"Do the names Mo and Solly mean anything to you?"

The stable master's eyes widened a bit, but he tried to mask it with a cough and shrugged. "There are lots of gardeners who come and go."

Val folded his arms. "The Prince didn't say that either of them were gardeners."

The stable master put a finger in his collar and began to sweat. "Well, what else could one of them be?"

Pol couldn't believe how the stable master had just admitted that he knew that only one of the thugs was a gardener. "Can we make him talk?" Pol said.

Val nodded and looked at the stable master with an unfocused eye. "Go ahead."

"Who paid you to arrange for the beatings of Siggon and Paki?" Pol asked.

"I, uh, uh," the man struggled to keep his mouth shut, but in the end said, "A South Salvan in King Astor's employ."

Pol wasn't surprised, but now he had to ask the question he dreaded. "Who ordered the soldier to hire you?"

"The two other Princes."

"Both of them?"

The stable master wrung his hands as he nodded. "That's what he led me to think."

Pol had to take a few steps back to lean against a worktable. It didn't surprise him, but hearing it from someone else hurt.

Val didn't waste any time and slipped a needle like weapon into the stable master's chest. The man went straight down. Pol's jaw dropped at Val's act.

"Why did you do that?"

Val pulled the sharpened sliver of steel out of the dead man's chest and slipped it into a sheath built into his boot. "He was no longer among the living once your friend Bibby told us of his animosity. I'm not interested in a trial. Either your brothers will talk your father into freeing the man, the most likely case, or they will order him killed, which is what the South Salvan agent would likely do. We save them all some time, and I'm under orders from the Emperor to take whatever steps are necessary."

Pol didn't know what to make of Val's words. He couldn't gather his thoughts to respond. He found his heart beginning to beat heavily and clutched his chest. "Won't you be arrested?"

Val shook his head. "King Colvin knows who I work for."

The stable master lay on the floor of the stable, but Pol couldn't even see any blood on the man's shirt.

"Is that a magic weapon?"

Val smirked. "No, but I did stop any bleeding with a spell. Can't have too many questions. Poor man must have had a heart attack."

Pol had to step outside. Val followed him and called out for help.

Kelso congratulated Val on his deductions.

"Not mine," Val said. "Pol conducted the investigation, including seeing a gardener first to verify that the stable master had a grudge against Siggon. The pattern fit too well. When we questioned the old man, he clutched his chest and died on the spot. Probably guilt."

Kelso curled one side of his mouth and looked at Val. "Heart attack it is, then."

Pol had remained speechless and only responded with nods, grunts, or shakes of his head. He had to process the casual killing that Val had done. It was an execution, pure and simple. When Pol fought another man, it was like a challenge, a tourney match, each person had a chance to defend himself, but no chances existed for the stable master.

The death brought conflicting feelings into his mind. He wanted to avenge Siggon's death and Paki's beating, but Pol didn't like the method. He looked at Val and felt a return to his fear of the man and uncertainty of his bodyguard's motives.

"Our investigation is over?" Pol asked. "Can we find the South Salvan soldier?"

"Assassin," Val said. "He could be the pea-shooter for all I know, but you are right, we are finished for now. We know enough to be aware of what happened, but to pursue the facts any further brings us peril, deadly peril."

Pol wished he could proceed, face the peril, so he could live a freer life, but that didn't seem to be possible since his father protected the sources at this time. To go further would endanger everyone. He thought they had made progress, and he had learned a lot, but Pol knew he couldn't take a life as easily as Val had just done.

"So I am done for the day?" Pol said.

Val nodded. "You have enough time to meet with Mistress Farthia."

He'd been so wrapped up in the investigation that he forgot all about his regular studies. "I'm very late! I'll be going."

"We'll be going," Val said.

Pol didn't tell Farthia about their recent activities. The stable master's killing still bothered him. He was glad that Val let him attend his studies without his presence.

Farthia rubbed her hands and looked across her desk at Pol. "Anything you'd like to talk about today?"

After running his finger along the front edge of Farthia's desk Pol looked up. "I'd like to know more about the ethics of assassination."

His tutor looked flustered and turned red. "You mean murder?"

Pol shook his head. "Well, you can call it political murder. How do people justify the killing of others for political reasons?"

"Did anything happen to bring this to your attention?" Farthia said.

Pol related his story of the last two days, including the killing of the three thugs and Val's execution of the stable master. "What is the difference?"

Farthia sat back. "You have me at a disadvantage. I can't speak of this in an objective manner. My father's business…"

"You said Val has worked for him, right?"

Farthia looked at Pol with a sad expression and nodded.

"Do you think Val considers himself a murderer? I can't see any remorse for what he did to the stable master. Does that make him a monster?" Pol said.

"I can't speak for Valiso, but that aspect of my father's work brings him no joy. It's a disagreeable part of his job. You've killed twice in your young life. Do you consider yourself a murderer?"

Pol stood up with his fists clutched tightly at his side. "I defended myself."

"Doing what was right?"

He nodded.

"What about the two men you killed? Do you think they were both the embodiment of evil?"

Pol knit his eyebrows together. "No, but they were trying to take my life."

"Did the stable master deserve to die?"

Pol suddenly understood what Farthia was getting at. "He did, and he should have been executed for his role in Siggon's death." He had to admit that he wouldn't. Pol jammed his eyes shut with frustration. "Life should be simpler than this." He didn't want to admit to Farthia that he hated this conversation, but he knew this perspective was what he needed. It hurt him to realize that the motives that drove his siblings, his father, and Valiso weren't as easily categorized as he had thought.

"Did you just learn something unpleasant?" Farthia said.

Pol glared at her as his mind filled with confusion and angry thoughts. He couldn't stand talking about this anymore and ran from the classroom. His feet clattered on the corridors as he fled from Mistress Farthia and quickly sought out the Royal Garden as a refuge from the complicated truth that he had just learned.

He found a secluded spot that had a curved bench. Pol had worked in the garden in this little section. It felt like he was alone, even though the castle grounds surrounded him.

He leaned over and put his head in his hands. His breathing and heart both labored to keep up, and that allowed Pol to lose his tortured thoughts in the rhythms of his body calming down. Pol didn't know how he could continue to live. His friends were killed or beaten, his mother attacked, and yet, when Val took the role of an executioner, something seemed to snap inside.

He shook his head, still cradled by his hands and moaned in emotional pain. The patterns of behavior and motivation of all around him seemed to crumble and fall apart in his mind. His breathing became labored again. Pol gasped and put his hand to his neck, fighting for breath.

Amidst his distress, Pol heard footsteps in the gravel.

"Poldon, my Poldon," Molissa, the queen mother, said. "Farthia said you were very upset."

He looked up at his mother, feeling lost and afraid. She sat down beside him and pulled his head down onto her lap, stroking his hair.

Pol made an attempt to sit up, but his mother held him down. "Just relax, my son. Sometimes I feel the way you probably do now. Life isn't fair. It never was. We exist in our own little cocoons and ignore most of the disagreeable parts, if we can. Your siblings dislike your existence because it intrudes on their cocoons, if you will."

His mother's hand on his head felt reassuring, even though her words weren't, not really.

She continued, "You dislike their treatment of you, and it is unfair. It is grossly unfair, but you represent a challenge they would just as soon not face. Your investigation with Val—"

Pol rose, feeling more calm and in control. "You know about that?"

She nodded and gave Pol the saddest smile he had ever seen on her face. "I asked Malden to keep me informed a few times a day since your friend Paki was attacked."

"We've hardly seen Malden."

"He's been around more than you think," his mother said. "Malden is one of the few in the castle who is exactly as you see."

At this point, Pol couldn't really trust anyone, even his mother. "Did he tell you who has died?"

"The attackers and the stable master?"

Pol nodded, shocked that Malden would give such unpleasant news to his mother. But then, if Malden were as open as his mother said, he would tell her if she asked him…maybe.

"I killed one of them. Did he tell you that, too?"

His mother looked across the garden, and then turned her head to him. Pol struggled to keep her gaze. "He did. You might question everybody and every motive, but you three, including the cobbler, saved each other."

Pol didn't know how much saving he had done, but he couldn't help feeling bad for the stable master's quick death. "I don't agree with the stable master's assassination."

Molissa gave her son a hard look, so hard that Pol shrank back. "It was not an assassination, and I think that perception is what has my son so upset. Valiso Gasibli has dispensation from the Emperor himself to take the life of those who threaten the Empire. Knowing how you loved Siggon and how you regard Paki, I would think you would support the death of one of those responsible."

"But he's just following orders from someone who is probably paying him well," Pol said, not wanting to pursue the thread of money all the way to his brothers in front of his mother.

"And we know who that someone is. Would you do the same?"

Pol shook his head. "Why do you think I'm out here, all upset? Of course not. I wouldn't, but just about everyone else would. Would you have killed the stable master?"

His mother didn't answer, but looked away. Why did Pol feel so alone in protesting the stable master's casual killing? Was it just the cold-blooded way it was done?

Her hands running through his hair calmed Pol down. After a while, he gritted his teeth and stood, frustrated that her ministrations could calm his distress so easily. "Thank you for being here. I'm much calmer now."

"But you still feel the way you did when you came down here?" She looked up at the castle in the background, and then at him.

"I do, but I'm not…not emotional, now. I'll have to think about everything." Pol knew he faced the dreaded task of rebuilding the patterns of motivation of all those he knew in his mind, although doing so could result in learning something that would continue to make him uncomfortable.

~ ~ ~

Chapter Twenty-Five

~

"HONNA AND GROSTIN," MALDEN SAID, "Val told me not to tell you, but I thought you should know. There is no evidence of Landon's involvement."

Pol sat in the magician's chambers, pressing his lips together. He had expected another lecture on patterns, but Malden had answered a question that had been eating at him for the past week. He hadn't had a session with Malden since before Paki's beating.

"Val can't execute them, though, can he?"

Malden shook his head. "Not those in direct line of succession. That requires a specific directive from the Emperor and with Hazett III, that is very, very unlikely. You knew your siblings were behind Siggon and Paki's assaults anyway." Malden said it as a statement, but Pol nodded. "Does confirmation change anything?"

Pol played with a paperweight on the table for a bit before looking at Malden. "Not really, I guess. I'm having trouble with making new patterns, though."

"New patterns?" Malden furrowed his brow.

"I constructed patterns of how people think, and some of them fell apart during and after the investigation," Pol said. He sighed and clutched one of his fists tightly to maintain control.

"Such as?"

"Val killing the stable master."

Malden nodded and pressed his lips together. "You've grown to like Valiso?"

"I try to like my tutors," Pol said. "I learn better from someone I know and trust."

"He disappointed you? More than disappointed you, he shattered the placement of your values over his."

Pol sat up straighter. "Is that what I did?"

"Explain what you might have done, My Prince," Malden said.

"I…I might have done what you said." Pol looked away and focused on the paperweight as he scrambled for an answer in his mind.

Malden broke Pol's train of thought with laughter. "Don't take me wrong. We look for those who agree with us, but people aren't exact matches. Everyone is different. That you see people as patterns is an encouraging sign."

"How can that be encouraging?"

"Creating patterns is a process. Generally, a training magician doesn't confront these problems until they are more advanced, but if you can quickly develop a pattern of someone, that can help you interpret their actions. Bear in mind that it is easy to introduce bias into the pattern, and that is what you have done."

"Bias? Oh," Pol said. He remembered a previous conversation that he had had with Malden and another with Val. Pol had fallen into the very trap of applying his own bias to a situation.

"Overlaying your pattern on someone else. Everyone is not the same, so if you don't change the pattern to match what you observe, there will be a discontinuity."

"Discontinuity?" Pol thought he knew the word, but he didn't understand how it applied here.

"The pattern in your mind doesn't match reality, and when the person you are patterning does something outside what you would do that should be consistent with that person's pattern, you get a discontinuity. It doesn't match. Val's quick execution of the stable master was a huge discontinuity. You would have never thought of doing that, and that invalidated the pattern of Val that you constructed. Rather than using the information to evaluate Val's true pattern, you went into a kind of shock. I'd put it down to deep disappointment," Malden said looking intently at Pol.

Pol had difficulty making eye contact with the magician. "You talked to my mother, too?"

Malden smiled. "I did. I constantly update the patterns I've made on people, so I needed to know how you reacted."

"That's not magic," Pol said. He felt a touch insulted by Malden's words.

"It isn't meant to be. You create patterns of things. I told you that all good magicians do. Patterns aren't just for magic, although if a person can't fabricate a pattern, they won't be able to tweak very effectively."

"Does that mean that I have to change who I am?" Pol could see this as an extension of that older discussion. Why did this pattern business have to be so convoluted? When he first thought of patterns, the concept seemed so simple.

Malden shook his head. "Not at all. You just have to learn to be a bit more flexible in your establishment of patterns. Allow for deviations...no, expect deviations and accept them. Do you think your behavior is always acceptable to your siblings?"

Pol took the paperweight and tossed it from hand to hand. "No. They don't like me."

"Are they wrong not to like you?"

Malden's comment got through to Pol. "I see. I need to look at the pattern from different directions."

Malden nodded. "Right. Another word might be looking at the pattern from different perspectives. It's like looking at a forest from one position. Every tree could hide something unexpected, but if you change your vantage point and look from behind and from the sides, you can get a better feel for what is there—"

"Or what is not," Pol said. That way of thinking wasn't entirely foreign to him, since Siggon had talked about tracking in the forest and said something similar, but Pol had never thought to put the concept into anything other than hiding and tracking and definitely had not applied it to the practice of creating patterns.

"You seem to understand what I've been talking about," Malden said.

"How do I apply it to magic?" Pol felt like he might have to start his magic training all over again. He sighed as he said it.

Malden rose and looked out the window that overlooked the castle town of Borstall. "The more accurate the pattern, the more powerful the magic. It takes years of practice. That is why a monastery is still the best place for you."

Pol tried to evaluate the pattern that Malden had let him a glimpse. "So you can remove me from behind a tree here in the castle and send me away? Are you truly a friend?"

The magician turned, the window's light held his face in bold relief, and Malden seemed stronger than Pol had ever seen him. "I am. You learn so well, Pol. You are wasted as the last heir, but there is nothing we can do. Yes, you stand a chance to survive longer if you go. You are still younger than what the monks of Tesna accept. Another year, at least. They generally won't accept a boy of fourteen."

"I'm almost fifteen," Pol said, but he didn't know why he tried to defend his age. Pol dreaded leaving Borstall and his mother and Paki.

"We've talked of this before, and I've written for permission to enroll you early, but it will still be weeks before the letter arrives. They have to make a decision and send back word," Malden said. "Until then, we can still work on patterns."

"Will I be able to tweak them?"

Malden nodded. "Just little things. You've already demonstrated the ability to levitate, but you've just touched the surface of what there is to learn."

Before dawn, Pol felt a hand grip his arm. He sat up in bed and looked directly into Val's face. "What do you want?"

"You," Val said. He looked into Pol's eyes. "We will train in the darkness for awhile. Get dressed."

Pol followed his bodyguard to the smaller training room adjacent to the armory where he had previously learned knife skills.

"Paki!" Pol said rushing to his friend's side. "You can work with us?"

Val stepped up to the both of them. "He can, since this phase of your training is not going to involve a lot of physical strength, but coordination and mental toughness."

"Sounds good," Paki said, grinning and rubbing his hands. "Anything to get out of the house. My little sisters were driving me crazy."

"You'll soon be back out in the gardens," Val said. "But you can extend your time off, by spending a few more days working for Kelso."

Paki's eyebrows shot up. "I can?"

"Not training to be a guard, but cleaning up from the mess the guards make while they train, and you can also spend some time straightening out the armory."

After rolling his eyes, Paki said, "Anything but weeding on my hands and knees." He grinned at Pol. "Now what are we doing?"

Val stood in front of the pair of boys. "Siggon might have had you do some of the same things, but we will continue to practice silent techniques. I'd like to see how much he taught you and what you remember. I want you both out in the woods next to the gardens trying to find each other." Val looked at Pol. "Practice whatever kind of woodcraft you know, and I will observe. Take turns."

They walked through the gardens to the little wood, and Pol volunteered to be found first.

"Count of ten," Val said. "Go. I want you both to have a few turns before dawn."

Pol ran into the darkness, not caring about Paki hearing his steps until he was further into the wood. He remembered about how he had set up diversions when he successfully hid the rod before the tourney. He sighed as he remembered the praise that Siggon had given him.

Using the same technique wouldn't work, but the dark woods made different patterns of possibilities blossom in his mind. He found a low branch and used it to climb up a few limbs and waited, trying to will his breathing to stop.

He used his magic to locate the trees and watched for Paki to enter the woods. He identified Paki and another enter the woods. Val must be walking right behind Paki. He remained silent in the tree and smiled when a breeze began to rustle the leaves, hopefully masking his breathing.

Paki investigated the areas close to the gate. He must have remembered what Pol did to hide the rod. The pair of them eventually walked underneath Pol's tree.

"Do you give up?" Val said.

Stopping by Pol's hiding place wasn't a coincidence. Val must know the location technique that Malden had taught him.

"I guess. I don't know how anyone could find something in the dark like this. I wish I had a light."

Val paused for a moment. "And let the person you are seeking know exactly where you are?"

Pol could even hear Paki scratch his head. "I guess the best thing to do is wait until it gets lighter."

"Is that what your father taught you?"

Another silence.

"No. He would just tell me to find a spot to wait until I heard something, I guess."

"Did he guess right, My Prince?" Val said. He created a magic light. "You can come down."

Pol could see the amazement on Paki's face when he dropped to the ground. Pol's heart still beat a bit faster after being caught so easily. "He's right. When you're hiding you have to be patient, too."

"Not if your pursuer is as skillful as I am," Val said.

Pol knew he meant skilled in magic. "My turn?"

Val nodded. "Find a good spot, Paki."

Val and Pol didn't say a word until they were out of the woods.

"You used magic to find me."

His magic light went out. "Of course. It's a tool to use. I want you to use it, but whisper to me when you've located your friend."

Pol hadn't used the locator spell since the tourney. He closed his eyes, even though dawn wasn't close. He could see Paki's color towards the back of the little wood.

"I can see him now," Pol whispered. He smiled at his little joke.

"You can?"

Pol could tell by Val's voice that he had impressed Val. "Follow me."

He walked into the wood and led his bodyguard to Paki's spot, but Paki was now on the move. "He's over there."

"Indeed," Val said. "Continue."

Pol moved towards Paki, but something didn't feel right. He stopped and re-thought the pattern and noticed a faint spot to his right that wasn't moving. Pol turned abruptly and silently circled around to approach the faint color from behind and clapped Paki's shoulder.

"Val said you wouldn't be able to find me!" Paki said.

"I did," Val said. "Now you know that there are counters to your location spell."

Pol nodded in the dark. "I've already learned that there must be a lot I don't know."

"A lifelong lesson," Val said. "I thought my compliment would make you overconfident. How did you know?"

"The lack of movement. I couldn't hear Paki's movements and something didn't feel right. Something wrong with the pattern that I saw."

"Excellent. I'll have to try harder to trick you in the future. It's a good thing that neither of you have forgotten what Siggon taught you about moving in the woods." He lit another light. "It looks like I won't have to get up so early again. A blindfold will do for you, My Prince."

"What about me?" Paki looked disappointed.

"Would you rather get up early and stand by yourself in the training room?"

Paki furrowed his brow. "No."

"So you're included. No more night games for now," Val said. "I'm ready for breakfast. Why don't we go to the kitchens?"

Val gave Paki instructions on what he was to do to reorganize their training room for the next morning while they walked to the castle. Pol liked eating in the kitchen better than maintaining his composure if he met up with his siblings in the family dining room, especially now that Amonna was in South Salvan.

After breakfast, Val and Pol walked up to his rooms. "I want you to spend this evening, haunting the halls of the castle. Malden said you've done it before, and I want to see how well you do. You lead, and I will follow."

~~~

Chapter Twenty-Six

~

MALDEN HAD SENT A MESSAGE that they wouldn't be meeting in the late afternoon, so Pol prepared for his tour of the castle by finding a suitable outfit in black.

"Why do you wear black if it will be dark anyway?" Val asked, looking over Pol's shoulder.

His bodyguard was in tutoring mode with that question, Pol thought. "So light won't reflect off my clothes. Merge with the shadows. That's why you wear dark greens and browns in the forest when you hunt. From a magical point of view, it would be becoming part of the pattern."

"That's not a magical concept. Many animals use camouflage as a defensive measure. They are born to wear their camouflage, but the same isn't the case with humans. Hiding with the pattern. Remember that. If you pursue your magical training, you will learn that magicians don't solely rely on magic. Live magicians, that is."

"How much magic do you know?" Pol said as he finished making his choices.

"Enough so that I use my powers more sparingly than most. In my line of work, power can be a hindrance and can get in the way of what I'm trying to do."

Pol began to change his clothes. "And exactly what is your kind of work, other than being my bodyguard?" Pol left unsaid the element of assassination.

"I do a little bit of this and a little bit of that in the background," Val said. His face lost the smirk it usually showed. "I'm my own man, but I take on many jobs for Farthia's father."

"Like this one?"

Val nodded. "The Emperor can order strange tasks, and protecting your mother and you is one of them."

Pol let that slide. He might engage Val in asking the details of this and that part of his duties, but for now, he tried to cast his doubts aside as he prepared for practicing more stealth in the castle. He had done it before on his own, but now he'd be tested.

At least he could sneak around the castle as well as anyone older. Pol didn't need to be strong or tall or anything but a bit nimble and smart. He knew he could do the nimble part for short stretches, and he already had accepted that his intelligence was a notch or two higher than most.

Being smart didn't make him better than anyone, because Pol was learning that there were a lot of different kinds of 'better' among people, and people had their own ideas of what that was. His siblings certainly didn't think Pol was better than they were. Thinking of patterns had given him a more realistic view of how others thought. Pol knew he thought better than many, but better didn't mean he'd live longer, either, Pol thought as Siggon came to mind.

Val yanked the servant's rope. "We'd better get some food in us before we start. I want you out and about for much of the night. You can take a nap after we eat."

Pol didn't have much of an appetite. He didn't think he'd feel nervous, but he found himself fidgeting with his hands after he had eaten.

"Nap time." Val said as he lay down on the couch. "I'm going to take one. Follow my august example."

Pol smiled at the request and felt a little lighter as he went to his bedroom and closed the drapes, darkening the room. He drifted off thinking about the coloring of various animals he had seen in the wild with Siggon and Paki.

A hand grasped Pol's shoulder, and he cried out.

"Quiet," Val said, a finger to his lips. "Our goal is not to say a word once we have left your rooms."

Pol nodded and kept his mouth shut. He would do everything he could to follow Val's instructions. As he rose and followed Val to the door, Pol could feel excitement begin to build, displacing his anxiety.

He cracked open the door and looked to one side, and then the other. No one populated the corridor in front of his rooms. Ignoring Val, as his bodyguard had instructed, he padded to the opposite side of the corridor and began to scurry from shadow to shadow in the corridor, gradually moving further away from his rooms.

Footsteps intruded on the silence of the night coming towards Pol. He found a darker shadow in the crease of an internal wall and collapsed into it, with the visualization of becoming part of the darkness. A shock of light appeared, making Pol hug the wall closer after he pulled up the black scarf that he had worn around his neck.

Grostin turned the corner and walked right past Pol, looking neither right nor left. He followed his brother through the castle until Grostin stopped at his mother's rooms.

The Queen's bodyguard sat in a chair at the side of the door and held up her hand. "You wish to see the Queen at this hour?"

Grostin nodded. "Ask her. She'll see me."

"Stay here," the woman said and disappeared through the door into the darkness beyond.

Pol could see light suddenly emerging from the bottom of the door, and the bodyguard appeared.

"You may enter. Watch yourself, My Prince. I will tolerate no sudden movements, even by you, in the presence of the Queen. Understand?"

Grostin's face showed a tinge of fear, but nodded as he walked in, followed by the guard.

Pol looked around the corridor. He couldn't see Val with his eyes, but used his magical sense to see a faint dot of color in his mind not far away. Val had used magic to conceal his presence. Pol wondered if his mother's bodyguard could do the same.

He tossed that caution aside and slipped to the door, crouching down into the darker shadows lower on the wall. and listened. Farthia had taught him about sound in a nature lesson, so Pol tried to think of a pattern that sound made, bouncing around inside a room. He caught the pattern and amplified it in his mind.

A smile creased his face as his spell succeeded. He could hear the conversation.

"You shouldn't have come here," his mother said.

"But Honna just got word from Yastan that the Emperor might not approve Father's petition. What are we going to do?"

Pol noticed silence. The fact that Grostin had come to speak with his mother set Pol on edge. Why? He could feel his face burn with emotion. He scattered such thoughts from his mind so he could concentrate on what they had to say.

"Leave Poldon alone, for now. Your meddling has cost lives and put Valiso Gasibli on alert. He is the most dangerous person in the castle. It was so stupid to abduct Pol's friend and beat him nearly to death. It only makes Pol more defensive."

"You are just trying to protect your son."

Another silence. He pictured his mother glaring at Grostin in anger, and it showed in her voice as she said, "You know my motivations to protect Listya are as strong as my interest in Poldon, especially since the Emperor now has an interest in him and we have to move more carefully." Another pause.

"What about the Emperor's bodyguard?" Grostin said.

The words shocked Pol since the woman was standing right there with them. "Don't worry about her," his mother said. "Worry about yourself. If you want Landon as King of Listya, that only solidifies your line to King Colvin's throne, and I will do what I can to help, but stop toying with my son. He won't last to his twentieth birthday."

"So you say," Grostin said.

"So a number of physicians say. Talk to Malden Gastoria. He never lies. Now, as to the petition, if the Emperor won't approve the elevation of Landon, Colvin can just make him regent. In five or ten years, Hazett will approve his elevation to vassal-king as a matter of form."

"How can I believe you? Father has told me something much different. He refuses to take no for an answer from Hazett III."

Pol began to breathe heavier. He closed his eyes and tried to calm down.

"You need to learn to exercise some patience, Grostin. It will be the death of you, if you don't."

"Are you threatening me?"

Queen Molissa laughed. "No. Quite the opposite, I'm giving you a warning for your own good. I think we are done here. Remember your father has alternatives to follow should the petition be denied. I suggest that you help him follow the least destructive one."

Pol rose to his feet. He had learned more than he wanted, and now he had to get back to his rooms. He wheezed and covered his mouth. He padded back across the hall and found a shadow.

The door opened, and his mother's bodyguard examined the corridor before returning to the Queen's quarters.

As carefully as he could, Pol made his way back to his rooms and collapsed on the couch. His head hurt, his body struggled with the shock of what he had just heard. Pol then sat up and leaned over with his hands on the edge of the couch, taking in huge gobs of air as Val entered.

"Did you hear what they said?" Val shook his head. "Of course you did." He put his hands on his hips. "You learned a new magical technique tonight, didn't you?"

Pol nodded and continued to struggle for breath. "Water, please," he croaked. His heavy breathing intensified until he took a drink of water, and Val began to massage Pol's shoulders.

"Relax, just relax," Val said as his hands began to move in a slower rhythm than Pol's breathing.

His ministrations worked, and Pol leaned back against the couch, his energy gone. Val stopped and let Pol calm down.

"Now what did you learn?"

Pol blinked. "About stealth?"

Val shook his head. "No. What caused your attack?"

The shock of the words still ran through Pol's mind. "My mother is in league with my siblings."

"What?" Val said. "That's unexpected."

Pol nodded. He took some more time to breathe and get in control. "She said she expects me dead before I'm twenty, so Grostin doesn't have to worry about destroying me." Pol looked up at Val. "The petition to install Landon as King of Listya might be denied, so Mother told Grostin that all Father had to do is appoint Landon regent, and wait a few years and it shouldn't be too much trouble to get the Emperor to agree to make Landon king. That leaves Grostin as heir to the North Salvan throne."

Val looked angry. "That's what they think. What did Grostin say to all of this?"

"Mother told him to be patient, but he told her that Father won't be patient. He is intent on having Landon sit on the Listyan throne." Pol shook his head. "My problem might originate with my father's obsession to have Landon rule."

Val sat down on an easy chair. "She is still protecting you, Pol."

"But she's working with my siblings."

"They are her children by law, you know. Don't you think she should care about them, too? She probably feels she's only got seven or eight years to keep you safe, and then you'll be gone."

Pol furrowed his brow. "So she is protecting herself by working with them?"

Val nodded. "Patterns, My Prince. You need to see a larger pattern than what exists solely between the Queen and you. Her true motivations are likely very complex."

Broadening the pattern. That was a concept that brushed through Pol's mind. He hadn't given it much thought, but it matched with looking at the pattern of the trees versus the pattern of the forest. He shook his head.

"I need to rest. This is all too much for me," Pol said. He had just been rudely reminded of the limited horizon of his future through what he learned tonight, and Pol didn't want to think of that right now.

Pol woke up some time after dawn. Val had let him sleep in. The issues of the previous night hadn't gone away, but Pol needed a bath and some time alone to think about his predicament. He decided that he would take a chance to use the family dining room, and Val accompanied him.

"It looks like we are alone. Do you want to join me?" Pol asked.

"Thank you, My Prince, but I've already eaten."

"Sit anyway. I need to talk."

Val nodded and sat across the table from where Pol pulled out a chair. A serving maid entered the room, and Pol let her know what he wanted since the breakfast buffet had already been cleared.

"I am upset about two things," Pol said, "my mother's alliance and my short time left. I don't know which is worse."

"I will never know since I always just assume tomorrow might be my last day alive."

Pol didn't quite know how to take that comment. He thought a bit. "So you can't plan out your life? No pattern to use? It seems you live a dreadful life, thinking like that.".

Val shook his head. "It's not that I don't plan ahead. There is a pattern to my life, but it could end at any time. Thinking that way makes some of what I do easier."

"Like what?"

Val shifted in his seat and looked out the window. Pol noticed that he didn't look him in the eye. "I'm not going to tell you. Perhaps when you are older, we might share a mug of ale in a pub somewhere, and we can trade stories, but this is not the time. You've got some idea, anyway."

Pol knew enough to leave Val alone. The comment about sharing an ale seemed a soothing comment, since it seemed likely that Pol might not ever be old enough to join Val in a pub. He did have a positive thought burst in his mind.

"So living your life one day at a time, that's it, isn't it?" Pol said.

Val nodded.

"It doesn't depress you, does it?"

"Not at all. I think you're smart enough to understand this: I try to live outside of a pattern."

That comment didn't ring true to Pol, but perhaps there was something in that. Pol's life included Val in his own current pattern, so Val meant something different. Perhaps his bodyguard thought about long-term patterns. Val might be thinking of living constantly in the shadows, behind the trees that most people saw from one perspective.

"I don't think a person can live outside of patterns, but you can make yourself less discoverable in a pattern," Pol said.

"You do understand." Val smiled. "Don't give up hope of living a long life."

"But you have."

Val shook his head. "I didn't say that. I just don't have entanglements that can affect my judgment."

Now Pol understood. "So your own personal pattern is very flexible."

That brought a grin to Val's face. "Right. That's probably a better way of putting it than I did. Good for you, lad. You should do the same. Your mother doesn't really know if you'll die young or not. People have told her that you will, but does that make your early demise a reality?"

Pol shook his head. "No, it doesn't." A flood of relief overcame Pol. He kept quiet as the serving girl brought in his breakfast.

Val stole a slice of bread. "It's been a bit since I ate." He smirked and took a bite. "You look a bit more relaxed."

"I need to talk to Malden about my health. He knows me better than I do."

~~~

Chapter Twenty-Seven

~

POL HAD BEEN UP AND DOWN SINCE HE HAD TALKED TO VAL at breakfast. Malden had agreed to share his midday meal with him in his chambers.

Pol knocked on Malden's door and opened it when Malden told him to enter. Val stayed in the corridor.

"It's better you talk to him alone, I think," Val said.

Pol nodded and closed the door behind him.

"If this is to be a private meeting, at least let Val get some food," Malden said.

Pol felt a bit embarrassed and opened the door. "Get something to eat, first."

"I am glad you noticed me in your pattern," Val said with some sarcasm.

Pol twisted his lips. "Actually, Malden did."

"Does it matter?"

Pol shook his head and let his bodyguard in. Malden and Val exchanged a few pleasantries. Pol wondered where they had met to become such good friends. Val left Malden and Pol facing each other across the magician's small dining table.

After being totally honest with Malden about what he had heard the previous night, including his conversation with Val. Pol finally took a bite of his lunch. He wasn't that hungry having eaten a late breakfast, but he felt driven to talk to Malden.

Malden had a few bites before he spoke. "This business with your mother bothers you, doesn't it?"

"What do you think?"

Malden pressed his lips together. Pol could see that Malden felt sympathy for him, but Pol wasn't interested in sympathy. He needed some perspective, so he could rebuild his pattern, at least that was how he thought of it.

"I think Val has it right. Your mother sees you as temporarily by her side, but then she has to live with your siblings. Can you trust her? Certainly with most things. It appears she has accepted the fact that Landon will be taking over Listya. I see Grostin's role as providing information, but your mother understands his penchant for hasty action. I don't expect Grostin to stop attacking you. Impetuousness is part of who Grostin is."

"What about my dying before I'm a man."

Malden thought a bit more. "It is certainly a possibility. You must know that. You had an attack last night. The attacks won't stop if nothing is done, but there are remedies. Perhaps you should consider going to Deftnis rather than Tesna. The Deftnis monastery has much better healers. I can't say they will be able to make you right, but I don't think you'll get better here, and I lack the understanding of all the body's patterns that their healers have."

"You really think I might live longer than eight more years?"

Malden shook his head and took a drink of watered wine. "You can't live your life like that, Pol. If you do, all your focus will be on some kind of morbid vigil, waiting for your body to quit. You have a lot of living to do in all of that time. What I'm saying it that your condition has a chance to get better with advanced healers. I am nothing compared to them."

"So when shall I go?"

"You've changed your mind about going to a monastery?"

"If my mother is in league with my siblings, then I don't need to protect her."

Malden took a few more bites. "As long as your siblings live, your mother is in danger. I worry about King Colvin's obsession with Listya and Landon. It has affected his judgment, and that means his siblings will have more latitude for mischief, not less."

Now Pol was confused. He didn't know if he should stay or go, but if he went, it sounded like Deftnis might be a better place. "You sent a letter to the Tesna monastery. Have you heard anything?"

"No. I don't worry about acceptance at Deftnis. If Val is there to vouch for you, there is no question about acceptance. Don't tell anyone about the prospects of switching monasteries. As far as anyone knows, it's Tesna, unless I get a rejection."

"So I may not die before I'm twenty, and my mother is not in immediate danger?"

"Nothing is certain in this world, and patterns can quickly shift on their own accord."

Pol nodded. "I realize that, but now I don't have to wait for my own death."

"You should never wait for your own death. All of us have a finite time to spend, and it's up to us to make whatever time we have count."

"Val does it day by day."

Malden raised his hand. "It's something taught at Deftnis."

"Have you been there?"

Malden looked past Pol at the wall behind him. "I taught at Deftnis for a few years when I was younger. That's where I met Val." He raised his hand to Pol. "Don't ask me about what is taught there. You know as much as I want you to know, and Val won't tell you any more than I have. Now describe how you figured out the listening spell."

A knock on the door interrupted their meal and their discussion.

"The king requests your presence, Magician Malden," a page said.

Pol had seen the messenger boy around. He was just a bit older than Paki and had fought in the tournament. His friend had barely beaten him, Paki claimed.

Pol sighed. It looked like lunch had just ended, so he gathered Val, and they returned to his rooms where Pol lugged out the book on religions. He had another hour before he would have his session with Mistress Farthia.

After waiting alone for quarter of an hour, Mistress Farthia rushed into the classroom.

"Forgive me, My Prince," she said, a bit breathlessly. "The Taridans have stepped up their incursions on the northern border, and it has the castle buzzing."

"An invasion?" Pol said.

Farthia shrugged. "No one knows at this point, but King Colvin isn't going to wait. He's sending an army up to the border."

"When will they leave?"

"Malden is shut up with the King and Banson Hisswood. He is recalling General Wellgill, but he's a week away, so expect nothing for that long."

"What about Imperial troops?"

Farthia laughed. "What have I told you about the way Hazett administers the Empire?"

"Loosely. He won't intervene to stop border skirmishes, only kingdom consolidations."

She nodded. "Right. So it's likely that your father will send a force, to slap the Taridans' hands. Don't you worry, there won't be a full-scale invasion that threatens Borstall. Now," Farthia took a deep breath to calm herself, "what is going on in your life? You look a bit harried. Have your siblings launched another campaign against you?"

Pol shook his head. "Their campaign hasn't stopped, but I overheard my own disturbing news."

"Are you going to share?" she said.

"I don't think so. Not at this time. I've talked to Malden and Val, and they've helped."

She raised her eyebrows and looked down at her hands. "So?"

"I do have a question. What do you know about the Deftnis monastery?"

Pol learned little more than what he had picked up in his readings and from Malden. They had the same age requirement as all monasteries did, sixteen years, however the magician seemed confident about getting him in.

"Why the interest?"

"Malden said they had better healers."

Pol picked up on that statement. Malden and Farthia had been talking about him. Should he get upset? Pol decided not to since, along with Val, they were the only adults in the castle to be trusted.

"From what I know, no one would care you're a prince, and from what Malden has revealed, it's not a fun place to be."

Pol wasn't looking for a fun place, and he knew he wasn't prepared to live day to day like Val.

Ten days later, a page escorted Pol into his father's study.

"I'm sending you north towards the Taridan border. You will be switching body guards with your mother, since Malden reminds me that her body guard has experience on the border," his father said. "You can take your gardener friend, Pakkingail, with you."

Pol was excited to leave the castle, but he wondered why Val wasn't coming. Malden had distinctly said Val had helped with the last border war with Tarida.

"There is a unit leaving tomorrow afternoon. Make sure you are ready to go. I suggest you visit your mother before heading out. You're just an observer and are not fighting. Understood?"

Pol nodded. "Are my brothers going?"

"No. Landon left this morning for South Salvan to bring back Amonna, and Grostin will stay here, by my side, learning from me."

"You aren't going either?"

His father lifted a corner of his mouth in something that didn't quite resemble a smile. "My father died on that border. I'll not do the same. You are dismissed." King Colvin flicked a finger towards the door.

Val stayed at Pol's side while they walked back to his rooms.

"I'm getting my mother's bodyguard. And you are switching with her."

"Kolli?"

"You know her?" Pol said.

"She's a good woman, although she is too dedicated to your mother." Val nodded. "I'll have a word with her before you leave."

"And that is tomorrow midday. Why don't you come with me?"

Val shrugged. "I think Malden would like me here to help him with the King. What about your brothers?"

"Grostin stays here to learn at my father's feet," Pol snorted. "Landon has gone south to bring back Amonna."

"He'll take his time," Val said. "I don't have to tell you to be careful."

"You don't," Pol said. "I can take Paki with me."

"Good," Val said. "He can watch your back when Kolli isn't watching."

Pol had a sinking feeling in his stomach that circumstances were getting out of his control. He had no idea what patterns would help him in a war. Malden had told him that court magicians had no place in the army, and Pol easily extended that to include fourteen-year-old apprentice magicians.

~ ~ ~

Chapter Twenty-Eight

~

KELSO HELPED POL WITH BITS AND PIECES OF ARMOR. He had used some of the items during the tourney, but Pol felt the necessity to protect his body from arrows coming from the front and the back, thinking how his grandfather had been killed. Kelso fitted Paki as well.

At least Pol had some experience spending time in the outdoors, and he tried to remember as much as he could as the columns of soldiers started out. Pol, Paki, and Kolli were relegated to the rear of the column, just in front of the supply wagons.

Kolli told them it would take ten days to reach the border, so Pol spent his time observing the patterns that the soldiers made. He constructed a simple framework of what Kolli called the logistical train and the columns of soldiers. Most of the officers rode up front, so they wouldn't be swallowing the dust of marching soldiers.

Paki and Pol quickly followed Kolli's instructions on how to make a dust mask to cover their mouths and noses. She joined them. Pol had to smile because the three of them looked like bandits to his eye.

When they stopped, they pitched their tents away from the other soldiers. Kolli had brought a small tent of her own, and Paki's horse carried a tent for both boys to share.

"They aren't treating you with any respect," Kolli said on the second evening when everyone had stopped for the day. "The officers eat well in their own section of camp, but you are left to scrounge what you can from the mess wagons." She looked a bit upset. "Well, there is more than one way to live while marching through your own country. Set up the tents, leave your armor behind underneath your blankets, and follow me."

Paki gave Pol a mischievous grin, and off they rode into the woods. A half an hour later, they approached a good-sized village.

"We'll spend the night here," Kolli said, dismounting in front of an inn. "I've got money to pay for rooms. You two can share a room, and I get my own." She grinned at both of them as they walked up the creaky wooden steps into the inn.

The buzz of the crowd quieted down as the three strangers walked in.

"Two rooms. One for my boys and one for me. Can you handle it?"

"Kolli Haverhill. It's been awhile," the woman innkeeper said. "You're not married, nor are you old enough for these two."

After a bit of shared laughter, Kolli said, "These bumbling bumpkins are apprentices to the army scouts. I was told to take good care of them, and that means tonight I'm treating them to meals and beds."

"As long as the money is paid. You want a bath?"

Kolli looked sideways at Pol and Paki. "Just for me. I want to keep the boys smelling a bit ripe for awhile." That got a laugh for all those listening in.

Pol was just fine not having to take a bath. Kolli led them to a table and sat them down. "The food is edible, but they have good ale. Want to join me?"

Paki nodded enthusiastically, but Pol knew Malden didn't want him drinking a lot of alcohol.

"Fruit juice, if they've got it," Pol said. He doubted the inn served the watered wine he was used to.

A serving maid who seemed to know Kolli brought stew, bread, a bit more stale than Pol was used to in the castle, but much softer than the rock-hard loaves they had been given to eat during the first days of their trip. Paki seemed to enjoy it.

"Not what you are used to?" Kolli said. He could detect the tease in her voice.

"I've had worse," Pol said, remembering the awful bread that Siggon had insisted on when they went camping. He looked at Paki who shrugged and nodded.

The stew was better than the bread, and Pol quickly ate his fill. "Why are you helping us? Weren't you given instructions to make our lives miserable?"

"Ah," Kolli said. "You caught on, did you?"

Paki looked up from his meal. "Caught on to what?" He had no idea they were being mistreated on purpose.

"Did my father order this as punishment?"

She shook her head. "Grostin suggested that you could use some toughening up, and General Wellgill agreed to do it. Your father agreed as well. Don't consider it mistreatment. In the army mistreatment is much worse than marching at the end of the columns and eating the same food as the infantry. You don't have to dig latrines, help the cooks with menial chores, or do night watches."

Pol hadn't thought about any of that. He felt ashamed and misinformed at his creating a faulty pattern. He hadn't observed enough.

"So it's permissible to leave the army camp?"

"You are a Prince of the Realm?"

Pol nodded. "I am."

"Then you can. Did you swear an oath to follow General Wellgill's orders?"

"No, did you?"

Kolli laughed. "I left the army to serve your mother and now to serve you. I follow your commands."

"Or anticipate my wishes?" Pol said.

"This time that is exactly what I did." She looked around at the inn as the sound level began to increase. "We have to leave early tomorrow, so it's time for bed."

Pol later admitted to Paki that he preferred a bed to sleeping outside. His friend admitted that he agreed. They didn't take long to get to sleep, and to Pol it only seemed like minutes when Kolli woke them up in the pre-dawn light. They walked down to a hastily prepared breakfast by the groggy staff and rode back into camp.

Kolli led them to their tents in a somewhat roundabout way, missing the sentries that the General had posted. When they arrived at their tents, she whistled softly.

"It looks like we had visitors," Kolli said.

Pol surveyed the damage. Both of the tents had been torn down and the fabric slashed with long cuts. The armor had been strewn about their little camp.

"This has gone too far," Kolli said. "Mount up. It's time to wake the General up." She picked up the remains of her tent and galloped to the General's camp quarters and burst into his tent.

"What is the meaning of this?" the General said. His hand held a straight razor and his face was half-covered with dripping soapsuds.

Kolli threw the shredded tent at the General's feet. "Someone attacked our camp. If you didn't remember, a Prince sleeps there."

"This is yours, Haverhill?"

She nodded. "The Prince's tent is worse. Our armor was thrown about and stomped on by horses. Was this by your command?"

"See here. Just because you are no longer under my command doesn't mean you can accuse me of something so dishonorable." The general's face began to get red. It only made his white beard stand out.

"And setting the Prince at the back of the train is?"

The General cleared his throat. "Well, we all have to follow orders." His anger seemed to turn to embarrassment. Perhaps he wasn't to blame. Pol tried to make sense of the shifting patterns.

"Orders?" she pointed to the remains of her tent. "Luckily, I suspected something like this, so we spent the night at the inn in Bancor's Lift."

"Ale still as good?"

A ghost of a smile flitted across Kolli's face as she nodded.

"What are you going to do?" she said.

"We have extra tents, and today you will ride just behind the officers and the knights." General Wellgill's gaze turned on Pol. "Is that acceptable?"

Riding in front didn't remove the peril that Pol faced on this trip. "What about those who destroyed our camp?"

"Haverhill?"

She looked at Pol. "We don't have any idea who did it."

Pol held his tongue. "We will sleep with the officers as well. Is that acceptable General Wellgill?"

"Of course, My Prince. The attack changes things."

"Indeed," Kolli said. "Thank you, General." She nodded to him. "I am sorry to disrupt your morning preparations."

Paki and Kolli left Pol still standing in the tent. "I intend on returning to Borstall with my life, General. There are those who have other ideas. Kolli is my bodyguard and will defend me against any who threaten. Any who threaten. Do you understand?"

The General raised his eyebrows at the threat that Pol struggled so hard to give. "I do, My Prince."

"I am also sorry to have bothered you." Pol turned around and left. His hands were beginning to shake and his breathing had become more labored, but not until he was out of the General's sight.

He slowly walked to the horses where Paki held the reigns and mounted. "I wouldn't be so sure there isn't any evidence at our camp," Pol said. In his mind he was following the investigative pattern that Val had so vividly set in his mind.

They rode back and surveyed the damage.

"Let me look at the damage by myself," Pol said.

"You really think you can find something?" Paki said, the disbelief plain in his voice.

"I won't know until I look for evidence. Val and I found that South Salvan Lion, remember?"

Paki nodded. "Oh. You did."

Kolli looked at Paki. "What?"

"I'll tell you all about it while Pol looks at our tents."

Pol hoped he knew what he was doing. He squatted over the ground and looked at footprints and hoof prints. He carried a charcoal and a wrinkled sheet of paper and began to write notes about what he observed. Pol looked at the armor and noted how it was destroyed and then examined the shredded tent that he shared with Paki.

Then he walked over to the pair of them. "I have a list. There were five men, all mounted. That means they weren't foot soldiers, doesn't it?" Pol looked at Kolli.

"It does. Go on," she said.

He showed them a sketch of two horses hooves. "This one has lost a shoe. So we look for a shoe put on this morning or it may still be off the horse." Pol pointed to another. "This horse has a cracked hoof. I think that they get patched with a metal plate and screws? I can't quite remember. So at least a hoof with a crack right here." Pol pointed to the hoof. "I can show you the prints. All of the men had sharp swords."

He brought over the remains of the tent. "See the slashes? They start from the top. None of the men dismounted while they cut the tents to ribbons. That means mounted soldiers."

"Knights, officers, and squires," Kolli said. "Scouts generally carry shorter swords, and I can't imagine them leaning over far enough to make a cut down so low. Few in the infantry carry sharp swords. Their weapons are more like the practice swords you used to train with for the tourney. So we have an idea of who our enemy is."

Pol liked to hear her say 'our enemy'. "Do soldiers wear different boots?"

"More evidence?" Paki said. "Where did you learn to do this?"

"From Val," Pol said. He didn't mention the pattern discipline that Val and Malden had taught him.

Pol looked at Kolli. "Taller heels?" Pol lifted up his leg to show them the bottom of his riding boots. "Like this? Now look at Paki's shoes."

Paki's boots had a much lower, flatter heel. "That is what the infantry walked on, am I right? Unfortunately I didn't see any boot patterns much different than mine. They were all about the same size."

"You've done enough. The hooves are the best lead. I'm afraid your evidence isn't going to be enough for General Wellgill," Kolli said.

"We've already eaten, so we should pick this mess up and head over to the officer's horse line and start looking at hooves," Pol said.

They quickly found the patched hoof. As Pol had described, there was a metal plate screwed to the hoof, and the crack was in the right place.

A soldier wearing a farrier's badge brought two horses to the line.

"Did these just get re-shod?" Kolli asked.

The young man nodded. "One had a loose shoe and the other threw hers."

"Who do these horses belong to?" she said.

"This one is Sir Gilbott's, and this is Sir Northbell's."

Sir Northbell rode the horse that threw a shoe.

Paki walked up. "You should check the shoe of this horse, too." Paki pointed to the horse with the patched hoof.

The farrier shook his head. "This poor horse shouldn't be on an expedition with a patched hoof," he said, "but Earl Caster..." The soldier leaned over. "This seems okay to me."

"Maybe I looked at it wrong," Paki said.

"Could you look at our horses' hooves? That's why we came over here," Kolli said. "The Prince is riding with the officers today, and we don't want any mishaps."

"Prince?"

"I am Prince Poldon," Pol said, bringing over his horse.

"You don't dress like the other officers, My Prince," the soldier said. He looked at their hooves and pronounced them sound.

"I'm here to observe, not to fight," Pol said. "Thank you for your assistance." He gave the soldier a short bow, making the man color a bit.

"Anything you need, My Prince." The soldier bowed more deeply and quickly left.

"Northbell and Caster," Kolli said. "Bootlickers, both."

"Along with three others," Pol said.

Kolli nodded. "We will have to stay observant. If it were up to me, I would head back to Borstall immediately, My Prince."

"It's not up to you," Pol said. For the briefest of moments, Pol wished Val were with him to keep a cold, cruel eye on the two officers. "We will have to be vigilant. Do you know who might be friends with the knight and the earl?"

"Oh," Kolli said, "you are smarter than I am."

"You know more than I do," Pol said. "I'm just applying what little I learned from Val."

"Valiso is a lot smarter than me," Kolli said. "I wish he were here."

The next few days were long and hard, but Pol took the opportunity to expand the flexibility of his patterning by riding next to different officers and talking to them. He had the opportunity to converse with Sir Northbell and Earl Caster. Both men had seemed uneasy, but then how often had they ever talked to a fourteen-year-old prince, no matter how precocious?

Sir Northbell struck Pol as a man of plodding intellect, but an experienced fighter. The earl reminded Pol of Grostin. The man was suspicious of Pol and he never volunteered the boastful stories that Northbell had. In talking to the other men, Pol had six others who he thought might be candidates.

He didn't tell Kolli of his suspicions since he knew he didn't have the breadth of experience in talking to these men and had no idea how to evaluate their interactions with the other men in the officer train.

At the end of the fifth day from Borstall, a scout galloped into camp, his horse lathered from a hard ride.

Pol managed to be in the proximity of the General's tent when the man rode in. He entered the tent as the scout delivered his message.

"Five hundred men have crossed the border and have begun to fire villages. Baron Forest has driven them back, but more men are assembling."

The General rolled out a large detailed map of the border as officers filled up the tent. "Where?"

"Here and here, General, sir." The scout pointed to a spot northeast of where they were currently heading.

"Then we will split our forces. Earl Caster, take your command straight north to the garrison. I will move the remainder with this scout." The General eyed Pol. "Prince Poldon, you will go with the Earl."

The thought of traveling under the command of a man who might have tried to kill him, nearly brought Pol to his knees with fear.

"I'd rather go with you, General Wellgill. There is danger all along the border. I'd feel safer with the largest force."

Pol could tell that his request had no effect on the General's decision.

The General appeared to get angry. "You will do as I say. Is that understood?"

It looked like Pol had no alternative, so he pursed his lips and didn't say another word. Now he would have to rely on Kolli to survive. Pol looked over at the Earl, who gave Pol a smirk. That smirk fit the pattern that Pol had constructed about those who attacked their camp.

"Those are your orders. Prepare your soldiers to leave at first light," the General said. "Prince, you stay behind. I'll have some more words with you."

Pol endured the stares from the officers as they filed out of the tent. The Earl continued his smirk as he walked past.

Wellgill sat down and offered a seat to Pol.

"I noticed the Earl's face when I put you in his company. What is there between the two of you?"

The General surprised Pol by his expression of concern.

"Five mounted men cut up our tents and trampled on our armor when we spent the night at the local inn. We showed you the evidence of their malice. One of them was Earl Caster. Sir Northbell was another."

"If you were gone, how did you know they did it, and why didn't you report it to me?"

Pol considered not answering, but he needed the General's help. "I didn't think you would believe me. Our evidence is not strong." He described what he had found at the site and how he had found the owners of the two horses.

The General leaned back in his camp chair. Pol looked around at the tent and noticed that the man lived no better than common soldiers, taking into consideration that he needed more space in his command tent. He saw the cot with a single blanket neatly folded at its foot. The General did have the comfort of a pillow.

"You aren't asking me to arrest the Earl, then, are you?"

Pol shook his head. "I know I don't have enough evidence to bring against Earl Caster, but I don't want to travel with him."

Wellgill put a hand to his chin to fondle the chin beard that the General affected. "Very well. When we leave tomorrow morning, you can travel with us. Put yourselves back among the supply wagons." The General raised his hand to stop any objection. "I want you there for protection, not to make you uncomfortable. There will be fewer soldiers in the column, anyway. I'll send a messenger to Caster once we are underway. I'm sorry I was so short with you, My Prince. I had thought you were challenging my command."

Pol didn't know how to respond to the compliment other than to say 'thank you' and left the command tent. By the time he found Paki and Kolli, Pol was exhausted.

"We leave tomorrow," he said, and then he relayed the contents of the short meeting and his conversation with General Wellgill.

"We are still in danger," Kolli said.

"I meant it when I said we were in danger no matter which part of the army we joined. But at least one of the attackers, and I would guess most if not all, will be in Earl Caster's command. Doesn't that sound right, Kolli?"

"My faith in the General has just been restored," she said. "But I don't like to depend solely on others for my survival. I agree we are less exposed in the middle of the supply train, but that doesn't mean we can let up on our vigilance."

Paki looked very concerned. "Why don't we just turn around and return to Borstall? We can't be expected to fight enemies inside and outside the army."

"You are just here to observe," Kolli said. "Neither of you have a chance against any of the officers who slashed our tents, and it's my job to keep you out of any battles."

"So we should stay with the wagons?" Pol said.

"From here on out. I'm sure you'll trade safely eating a bit of dust to being in the vanguard with the officers when the Taridans attack."

Both boys nodded.

"Make sure you're wearing your armor, especially your chest protection," Kolli said.

~ ~ ~

Chapter Twenty-Nine

~

POL WOKE TO CHAOS AS THE ARMY SPLIT INTO TWO. He scrambled out of the tent he shared with Paki after shaking his friend awake.

"Hurry," Pol said. "We can't be left behind."

"No one's going to leave us behind," Paki said. "We're in the back, remember?"

"Well, you go hungry then," Pol said.

That was enough to get Paki into motion. The two boys quickly donned their armor and broke down their tent. Pol noticed that Kolli sat on a log, watching them work as she sipped from a waterskin. She gave them a little wave.

"I've already pulled your horses from the line." She pointed to the three horses tied up on a bush. "Hurry and eat. I want to check out your armor."

Pol and Paki hustled to the end of the meal line. Breakfast consisted of a mush that was cold by the time the boys got theirs. They wolfed it down anyway as they walked over to Kolli.

"Take off your armor," Kolli said. She got up and gave them both hard leather vests. "These go underneath your chests. Your armor is so beaten up that no one will notice the difference."

"But I'm going to get awfully hot," Paki said.

"Better that than getting awfully dead," Pol said as he thanked Kolli for his vest. "You've got one on, too?"

She nodded. "I might be the one an attacker might go after first."

"Where did you get these?" Pol asked.

"Val suggested that I bring them along to wear when we drew nearer to the border. I agreed with him. I wish there were three or four of me to protect you, My Prince."

"I'm here," Paki said.

"You certainly are," Kolli said, laughing. Her laugh carried genuine amusement, whereas Val's laughter always had an edge, Pol thought.

For the first half of the day, Pol rode next to Kolli, while Paki stayed behind a length or so at Pol's request.

"I have a question for you, if you are willing to answer," Pol said. He described the night he saw Grostin enter his mother's suites. "Why did you let my brother in to see my mother?"

"That has been bothering you all along, hasn't it, My Prince?" Kolli said. "Valiso told me you listened in that night."

Pol nodded. "I'm, uh, disappointed that my mother would align herself with my siblings against me. Why has she?"

Kolli laughed. "Do you think I'm her confidant? I follow her orders, just as I now follow yours. Your mother is experienced in the noble game and must work with what she finds to secure her position. It's no secret that you are ailing and under attack from your brothers and sisters."

"Amonna isn't attacking me."

Kolli gave Pol a look that chilled him to the core. "Don't be so sure that will always be the case. Would your mother act differently if you were a healthy prince? I think she would. If you think she is one with your siblings, think again. Molissa is as exposed as you are, except she is King Colvin's wife, and that provides her with a bit, only a bit, of protection."

Pol sat back in the saddle and gritted his teeth. He tried to expand the pattern of his family and put more perspective into the model of the pattern in his mind. What he came up with scared him. He still thought too much from his own point of view, and he knew that kept him from getting a good grasp of his own situation. He had never tried to establish what his mother might be facing, and now that made it even more important for him to get more perspective.

The disappointment that he felt continued to bother him, but now with the information that Kolli had just given him, he felt bad for his mother. He recognized that he often thought of his own survival without regarding hers. Would she be disappointed in him? He didn't think so. He vowed to have another conversation with his mother when he returned to the castle.

"Thank you for your frank answer," Pol said. "It has helped me."

Kolli smiled at him, but he could see a touch of sorrow. "Don't dwell on castle politics while you are out here. You are remarkably observant, so turn that skill to our present situation."

The compliment surprised Pol, and he really appreciated her words, because as far as he could tell, she meant it.

The long column finally halted mid-afternoon for a break and to give the soldiers a chance to drill before entering into battle, which Kolli had heard they would encounter the next morning. Kolli, Paki, and Pol practiced in a little clearing out of sight of the soldiers.

Kolli pulled a package out of her saddlebag and tossed it to Pol. "Something from Valiso Gasibli and Kelso Beastwell."

Pol untied the string and unrolled a set of ten throwing knives, each one having a thin sheath. A little note popped out.

"What does it say?" Paki said.

Pol read it first. "A little extra protection. Don't hesitate to use them," he said to Paki.

"I also have a set for you, Paki." She tossed a smaller bundle to Paki. "Valiso said that you haven't mastered the throw since you've been injured."

Paki unrolled his and looked for a note, showing a bit of disappointment on his face. "No note?"

"Be happy you got those."

Pol looked at Kolli. "Do you have any of these on you?"

"A girl has to keep her secrets, My Prince," Kolli said with a smirk on her face. "I can give you some idea where to put these. They are easy enough to hide."

Pol pulled one out. He noted the style of the knife. The knife was flat. The hilt fit his palm. The leaf-shaped blade was sharpened on both sides. He stood and threw it into the center of the bole of a nearby tree.

"You're accurate enough," Kolli said, getting up to inspect his throw, "but make sure you aim for flesh. You don't throw hard enough to get through metal, and against leather, it won't penetrate deeply."

Pol nodded. "That's what Val said."

Paki threw his knives at another tree. He missed the trunk with one of the knives and had some difficulty removing the blades. "I don't have the same kind of problem."

"You certainly don't," Pol said, laughing.

Pol could feel the tension in their air when he woke up. It seemed that half of the camp was already awake. He walked through the soldiers sharpening their weapons or writing final letters that would go into bags that one of the wagons would carry, to be sent if they died.

He shared in their nervousness. Kolli had told him that in the fury of war, strange things happened. Pol's grandfather had died in a flurry of arrows from an unexpected direction. Pol wondered if the arrows were from Taridans or North Salvan archers. Pol and Paki checked each other's armor and re-cinched their saddles.

Pol heard riders approaching him, and he turned to look up at General Wellgill and his staff.

"Stay among the wagons, My Prince. It is not unknown for the enemy to attack the supply wagons; however, we are close to a town and a few villages, so their loss won't be critical to us. I doubt if you will be attacked, but be prepared." The General took a long look at Kolli and nodded to her. "Take good care of your charges," he said before turning and riding back to the head of the column.

"Mount up," Kolli said.

Pol wondered what the woman thought about playing nursemaid to two boys going into an actual battle. He closed his eyes and thought about patterns, and ended up concentrating on what kind of patterns would be a threat. He couldn't predict what the Taridans would do, but he could picture what Earl Caster might attempt.

He wished he knew what the battlefield ahead looked like. Pol hadn't attended General Wellgill's last meeting the previous night since his participation was limited to staying with the wagons. He mounted and moved his horse next to Kolli's.

"We should be looking in all directions," he said to Kolli, who nodded. "I can concentrate to the right. You can look towards the left, and Paki can look behind. Does that sound right?"

Kolli gave him the ghost of a smile. "That works for me."

That wouldn't hurt, since Pol felt an attack would likely come from a flanking position. He intended to use his magic to locate anyone lurking on either side.

The column began to move forward, and soon Pol could see smoke up ahead above the trees. He hoped that the North Salvan units would still be functional by the time they arrived to close with the enemy. He had no idea what kind of information the General had received from his scouts.

The road widened, and Kolli positioned them within four wagons driven in a diamond configuration, one in front, one in back and two on either side. Pol felt hemmed in, but there were openings between the wagons to exit if he needed to. He looked at Paki and nodded nervously. His friend looked as frightened as Pol felt.

Why did his father insist on his going north? He had no function other than to be an impediment to the General, but then Wellgill had pretty much ignored him.

A woman rider rode to the rear alongside the soldiers, and as she passed the pace increased. She arrived at the wagons.

"Fighting up ahead. The forces we are to join are under duress, but mostly intact. We are to move forward with speed." She passed the message to the very last wagon and turned to ride into the woods on the left.

Pol asked Kolli, "Do you know her?"

"I do. If I hadn't been called to the castle it might have been me passing on the message. Now she'll be ranging through the woods on that side, looking for the enemy."

"That won't help us if the Earl's men are waiting for us."

She nodded. "It won't." Kolli turned her horse around and rode alongside the last wagon and pulled out two small shields. She had them ride out of their protection and stopped on the side of the column.

"Another surprise gift. This is from your Mistress Farthia. She didn't want you burdened with them until you were in battle. The straps are adjustable so you can carry a shield with your arm or wear it on your back."

Pol took the thing from Kolli and could feel the weight of it on his arm. "I can't hold this up for long."

"Then back it is. Wear it like a backpack." She adjusted the straps and helped Pol put it on. The shield was short enough to just clear the saddle.

Paki took his and threaded his arm through the strapping inside. "I'm good with it this way. Where is yours?" he asked Kolli.

"Don't worry about me. I've got extra armor on, just like you. Any more, and I won't be able to fight."

Pol felt like a turtle with the shield on his back, but he lacked the strength to fight for long from his horse. He worked his arms and found the shield didn't restrict his throwing arm very much.

They caught up to the wagons and resumed riding within their diamond of rolling protection. The soldiers had begun to pull away, but the wagons only increased their speed just a bit. Kolli pulled out her sword and Paki did the same. Pol made sure to locate the easiest throwing knife that he had, one of the two at the top of his right boot.

As they continued, Pol heard the roar of battle in front of him. The wagon drivers had taken out swords or strung bows that they made readily accessible. Pol began to monitor the woods on his side. He closed his eyes trying to figure out the pattern of the trees and began to focus on the trunks. He opened his eyes, still able to sense the trunks. He didn't notice anyone within his range, which being in the center of the path of the army, didn't extend too far into the woods.

The sounds of battle became louder, and the front wagon called a halt. Kolli told them the wagons wouldn't advance until commanded. Pol could feel tension building inside. His palms began to dampen, and he felt exposed sitting on his horse beside Kolli and Paki.

He looked around at the anxious faces of the drivers and the cooks and quartermasters who rode alongside. A few nervously held their weapons, while others paced alongside their wagons.

"What do we do?" Paki said.

"Point your shield towards the woods and try to be as patient as you can. I'm as nervous as you. I've never had to wait like this before," she said. "It's easier to ride through the woods than it is to sit exposed."

Pol could see a look of frustration, not fear, on her face. He concentrated on the woods again, and four spots of color appeared within range on Kolli's side. Pol couldn't detect anything on the right.

"Possible invaders on the left," he said. Now he wished he didn't wear a shield on his back as his focus turned past Kolli to the woods.

"Movement," one of the men on the wagon said.

"They are ours," another driver said.

"Be prepared," Kolli said.

Just then Pol sensed faster moving dots in his mind on his right. "Invaders on the right! They are closing quickly."

Pol kept his back to the right, using his shield to protect Kolli as well as himself. He heard a thunk at the same time that something pushed him forward. He was sure an arrow had struck his shield. Another whizzed past his helmet.

"We're under attack!" Kolli said.

"No, we're not," a driver said. That's our men." He gagged as an arrow caught him in the throat, throwing him from the wagon.

"Down, all of you!" Kolli said. "They are after Prince Poldon." An arrow clipped her arm, but it didn't penetrate. "Off your horses," she said.

Pol frantically tried to locate the invaders in the woods, but fear had gripped him, and his ability to locate anything faded as his anxiety grew. Another arrow buried itself in the side of his shield. He could feel a splinter strike his neck.

He drew his sword as nine men emerged from the woods. The four men on the left were unmounted, but the faster moving dots proved to be mounted men. Pol recognized Sir Northbell.

Pol pulled out a throwing knife, and as the knight began to close on the wagon, he threw the knife into his neck. The knife buried itself underneath the knight's chin. Sir Northbell gurgled, clutching his neck, and fell off his horse.

Pol drew another knife and found the neck of one of the soldiers on the left, running through the opening made by the first wagon. He didn't have time to check on his friends as he kept drawing knives and accurately threw the first four.

His breathing began to labor, and he began to hear his heart in his ears again. Pol could sense himself losing strength. He turned to see a soldier raise his sword to strike Paki. Pol quickly found the pattern and tweaked. The soldier jerked backwards and up, as if a giant hand had grabbed him by the scruff of the neck and tossed him towards the wood.

Pol felt himself begin to black out. He had a knife in his hand and threw it feebly at an attacker. Through hazy vision he saw that he had distracted the man enough for Kolli to run him through. Pol lost all strength and dropped to the ground. He struggled to roll off his back, impeded by the shield and scuttled underneath a wagon, where he struggled to stay conscious amidst the battle.

A new fighter entered the fray, and the attacking soldiers began to thin. He vaguely heard the cheers of the drivers as the battle ended.

Pol shook his head as he was dragged by the feet inside of the diamond. Someone had led the horses out, but one seemed to have been killed. He tried to focus on the bodies, hoping that Paki and Kolli weren't among the dead.

The spout of a wineskin was thrust in his mouth, and Pol fought to clear his vision. His gasping had begun to slow, and his heart finally stopped filling his head with sound of pumping. He closed his eyes to concentrate on calming down.

"Are you all right?"

Where had Pol heard that voice before? His mind began to clear. Valiso!

He blinked his eyes open. "I am very, very tired, but you should be at the castle."

"Do you want me to return?" his former bodyguard said.

"No. We won, didn't we?"

"I'm sorry I was a little late. I was unavoidably detained by fighting more of these soldiers before they reached you. It looks like I arrived in time to keep them from accomplishing their mission."

Pol struggled to stand. "Sir Northbell?"

"Dead," Kolli said. A driver was winding a bandage on her upper arm. She had blood running down her face, but her voice seemed normal.

"Paki?"

He heard his friend's voice from the other side of the wagon. Pol knelt down and looked underneath. Another person was bandaging his leg. "I took an arrow in my leg. It didn't go deep since it bounced off of my shield. Don't look at me like that. You're bleeding, too."

Pol put his hand to his neck and felt the stickiness of blood. "A splinter from my shield. Help me get this off."

Val pulled Pol to his feet and loosened the straps. Three arrows had struck his shield from the back. Only the stubs remained. The one that hit the side still stuck out. "Mistress Farthia saved my life," he said, more to himself than to anyone.

"All of you were lucky. After the shock, the soldiers on the wagons fought, once they realized that they were targets of their own people. Two of them died," Kolli said. "Just rest a bit."

Pol sat back down and leaned against a wheel. "When will this end?" he said.

"Probably never," Val said. "Malden and I thought it would be better for me to track you rather than ride with you. I'm glad I did. You detected the attackers soon enough not to be overwhelmed."

"We were overwhelmed, anyway," Kolli said. "Or didn't you notice?" She kicked the leg of her dead horse after she got up and walked outside inspecting the damage. She shortly returned and presented Pol with six knives. "You were accurate with five," she said.

"I don't know if I was even conscious with one of them. I lost my energy."

"Not before saving me from a deep, deep cut," Kolli said.

Pol sat for a bit, and then Val helped him up and assisted him as he walked around the wagons, inspecting the carnage. "I counted nine." Pol said, looking down at six bodies. One of the attackers was still alive after being slammed into the trees by the force of Pol's magic. No one mentioned his act, and Pol didn't bring it up. "Two got away?"

Val nodded. "Two of the mounted men. All those on foot were killed except for the one that we found at the tree line. The three dead mounted men were all part of Earl Caster's officer corps. I can't see how General Wellgill can ignore this."

"Grostin won't be caught," Pol said. He felt hollow inside for he knew that his brother would not face the justice he deserved. Three nobles had died this time. Two, it appeared, by Pol's knives. All he remembered was throwing his knives at exposed flesh. His mind cleared a bit. "What of the battle?"

Val looked down the road. "It's over. I'm pretty sure the General prevailed. Perhaps you'd like to visit him?"

Pol put a hand on his hip and another on his forehead. "I just don't have the energy."

~ ~ ~

Chapter Thirty

A FTER PERSUADING GENERAL WELLGILL that Pol had seen the campaign closely enough, Val and Kolli took Pol and Paki back to Borstall. Kolli hired a wagon to transport Paki, whose leg wound didn't allow him to ride a horse very well.

At least they were able to stay at inns every night on their way back to the castle. Pol had another nice scab on his neck to show his mother. Kolli felt best with her arm immobile, and Paki's leg had improved to the point that he was able to ride the last day. His friend boasted about his prowess in battle, but Kolli had said that Paki had gone down with the arrow in his thigh shortly after Pol had blown the soldier away with his magic and had spent the rest of the battle poking at the feet of the attackers.

Val hadn't taken Pol aside to ask him about his magic, so he thought that Val didn't know he used magic and he felt ashamed that the act had incapacitated him, just like every other time when he tried to do too much.

Pol looked upon Borstall Castle with trepidation. If Grostin had so aggressively tried to assassinate Pol in the North, then what would stay his hand when Pol was so close?

"You don't look very happy to return to Borstall," Kolli said.

Pol couldn't help but sigh. "I'm afraid I'll only be fighting off another assassination attempt. Perhaps I should just give up and let them kill me." Pol really didn't feel that way, but he wanted a bit of sympathy, and Kolli would be more likely to give him some than Val.

"You can always go on the offensive," she said.

"No, he can't," Val said from behind them. Had he been enhancing his hearing? "King Colvin tolerates the siblings' misbehavior, but he looks at Pol as a temporary fixture, and if Pol strikes back too hard, he'll have Pol quietly put away."

"He wouldn't!" Kolli said.

Val nodded with his eyebrows raised. "Think about what has happened so far. Did the General execute Earl Caster? No, he took away his command, but the Earl still lives for leading an assassination attempt against a member of the royal family. Events are stacked against Prince Poldon."

"What if I abdicated my rights to either throne?" Pol said. "Then my siblings wouldn't have any reason to attack me."

"Talk to Malden about that," Val said. "I've already said too much." He didn't respond to any more of Pol's questions on the subject all the way to the castle gate.

Pol said goodbye to Paki at the stables, and both Kolli and Val helped carry his armor to the classroom where Pol had learned all about knives. He had regained his strength, so he felt that he could carry the rest of his things to his rooms, but the pair of bodyguards insisted on helping.

Malden stood at Pol's window when he opened the door.

"Ah, again the hero has added more accomplishments to his ever-growing list," the magician said with a twinkle in his eyes. He turned to Kolli. "Thank you for your efforts. There will be suitable compensation for your trouble. I think the Queen is waiting for you."

Kolli actually curtseyed wearing trousers and smiled at Pol before she turned and left Pol with his two mentors.

"General Wellgill sent a bird with the bare minimum of information. I'd appreciate a full report, Val. Feel free to chime in, Pol."

Val surprised Pol by describing the destruction of their camp the night Kolli, Paki, and Pol stayed at an inn.

"I didn't know you were watching us so early."

Val snorted. "And a good thing. The timing wasn't right to let my presence known, then."

"It wasn't right when you did come to save us," Pol said.

"I'll continue, if you permit, My Prince," Val said a bit too dismissively for Pol's taste.

Val didn't know about Pol's magical blast, but he did surmise that Pol had used magic to detect locations. Most everything else was thorough enough.

"There is one other thing," Pol said. "I used magic to save Paki."

"That makes sense," Val said. "I suspected as much, but you kept it a secret."

Pol's face colored. "It incapacitated me," he said. "I couldn't let my friend die."

"And you did the right thing," Malden said. "Val was closing in by that time, right?"

Val nodded. "I arrived just after," the man grinned, "but I would have liked to have seen it. The soldier suffered enough injuries to put him out of the fight, but he was sufficiently alive to tell General Wellgill all about Earl Caster's plot."

"All the Earl received was a demotion," Pol said. "It isn't fair. I want permission to attack Grostin with Val."

Malden glared at Pol, but softened his look, still standing by the window. "I keep forgetting you're not quite fifteen. Your life will end if you try to assassinate any of your siblings. Val and I have gone through such scenarios, and knowing Colvin as I do, he would take your life, and maybe your mother's too."

"My mother?"

"Guilt by association. It happens often enough in the Empire," Malden said.

"Can't the Emperor stop it?" Pol looked from Malden to Val.

Both of them shook their heads. "No," Malden said. "He won't go that far. It's a light touch that has kept the Empire intact for all of these hundreds of years."

"What about if I abdicate? Won't that save Mother and me?"

Malden looked out the window and took a seat. "Probably not. In North Salvan, the king can reinstate an abdication at any time. It's the law, and Colvin wouldn't think of breaking it. That means you will remain a threat."

"What if Father disinherited me?"

"What?" Val said.

"A disinheritance is different from an abdication. I read all about it before we left. Since it is the king doing the disinheriting, it isn't something he can just change on his own. That's in the law, too."

Malden rubbed his chin. "It is. But if you're disinherited, you won't be a prince any longer. You won't live in the castle or have any of its advantages. Abdication just means you are taken out of the line of succession."

"And you said abdication isn't good enough. You want me to go to a monastery.. I'd be spending the rest of my life out of the castle anyway. I could be dead in seven years, as it is."

Malden looked confused, but then he understood Pol's comment. "You mean you will die in seven years?"

Pol nodded with a solemn face.

"We've gone over this before. Not if you get decent medical treatment." Malden pulled a paper out from his coat. "By the way, you've been accepted to Tesna. They have competent healers that exceed my capabilities. You won't have to worry about dying."

"But everyone dismisses me because I'll be dead. I'm weaker than everyone anyway. If I do a big tweak, I nearly faint."

"You faint," Val said.

"I'll talk to the king, if you are truly willing to give all this up. You might not get to see your mother again."

That changed things. "Not see Mother? I, I don't know if I can do that."

"Then let's set the option of disinheritance aside for now," Malden said. "Val is back to being your bodyguard."

Pol looked from Malden to Val. "He never left."

~

Pol and Val kept to Pol's rooms except for more practice at throwing different kinds of knives and learning to use his magic to fight in the dark. Dark consisted of a blindfold, but Pol had to hone his magic in order to sense more than just a colored dot, so Paki did not attend these sessions. Paki was far from being able to use magic at any level.

"You have to sense an entire body from four or five paces away," Val said.

Pol knew Val taught him assassination techniques, but Pol rationalized the technique as a way to fend off assassins.

Val had Pol walk through a maze that he had set up. Pol could detect still objects well enough, but visualizing a moving person eluded him when he started. The effort drained him every time, but he recovered well enough in half a day.

He sat drinking some fruit juice after a session when Kolli walked in followed by his mother. Pol immediately stood. He hadn't seen his mother alone since before he had gone north.

Val offered her a seat at the table where Pol sat. He bowed to the Queen and left with Kolli to give them privacy.

"How have you been, my dear prince?"

"Paki has recovered, and it looks like Kolli has, too."

"What about you?" she said.

Pol pointed to the small scar on his neck. "My only wound, a splinter."

"From an arrow striking your shield. Kolli gave me all of the details. I hesitated visiting you until after the shock of your return settled down in the castle. I had confidence that you would come back."

"You planned this with Grostin, didn't you?"

Queen Molissa pursed her lips and played with the cup of fruit juice that Val had given her before he left with Kolli. "We talked about getting you out of the castle by going north, but not the assassination attempt. Please believe me when I say I would never condone such a thing. Kolli also told me of her conversation with you about me."

Pol couldn't help but blush. "I, I—"

She put her index finger over her son's lips. "Don't say a thing. It is fine that you know. I wanted Grostin to think his success was easy and assured. Malden and I talked about what might happen, so he sent Valiso Gasibli, the one-man army." She smiled and took a sip of the cup.

"Has no one told me the truth?" Pol said, getting a little angry with all of the plotting behind his back.

"What would you have done if you had known?"

Pol looked away and thought about her questions. "I would have acted differently."

"And let your adversary know that you expected an attack? Earl Caster would have sent three times more men, but just the three of you lured him. If you were healthier, I think you would have had a good chance of fending them off, even without Gasibli," she said. "As it was, Valiso showed up in time to reduce the attacker's numbers before they even closed with you. His job was to make sure that you survived and prevailed."

"Four arrows hit my shield. Without it, I wouldn't be returning." Pol wondered if she had been told about his magic. He took a deep breath and decided to tell her. "I can do magic." He looked into her eyes for the surprise that was certain to come.

"I know, dearest one," his mother said without surprise. "Another reason why a stronger Pol could have prevailed. As it was, you turned the tide with the skills that Malden and Gasibli have taught you. Your knife throwing and magic killed or incapacitated five of the nine. That was you, Pol, not Val."

Pol opened his mouth to protest, but his mother's finger found its way to Pol's lips.

"Accept what you are, but you must get stronger, and that is why you have to go to a monastery. They can increase your power and, hopefully, extend your life."

"But I need to protect you," Pol said.

"Malden and Kolli are here to do that," she said. "Malden told me of your fears about leaving the castle. Set them aside. King Colvin loves me, and while he does, the children are no threat."

"But they attacked you on the streets of Borstall." Pol obviously feared more for her life than she did.

Molissa shook her head. "They attacked you, Pol. I was never in danger. Grostin quite enjoyed telling me all about what he had planned."

"But what if I hadn't prevailed?" Pol said.

"Then the fates would have spoken differently. However, I believe, quite strongly, that you have a destiny to succeed many times during a long life."

Pol shook his head to straighten out his confusion. His mother had more faith in Pol's ability to survive than he did. "I could have been killed any number of times since spring."

"You weren't. I see my son, Poldon Fairfield, sitting in front of me. You have a few scars to remind you that the dangers have all been real. Don't condition your life to please me or protect me. You will lose strength if it becomes an obsession, blinding you to good, common sense decisions. I am dealing enough with your father's ever-growing mania about Landon sitting on the Listyan throne. He only gets worse, and I think King Astor adds to it."

"But I don't want to lose you," Pol said, thinking about being disinherited.

"You won't lose me. I am always a part of you. That is something a mother passes along to her children."

"And Father?"

"At the present, he doesn't care about you like I do. You understand that, don't you? Colvin's regard for your safety has largely diminished."

Pol finished off his juice and rolled the cup between his hands. "It has diminished to nothing. I understand that, painfully so."

His mother took a deep breath and pulled out a necklace. A large amulet hung from it.

"What is that?"

"Your real legacy," his mother said. "You aren't entirely human, Pol."

"I'm not. I'm a sick human."

"No. You have within you the remnants of a race that arrived on Phairoon from the sky and settled in northern Volia. Your blood has been diluted over the centuries, but—" his mother looked around the room, "your real father is not King Colvin, but a countryman that I met in Listya. He looked so much like you, and he had the whitish hair that you and I share. From the two of us, you probably possess more of your alien ancestors' blood than any in generations."

Pol sat back in his chair, amazed. "Does King Colvin know this?"

Queen Molissa shook her head. "He does not. I was careful to hide the possibility of paternity from him."

"What happened to my real father?"

"Died. He had a heart not much better than yours and I received word that he died in Finster not long before you were born. He told me a bad heart was a defect that the ancients somehow passed on to the human males they bred with." She shrugged her shoulders. "The weakness didn't pass on to me, but you inherited his. The full story is lost. This, however, is made of an unknown material." She dangled the amulet in front of Pol.

He looked at the silvery object. It looked more like a star than anything else.

"Are you going to give this to me?"

She put it in his palm and closed his fingers around it. The metal felt cold to the touch and didn't seem to warm up while he held it. "He gave this to me and said he would take it when his health recovered to go to north Volia to find where our ancient ancestors lived and thrived. He never made it."

"And I might not either," Pol said.

His mother leaned over and held the hand that clutched the amulet.

"I knew nothing other than I had unique ancestors. Cissert, your father, had studied the amulet." She shrugged. "That's all I know. Your father had magical talent, too, but kept it secret from the Emperor. He was unschooled, but had taught himself something of the patterns and performed little tricks for me."

"That's what attracted him to me when I was a teenage princess in Listya." She sighed with the memory. "I love the King, though," she said. "Don't forget that."

"I won't," Pol said, more confused by her words than comforted by them.

She rose. "This is a secret between you and me. Don't ever tell anyone, and that includes Malden or Val."

Pol nodded. "I won't."

~ ~ ~

Chapter Thirty-One

~

CISSERT. WHAT KIND OF A NAME WAS THAT? Pol thought a few days later as he perused the texts in his classroom waiting for Mistress Farthia to appear. He found a similar last name of a historical ruler of a country in Volia, but Pol figured he'd have to travel to that continent to ever find out.

He couldn't help but sigh. Such a trek would probably never happen. Pol knew that, despite all reassurances, that he expected to live only six or seven more years, and then he would die, just like his real father. The notion depressed him.

So King Colvin wasn't his real father, and if the King knew, then no wonder he let his own children go unpunished. He realized that no matter who his father was, Pol was still a prince just by being born to his mother, the Queen. Farthia had thoroughly taught him the rules of succession. He wondered what would have drawn his mother to another man? The answer exceeded his ability to answer. There were some things that were too far beyond the grasp of a fourteen-year-old, and that was one of them.

Pol pulled out the amulet. The metal looked different than any he had seen. It was bright and hard, but it had a different finish. It looked like a cross between silver and steel. The necklace was made of the same material, and Pol had never seen such intricate links. Even the device on the amulet was strange.

The door opened, and Pol quickly jammed the amulet in his pocket just before Mistress Farthia entered and opened the book on religions that sat before him.

"What have you been doing?" she said. "Your face looks like you've been caught doing something you shouldn't."

Pol looked away from his tutor. "I, uh, just opened the book when you entered the room. Do I really have to read the whole thing?"

She narrowed her eyes and put fists on her hips. "How far have you gone?"

Pol looked down to find the bookmark. "I'm most of the way through." He used the bookmark to go to the last page he had read.

"You've been taking notes?"

He nodded and went to a bookshelf and pulled out a thick portfolio filled with his scribbles, including the doodles he made when the book got too boring. He really didn't want Farthia to look at the latest notes.

"Then finish up with the rest of the religions in the Empire, and you are done," Farthia said. "I don't have anything more for you today, other than to see your smiling face, although it wasn't smiling when I walked in." She looked at Pol with an expression that concerned him. There were too many thoughts behind that expression in his opinion. "Val is waiting outside."

Pol slammed the book shut and gave Farthia a little bow before he quickly made it through the door.

"Why are you in a hurry?" Val said.

"Mistress Farthia caught me daydreaming. I guess I looked guilty."

The bodyguard nodded. "You generally look guilty of something. Paki doesn't ever look like he's guilty, and he generally is, of something or other. Are you up for a field trip?"

"I thought I wasn't to leave the castle."

"We'll take a couple of guards with us. I made sure they were good cooks," Val said, the characteristic smirk returning to his face. "I even had a volunteer, a guard that you saved. Name's Darrol Netherfield. I've met Darrol before."

Pol vaguely remembered the guard when he met him right after the attack on his mother. No, Pol corrected in his mind, the attack on him.

"When are we leaving?"

Val nodded. "I suppose that means you agree. Right after the midday meal. You have enough time to gather some clothes. Not court clothes.

Consider it a testing of what you've learned so far."

Pol grinned. He liked this kind of test. "I suppose you don't want me to tell anyone."

"Not a good idea. The guards think they are escorting one of the Queen's ladies-in-waiting to her home village," Val said. "I would expect word to get to Grostin, but we will also be covering our tracks. Still, it's always good to be prepared for anything."

At this point, Pol expected attacks at any time. He might as well have some fun waiting for the inevitable. He wouldn't mind some time sitting in a saddle, thinking about what his mother had told him.

Leaves on some of the trees had begun to turn, as summer seemed to have lost a bit of its power. Pol looked out at the ripe fields and orchards and wondered what his fifteenth birthday would be like. His life in the castle had never been fully comfortable, and now Pol felt like he was constantly under siege.

He still entertained thoughts of petitioning King Colvin for disinheritance. He'd have to give up his rights to the Listyan throne, as well as North Salvan. With his limited life span, he wouldn't be allowed to rule no matter what happened, and no matter what his mother said, Pol thought the pressure would be off both of them.

Pol looked ahead and saw Val reach up and grab an apple from a tree just off the side of the road. Paki tried to do the same, but lacked the reach.

"You want one, My Prince?" Darrol Netherfield said, as he rode just behind Pol.

"I would. Get one for yourself."

"My pleasure." Darrol stopped his horse, but Pol walked his on. "Here," Darrol said, offering a big apple to Pol.

"Many thanks," Pol said as he wiped the apple on his dark linen jerkin. He bit into it. Nice and sweet. Pol smiled and savored the moment. He thought back to what Val had said about living day to day. In a sense, that was what this trip was about for him. He wouldn't worry about his future in the castle and would try to keep the recent darkness in his past from destroying this interlude.

Despite his vow, Pol's mind drifted to his mother's talk. Pol's hand went to the amulet, which he wore underneath his shirt. How could he be from another race? Other than his white-blond hair, he didn't look different from anyone else. His heart condition made him puny and weak, although he had made the effort to minimize his strength disadvantage.

He had fought and defeated enemies, but not by usual means. Was his magical talent a vestige of centuries-gone ancestors? What had his mother said? Cissert and she were both descendants, and that made Pol more alien than anyone born in the world for a long, long time?

Pol looked at his free hand. It looked normal to him. He shook his head. Maybe the amulet was of magical origin, but he couldn't quite accept his mother's words. His discomfort brought a weak laugh out of him.

"My Prince?" Darrol said.

"Nothing, just musing how much I liked the apple," Pol said. He chided himself for making such a simple lie. If he was going to lie, it should be bigger, bolder, and mean something.

Val had stopped his horse, waiting for Pol to catch up.

"Our pleasant interlude is about to stop. We will ride through that field. Follow me closely as that group of riders passes us by," Val said.

Pol looked ahead at a tall stand of corn and then at a group of riders. There must have been ten or more in the group. Pol could barely make out the uniforms of North Salvan. Val had insisted that the guards change into civilian clothes after they had left Borstall.

Pol followed Val. Paki and the two guards trailed behind them as Val led them directly off the path at a trot and then plunged into the cornfield at an angle. "No one will see where we entered the cornfield from the road.

Pol looked back and saw only corn. Just a few strides into the field and it appeared that they were transported to a different place. He had never ridden in an environment like this before. Val went slowly, forging a pathway through the rows. He turned suddenly every so often after looking up into the sky.

They reached the end of the field, and Val headed towards another one. They seemed to be moving northwest of the road. After a string of four cornfields, they emerged onto a different road heading southwest and stopped to rest the horses.

"Is this where you intended to be?" Pol said.

Val nodded. "Use your senses and cast them out behind us."

Following Val's instructions, Pol closed his eyes and opened them without focusing on his surroundings and tried to feel the surface of the earth the way he did during his time with the army. It took a bit of time, but the cornfields appeared in his mind. He couldn't reach out to the other road, but he could sense the disruption in the pattern of the cornfields, tracing their route to where they now rested.

"I can't go out more than three fields."

Val gave Pol a smirk that was a bit more smile-like. "You will. It takes practice and a bit of growing up." He addressed the other three in their group who sat in the shade of an oak tree. "We'll go southwest for another few hours until we reach tonight's destination." Val looked at Pol and told him quietly, "Observe your surroundings. Practice increases your range."

His bodyguard did tell him their excursion was a field trip, not an idle ride through the North Salvan countryside. Once they had mounted after eating, Pol rode right behind Val. If he truly lost focus, his horse would just follow the one ahead. Siggon had taught that to him long ago, saying that fact saved his late friend the considerable embarrassment of veering off the path a few times while Siggon rode in a column of horses.

He saddened at the thought of Siggon and looked sharply at Paki, who hadn't seemed to have changed with the loss of his father not so long ago. Pol shook his head and looked at the horizon, a band of trees stretching across the road. Bandy Wood, he thought, one of the larger forests in North Salvan. The wood ran over a rocky ridge of hills that ran north and south. The ground had proven unsuitable for cultivation, so it was left as woods for the hunters.

He closed his eyes and then opened them with less focus. He picked up multiple patterns overlaid on the land. Being more relaxed than when they had traveled through the cornfields, Pol could detect a few farmers working their land. There were no cornfields, and he discovered that the cornrows had reduced his range. Now he could sense activity in more directions, even as far as the very edges of Bandy Wood up ahead.

Pol felt the heat of the sun on his fair hair and put on the hat he had stuffed in his jerkin when they rode through the cornfields. Back to his focus, he sensed more colored dots. Horses? Dogs? As he sought out more activities, Pol noticed that his sensory range diminished. He wondered how much Val and Malden could sense. Malden was a full magician. His range must be extensive, Pol thought.

Something tickled his senses to his rear. "Riders coming from behind,"

Pol said.

Val nodded. "We'll move more quickly," he said, spurring his horse to a gallop.

Pol's expertise with a horse diminished the faster his mount moved. He fought to control his horse as it jumped ahead to keep up with Val. Suddenly it bolted and sped past Val. Pol had lost control.

He fought with the reins. The horse kept to the road, but Pol could only hold on to keep from being thrown, not having the strength to fight with the reins. His heart began to beat in his ears, and he gasped for breath as his condition sapped what little strength he had.

The horse didn't stop as it entered into the dappled shadows of Bandy Wood but its hooves began to thud on the softer surface of the forest road. Pol wished there was a lake or a river to slow the horse, but through his physical distress, he realized that was a pattern he might employ. He projected a thickening of the air and the horse began to lose speed and suddenly stopped in the middle of the road, just as Pol fell from his seat to the ground below.

Pol woke while his body jerked up and down. Burly arms surrounded him. He blinked his eyes open and turned to look into Darrol Netherfield's face.

"You feeling better, My Prince?" the guard said.

Pol nodded. "How long have I been asleep?"

"It's hard to know with the pace that Gasibli fella has been pushing us. An hour, maybe?"

Pol sat up a bit straighter. His breathing seemed normal, but after his spell, as usual, he had lost all his strength. "We're not on the road."

"We are not. As soon as we caught up to you, Val took us off the road, and we've been threading our way through the trees."

"Is he awake?" Val called back.

Pol noticed that Val led his horse.

"I am," Pol said.

"Good. Let's rest for a bit before we continue on."

Val quickly found a little meadow. Pol now knew that he could find such things and realized that there were more uses to sensing locations than finding one's enemy. Darryl helped set Pol down next to a fallen log.

"You can sit here. I'll go find a stream to water the horses," Darrol said.

GUY ANTIBES | Page 261

He nodded to the other guard, Lirro, and they took all five horses towards a spot that Val pointed out to them.

Pol tried to find the stream, but didn't know how and gave up. Even that effort seemed to drain his energy a bit.

"Now, what did you do to stop your horse? A spell of some kind?" Val said.

Pol couldn't detect any accusation in his voice, so he didn't hide the truth. "I had a breathing attack. I think the horse's bolting made me too nervous. My horse showed no signs of stopping, and I didn't have the strength to fight the reins, so I thought that a lake would slow the horse down. I visualized a pattern of thick air like water, and the horse slowed and then stopped. I think I dropped off the horse as soon as she stopped."

"You keep finding ways to save yourself, but fainting after every spell leaves you utterly defenseless."

Pol looked at Val. "I know, but I'd be injured worse if I fell while my horse was out of control."

Val patted Pol on his head. "Here's your hat. You did the right thing. I didn't stop to think you'd have limitations on our ride. I'm sorry, My Prince. I won't make the mistake again."

His bodyguard's contrition surprised Pol. "Maybe I'll have to ride with someone if we have to gallop. I was fine until we all went too fast."

"We can do that. I keep underestimating the power your siblings have of influencing their father to send out so many men. Kelso specifically told King Colvin that we were on a riding tour. It's not as if you were abducted."

"They are all against me," Pol said reflexively, but he knew it to be true. Even his mother, in her own way, had abandoned him. "We can return to the castle, now."

"Is that an order, or an expression of a possible option?" Val said.

Pol considered his words. "A possible option. Can we be safe anywhere?"

Val nodded. He walked across the meadow to the guards and the horses.

Paki sat down next to Pol. "You used magic again, eh? Saved your life. That horse of yours is a lot faster than the rest. None of us could catch up, not even me," Paki said. Pol was very aware of his friend's boast. Paki was lighter than any of the other riders, with the exception of Pol. Siggon had been teaching Paki riding skills since his friend had learned to walk.

"Had to," Pol said, watching Val stomp across the meadow with something in his hand. "I made the air thick. I guess it worked."

Paki nodded. "It did. The horse just slowed right up and stopped. I could see the very end of it. You just dropped out of the saddle."

"Lucky I didn't land on my head," Pol said smiling. "I'm better now." He got to his feet when Val reached him.

Val spread out a map over the log that Pol had sat against. "We are here. There are five villages in riding distance before sunset." Val looked at the second guard. "Pick one," he said.

The guard rubbed his chin and picked the one that was southeast of where they were.

"Good enough for me. We will spend the night here," Val pointed to a different village closer to Borstall and out of the woods.

"Why didn't you pick the one the guard chose?" Paki said.

"I was just verifying that our pursuers would likely think we would be heading further east. They probably won't think to backtrack. It's not like we are in enemy territory," Val said.

It sure felt like enemy territory to Pol, but he saw Val's point. He just showed how to tweak the pattern without magic. Do the unexpected. He had read about the concept before, but this was the first time he had ever actually seen it in practice out in the open in a real situation.

Val had Pol and Paki climb up the back stairs to their rooms and had promised to send up some food. Pol collapsed on the bed at the inn after removing his boots, totally exhausted. He hadn't told anyone that his energy had been completely tapped out by the time they reached the village.

Paki had gone ahead of Pol, and even he was starting to snore. Pol couldn't go to sleep. His body was out of energy, but his mind kept replaying the events of the last few days in his mind. He knew that his thoughts were muddled, so he tried to focus on one thing. He pulled out the amulet and clutched it in his hand, going over again the conversation with his mother.

He lay on the bed and examined his other hand. It didn't look any different from any other, but if his mother told him the truth, he had otherworldly blood coursing through his veins.

Pol frowned. He didn't have anyone to leave the amulet to. In fact, he considered returning it to his mother since she would probably survive him. He wondered if the amulet had been Cissert's. He would ask his mother when he returned to the castle, whenever that was.

Pol sat up at a knock on the door. He padded over and opened it, revealing Darrol carrying a crude wooden tray with three bowls of food and three tankards.

"Come in," Pol said.

Darrol put the tray on the small table in the room. "Val thought it would be a good idea if I joined you and stayed until the both of you had finished your food and gone to sleep."

"Food?" Paki rolled over, rubbing his eyes. "Food!" He jumped off of the bed and pulled up one of the four rickety stools that surrounded the table.

"I thought sleep was what I needed, but I need something else. Is that ale?"

Darrol chuckled. "Ale for you and me and fruit juice for Pol. It's a bit fermented, My Prince. That's the way they make it in this village."

Pol didn't really want to eat, but after the first two spoonfuls, he discovered that he did have an appetite, after all.

"That was quite a trick with that horse, My Prince," Darrol said after he had nearly finished his bowl."

"Trick?" Pol hadn't mentioned his magic to either Paki or Darrol.

"I knows magic when I see it, I do," Darrol said. "You did something to that horse. Impressive. That was why you fell off. Any dolt knows that."

Pol didn't think that was possible when he started the trip.

"How do you know so much about magic?'

"You're looking at a former Deftnis acolyte," Darrol said. "I didn't stay very long. They want too much book learning, so I only lasted a few years. Learned how to twirl a blade better than most. There's plenty with the talent at Deftnis. I met Valiso there, but he had already moved on. I think he still visits the monastery from time to time."

"He took someone there before the Emperor came to Borstall and returned as my bodyguard."

Darrol wiped the bowl with a scrap of bread that had originally been on top of the bowl. "He's no ordinary bodyguard. More of a teacher and a minder, if you ask me."

Pol looked at the guard. He wasn't the bumpkin that Pol had thought.

"I'm contemplating going to Tesna Monastery. Magician Malden has received a dispensation for me."

"What's the dispensation for, your tender age?"

Pol nodded.

"Deftnis would suit you better. Life is more than playing with the patterns."

"You know about patterns?"

Darrol nodded. "I have a tiny bit of talent, truth be told. Not enough to do much more than light a campfire, but enough to earn me a few lessons at Deftnis.

"Does Val know?"

Darrol took a drink to wash down the last of his bread. "He does. That's one reason he let me come with you."

"What about the other guard?"

"Lirro's a good man. Ordinary, stolid, and loyal to Kelso Beastwell. To a fault, in my opinion, but Valiso can trust him. It's time to tuck you two into bed," Darrol said. He stacked the empty bowls together and waited for Paki and Pol to finish their drinks. "I'll be letting you two go to sleep on your own. Lock the door after me."

"What's Deftnis? I don't know anything about monasteries," Paki said.

"Monasteries are places of learning. Those who do most of the teaching are called monks, and those who are taught are called acolytes. They once had religious significance, but Baccusol monasteries no longer adhere to any set religion."

"So what's Deftnis?"

Pol laughed, since he hadn't actually answered Paki's question. "Deftnis teaches military skills. It also has a group that teaches healing. Battles and healing sort of go hand-in-hand."

"I have first-hand experience with that," Paki said. "There was another you mentioned. Tesna?"

"That one is in South Salvan. It trains magicians."

"So you're headed to Tesna?"

Pol nodded. "That's where Magician Malden would like me to go," Pol said.

"I like Deftnis better. I bet I'd make a better scout going there."

Pol would like Deftnis better, too, he guessed, if he had any level of the stamina an armsman needed. "Tesna is a better choice for me," he said. Pol could feel his eyelids drooping a bit. "I'm going to bed."

Paki jumped up on the bed before Pol. "I'll beat you to sleep"

~~~

Chapter Thirty-Two

~

B ACK ON THE ROAD, Val didn't take them very far. They headed due
south from the village on a road that was barely a farmer's track. He led
them to a clearing in the middle of a thick wood.

"This will do," Val said.

"Lirro, would you return to the village and get supplies?" He handed
Lirro a list.

The guard puzzled over a few of the words, but Darrol helped him
interpret Val's handwriting. He left with a small purse of money.

"Now, let's sit down and talk about your futures," Val said.

Pol dreaded these kinds of talks. He had had them with Kelso, Mistress
Farthia, and Malden before. They only made him depressed since everyone he
talked to would outlive him.

"I talked to them about Deftnis last night, as you requested," Darrol
said.

"Not really." Pol picked up a stick and began tracing designs in the dirt.
"I mean I already know they teach military skills and healing, but I don't
know why, and I don't know why this applies to me." Suddenly he felt sorry
for himself. "Malden has already arranged a spot at Tesna."

Val looked away from Pol and then back. "Tesna isn't the right place for
you. It will end up being more of the same environment that you're struggling
with at the castle. There are politics everywhere, but at Tesna, everyone has
their own agenda."

"I can't fight. You saw me run out of energy on the Taridan border. Military training is wasted on me. I won't live to use it anyway."

"You really are a pathetic human being when you feel sorry for yourself," Val said. His bluntness surprised Pol. "What if you wake up tomorrow and your malady is gone? You'll be stuck without a plan."

No one had talked to Pol quite like that before. It made him angry. "Plan? Why should I plan? You said, yourself, that you live from day to day."

"Don't turn my words against me, lad," Val said, eyes narrowing. "I gave you that advice in context of your past. Your past shouldn't dictate your future." Val waved his hand for emphasis. "I thought you were smarter than that, but I guess that you aren't."

"I'm smart enough," Pol said, feeling very defensive.

"No, you're not. You are letting your past, your trouble with your family, and your lack of health, determine what you are in the future. That is exactly the opposite of my point."

Pol blinked in astonishment at Val's attack. "So?"

"So?" Val mocked Pol. "You need to plan enough ahead so that your actions are not predictable to your enemies."

Pol did see the wisdom in not revealing patterns. "Are my actions predictable?"

Val nodded, and so did Darrol. "We go for a jaunt in the woods and what happens?"

"My enemies attack us."

"Were we attacked?"

Pol was confused. "No, we evaded them."

"Were we attacked?" Val repeated.

"No." Pol didn't understand why Val was pressing him so hard.

"No one was after us," Darrol said. "I know enemies when I see them, and I never saw enemies. All I saw were riders on the same road as us, twice."

Confusion still filled Pol's mind. "Then why did we take all of those evasive actions?" The reason blossomed in Pol's mind. "This is a demonstration."

Val finally smiled. "Ah, the boy finally gets it. I told you it was a test."

Paki still looked as confused as Pol had just felt.

Turning to Paki, Pol said, "This is as real life as Val could make it."

His friend's face finally smoothed with understanding. "Game playing?" He grinned. "Fun."

Pol didn't agree with him. Game playing was not fun when you didn't know you were playing games. He had to agree that he would have reacted differently if Val had just shown them the various techniques that he used to evade the imaginary enemy.

"What have you learned?" Val said.

"I liked the cornfield thing," Paki said.

Pol let Paki continue on for a bit until he ran out of overly enthusiastic things to say. Paki had commented on what they did. Pol thought a bit and felt that Val wanted him to respond to the concepts.

"Early detection of the first set of riders allowed us to cover our tracks in an unexpected way. We didn't have a set destination, so they wouldn't just run ahead of us on the road. Keeping our travel plans flexible and secret let you lead us through the cornfields which provided cover for our flight, as well as a good opportunity to lose them."

Val nodded. "Go on."

"Our travel through the woods was more hasty and only because of your ability to locate a path through the trees did we have the chance of evading the enemy. Your ability to think while improvising gave us the edge against our imagined enemy. We were also careful at the inn, not to show Paki or me, since we are more noticeable that three adult male travelers."

'Is there more?"

Pol shrugged his shoulders, but then he looked at the two men. "You sent Lirro back to the village to get supplies alone. Again, you tweaked the possible pattern of three men traveling together. It's not a matter of just living one day at a time, but living from one moment to the next, looking for any chance to avoid revealing a pattern."

"You do understand, as always. For a while there, I thought you missed my point," Val said. "Mistress Farthia would have given you high marks. Ranno, her father, would have, too."

Pol had a quick thought about possibly dying falling off the runaway horse, but he didn't think Val would look favorably on any whining about what might have happened. Pol had solved that dilemma on his own, anyway.

Darrol looked at Val. "He'll be a waste at Tesna."

"I agree, but it's Magician Malden's call, not mine," Val said. "Darrol and I are going to set up camp. It's up to you two to provide us with some fresh meat. Lirro's list didn't include any."

Paki sighed.

"Siggon taught us how to fend for ourselves. Let's go," Pol said. "There is still enough light to find something."

Four rabbits sizzled over the fire that Darrol had prepared. Pol munched on a piece of bread given him to stave off his hunger until the rabbits finished. He looked over at Paki, doing the same, and wondered how Siggon's son could forget how to make snares. Pol had to do it all with Paki complaining over his shoulder. The complaints turned to compliments after the two boys checked the seven snares they had laid. The forest had to be overrun with rabbits.

Lirro stirred the pot of vegetables and herbs that he had bought in the village where they spent the night. Pol knew it would have been just as easy for the man to purchase meat, but Val obviously wasn't through with their testing.

The camp took on a familiar aspect. Siggon had taken Paki and Pol out a number of times into the Royal Woods on camping trips, the last one during the spring had ended in near-disaster with the poisoning. The next day, Val put them through the same exercises that they had done in the little wood on the castle grounds, but this time, Darrol and Lirro were the targets for finding and the seekers when Paki and Pol hid in the woods.

Lirro had just returned from the village with a few additional supplies when Val told Pol and Paki, "Tomorrow morning we will head back to the castle. We celebrate with fresh supplies,"

Just when Pol had shaken off his anxieties and begun to really enjoy being out in the woods, they were leaving. He knew that they couldn't stay outside the castle forever, but he still felt disappointment when Val made his announcement. A quick look at Paki told Pol that his friend felt the same way.

Lirro cooked two chickens over a spit. He had purchased some seasonings and mixed them with butter to baste the birds. Pol had never eaten such tasty chicken. What made the meal even better was that the older men had treated Pol and Paki like peers, not little boys.

Was this what life was like outside the castle? Pol thought. He knew people worked hard for their living, and plenty of his father's subjects often went hungry, but Pol could just take this night, this trip, and enjoy it for what it was. He enjoyed thinking about the day and not worrying about the past or the future.

He had learned more than he thought he would, and little of it could have been taught in Mistress Farthia's classroom or in Malden's chambers. Pol's eyes drifted to Paki. If Siggon still lived, they would be having an even better time. Pol sighed and put that thought in the back of his head as he concentrated on a story that Lirro had just begun.

Another few hours and Pol would be back in the thick of royal intrigue again, looking over his shoulder and wondering what plans Grostin had in store. Val had them taking little lanes and heading straight across farmlands to avoid the main roads.

"We will assume that there are men posted around the roads leading to the castle, so we will take measures to avoid confrontation," Val said.

Paki grinned at the comment when they first left the road, but his smile had long since disappeared when the grind of having the horses pick their way through the countryside began to get old. Pol's thoughts turned back to the amulet and his hidden heritage.

They traveled through a stretch of trees not far from the road they had taken to leave the castle when Pol sensed a few men ahead. He rode up to Val. "Men ahead, in the wood over there." Pol pointed to the northeast.

Val nodded. "There are more towards the road that leads to Borstall. They are not part of the trip. Shall we move past them or see why they are camping in the middle of this forest?"

"A final test?" Pol said, not knowing if Val was telling him the truth or not.

"Not an intentional one," Val said. He looked back at Lirro and Darrol. "Unknown strangers ahead. We will dismount and investigate. This is not practice, so be prepared for anything."

The two guards nodded. The amiable expressions on their faces had instantly hardened into grimness.

Val had them tie up their horses when they were about one hundred paces from what might be an enemy camp, so that they could quickly mount and flee. Pol could now confirm that there were three people in camp, and far away there might be five or six more in a rough line that probably meant they were positioned along the road. Perhaps they intended to ambush travelers.

"Bandits?" Paki said, grinning. "We can do King Colvin a service."

Val glared at Paki. "We will approach the camp with all seriousness. We don't know who is in the camp or why, but we can't go in expecting a fight, although we need to be prepared."

Pol's friend nodded and looked at the others. Pol put his hand on Paki's shoulder as sign of encouragement.

"Darrol, you go in with Lirro. We three will stay concealed," Val said.

Pol wondered why Darrol wouldn't take Paki or him. That might disrupt the pattern better, but this encounter might not be practice, after all. Val gave Lirro and Darrol a few minutes before he sent Paki to his right and Pol to his left.

"Don't engage with anyone unless Darrol and Lirro need help. They are capable fighters, especially Darrol," Val said.

As long as he doesn't trip, thought Pol.

Pol and Paki nodded and moved as quietly as they could towards the camp. Pol concentrated on locating the three campers and Darrol and Lirro in his mind as he slid through the forest. Even if this were another practice session, Pol would treat it as the real thing.

He continued to move away from the camp at an angle and then would use trees as blocks. Pol stopped and located the barely-noticeable colored dot of Val finally moving. He was about to converge on the campers when he noticed another faint color up ahead of him. The person remained still just outside the camp.

Pol reached within the pattern that he saw and tried to make himself invisible, like Val and this other magician. Val hadn't mentioned him, so he might not have detected the man's presence. Four against three men and two boys might have changed Val's mind, but it was too late now.

He sneaked closer to the faint dot and concentrated, finally seeing his quarry, looking this way and that. Perhaps Pol's concealment spell worked. As Pol worked his way closer, the hidden man had a strung bow in his hand.

He looked closer and realized he might be the peashooter that had presumably left with King Astor. So the man was a magician as well. Pol slid his sword back into its sheath as quietly as he could and drew two throwing knives. He would have to get closer to his quarry to get in range.

Voices broke the silence of the wood. Lirro and Darrol were talking to the three men. Val was out of sight, and Paki seemed to have stood still as well. The archer began to move towards the camp. He looked around him, searching for Pol's location, showing frustration on his face, but he moved closer to the edge of the clearing and nocked an arrow.

Pol couldn't wait any longer and padded towards the man. He cocked his arm to throw the knife and hesitated. He thought of the man breathing, living, and questioning thoughts ran like lightning through his brain. He had felt fear before, but now the taking of the man's life without being threatened had stayed his hand.

The twang of the bowstring jerked Pol from his doubts, and he threw his knife, hitting his target in the side. The man looked at Pol with utter surprise on his face as he struggled to nock another arrow. Pol transferred his second knife to his throwing hand and let the knife fly beneath the outstretched arm of the archer. His knife sunk into the man's chest just below his ribs as an arrow let fly towards Pol.

Pol felt the impact of the arrow slide along his throwing arm, carving a streak of pain. He looked at the bloody sleeve of his shirt, ripped open, relieved that the arrow traveled outside of his arm and not on the inside. The sounds of fighting ceased in the clearing as Pol gasped for breath and his heart began to pound in his ears. He had held off the inevitable attack as long as he could. He sank to his knees and tried to gather himself as quickly as he could. He looked over at his foe and worried that the man wasn't dead.

With his sword in his left hand to assist, Pol knee-walked over to the archer and prodded the body to see if he was dead. The man, lying facedown, didn't move, but Val arrived and gently pushed Pol aside. His bodyguard pulled out a long knife and pushed the archer over. Pol gasped at the glassy eyed stare of surprise.

"He was a magician, like me," Val said. "I didn't notice him, but you did. Good work." He began to quickly search the body and pulled out two purses. One held North Salvan coins and the other South Salvan. The South Salvan purse had a small leather tube that held five South Salvan Lions, with room for more.

"We can assume that this man paid for Paki's beating. I think he is the pea-shooter," Pol said.

"Undoubtedly. Lirro's dead." Val said, continuing his search until he pulled out a blowpipe, evidence this was the peashooter. "The man was an expert bowman. You were lucky." He pocketed the purses, pulled out the throwing knives, and helped Pol into the clearing, but the worst of his short attack had ended. Four men were dead. Paki stood apart from the bodies, his sword still clean.

"We'll look like bandits," Darrol said holding onto a fistful of purses. "We need to move out now."

Pol located the other ambushers with his mind and they hadn't moved from their positions.

"We should take the pea-shooter in. Now they'll believe us," Pol said.

"Believe what? The King knows what happened. How will this man's body change anything?" Val said.

"I…" Pol furrowed his brow and thought for a moment. "It won't change anything, other than vindicate me." He felt deep disappointment well within him. "If we leave him here, we might not be suspected."

Val only grunted. "I'll wrap your arm first," Val said, pulling a roll of cloth from his pocket. "You should always carry something to bind wounds when you are out and about." Val pulled back Pol's sleeve and used a little bit of magic to close up the wound. "You've just seen the extent of my healing talent."

They walked back to the clearing and looked at the bodies. "I suppose they were counting on us coming from west. Not a bad guess, but we didn't stick to their pattern, did we? Good for us, bad for them."

The way Val said it made Pol shiver, but he felt better having his wound bound up, and there was no blood to immediately soak the cloth.

"We won't waste any time getting you back to the infirmary. I think we are all a little nicked up, except for Paki. It's better we keep our wounds to ourselves. Why, Pol?"

"So we aren't connected to the pattern in this camp?"

Val nodded.

Pol's friend looked a bit sick as he helped Darrol drag Lirro's body onto one of the bandit's horses. Pol had been there when he lost Siggon, so he knew what it was to see a friend die. Val pushed them onward to their own mounts and found a suitable pathway to the road a mile closer to the castle from the ambush, where they rode the rest of the way to the castle without incident.

~~~

Chapter Thirty-Three

~

MALDEN EXAMINED POL'S ARM. "It might as well have been a knife, the cut is so straight and clean. Val did a fine job of sealing this up. Your collection of scars just grows."

"I didn't get them on purpose," Pol said. "I'm just lucky to be alive. I guess my throw put me or the pea shooter's aim off enough to save me."

"No one will ever know which."

Val looked up from dozing in a chair in Pol's bedroom. "Pol saved himself by locating the archer. The man's location spell hid him from me and from Pol until the Prince was closer."

"I tried an invisibility spell, and I think it worked," Pol said. "He was looking all around for me and didn't find me until I had slowed him up." Pol turned red as he remembered his hesitation. "I'm sorry."

"For what?" Malden said.

"I could have thrown my knife before he shot Lirro. It took me a few seconds to work up the nerve."

"Don't be sorry. If that arrow was nocked and ready to shoot when you first hit him, he might have had enough strength to turn and shoot straighter, right at you," Val said.

"I don't—"

"Right. Don't fixate on what might have been. I could have gone in with Darrol and Lirro and been the one to be killed. I'm sorry one of us had to die, but I'm not upset that it wasn't me," Val said.

Pol had to gulp at Val's coldness. However, his philosophy made even more sense this time than it did when he first talked to Pol. What Pol took for a cold heart seemed to be more of a practical approach to fate, now that he had been in the midst of it. He didn't know if he believed in fate, but he knew a lot more about it since he had been assigned to read the religion text.

"Still," Pol continued to think about their trip. He had learned a lot more accompanying the army to the Taridan border about being out in the field. Pol had considered traveling with Kolli very instructive.

"Still what?" Malden said.

"I've been through more than any fourteen-year-old should have to go through," Pol said.

"Have you ever starved? Have you ever been sick when there wasn't enough money to get a healer? Have you lost a close family member?" Val said, but then he softened up. "I'm sorry about that. Siggon was like an uncle, wasn't he?"

Pol nodded. "I guess I've had a different set of troubles."

"I'll agree with that," Malden said. "Nothing physical for a few days. Give your arm a chance to heal inside. Val has given it a head start."

The door opened to Pol's rooms. Val stood up with his hand on the hilt of his sword.

"King Colvin and Queen Molissa are here to see their son," a voice announced from the sitting room.

Val straightened up his clothes as the King and Queen of North Salvan entered Pol's bedroom. Malden moved to stand beside Val next to the window.

"Poldon," Pol's mother said as she took her son's hand, looking at the bandage on his arm. She turned to Malden. "Is he still doing fine?"

Malden nodded.

"Malden told us not to worry, but this…" his mother said.

"Did the boy good. I never did think he got enough seasoning on his trip to the north. Malden told me you took care of the man you suspected of hiring the thugs that beat up your friends?" the King said.

Val stepped forward and put the purse of South Salvan money into the King's hand.

"Even some Lions." King Colvin shook his head. He stood silent moving his finger through his southern ally's coinage. "I'll keep these."

Val cleared his throat. "Your Majesty, perhaps a Lion to Pol as a souvenir to remember his trip."

The King looked at Val uncomprehendingly for a moment and then blinked his eyes. "Of course." He brought out the little purse and put a Lion in Pol's hand. "This isn't payment, but a symbol." The King turned red. Pol wondered what would cause his father to become embarrassed by his words. A symbol of what, treachery by an ally?

"Other than this, I'm fine. We had an exciting trip, but it's better not to talk about it," Pol said, showing them the thin red scar on his arm.

"As long as you learned what you needed to know," King Colvin said. "We will be leaving now. Visitors are arriving tomorrow, and your mother has preparations to attend to."

Pol wondered what his mother would have to do at night that servants couldn't do.

Dressing the next morning was a challenge for Pol with the stiffness still inside his arm, so he had to have Val help him with his clothes. Pol rang for a meal, but a servant came instead, requesting his presence in the family dining room.

"That's odd," Val said. "Be prepared for anything. I don't look on this as a positive."

Pol agreed, and the two of them stalked through the corridors. Pol concentrated on even breathing, although he was certainly nervous enough to be tied up in knots.

An attending servant opened the door to the family dining room to show that Landon had retrieved Bythia and Amonna from South Salvan. His siblings and Bythia abruptly stopped laughing when Pol entered. His mother sat at the head of the table, but his father wasn't in evidence. So his mother must have left him last night to prepare rooms for Bythia, and that meant she might be at Borstall for an extended stay.

"Pol, come in and greet your sister and brother," Molissa said.

Pol took a deep breath, remembering to school his thoughts the way Mistress Farthia had taught him, and bowed to them.

Grostin noticed Pol's wrapped arm. "Hurt yourself, did you? Fall on something?"

"The pea shooter at the Tourney did it," Pol said, throwing caution to the wind.

His brother looked confused. "Where is he?"

Pol shrugged. He struggled to maintain his composure. "Most likely moldering on a forest floor where I put his conniving to an abrupt stop." He hoped his words came out evenly.

Bythia shot a concerned glance at Grostin and then at Landon. She obviously knew everything. He looked at Amonna, and she looked nearly as shocked as Grostin. His heart sunk. They had finally all united against him.

Pol walked to the buffet where food had been set out and filled his plate. He sat next to Amonna and began to eat. Val stayed by the door, sliding just off to the side, observing Landon, Bythia, and Honna.

Pol closed his eyes at one point to collect his thoughts. His mother gave him a sympathetic glance, but smoothed her face shortly thereafter.

"We expect an answer from the Emperor in the next few days," Landon said. A bird arrived from the border letting us know of an Imperial messenger on his way from Yastan.

A few days, thought Pol. Would anything change with the message? His mother had already told him that the King would install Landon as King of Listya or place him as regent, so practically speaking, the Emperor's decision would have little effect. The conversation with Pol in the room had obviously changed when he entered. Whispers had taken the place of open conversation, and Amonna virtually ignored him.

They were still friends when he left, but his younger sister's lack of curiosity proved otherwise. Pol asked her about her stay in South Salvan, but he only got simple sentences for answers. He bolted his food down, and before anyone had left, he rose.

"I hope you have a pleasant stay in Borstall." He bowed to Bythia and his mother and left.

Val followed him out. Pol needed to sit out of sight of the doors to collect himself, and then he realized that Kolli wasn't around.

"Where is Mother's bodyguard?"

Val pursed his lips and didn't respond but helped Pol stand and headed him back to his rooms. "She's been dismissed," he finally said.

"Mother's doing?"

Val looked out a window as they passed. "I don't know, but I heard this morning that she had headed back north to re-join the forces as a scout."

Pol was confused. "I thought Ranno paid for her presence."

"I heard her family was threatened, but that might have been a rumor," Val said.

"That is disappointing," Pol said. "The danger hasn't passed."

"No, it hasn't." Val didn't prolong the conversation.

Pol felt something ominous was going to happen, and he doubted there was anything he could do to stop it. Or was there?

"I want Father to disinherit me," Pol said to Malden. "I'm afraid for Mother."

"You should be afraid for yourself, instead," the magician said. "No matter what comes from the Emperor, with Landon and Bythia here, the marriage is a sure thing, and that means King Colvin will have them wed and sent west to Listya as soon as he can."

Mistress Farthia sat up in one of Malden's easy chairs. "I don't know how effective disinheritance will be if you stay here," she said. "I had an interesting conversation with Amonna this afternoon. She acted as peacekeeper before, but now…" Farthia shook her head. "I would say she sees you much in the same way as your other siblings. Bythia is a hateful girl. I suspect she will be running Listya while Landon is playing soldier or something."

Pol blinked his eyes in amazement that Farthia would be so frank in his presence. "I can't do anything else. I've fended off attack after attack, but they will be successful, even with you around." Pol looked over at Val, leaning against the wall. "You three are all I've got."

"Conditionally, you've got Kelso, but we all know that he can be influenced," Malden said.

"Darrol will follow you to the end of the world," Val said, which surprised Pol. "If you want to escape, there is Paki, Darrol, and me. I really don't work for your father, and Ranno gives me wide latitude."

Farthia snorted. "Until you get yourself killed." She looked back to Pol. "We will help you petition for disinheritance, but you must promise to depart for Tesna as soon as possible after the King accepts or rejects it."

Pol sighed and rubbed his hands together. He didn't want to make this kind of decision, but Pol wanted his mother to outlive him. "Let's do it then." He looked at Malden. "What are the chances Father will accept my petition?"

Malden swirled wine around in his goblet. "He probably will, but he's not who will attack you."

"He will acquiesce to any attempt by my siblings," Pol said.

Mistress Farthia smiled approvingly. "Good word, Pol."

Malden glared at Farthia for a second. "Your mother won't be of any use," he said. "She just wants everyone to get along, and that won't happen."

Pol looked at the three in the room. He had to admit that these were his acting parents. His mother, as much as he loved her, had to play her own game to survive and had told him so. Malden, Farthia, and Val had all, in their own ways, always acted in Pol's interests. Oddly, it made Pol feel more isolated than a member of their group.

"So I should just accept the fact that I'll be heading to a monastery?"

Val and Malden nodded. Mistress Farthia just looked worried. "It has been a horrible summer, hasn't it?"

Pol thought for a moment. "I've learned more about life than I wanted to. There are more scars on my body." He lifted up his arm. "I've been injured more this season than at any other time in my life. I wish I could say everything is over, but it isn't."

"No," Val said. "But then your life isn't over."

Pol looked at all three of them. "Not yet."

The Imperial messenger rode into the castle courtyard. Pol looked down from the classroom window, the best private vantage point available to Pol. His father and Landon stood on the third step leading up to the main doors. The messenger dismounted and walked up to the King and gave his father a deep bow. He pulled a large envelope from the leather bag slung across his chest.

Pol could barely make out the expression in his father's face from this view. As King Colvin read the decision, his face turned red. He turned to Landon with an enraged expression and shoved the letter into Landon's arms, and stalked up the stairs and into the castle. Landon spent a bit more time reading and re-reading the letter.

Kelso took the messenger aside and signaled to a guard to take the man's horse. He'd not be a friend of the King this night. Landon trudged up to the door and disappeared into the castle.

A feeling of unease settled upon Pol. Something bad was going to happen, and he didn't know if it would happen to him or some hapless servant, but there would be an unwilling object of the King's displeasure.

"Nothing good will come of this," said Mistress Farthia, who had been watching from the other window in the room. "Make sure that Val is close by."

"Aren't you worried? My siblings have to know you are on my side."

Farthia emitted something between a laugh and a giggle. "They all know my father. If something happens to me, Ranno won't rest until the perpetrators are done for."

"He's a cold man, your father?"

She raised her eyebrows. "In some ways. Towards me, Ranno Wissingbel is just like any other doting father."

"You said doting father. That's something I don't have." Pol tried to keep the whining out of his voice, but he didn't think he succeeded.

Farthia put her arm around him. "You don't, and your mother must carefully measure her expressions towards you. This will become an even more hostile place. The rejection will make him more obsessed about putting Landon on the throne of Listya."

A feeling of hopelessness descended over Pol. He couldn't say another word.

"You haven't much left in your religion book. Finish it before you retire." Without another word other than a pat on Pol's shoulder, she left the room.

Pol peeked out the door to see Val sitting on a chair across the corridor. His bodyguard gave him a salute. Pol went to the book and thumbed through the pages. He finished a few hours later and turned back to the Sleeping God chapter. The cathedral was in Fassin, near the Penchappy Mountains, where his mother said their alien ancestors might have arrived. He wondered if he would find any clues in Fassin about his heritage. He sighed as he concluded that wouldn't happen.

Pol closed the book. It had taken him all summer, but he finally had slogged his way through it. The end of the book at the end of summer. What else would soon end? Pol felt morose as he looked up to see the orange light of the setting sun in the classroom. He opened the door to find Val still sitting. He wondered what his bodyguard had been thinking of while he sat there for so long.

"We'll eat in my rooms, tonight," Pol said. "I don't want to be around anyone with the bad news floating about."

"Not a bad idea at all," Val said. "The King is beside himself, and the message stirred up all of the siblings, including Landon's Bythia."

"You learned a lot sitting outside in the corridor?"

Val gave Pol a cold smile. "People do stop by to talk from time to time, My Prince."

~ ~ ~

Chapter Thirty-Four

~

POL DIDN'T HAVE MUCH APPETITE, but ate enough to fill his stomach. Val finished off both plates of food and suggested that Pol retire early.

Val woke him late in the night. The look on his bodyguard's face alarmed Pol.

"Your mother has been poisoned. You've been summoned to her bedside."

Pol jumped out of bed and shook the sleep out of his head. He threw on clothes, not caring what he looked like, and ran with Val to his mother's chambers. Pol had to collect his breath before he entered.

He could hear sniffling and crying sounds. Probably from her ladies-in-waiting. Pol entered and saw Malden holding his mother's wrist. The magician called him over and had him take her hand.

"She is barely holding on," he said.

Pol took his mother's hand and looked at her pale face. A trace of foam coated her lips, and Pol could smell the traces of vomit on her clothes. He squeezed her hand and just sat by her side, listening to her struggle to breathe.

She barely opened her eyes and tried to speak. Pol put his ear to her lips, hoping she would say something he could understand.

"I love you, mother," Pol said through watery eyes. "Please don't die."

Molissa's eyes grew wide, but then settled down. Her lips moved again. "Amonna," she breathed.

Pol looked around for his sister and was surprised that none of his siblings or the King were in the room. He looked back as his mother's eyes widened again. She shuddered and slowly exhaled. His mother had died. The shock of her passing was nearly too much for Pol. He wailed and clutched her body, but then his heart began to pound in his head, and his throat began to constrict. He began to wheeze, as he couldn't catch his breath. Splotches of black began to pulsate in his sight until everything became black.

Pol blinked his eyes open and sat up in the dark. He was in his bed, only in his underclothes. His breathing had returned to normal, but the panic of not being able to breathe had shocked him. His next thought was of his mother's widening eyes. He could tell she wasn't seeing anything, and then that long exhale. He began to whimper and couldn't stop. His breathing remained under control when Val opened the door to his room.

"Are you well?"

"How could I be well?" Pol snapped back. "She's dead, isn't she?" The anger quickly turned to a numbness. Pol didn't want to move from his bed.

"We are all sorry. Your siblings didn't waste any time. Your mother still carried the rights to the Listyan throne, and they put a quick stop to that as soon as the news of the declined petition arrived."

The Emperor quickly became an object of Pol's hate. "If he hadn't rejected Father's petition…" His hands tightened around his bedclothes. Pol knew he wasn't thinking straight, but he was powerless to clear his mind.

"She'd still be dead sooner or later. Your father or your brothers and sisters wouldn't have stood for her existence for very long."

"I'm petitioning for disinheritance," Pol said. He said it, but realized that becoming disinherited was too late for his mother. He stifled a sob and just wanted to go back to sleep.

"Malden has already submitted it. Farthia worked on the petition while you read that religion textbook this afternoon. It may not save you, but I am finally seeing your point about doing all you can."

Val left him in the darkness, and Pol could hear him rummaging around in his sitting room. Although his eyes wanted to close, the vision of his mother dying in front of him kept all other thoughts away. Pol knew he wouldn't be able to sleep. Pol walked into the sitting room and sat down. "I'm not tired anymore."

"Good. Get some clothes on. They are setting up the pyre right now."

"My mother's funeral? Now?"

Val shook his head. "No funeral, just a pyre. I doubt the King or your brothers and sisters will be attending. They told Malden that they want her body burned as soon as possible."

Pol couldn't believe his ears. "She was married to the King for fifteen years, just after Amonna was born. My mother was the only one she knew. All of them really, even Landon." The hurt just overwhelmed Pol until he sat down hard on one of his chairs. "Were you going to wake me up?" Pol said in a moment of clarity.

Val nodded. "You needed the sleep. I was afraid you'd be joining your mother the way you reacted when she died."

"Malden must have saved me."

"Nope. When you fainted your struggling stopped, and you began to breathe more easily. So I carried you to your bedroom."

Pol clutched the amulet underneath his nightshirt. His mother couldn't possibly have intended him to keep it, since he would die in a few years. Now, he felt guilty that she hadn't outlived him. "Her last word was 'Amonna'. I heard it as clearly as you can hear me."

"Amonna? I wonder. Don't let anyone into your rooms until I get back," Val said and left.

Pol locked the door and lay down on the couch. His mind seethed with emotion. There was no question in his mind that one of his relatives had hired someone to poison his mother. He was somewhat disappointed that the last person she mentioned was his younger sister, but then Pol recalled that someone had told him mother-daughter relationships were stronger than with sons. His mind was whirling too fast to recall who.

He walked back into his bedroom to put on something plain to wear at his mother's burning. His princely days were over, indeed, he felt like his life had already been snuffed out by the poison that his mother had taken.

He looked around the sitting room and realized that he had no more ties to Castle Borstall. His real father and mother were dead. His siblings weren't really siblings at all, but vicious Fairfields trying to rid themselves of him and his mother so they could take over Listya. He wouldn't stay in the castle any longer than he needed to, but would Val and Darrol be willing to travel with him all the way to the Tesna Monastery? He hoped they would.

Memories of his mother began to flood through his mind. He clutched again the amulet that he wore under his shirt and wondered about his father Cissert. Since that was a last name in the brief passage that he had read, Pol decided that when he left the castle, he would cast off King Colvin's surname of Fairfield, and he would go by the name of Pol Cissert.

It seemed like the right thing to do. He wondered if monasteries charged a fee, a tuition, he thought it was called. Would King Colvin pay? He would have to ask Val. He shook his head at the random thought. Malden would have already taken that into account.

Pol jumped up at a knock on his door.

"It's me, Val."

Pol unlocked the door, and Malden walked in followed by Val, who left the door half open.

"Your mother will be burned in little more than an hour. You should get dressed. There will be few in attendance," Malden said. "The king has accepted your petition and wants you out of the castle within a week's time. I suggest you leave first thing tomorrow with Val. He will take you to the Tesna Monastery."

Pol looked at both men's faces and began to shake in fear. The time to leave had really come. "What about my tuition?" Pol's battered mind sought out something else to worry about.

"What?" Malden looked at Pol blankly.

"I'm not a prince anymore. How will I pay for anything?"

Val barked out a laugh. "You've got your Lion. That will get you to Tesna." Val looked at Malden and nodded. "But monasteries don't accept fees if you can pass magic tests. You are certain to be accepted, so there won't be anything expected in return."

Pol looked out through the half-closed door and saw a few frightened faces that quickly disappeared. The anxiety level decreased a bit. The entire night had upset and distracted Pol from rational thought. His mother's face flittered through his mind, and he put his hands to his face, trying to keep from crying all over again.

"We should spend the next hour packing. Tomorrow, you'll not be returning to this room, ever," Val said gently, and left again.

Pol didn't want to stay, and he grabbed onto Val's command to pack as a much-needed diversion from his grief. He began to gather his things, but realized he wouldn't need court clothes or any other of his princely trappings. He had nothing in the way of jewels and chains, unlike his brothers, so by the time he was ready to go, he had a bag with his throwing knives, and a few changes of clothes.

Even so, he found a few things of value to take, but the memories of his mother and the better times of his life in Borstall would remain in his mind forever. Val knocked on his door again and stood carrying a bag no larger than Pol's.

"A change of plans, we will leave tonight."

"What about all of your weapons in the armory?" Pol said. He didn't even know why he brought that up.

"I'll let Kelso know where to send the rest of my things. We will be leaving our bags with Darrol, who will get the horses ready during your mother's last rites," Val said.

"Last rites? She wasn't religious." The numbness returned.

Val just shook his head and put his hand on Pol's shoulder. "It's time to go, lad."

No 'My Prince'. He would likely not hear that honorific again.

The pyre had been set up in the stable yard. Pol thought that was a final show of disrespect for his mother. He felt anger begin to build within him at the way his stepfather treated his mother at the last. Stepfather. Pol had known bad things would arise from the Emperor's action, but he never thought his life would be crumbling so quickly, so completely.

Someone had already arranged his mother's body on a plank amidst a pile of branches. The area around her head and shoulders was covered with flowers. She would like that, Pol thought.

Darrol stood with Malden and Mistress Farthia. Two of his mother's ladies-in-waiting wailed while Kelso held a branch out to Malden, who lit it with magic. Kelso handed the burning branch to Pol.

He didn't want to take it, but all of them encouraged Pol. He walked to the pyre and set it aflame. Pol felt tears stream down his face as he stepped back and sobbed as the fire caught and consumed his mother. Farthia took Pol by the shoulders and led him back from the flames.

Malden walked up to Val and gave him a small bag, and then he approached Pol.

"Here is a book on magic. You'll need it at Tesna." Malden said loudly. Pol didn't think that the pyre was that loud, but then he didn't care about much of anything right then. Malden took Farthia's hand. "You can always rely on us. Ranno will know where we end up. I can't stay in your father's service any longer. Not after this. Since you're leaving, my biggest reason for staying," he looked at Farthia, "will be asked to find a position elsewhere. We might end up in Yastan. Who knows?"

"As you said, Ranno will," Val said.

"It's time to end this," Malden said, taking a deep shuddering breath.

They all watched silently as Malden walked up to the pyre and raised his hands. Molissa's body flared in a green flame and disappeared. Nothing remained of the Queen's remains.

"What did you do?" Pol said.

"There are no ashes for the King or his children to desecrate. I wouldn't put it past their vindictive souls," Malden said.

The magician's emotions were raw for the first time that Pol had ever noticed. Kelso stayed by the pyre, but Malden, Farthia, Val and Darrol walked with Pol to the stables.

"It's time to fly," Val said. "Here is your bag."

Pol took it. The book had added noticeable weight. "Can we just take the horses?" Pol didn't care about his random thoughts at this time.

Malden nodded. "Consider it a final consideration for a disinherited prince to leave North Salvan. You must leave quickly."

Val mounted while Darrol helped Pol on top of a large horse. It reminded Pol of the big warhorse that Siggon had taken out when he was poisoned. That seemed like years ago, in a long-past part of Pol's life.

"This isn't my horse," Pol said.

"You'll take what you're given," Malden said as he helped Pol mount the tall horse.

"It's too big for me," Pol said as he grabbed the pommel of the saddle. Someone had already adjusted the stirrups. All Pol could think about was what was happening in the next few moments as he held back a torrent of worse thoughts.

"He won't always be,' Val said as he secured Pol's bags.

Darrol joined them. "It's time to go," he said.

Val nodded, and the three of them trotted out of the stable yard. Pol waved to Malden and Farthia as they held onto each other.

The streets were nearly empty in the dark of early morning as they trotted along the city's streets. Pol looked around, knowing he wouldn't be returning to Borstall, his home for nearly fifteen years.

He wondered where Paki was. Probably sleeping through all of the night's events. Pol would miss his friend. It wouldn't work for Paki to go with him to Tesna, at least not now with the haste of their departure. Pol couldn't help but sigh. He wondered how many times he would do so on his way south.

They passed through Bangate, heading south and west. Pol looked back at the darkness of the town. Even the castle had few lights showing. He wondered if any of his siblings had bothered to note his mother's death.

Pol found his mind clearing as they picked up their pace. Amonna. It dawned on him that his mother hadn't said her name as last words of endearment, but she identified the person who delivered the poisoned meal or whatever it was that killed her.

"I know who killed my mother," Pol said to Val.

"You do," Val said. "Your youngest sister, Amonna." Val had been ahead of him and turned in the saddle. "The ladies-in-waiting all admitted that Amonna brought a late night drink. Everyone knew. It was an open assassination, pure and simple. The King didn't even bother to stop his daughter, and Amonna's act will likely be celebrated in Castle Borstall this morning."

Pol's heart sank. What betrayal! He couldn't believe how vile everyone in the castle had been with the exception of those few loyal to him. The only person, who had shown him any courtesy at all as he grew up murdered his mother. How could a person change so much in the course of a few months? The horror of her act brought tears to Pol's eyes yet again.

A dark shape rode up to them from the woods that they had just entered.

Pol pulled out a throwing knife, although he wouldn't be very accurate in his current state.

"Sorry about your mom, Pol," Paki said as he guided his horse next to Pol's. "I would have been there at the stable yard, but Val wanted to make sure no one had set up an ambush."

Pol noticed that Paki led a horse laden with supplies.

"You anticipated this?" Pol said to Val.

Val nodded. "I've been prepared to leave ever since we returned from our little trip. Follow me closely, all of you, it's dark."

They left the road and traveled through the woods throughout the rest of the early morning. They emerged from the forest, far from any road, just before dawn. Val led them on a track up to the top of a hill high enough to see Borstall in the distance.

"We'll eat a cold breakfast and rest the horses," Val said.

Pol needed help getting off from his new mount. "Do you know this horse?" Pol said to Paki.

"I do," Paki said with a grin. "Landon bought him for a lot of money in South Salvan. It's a rare horse breed that the Shinkyans won't let leave their land. I don't know how he was able to get one, but rest assured, your brother will be furious when he finds out."

Taking the horse would only make life worse for him in the monastery in South Salvan. He could always send him back after they reached Tesna. He didn't think anymore about it, sitting down with the others while Darrol passed out bread and cheese. Darrol gave a skin of fruit juice to Pol, while the others drank ale, although Paki complained that his was too watered down.

"There they go," Val said.

Pol looked towards Borstall. Far away he could see a cloud of dust in the far distance across the farmlands below, as a cluster of riders he couldn't really see sped along the Southern Road.

A feeling of confusion hit Pol. "That's where we should be," Pol said. He got to his feet and looked around. "Why aren't we heading south to Tesna?"

Val chuckled. "Because we aren't going to Tesna. You, my lad, are Deftnis-bound. Always were. A few times last night, Malden made it plain to any that wanted to hear, that you were headed to Tesna. Think of it as a non-magical tweaking of the pattern. Those riders will be disappointed that they never catch up to us. The monks there are in King Astor's pocket. You wouldn't last a week in that nest of snakes." Val pointed to the riders. "But I don't think you were intended to make it out of North Salvan alive."

"Deftnis. So Paki can stay there with us?"

"With you and Darrol. I'll be on my way once you're delivered. We came this way just because I wanted to see the pursuit," Val said, shaking his head, still chuckling. "Mount up. We won't be traveling on many roads and certainly won't be staying at any inns on our way out of this cursed kingdom."

"How do you feel, Prince Poldon?" Darrol said.

Pol felt a shock of ice flow through him. "I'm a Disinherited Prince, remember? From now on I want you to call me by my new name, Pol Cissert." He clutched the amulet beneath his shirt and vowed that some day he would make all the Fairfields pay for what they had done to his mother and to him.

~~~~

An excerpt from Book Two of the Disinherited Prince series follows. If you liked this first volume, please leave a review at the place where you purchased it. If you'd like to know about future books in this series, check out the Guy Antibes website, www.guyantibes.com

Excerpt from Book Two of
The Disinherited Prince Series

The Monk's Habit

Chapter One

~

A COOL WIND WHIPPED THE CLOAKS OF THE FOUR RIDERS looking out over
the estuary towards the large island that held their final destination,
Deftnis Monastery.

"There it is," Valiso Gasibli said. His dark curly hair flitted this way
and that in the wind. "It's a bit of a boat trip, but I'm sure you are all up to
it." He turned his mount and kicked the sides of the horse to urge it on back
towards the coastal track that led down to the fishing village, which served as
the mainland port for those heading to Deftnis.

Pol Cissert, a refugee from Borstall Castle where his mother had been the
Queen and he a prince, looked at the whitecaps on the angry sea and blinked
his eyes. For all his time as a prince of North Salvan, the nearly fifteen-year-
old had never ridden in a sailboat on the ocean. His gaze lingered on the little
craft coming in from the island and worried about all the bobbing. He didn't
look forward to the final leg of his escape.

"Worried about a little boat ride?" Paki said. His fifteen-year-old
companion rubbed his hands in anticipation before taking off after Valiso, or
Val, as the boys called him.

Actually Pol thought that 'terrified' described his current emotional
state. His large horse quickly caught up to Val, Darrol Netherfield, his sworn
man, and Paki. Pol wished he could feel the relief of reaching the refuge of the
monastery, if it wasn't for that boat ride.

"What's the matter with you?" Val said. He followed Pol's eyes out to the ocean. "Does the little trip out to the monastery worry you? Think about your horse who will have to follow you in that big barge sitting at the dock."

A barge with ungainly sails bobbed in the water at the end of a stone dock. Pol instinctively reached down and patted his mount's neck. He had yet to name his horse, once the property of his step-brother, Prince Landon. It had served him well in the two weeks they had been on the road. Their flight from Castle Borstall, where Pol's mother had been poisoned and he had been disinherited, had been slowed up by the necessity of traveling cross-country rather than using North Salvan's roads.

At least Pol's fragile constitution had held up during their ride. He wasn't so sure what would happen on that boat, but that monastery was the only sanctuary available to Pol. Val thought the healers at Deftnis might be able to cure his heart and lung problem. As it was, Pol was convinced he would die before he reached the age of twenty, if he made it alive across all that water to the island.

They stopped at a stable yard serving the monastery and removed their bags. Pol regretted leaving his horse in the care of someone else, but then his horse along with Darrol's and Paki's would make the crossing later when the sea had calmed. Val told them that he intended to stop just long enough to see him settled at Deftnis, and then he would be heading due north to the Imperial capital of Yastan.

"I'm hungry," Paki said, earning a scowl from Darrol.

The former Borstall palace guard clapped Paki on the side of his head. "Not until we are across. You might lose whatever you shove in that bottomless maw of yours, otherwise. I know, I've made the crossing in conditions as bad as this and fed the fishies."

Val smirked, the shape of his usual smile, and called them over. "I can put you under during the crossing, but my magic works only if you're willing."

Paki shook his head. "I'm brave enough."

Pol thought his friend looked a little uncertain of his claim. Pol had no desire to make a fool of himself for the sake of bravado. "I'll take you up on that. Maybe another time I will take a chance." He worried more about his heart beating out of his chest with anxiety and losing his breath if the ride made him nauseous than losing whatever he had in his stomach.

The boat they had seen from the cliff had put in alongside the dock and let passengers off. Three men wore the gray robes of monks, but Pol could see the men wore swords and had boots with spurs hiding behind the folds of thick cloth. One of the monks had to be assisted off the boat, then threw off the helping hands once they reached the solid footing of the dock. The monk continued to walk a bit unsteadily right past them. The men nodded to Val, maybe recognizing him since Val had trained for years at the monastery.

Pol looked at Paki, who swallowed a bit, but took a deep breath and gave his bag to one of the sailors on the boat.

Once Pol had sat on the boat, Val joined him. "Are you ready?" Val said. Pol nodded.

A bump woke up Pol. The boat bobbed against a thick wooden pier. "Are we here?"

Darrol put Pol's bag on his lap. "This is yours, but I'll carry it up to the dock. Val will do the same with Paki's. You might want to help your friend up the ladder."

Pol looked over at Paki, whose pale face held a sorrowful expression.

"I'm a fool. I'm a fool. I'm a fool," Paki said as he struggled up the ladder.

Pol followed him and helped his friend walk around on the pier for a few steps.

"Did you feed the fishies?" Pol teased.

Paki nodded, and Darrol laughed. Pol looked back at the angry stretch of water knowing he had made the better decision.

Val didn't seem to pay any attention to them and stalked off the pier and into the village that made up the little port on the Isle of Deftnis. "Don't bother about gawking. You'll be down here often enough," he said. "I want to get to Yastan before the month is out, so I can't waste time."

It was a struggle to keep up with his former bodyguard, but they all followed Val like ducklings following their mother. Darrol had spent a few years in the monastery, but even he still examined the buildings as they trod through the village to an inn. A carriage that looked more like a covered cart stood in front.

"We'll take that the rest of the way," Darrol said, as he put his bags in the back of the conveyance. Pol did the same, and soon his teeth shook and rattled as the cart made its way up the rough cobblestones that went to the Monastery sitting at the top of a hill overlooking Deftnis Port.

As they approached the monastery dressed in black stone, Pol thought the place looked sinister and unfriendly. "It looks foreboding," he said.

Darrol pulled on his lower lip and looked at their destination. "It's not a particularly happy place, but I have mostly positive memories."

Pol shuddered at the term 'mostly positive'. He expected to be worked hard with a monastery filled with men as severe as Val. "What are you going to do now that you are back?" Pol asked Darrol.

"I may teach arms to the young things," Darrol said, "or learn a bit more about Seeking." He looked at Val. 'Or both." His face broke into a smile.

"Pol can help you with that," Val said. "He'll do well in the Seeker category."

The way Val spoke put an end to the banter. They rode on in silence and finally clattered underneath the portcullis of the monastery gate. It looked more like a castle than a spiritual refuge. Pol remembered that monasteries these days were mostly secular orders in the Baccusol Empire.

"Stay here," Val said as he left his bag with them in the large courtyard, and walked up the stairs into a newer-looking building on the castle grounds. Pol just absorbed the feel of his new home. He might die on the monastery grounds, he thought, unless the healer-monks cured him.

A short time later, Val emerged along with three older monks. They all shuffled down the stairs in their gray robes. Again, Pol thought it odd that they wore swords and boots, but these didn't have spurs. They eyed the trio.

"Darrol, we know. You are always welcome amongst us," the oldest-looking of the monks said. "Pakkingail Horstel?"

Paki halfheartedly raised his hand.

"You are accepted by virtue of this letter of recommendation from Malden Gastoria, Court Magician to North Salvan." The monk waved a document in his hand and then turned to Pol. "You are the newly-disinherited prince, so Valiso says."

"I am, sire."

"Show me some of your power. Malden writes that you are somewhat of a prodigy."

Pol drew within himself and detected the pattern of the seven of them standing in the courtyard. "If you will excuse me," he said. He pointed to one of the monks and raised him six inches into the air, moved him backward and then forward before lowering him down onto the cobbled courtyard. "Will that work?"

The monk who had been moved smiled, once he shook off the shock of being transported. "You are what Val described."

Pol smiled and then collapsed to the ground. His heart beat too fast, and his breathing began to get out of control. "I can do more, but if I do, I will faint."

The monk helped Pol to his feet. "Val said you get overcome with fatigue. We will see what we can do about that. I'm sure you have stories to tell."

The old monk nodded. "That will have to wait. A quick meal for Val—"

Val held up his hand. "The sea is a bit rough today. If you don't mind, I'd like to enjoy my dinner only once, going down. I think I will be heading back on the next trip, after all."

"Well, we will let you leave before the boat returns to the Mancus shore. Say goodbye to your friends." The three monks returned to the building.

Pol looked at Val and really didn't want him to leave. "You really aren't staying?"

Val shook his head. "The Emperor must know the true story of what went on in Castle Borstall, even if he likely won't do anything about it. Your father plays a shrewd game, and the Emperor won't forget your mother's murder. He won't forget you, either. It's hard to get an audience with Hazett, but if you need anything in Yastan, you can contact Farthia's father, Ranno, for assistance."

Val looked around at the buildings in front of him. "I learned most of my craft within these walls. Neither of you will lack for training." Val put his hands on the boys' shoulders. "Work hard. I'm sure we will run into one another in the course of time." He threw his bag back on the covered cart and climbed up on the front seat. The driver turned in the courtyard and drove Val out of sight. The man never turned to wave, which disappointed Pol.

The sparsely furnished dormitory wasn't what Pol had been used to, but it met his expectations. Darrol merited his own personal cell, as they called individual rooms in the Monastery, but it looked like the boys would be sharing their living space with fourteen others, so Pol and Paki found two empty beds next to one another.

"Appreciate the solitude. A number of those identified during the

Emperor's processional are due to start arriving in a week or two along with our normal raft of new inductees. The dormitory will fill up. As far as I know, you two are the youngest pair of acolytes to be taken in at Deftnis in my lifetime, at least," Gorm, a younger monk, said. "Tomorrow both of you will be given a battery of tests to determine how you can serve Deftnis. There are a number of specialties, but you will be required to learn a bit of everything."

"What kind of specialties?" Paki said. Pol could tell his friend was getting excited.

"Archery, Swordsmanship, General Weapons, Seeking, Scouting, Healing, Strategy & Tactics, as well as a few others that we won't talk about today. This dormitory is for those with magical abilities. Magic has a training regimen all its own."

Pol thought. "Where does knife throwing come in?"

"Valiso taught you how to use knives?" Gorm couldn't hide the surprise in his voice.

The question brought a nod from Pol. "I needed to defend myself from assassins."

"I'll note that. It fits in a few of our categories, but I think you will be a special case." Gorm frowned and Pol didn't know why. Was it his frail constitution?

They both ate in the half-empty commissary. No one introduced themselves to the two boys, and Paki's presence became a comfort. Pol finally felt that he was safe.

They returned to the dormitory just after dark to find a few of the beds now occupied. Pol collapsed onto his. He had no idea what Paki dreamt of, but Pol kept waking up after having dreams about his struggles during the summer. He had had to fight for his life time after time, and his survival had come at a cost. Pol had more battle scars than any fourteen-going-on-fifteen-year-old should have. He pulled back the right sleeve of his nightshirt and ran his finger along the latest one. An arrow had skittered along his forearm and carved a line. He could feel the newly healed wound in the dark.

How many more scars would he collect at Deftnis?

~~~

~ A BIT ABOUT GUY

With a lifelong passion for speculative fiction, Guy Antibes found that he rather enjoyed writing fantasy as well as reading it. So a career was born and Guy anxiously engaged in adding his own flavor of writing to the world. Guy lives in the western part of the United States and is happily married with enough children to meet or exceed the human replacement rate.

You can contact Guy at his website: www.guyantibes.com.

†

BOOKS BY GUY ANTIBES

POWER OF POSES

Book One: Magician in Training

Trak Bluntwithe, an illiterate stableboy, is bequeathed an education by an estranged uncle. In the process of learning his letters, Trak finds out that he is a magician. So his adventures begin that will take him to foreign countries, fleeing from his home country, who seeks to execute him for the crime of being able to perform magic. The problem is that no country is safe for the boy while he undergoes training. Can he stay ahead of those who want to control him or keep his enemies from killing him?

Book Two: Magician in Exile

Trak Bluntwithe is a young man possessing so much magical power that he is a target for governments. Some want to control him and others want to eliminate the threat of his potential. He finds himself embroiled in the middle of a civil war. He must fight in order to save his imprisoned father, yet he finds that he has little taste for warfare. Trak carries this conflict onto the battlefield and finds he must use his abilities to stop the war in order to protect the ones he loves.

Book Three: Magician in Captivity

After a disastrous reunion with Valanna, Trak heads to the mysterious land of Bennin to rescue a Toryan princess sold into slavery. The Warish King sends Valanna back to Pestle to verify that the King of Pestle is no longer under Warish control. The Vashtan menace continues to infect the countries of the world and embroil both Trak and Valanna in civil conflict, while neither of them can shake off the attraction both of them feel towards each other.

Book Four: Magician in Battle

Trak saves Warish, but must leave to return the Toryan princess. He reunites with his father, but is separated again. Circumstances turn ugly in Torya, and Trak returns to Pestle to fight a new, unexpected army. Valanna's story continues as she struggles with her new circumstances, and is sent on a final mission to Pestle. The Power of Poses series ends with a massive battle pitting soldier against soldier and magic against magic.

FANTASY - EPIC / SWORD & SORCERY / NEW ADULT

THE WARSTONE QUARTET

An ancient emperor creates four magical gems to take over and rule the entire world. The ancient empire crumbles and over millennia. Three stones are lost and one remains as an inert symbol for a single kingdom among many. The force that created the Warstones, now awakened, seeks to unite them all, bringing in a new reign of world domination—a rule of terror.

Four Warstones, four stories. The Warstone Quartet tells of heroism, magic, romance and war as the world must rise to fight the dark force that would enslave them all.

FANTASY - SWORD & SORCERY/EPIC

Book One: Moonstone | Magic That Binds
A jewel, found in the muck of a small village pond, transforms Lotto, the village fool, into an eager young man who is now linked to a princess through the Moonstone. The princess fights against the link while Lotto seeks to learn more about what happened to him. He finds a legacy and she finds the home in her father's army that she has so desperately sought. As Lotto finds aptitude in magical and physical power, a dark force has risen from another land to sow the seeds of rebellion. It's up to Lotto to save the princess and the kingdom amidst stunning betrayal fomented by the foreign enemy.

Book Two: Sunstone | Dishonor's Bane
Shiro, a simple farmer, is discovered to possess stunning magical power and is involuntarily drafted into the Ropponi Sorcerer's Guild. He attracts more enemies than friends and escapes with his life only to end up on a remote prison island. He flees with an enchanted sword containing the lost

Sunstone. Trying to create a simple refuge for an outlawed band of women sorcerers, he is betrayed by the very women he has worked to save and exiled to a foreign land. There, he must battle for his freedom as he and his band become embroiled in a continent-wide conflict.

Book Three: Bloodstone | Power of Youth

When usurpers invade Foxhome Castle, Unca, the aging Court Wizard of the Red Kingdom, flees with the murdered king's only daughter, taking the Bloodstone, an ancient amulet that is the symbol of Red Kingdom rule. Unca uses the Bloodstone to escape capture by an enemy and is transformed into a young man, but loses all of his wizardly powers. Unca must reinvent himself in order to return the princess to her throne. Along the way he falls in love with the young woman and must deal with the conflict between his duty and his heart, while keeping a terrible secret.

Book Four: Darkstone | An Evil Reborn

As the 22nd son of the Emperor of Dakkor, Vishan Daryaku grows from boy to man, learning that he must use his unique powers and prodigious knowledge to survive. He succeeds until his body is taken over by an evil power locked inside of the Darkstone. Now Emperor of Dakkor, Vishan is trapped inside, as the ancient force that rules his body devastates his homeland while attempting to recover all of the Warstones.

As the amulets are all exposed, the holders of the Moonstone, Sunstone, and Bloodstone combine to fight the Emperor's relentless drive to reunite the Warstones and gain power over the entire world. The armies of Dakkor and the forces of those allied with the three other stones collide on a dead continent in the stunning conclusion of the Warstone Quartet.

Quest of the Wizardess

Quest of the Wizardess chronicles the travels and travails of young Bellia. After her wizard family is assassinated when she is fourteen, Bellia seeks anonymity as a blacksmith's helper. When that doesn't work out as expected, she flees to the army.

Her extraordinary physical and magical skills bring unwanted attention and she must escape again. After finding a too-placid refuge, she takes the opportunity to seek out her family's killers. Revenge becomes her quest that takes her to a lost temple, unexpected alliances and a harrowing confrontation with her enemies.
FANTASY - EPIC/NEW ADULT-COLLEGE/COMING OF AGE

The Power Bearer

How Norra obtained the power and the extraordinary lengths she went through to rid herself of it.

What's a girl to do when all of the wizards in her world are after her? She runs. But this girl runs towards the source of her power, not away from it. Along the way she picks up, among others, a wizard, a ghost, a highwaywoman and a sentient cloud. Through thick and thin, they help Norra towards her goal of finding a solution in a far off land that no one in her world has even heard of.
YOUNG ADULT EPIC FANTASY

Panix: Magician Spy

Panix has life by the tail. A new wife, a new job in a new land that has few magicians and none of his caliber. His ideal life takes some unexpected downturns and Panix finds himself employed as a spy. He has no training, but must make things up as he goes if he is to survive the politics, betrayal, war and, at the end, his own behavior.
FANTASY - ADVENTURE

THE WORLD OF THE SWORD OF SPELLS

Warrior Mage

The gods gave Brull a Sword of Spells and proclaimed him as the world's only Warrior Mage. One big problem, there aren't any wars. What's a guy to do? Brull becomes a magician bounty hunter until the big day when he learns he not only has to fight a war with the magicians of his world, but fight the god that the magicians are all working to bring into being. He finds out if he

has what it takes in Warrior Mage.
EPIC FANTASY

Sword of Spells

Read about Brull's beginnings and earlier adventures as a bounty hunter of magicians in the Sword of Spells anthology.
EPIC FANTASY

THE SARA FEATHERWOOD ADVENTURES

Set in Shattuk Downs, a reclusive land in the kingdom of Parthy. Sara Featherwood could be a Jane Austen heroine with a sword in her hand. There are no magicians, wizards, dragons, elves or dwarves in Shattuk Downs, but there is intrigue, nobility, hidden secrets, plenty of adventure and romance with a bit of magic.
FANTASY - YOUNG ADULT/COLLEGE
FICTION - WOMEN'S ADVENTURE

Knife & Flame

When Sara Featherwood's mother dies, her sixteen-year-old life is thrown into turmoil at Brightlings Manor in a remote district of Shattuk Downs. Life becomes worse when her father, the Squire, sets his roving eye on her best friend. Dreading her new life, Sara escapes to the Obridge Women's School. Seeking solace in education doesn't work as her world becomes embroiled with spies, revolution, and to top it all off, her best friend becomes her worst enemy.

Sword & Flame

If you were a young woman who had just saved the family's estate from ruin, you'd think your father would be proud, wouldn't you? Sara Featherwood is thrown out of her childhood home and now faces life on her own terms at age seventeen. She returns to the Tarrey Abbey Women's School and is drafted to help with the establishment of the first Women's College in the kingdom of Parthy. Now in the King's capital of Parth, life confronts Sara as she learns about family secrets, which threaten to disrupt her life and about resurgent political turmoil back home that turns her scholarly pursuits upside down as she must take action and use her magic to save her family and her beloved Shattuk Downs.

Guns & Flame

At nineteen, Sara Featherwood has done all she can to help establish the first Women's College in the kingdom of Parthy. That includes a pact with the kingdom's Interior Minister, to go on a student exchange program as payment for eliminating opposition to the college. Little does Sara know that her trip to a rival country is not what it seems and as the secrets of the true purpose of her trip unravel, she utilizes her magic to escape through hostile territory with vital secrets, but as she does, she finds herself drawn back to Shattuk Downs and must confront awful truths about those close to her.

THE GUY ANTIBES ANTHOLOGIES

The Alien Hand

An ancient artifact changes a young woman's life forever. A glutton gladiator is marooned in a hostile desert. An investigator searches for magic on a ravaged world and finds something quite unexpected. A boy yearns for a special toy. A recent graduate has invented a unique tool for espionage. A member of a survey team must work with his ex-girlfriend in extremely dangerous circumstances. A doctor is exiled among the worst creatures he can imagine.

SCIENCE FICTION

The Purple Flames

A reject from a Magical Academy finds purpose. A detective works on a reservation in New Mexico, except the reservation is for ghouls, demons, ghosts, zombies, and the paranormal. A succubus hunts out the last known nest of vampires on earth. The grisly story about the origins of Tonsil Tommy. In a post-apocalyptic world, two mutants find out about themselves when their lives are in imminent peril.

STEAMPUNK & PARANORMAL FANTASY with a tinge of HORROR

Angel in Bronze

A statue comes to life and must come to terms with her sudden humanity. A wizard attempts to destroy a seven-hundred-year-old curse. A boy is appalled by the truth of his parents' midnight disappearances. A

captain's coat is much more than it seems. A healer must decide if the maxim that he has held to his entire career is still valid. A fisherman must deal with the aftermath of the destruction of his village.
FANTASY

~~~

Guy Antibes books are available at book retailers in print and e-book formats.

Made in the USA
Lexington, KY
16 September 2017